SHARDS OF WIND

THE CROWNS OF TALAM

LE VAN VEEN

First edition June 2026

Published by Storied Stars Books

Cover Design by Story Wrappers

Interior Illustrations by Nathan Hansen

Copy and Developmental Editing by Becky Wallace

Line Editing and Proofreading by Jennifer Murgia

Map by Alyssa Hurlbert

Author Photo by Marigold Visuals Photography

ISBN 979-8-9892243-8-8 (e-book)

ISBN 978-1-972952-00-9 (paperback)

ISBN 978-1-972952-01-6 (hardcover)

www.LEVanVeen.com

To Luna,
thank you for being by my side for over fifteen years.
I look up at the moon and I think of you.

BOOKS IN THE CROWNS OF TALAM SERIES

Under Cold Moons
Blood of Ember
Shards of Wind

Fuar
GEIMHRIGH
Spuchar
FOMHAR
Tusnua Sea
BRIONGLOID
Caillte
EILEAN
Omra
N
W
E
S

World of Talam
Beannaithe Sea
Seambog
BITU
Seamall
EARRACH
Blathriel
SAMHRADH

THE VOICES OF TALAM

AISLING (AISLA) TARKIS

ash • ling, (ash • la), ee • ark • iss
Mathair Apparent of Eilean | The Gheall Ceann | The Mallaithe

WEYLIN MYRKOR

way • lynn, mur • core
Udar Apparent of Iomlan | The Young Wolf

RANIA DORCAS

ruh • knee • uh, door • cass
The Gem of Dreams

RUAIRI VILULF

roor • ee, vil • ulf
Eilean's Scout and Sailor

EIRE TRYGG

air • uh, trig
Eilean's Joy and Believer

CALLUM RONAN

call • um, roan • in
The Captain of the Udar Apparent's Personal Guard

EIMEAR SHEA

ee • mur, shay
The Eldest Daughter of Deaglan Shea

ESOS IN TALAM

ASHER
the esos of flames
begins with an itching of the palms

TSUNA
the esos of water
begins with the feeling of dry mouth

TERRAN
the esos of nature
begins with the chattering of teeth

ZEPHYS
the esos of winds
begins with a rush of wind in the ear

SHADOW
the dark esos
begins with a ringing in the ears

MENDER
the healing esos
begins with sounds feeling muted

SHIFTER
the esos of shifting
begins with transformation of body

PRYER
the esos of mind manipulation
begins with the eyes going white

SEER
the esos of future sight
begins with the hands growing cold

THE GODS

EABHA

ay • va

goddess of wisdom, mother of the gods

CION

kee • on

god of beauty, love, and fate

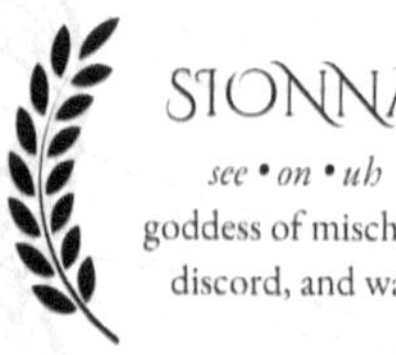

SIONNA

see • on • uh

goddess of mischief, discord, and war

LEIGHIS

lay • hiss

goddess of healing and harvest

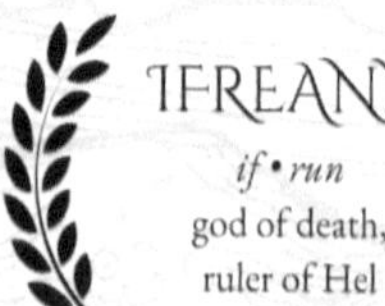

IFREANN

if • run

god of death, ruler of Hel

OF TALAM

TARAN

tear • in

goddess of thunder,
protector of mortals

MUIR

moor

god of the seas
and waterways

AIRDEALL

arc • dell

goddess of the heavens,
protector of ancients

REALTA

ray • all • ta

goddess of
celestial bodies

THE
NORNS

weavers of fate

THE GREAT

EILEAN

eye • lee • an

The Forgotten Realm

SAMHRADH

sour • rah

The Wolves' Den

EARRACH

are • rah

The Realm of Hope

GEIMHRIGH

gev • ree

The Frozen Realm

HOUSES OF TALAM

BRIONGLOID

[bring • loyd]
The Realm of Dreams

FOMHAR

[fove • err]
The Realm of Abundance

BITU

bite • oo
The Realm of Life

TAISTEALAI

It was not often that the messenger of the gods found himself in the wolves' den.

Taistealai had never been fond of the heat and the sand and the poor manners of the barons of Samhradh. But it had been an occasion that was worth braving the South. It was the day the Udar Apparent would breathe his first breath. The son of Faolan Myrkor—the reigning Udar of the seven worldly realms of Talam—would play a vital role in the ninth generation. He would one day inherit his father's throne and crown, and he would rule during the era of the *Gheall Ceann*.

There was an inherent dark cloud over the birth.

Taistealai could not help but assume he would follow in the footsteps of his father. He could only imagine the heir would one day rule the realms with a stern grip and an iron fist. Yet, Niamh Myrkor was known to be a kind woman.

She was loving and gentle. She was everything her mate was not.

It was a wonder they ever chose each other.

The mates of Udars before him were often as cold and cruel as their ruling half. One and the same, but that could not be said of Niamh and Faolan. Where Faolan was fire so hot it burned through the very veins of Talam, Niamh was a slow-running stream of cool water, content to be fed upon by the world.

If her child had a hint of her gentleness and the mercy she possessed, the realms would be in better hands than it had been for many generations.

Taistealai even dared to hold onto a thread of hope that the child would find the patience and wisdom to convene with the *Gheall Ceann* who was yet to be born, rather than raise their blade to her throat the moment they had the chance, as Taistealai knew Faolan would.

Despite what he believed, Taistealai still held onto that hope. And he would, ever as the gods preferred, turn a blind eye, ignoring the state of the realms altogether. They lived in a bliss that could not last. The ninth generation was upon them, and they were all aware despite the lack of conversation surrounding it.

The games would soon play out beneath their feet—games that could very well bring about their demise.

The small squirrel listened to the soft sound of his feet as he padded through the quiet halls.

The norns had arrived before him. He could smell the unsettling stench of life and death mingling on the stone that his paws grazed as he breezed through the dark corridors.

Taistealai longed to know the words they would sing to the Young Wolf, if even to get a glimpse into what would come of his own fate.

No one was safe during these times. And Taistealai found he was not ready to say goodbye to Talam.

The decor of wolves and colors of maroon and marigold flew by in his peripheral vision as he picked up his pace. He raced towards Niamh's quarters with his heart pounding in his chest. Niamh and

Faolan had never shared a bedroom, which was not uncommon among the lords and ladies of the realms.

When Taistealai finally reached the room that smelled of the birth of a babe, he paused to slow his heaving breaths. He hid in a corner beneath the heavy fabric of curtains, bathing himself in their shadows and the dark of the night.

His eyes adjusted, and he found the feet of Niamh's bed. Taistealai followed the dark wood up until he laid his eyes upon the beautiful female, whose skin was an odd shade of grey and sickly looking.

Taistealai tilted his head at a peculiar sight.

Niamh was not overcome with emotion as new mothers often were. She was not flushed red, and her eyes were not welling with tears of joy. She held her child in a swaddle of marigold cloth, but she did not look upon his face.

Niamh Myrkor gazed out the window at the night sky full of clouds—not a star in sight. Only the faint glow of Talam's dual moons.

Her face was entirely unreadable. Blank and emotionless. She continued to stare beyond the walls of her castle and into a sky so vast there was no end to it. She was as still as a statue as the norns closed in on her.

They reached out, and Verdandi's spindly fingers stretched into the air, as she clasped the shimmering golden thread that responded to her silent call. She pulled it down and touched the end to the young Myrkor's kicking foot where it attached.

Skuld reached for the other end and pulled it until it shot through the ceiling and went beyond where their eyes could see.

Taistealai had been too late to hear the words they had given to the Udar Apparent upon his birth. He was left to wonder if it was their prophesied song that had put Niamh in such a distant state as she gripped the cloth her babe was nestled inside of. The only hint of emotion showed in the way the tension turned her knuckles white.

The norns hummed gently and strangely for one beat . . . two beats . . . three beats, before the thread disappeared, and with it, so did the three ageless females.

Their absence left the room eerily silent.

Faolan sat beside Niamh's bed. Taistealai forced himself to look upon the male at last, his stomach turned the moment he found his amber eyes, full of smug approval as he watched his male heir. His arms rested not around his mate in comfort or celebration but folded across his chest.

Niamh continued to stare out of the window as though she was not of the worldly realms at all, but somewhere else entirely.

Taistealai silently cursed himself for not leaving sooner as he was left to puzzle over what it all meant.

The norns would never tell him either.

The words could only be spoken once. The words were only meant to be heard by those present at the birth. The words were meant to uplift or to doom, but given the pride of the father and the detachment of the mother, Taistealai could not begin to guess which the norns had granted the babe—born of duty, not love or tenderness.

Taistealai's heart tore at the seams with a sudden and overwhelming wave of grief for the young mother who had never wished for a life such as this.

He watched the light fade from her once bright eyes, not in a rush, but slowly, as though seeping through cracks she had held together for as long as she could.

The messenger of the gods began to pray that she'd saved enough love and tenderness to raise her son, as he'd receive neither from his father.

At last, the heir began to scream, shattering the silence of the too-still night.

PART ONE
CAGE OF DOUBTS

I
AISLA

Aisla Iarkis woke up wrapped in a warm blanket, in the beautiful deep orange of House Shea. Her arm was folded beneath her in a makeshift pillow, and when she moved, her hand brushed the cold floor of the castle's dungeon.

Her heart weighed heavily in her aching chest, carrying a range of emotions she did not have the energy or time to parse through. She reached out, allowing her fingers to graze the cobbles, grounding herself in a long breath. Aisla did not want to look over her shoulder to where the sleeping wolf lay in his cell. She thought, if she didn't, she could make herself believe for a while longer that it was all a dream.

A horrible, convoluted dream.

Aisla did not want to face what she had done—the mess she had created.

The *Gheall Ceann* did not know where her next step would take her, or even where to find the footing to take that next step.

She was afraid. And she did not know the way forward.

She only knew that Weylin Myrkor would have been able to find her the moment the shimmer of cursed gold had appeared, binding their souls together irrevocably and dangerously. The norns had made a joke of her fate by binding her to him as *searc*. She knew there had to be a way to use it to her advantage and had limited time to figure out how she could.

But now that Aisla had Weylin in a cell beneath her allies' castle, she was filled with guilt so heavy her stomach was constantly on the verge of upheaval.

The Udar Apparent was in her possession, and she had not the slightest idea how to proceed.

There was never a reality where Aisla could leave him alone in the dungeon. The Myrkors were no friends to the Sheas, and never had been, according to the world tellers' books. It was a known fact, even across the Tusnua Sea in Aisla's home realm of Eilean.

Aisla had seen what had been done to Ruairi at the hands of the Udar's men in a cell beneath the castle. She had not been there to prevent it, and that was something she could never forgive herself for. She would not be able to live with the guilt of allowing the same to happen to Weylin, no matter who he was.

Searc, or enemy, or complete stranger—no soul deserved the scars that Ruairi lived with physically and mentally—save for maybe the one responsible for them.

But Weylin was not. Because he was not his father.

So, Aisla slept on the ground outside of his cell. She had lost her trust in all the world, save for herself, Ruairi Vilulf, and Eire Trygg.

Aisla had not spoken a word to the male since she drove her blade into his flesh. He had made no attempt to speak to her, either. His hatred radiated from his all too familiar body like heat from a blazing fire. She brushed it off like stray embers that fell into a river.

Her bones ached, and her joints groaned in protest as she pulled her body up into a sitting position. Her fingers absentmindedly toyed with the familiar twine and wyvern tooth necklace that rested against her throat.

"Good morning," Weylin purred in a voice that dripped with malice. "That cannot have been a very comfortable sleeping arrangement. Surely the Sheas have better to offer their *Gheall Ceann*."

He spoke her gods-given title like venom on his tongue.

The hair along Aisla's spine rose in response to the familiar cadence of his voice as it met her ears. Her heartbeat quickened and her throat dried. Her mind raced with the memories of a time from before they had been declared *searc* by the norns. She inhaled a long, trembling breath before forcing herself to turn and face the male. His amber eyes danced with a challenge she didn't dare accept.

Not yet.

Weylin Myrkor perched on the edge of his bed, leaning towards her. His hands were clasped between his knees, and he wore a smirk of casual, unnerving arrogance as if she were the one behind iron bars and not him. His eyes gave him away, though. He looked weary, and a hint of nervousness indicated he was entirely out of his element. Exactly as she needed him to be.

A chill overtook Aisla as she held his gaze, fighting her instinct to look away.

Her lips remained pressed together. She feared what would come out if she opened them and dared to speak.

Would she curse him for the anger she held towards him during the sunrises that passed since their journey together, causing her blood burn to with fire? Would she whisper the words she tried to make herself forget? *I missed you.* Would she rattle the bars of his cage and shout with the rage of all of her ancestors until her throat was raw? Or would she fall to her knees and beg for his forgiveness? Because she had been the one to betray him in the end—hadn't she?

Aisla hadn't been able to forget that moment. When Weylin

leaned close enough for their lips to touch and spoke those words that rattled through her soul like a dam breaking free: *I could never hurt you.*

He had meant it, too. Aisla was certain of that, just as she was sure the moons lit the night sky.

And then, Aisla had betrayed him. She had stabbed him with her poison-tipped blade, leaving him vulnerable when he had already given her all that she had asked for. The thought made her stomach twist with guilt. She couldn't dwell on it.

She swallowed the feelings, pushed them as far down as they would go. Aisla gathered up the blanket that served as her makeshift bed without a word.

"Don't you know it's rude to ignore your guest, *banphrionsa*?" Weylin continued.

Aisla froze. The word carried the burden of a flood of memories that rushed through her veins, making her spine go rigid, halted by the weight of them.

"Or am I your prisoner? I do not know which to assume when you lock me up here but sleep at my feet."

Aisla bit her tongue until she tasted the metallic tang of blood. A guttural snarl rose in the back of her throat. He always knew the right words to say to get under her skin. He would find a way to twist her kindness into weakness.

She clutched the blanket closer to her chest, and the sound of crinkling parchment perked her ears. A corner of it jutted out from the folds. She furrowed her brows curiously, as she knew she had not fallen asleep with it.

Aisla shoved it deeper into the blanket, wishing to keep it out of the male's sight. She turned on her heel to leave, but his voice made her pause once again.

"What is your plan anyway? You know my father will not tolerate my absence for long, and I know you're fairly new here, but whispers on the wind travel fast on Iomlan."

Shame heated Aisla's cheeks as she prayed to the nine gods that she had not brought war to the Sheas' front door. A part of her wanted to admit this truth to him—to admit that she did not know—that she had no plan. But she could not let the Udar Apparent see her weakness. She could not admit that truth to anyone, not even her closest friends, and him least of all.

They were all looking up to her. They were all trusting her. They had all sacrificed for her. And Aisla feared most of all that it was a loyalty that had come to her unearned.

Aisla did not turn around but carried on towards the spiral staircase that would lead her back into the main castle.

"*Banphrionsa!*" Weylin called after her. There was even a hint of fear in his voice. A hint of desperation as he watched her disappear.

Good, Aisla thought. *Let him come to terms with the position he fell into. Let him acknowledge the control that he has lost.*

Aisla hurried up the stairs, ignoring the nagging feeling begging her to turn around. She had left with her dignity intact, and all it took was her complete silence.

She took the stairs two at a time as she hoped to make it back to her rooms without being seen. Whatever parchment had been tucked beneath her head while she slept was meant for her eyes, and she needed the privacy of her quarters to unfurl it.

Dawn light filtered through the thin curtains, and it looked early enough that the rest of the castle would still be asleep with any luck.

Aisla had nearly made it down the final corridor to her private rooms when a familiar voice called her name.

She winced before looking up to face one of her oldest and closest friends, Ruairi Vilulf. Her lips turned up in a small, false smile.

"Hey, Ru," she greeted, itching to push past him for a breath of time to herself.

"Ash, where were you? I went to your room to find you," he said, and the ever-present guilt in Aisla's gut fluttered.

Only Eimear Shea knew where Aisla had slept the previous night.

Aisla had asked her for help finding the castle's dungeon, and Eimear had led her there, no questions asked. For that, Aisla was grateful. The eldest Shea female possessed a kind soul and a gentle demeanor that was hard to find.

"Couldn't sleep. Restless night," Aisla lied, her guilt deepening like a gaping hole in her chest. One she hoped Ruairi could not see through. "Is there something you need?"

"I just wanted to make sure you were okay," he replied, gently and cautiously, as though afraid to spook her into running away.

"I'm fine," she nodded, feeling anything but.

"You don't have to lie, Ash," he said. Before she could protest, he continued, "But you don't have to tell me either. I know you have a lot going on, and a lot has changed, but you're still my best friend. Eire and I are here if you need us. You don't have to carry this alone."

Aisla's stomach twisted in knots. She would never deserve Ruairi's loyalty or his affection. The thought made her both angry and sad at the same time. It was a feeling she didn't know what to do with, and she hadn't known what to do with it for a while.

"I know, Ru. And the same goes for you."

Before Ruairi could say anything more, Aisla brushed past him towards her rooms. She didn't want to delay the mystery of the parchment any longer, and she was far too exhausted to talk to Ruairi about any of it—even though she owed him much more than she had given him.

The parchment felt too reminiscent of the letter her father, whom she had once thought was long passed on from the worldly realms, had translated for her in the library beneath the soil in Eilean.

She finally found her rooms that she had not slept in for several sunrises and took a deep breath as she leaned against the door. She was grateful for a moment of solace after so much had changed. In her life. In the political landscape of Talam. In the lives of those she loved from home, and those who hardly knew her but had taken her in.

Aisla closed her eyes and released a breath before crawling into the bed she had missed, even though it was hardly her own.

She settled in and shook out the blanket she had carried up from the dungeon. Aisla caught the wrinkled parchment as it fell from the creases. It had to be a message. Someone had found her sometime in the middle of the night and tucked it beneath her while she slept. She was certain she had not gone to sleep with it.

A dark foreboding feeling settled over her as she flattened it out in her lap. It was in the common tongue, Nua. The pressure in her chest lightened ever so slightly at the realization as she considered her journey to translate the runes of the letter from her grandmother. What Aisla had not expected were the words at the top of the page scrawled in the penmanship of someone running out of time.

To Aisling Iarkis, the one who was promised, the prophecy is yours at last.

Aisla's heart caught in her throat. Her breath rushed from her lungs as though she had taken a blow to her gut. Her hands began to shake until it was nearly too hard to read the words. She set it down, and her eyes poured over the riddle laid bare before her. She devoured each syllable as though they would disappear from the white sheet at any moment.

Under cold moons, the worldly realms will see an ember rise amidst blood already rife with power. An elf will be gifted with the esos of all nine gods to rise from the rubble and dust of circumstance and cruel winters.

The day the winds show their true force, a union or a dissolution of power will chart the course of vanished stars. A shattered glass will bring in a new age of esos and usher in the Mor War.

On the day that air turns to fire, children of darkness shall mark the downfall of an empire and a revival of wyverns to sunken earth. The dusk of the ancients will fall to the power of the blessed as fate hangs in the balance.

The words felt familiar, as though they resonated with Aisla's soul before she had ever seen them written on the page. At the same time, they felt distant—out of reach in a way she could not explain.

The words were about her, and Aisla could hardly begin to wonder at their meaning. It was vague and elusive. Aisla felt more lost than she had before she even read the letter.

She had been gifted the miracle for which she had prayed, but she didn't feel any closer to saving the realms or her destiny as the *Gheall Ceann*.

If anything, she felt farther from her fate, as though each step she took was a step in the wrong direction.

Aisla's stomach turned uncomfortably. She was afraid to continue down her own line of thinking.

She read through the words again, reading between the lines for any hint at who had delivered the message, but she found no clarity. Each read through seemed to cloud the already blurred direction before her.

Why would anyone give this to her?

She had half a mind not to trust it at all, but the words read like a distant memory. She knew it had to be the one and true prophecy—the prophecy that had never been written.

Why now? She couldn't help but wonder.

Her esos began to rile with frustration. It whispered through her hair and into her ears, but she shoved it away, knowing she needed to work on her control.

The only control she had previously known was the constraint Cliona had put over her esos to completely drown it without Aisla's knowledge. It was as if she was starting from scratch with her control, knowing that it had never truly been her own. Save for the brief time she had been on Iomlan and out of her grandmother's claws.

Even then, she had scarcely used her power, fearing it would give away her identity in the foreign land with no ash trees—the source of all elves' esos.

Aisla crumpled the damned paper as tears of irritation burned the corners of her eyes. She threw it at the wall, feeling like a child throwing a tantrum. The ball of parchment bounced off the wall and tumbled to the floor. Aisla didn't know what else she had expected.

Her gaze found the window, and she focused on the vast mountain range beyond it. They were smaller than the mountains of Caillte but beautiful all the same. The mountains were covered in a blanket of trees with leaves in beautiful golds, burning oranges, and rich greens.

Aisla pulled her knees into her chest and buried her face in them. She began to sob.

She was shaking before she could stop herself.

There were moments she wanted to break since she had learned that the Young Wolf was her *searc*. Moments when she could feel the grief and fear grip her heart like talons that squeezed so tightly, she feared her heart might burst into shreds beyond repair. Moments when she wondered how she had come to deserve this punishment of the gods.

But she held it all in.

Aisla knew she needed to see her plan through. A plan that she felt had taken a piece of her.

She held it together to be the leader the Sheas needed, so she was worth the risk. Given all they'd sacrificed for her, she had been the laoch Eire and Ruairi had anticipated.

But she could pretend no longer. Aisla was no leader.

She had no plan. No solution. No rally cry to shout for them.

Not even the prophecy itself had given her the answers she so desperately needed.

So, Aisla Iarkis fell apart in the bed loaned to her by the ravens of Fomhar. And the gods watched.

2
RUAIRI

The halls in Castle Orga were empty, and the air was eerily silent as Ruairi shuffled through the corridors.

He felt lost.

It was not that he did not know his way to the castle's dining hall, where they would serve tea and breakfast biscuits, and he didn't feel unwelcomed by the Sheas. But he did not know his place any longer. His fingernails were bitten down to the nub, and his cuticles were ripped as his unease ate at him.

He once should have been Aisla's right hand, helping her with the plans she devised, and walking with her every step of the way—no matter what mess they found themselves at the center of. But she had devised the plan to trap the Young Wolf herself, and he had found out alongside Eire and the Shea family.

Ruairi still did not understand how she knew where the Udar Apparent would be, or how she knew he would arrive alone. The letter she had left them explained very little, but Eire and Ruairi had convinced the Sheas to trust their friend.

It hadn't taken much convincing, as they already believed in their *Gheall Ceann* as though she were a god herself. It unsettled Ruairi in a way.

He had only ever known Aisla as his friend, and they had grown up side by side. She would always just be Aisla to him. But in another way, it made him proud to see her finally have support after all she had endured. First on Iomlan, and then through the translation of that cursed letter. The words that spelled the fate Cliona was willing to commit to. She would have sold Aisla to the Udar in exchange for power.

Ruairi's blood boiled when he thought of all that Cliona Iarkis had done to her granddaughter. While Cliona and Ruairi had certainly never seen eye to eye, he never imagined her to be capable of the evil revealed by her own words.

Ruairi had hoped to help Aisla through it. His heart ached to know she was in such pain. All it took was one look at her yellow-green eyes that were as familiar as his own to see the constant anguish she tried to hide. Yet, she pushed him away every time he took a step closer.

So, Ruairi waited, trusting she would allow him back in when she was ready.

It was selfish, but he found slight comfort in the fact that she seemed to be doing the same thing to Eire. It let him know that she wasn't upset with him, but was just sorting through it on her own, which wasn't entirely uncommon for Aisla.

On top of it all, being on Iomlan had returned the nightmares Ruairi had finally managed to get rid of back home. He hardly slept despite the comfort and luxury of the room loaned to him. His headaches had increased, too, as though the sinister forces that resided in Samhradh sensed his return to the main continent and were eager to sink their claws into him once again.

He felt like he was losing an uphill battle.

Ruairi found himself constantly looking over his shoulder, fighting against the paranoia that he was being watched. The place where his pinky had once been throbbed more often, too. It was the physical piece of himself he had lost within the castle walls to the Udar's laochs. Ruairi had to shake the fears. He had to move past it all if he was ever going to be useful in the war that was growing ever closer.

Aisla's ploy for a hostage wouldn't stall the Udar long—that much Ruairi was certain of.

"Ru!" Eire's frantic voice called him from his thoughts as he ambled through the corridors of the castle he was slowly becoming familiar with. "Did you hear?"

"Hear what?" he asked, looking up at her and meeting her piercing blue gaze.

"Bitu sent a ward to Fomhar to aid them during the Inevitable War."

"Bitu? They didn't even back Eilean during the Siege of Arden. Why would they do that?" Ruairi asked, immediately suspicious of the intent behind the action.

"Something about a debt owed to Fomhar. The Sheas say they called in the debt a couple of sunrises before we even arrived."

"Who is he?"

"Not anyone we would know," Eire replied with a hint of the sass that was an echo of her previous self. "Supposedly, he's the son of one of the noble houses in Bitu. His name is Kol Asulf, and he's a male elf around our age. He claims to be one of their top laochs. I don't know much else about him."

"What motive would he have for supporting the claims of an enemy to his realm?" Ruairi asked skeptically.

"He's sworn an oath before a priestess. The Lord of Bitu said so in the letter he brought with him for the Sheas. He will obey the order of the Shea dynasty until his final breath under the penalty of death. He has his own history in his home realm, unknown to me, of course, but he had to do something to be sent away from his family to fulfill the debt of his realm. And now, he'll never return to it."

"I can only imagine how pleasant he will be to be around," Ruairi grumbled. "I wouldn't be if I were sent to another realm against my will."

Eire gave him a flat look until he rolled his eyes in acknowledgment of the irony in his own words.

"Maybe he believes in Aisla," she added, too optimistically in Ruairi's opinion.

"We can hope," he agreed, but he felt indifferent.

"Regardless, we will take any of the help we can get. The Lady of Bitu, Bela Unfrig, assured the Sheas that Kol is a laoch who can hold his own."

Ruairi had never been to Bitu, but of all the realms, it intrigued him perhaps the most. It was the realm that was home to *Crann Na Beatha,* the tree of life, where it was rumored that Taistealai, the squirrel who served as messenger between the mortals and the gods, resided.

"Fair enough," Ruairi said. "How did you find all of this out, anyway?"

"Eimear told me."

"You seem to be fast friends," Ruairi noted with a suggestive raise of his eyebrows.

"Yes. She's pleasant and welcoming," Eire said, slowly. "But not like that. Not like that at all, Ru. It'll be a long time before it will ever be like that again."

Eire winced when she said the words, and Ruairi felt himself do the same. Eire hadn't talked about Fiona and what had happened to her, but Ruairi could put the pieces together well enough. His heart broke for the loss his friend had endured. He hoped she did not have to witness Fiona's passing on, but she hadn't told him one way or the other. All he knew was that she was still grieving, and would be for a long time.

"I'm sorry, Eire," he said, gently.

Eire looked at the floor, her face fallen.

"Have you seen Aisla yet? I figured she must be tired after everything. I still don't really understand what happened, but it isn't like her to sleep in this late."

"I actually passed her earlier. She woke up early and took a walk around, but she was heading back to her rooms when I saw her. She seemed like she was in a rush to get there, honestly."

"Should I talk to her?"

"If you want to," Ruairi said. "She's in her head again."

"I know. I wish I could pull her out of it," Eire replied with a sigh. "Let's go find the biscuits, shall we? I think we deserve them."

Eire turned her lips up in a smile that did not meet her eyes. She looped her arm through his—just like old times. They meandered down the hallways of Castle Orga, towards the dining hall.

Ruairi had to admit that of the three realms he had experienced, Fomhar had to be the most beautiful. The oranges, greens, golds, and reds used to decorate the castle's interior created an organic warmth that made the castle feel more like a home than a place for politicking. The only thing that made it feel less casual was the tradition of formal attire, where most castles had abandoned it to some extent. Ruairi didn't mind it much. He was grateful for the clothes loaned to him, and they fit rather comfortably for formal wear.

"Do you think the Udar knows where his son is, yet?" Eire asked the question that had been burning in the back of her mind since they had dragged the Young Wolf's unconscious body atop one of the Shea's horses. Hostage situations were new to them both, and Ruairi imagined to the Sheas as well, so he could only guess at where they would go from there.

"Doubtful," Ruairi replied. "They have no reason to suspect he would end up here, of all places. If Aisla and the Sheas act soon, they can send a raven with their list of demands in exchange for his safe return, and maybe they can stop the conflict on Eilean before it can begin."

Eire nodded.

Muinin had told Aisla that everyone was safe, for now. Things had not turned violent, but the island was surrounded on every shore by the Udar's laochs. Cliona was in talks with them, but nothing had been settled as far as Muinin knew. It had yet to be seen if war would break out across their home realm.

"What are they waiting on then?" Eire asked as a visible shudder racked down her spine. She had family in Eilean, as did Ruairi. It was terrifying to think what could happen in their absence. Ruairi found comfort in the fact that Cliona had made it clear in her letter that she was an ally to the Udar. While Faolan Myrkor might not have received the letter intended for him, surely she could find a way to reason with his laochs. But at what cost, Ruairi did not know.

At least Aisla wasn't there for Cliona to use as a bargaining tool.

"Aisla," Ruairi replied quietly. "I don't blame her, though. It's only the first sunrise since our return."

"Good thing I'm right here, then."

Ruairi startled at the sound of Aisla's voice behind them. He wondered how she could have caught up so quickly and how she could have walked up on them so quietly that Ruairi had not noticed even with his heightened elven senses.

"Ash!" Eire chirped.

Without hesitation, she turned and threw her arms around their friend. Eire pulled away to look Aisla in the eyes. Ruairi glanced over and saw a distance in Aisla's eyes that seemed to grow further with each passing heartbeat. He could tell the smile she wore was false the moment he looked at her.

"How are you feeling?"

"Lovely," Aisla replied, her tone dripping with sarcasm. "Never better."

"Where are you headed?" Ruairi spoke up, ignoring her snark.

He noted the way her face was set with determination, but a trace of fear lined her weary eyes. She wore a beautiful burnt orange gown with long sleeves that flared at her elbows. It was layered with a beige corset, and of course, Aisla accessorized it with the wyvern tooth necklace that Eire had given her all those moons ago. It felt like a different lifetime.

"Breakfast, right?" she replied, turning to look at him. She said it as though she always joined them for breakfast, but Ruairi could not remember the last time they shared a proper meal.

"Aisla, what's going on?" Eire interrupted before Ruairi could reply. "Enough of this act and the coldness. We know you have a lot going on—neither of us doubts that—but you don't have to pretend around us of all people. Save that for the politicking. Trust me, there will be more than enough of that to be had."

"What's going on is that I'm trying to save the worldly realms from their doom, not knowing if every step I take is for better or for worse. I'm racking my brain trying to figure out how to move forward with this situation that I've gotten us into. I'm trying to pretend I have half a clue where to go from here, but I was not trained for this," Aisla began, and the words poured out of her, as if she did not know where to end. "Give me a sword. Give me a bow. Give me a blade or allow me to wield my fists, but words meant for bargains and bribes have never been my method of weaponry. I have so little room for error. I wasn't meant for this. I don't know how I ended up here, and I'm doing all that is expected of me."

Aisla's voice broke on the final word as she looked up to meet their gazes. The three of them froze in the middle of the hallway, thankful that no one else happened upon them.

Before Aisla could say anything more, Eire wrapped her arms around Aisla again. This time, Aisla did not pull away or let go. Ruairi watched Aisla slump into her friend's embrace, needing the support although she did not know how to ask for it.

"I know," Eire whispered as she stroked Aisla's long, light brown hair. "But you don't have to pretend right now. You don't have to do any of this alone. We'll figure it out. We always have."

"How can you be so sure?" Aisla's voice came out as a cracked whisper.

Ruairi stepped forward to rest a comforting hand on her trembling shoulder.

"We can't," he replied, gently. "But when has that ever stopped us?"

Aisla pulled away from Eire and nodded slowly. She held open her arms and allowed Ruairi to pull her into his chest. He rested his chin atop her head and listened to the steady pounding of her heart.

For a moment, he was taken back to the shores of Eilean when he had to tell her he was leaving. Little did he know that he would never leave Eilean without her.

Yet, he should have.

Ruairi closed his eyes, longing for a time before that moment. Wishing things could be simpler, if only for a little while longer.

"The journey of endless sunrises begins with the very first step," he whispered the words to her, and tried to let them settle on his own restless heart, even as the persistent splitting headache returned.

He pushed it away, gritting his teeth against the pain.

3
EIMEAR

"Are you certain this is a task suited for me?" Eimear asked, allowing her exasperation to fill each syllable as she looked into her father's steely gaze with what were her best pleading eyes. "Surely Sorin or Cillian or even Roark would be better at this than me. I've no place in politics. I never have and I never will, Father."

"As I have already told you, simply keeping an eye on the ward from Bitu is not a matter of politics. Sorin is busy ensuring our laochs are ready for whatever comes our way when Faolan realizes where his son is. And Cillian is preparing to go north to speak with Lord Bastien and Lady Emil. And Roark—good gods, Eimear, your brother can hardly be trusted to keep an eye on Halli on a good day." Her father did not bother holding his own exasperation back.

He was not going to budge. Eimear's hope was fading fast.

"I don't want *anything* tying me here to the castle. I have my own baile—my own life," she insisted, gripping the arm of her chair as suddenly the room felt too small and the corset of her dress too tight.

"You were tied to this castle by your family name long before Kol Asulf ever stepped foot inside, whether you like it or not," her father said, sternly. "And what did you expect when you brought the *Gheall Ceann* to our realm? Did you really think life would return to normal? Yours or any other?"

"No, I suppose not. Do you wish I hadn't?" Eimear asked, fearing his response.

When Leighis had spoken of the *Gheall Ceann* and the danger she and her friends were in, she had told Eimear that Aisla would need a safe place to land, and that the Sheas assistance would be remembered and rewarded by the gods. Eimear had been excited to help. The goddess of healing and harvest had always been one Eimear thought to be good and wise and kind to the mortals of Talam. She had no reason not to trust her, and no time to consult her father on the matter.

And perhaps most of all, Eimear had no motivation to reject a god who could quite literally erase her from existence.

Fomhar had always been a friend to Eilean. And unlike the coward that was Brendan Dorcas, they would not turn their backs on the lost realm during the time of the ninth generation when it mattered most.

"No, my dear, of course not," her father said. She watched his light brown eyes soften, and he rested a hand upon her own that clung to the arm of her chair. She felt her muscles loosen as the comfort of his touch warmed the chill of anxious thoughts that coursed through her. "You obeyed a goddess, and for that we will be blessed. No one could ever fault you for such a thing. Even besides that, we are now able to help the *Gheall Ceann* save the realms. That was your doing, Eimear. Your name will be written about in the world tellers' books until there are no more eyes to read their pages."

"I never intended for my name to ink their pages," Eimear mumbled. She felt like a child, and she hated it.

"It seems as though the norns had other plans for you," her father said with a gentle smile. "And I have full faith that they picked the right elf for the job."

"I didn't mind that job," she said, attempting to push him back to her main point of grievance. "It's this new one that's been assigned to me by you, not the gods."

Her father loosed a deep chuckle that rumbled through his chest and shook his head.

"I'm only asking that you keep an eye on the male, Eimear. He may have sworn his life to us, but to some, their lives mean little. I do not want him running around our home unattended, especially now of all times. Would you rather trade roles with Sorin or Cillian?"

"I wouldn't mind going north," Eimear replied, brightening up.

She loved her cozy baile outside of the castle grounds, but what she loved most was not being stuck in place. Having a duty in her family's castle was the very definition of being tethered.

"You know that's not what I meant," he replied. Eimear deflated. She turned her gaze to the window beyond her father's chair and looked out upon the trees dappled in shades of maroon and gold. "And to be fair. The north would include a lot more politicking than either of the other roles would."

"Well," Eimear said with an audible sigh of defeat. "I definitely do not want that."

"I know, my girl," her father gave her an understanding smile, "but when Cillian returns, he can relieve you of your duty, how about that?"

"Deal. Must I stay here, though? What about my baile?"

"Unless you plan to make room for Kol there, then no," her father retorted.

"Absolutely not!" Eimear exclaimed.

"Then it is settled. Your rooms here remain exactly as you left them. You should feel right at home."

Eimear let out a puff of air that blew strands of her brilliant red hair out of her face. She settled into the cushioned chair, giving in to defeat. Eimear Shea preferred to spend her days however she pleased, free of responsibility and burdens. Most often, it pleased her to roam the forests of Fomhar, observing the animals and scouting for berries. She buried her nose in books and wrote stories of her own, set in lands far away. She flew low to the ground with her gryphon, Maira, and brought her watercolors with her to settle beneath large trees and paint scenes she dreamt up.

Eimear cherished her freedom.

She knew it was a selfish and childish thing to expect of her life, especially being born to the Lord and Lady of Fomhar, but still, she clung to it as tightly as she could.

"When is Cillian leaving?" Eimear asked.

Cillian had always been her closest sibling, and she would miss him dearly.

"That is still up for discussion," her father replied, suddenly distracted as he looked over her head to the doorway.

Eimear followed his gaze, and her breath caught in her throat as she met the wild and wide yellow-green eyes of Aisla Iarkis. The last time that Eimear had seen the female was when Aisla had shown up to her baile in the middle of the night with a dark brown cloak pulled over her head as she asked for directions to the cell where they brought the Udar Apparent. Her skin had been pale, and her eyes were tired—maybe even afraid. There had been a desperation in the question that the female had tried to pose as nonchalant. There was nothing sinister in her request, that much Eimear was certain of.

Eimear nodded, even though she did not understand at all. Something had told her it was not her place, and Eimear had never been one to pry. She led Aisla to the staircase that went down below the castle and did not ask any questions.

Standing in the doorway to one of Eimear's father's many studies, Aisla looked stronger than she had the sunset before. She looked confident and brave. She walked with a bit of swagger to her gait as she made her way into the room. Eimear couldn't help but wonder if she truly felt it.

"I hope I'm not interrupting anything," she said cautiously as she neared Eimear and her father.

"We were just wrapping up, actually," Eimear replied before her father could, feeling suddenly exhausted and thankful to end the conversation. "Anything we can help you with?"

"I would like to call a meeting," Aisla replied. Eimear felt her father tense beside her. "If that is okay with you, of course. I am ready to address the Udar. He will not tolerate the absence of his son for long. I think it is best we let him know where his heir is. I am ready to make our list of demands, but I would like a council to give input as well."

"That is very wise," Eimear's father said with a slow, grave nod. Eimear did not miss the admiration in his tone.

"My only request is that Ruairi and Eire join. And Eimear, as well."

Eimear's eyes widened.

"Why Eimear?" he asked in the same instant Eimear whined, "Why me?"

Eimear turned to look at her father and grimaced when she saw the amusement dancing in the depths of his brown eyes.

"I think you are wiser than you realize. And you are gods-chosen. It would be an honor to have you on my council. But if you object, I will not force the matter. Just know you have a seat at my table should you choose to take it."

The weight of Aisla's gaze was heavy on Eimear. Her skin began to itch with discomfort.

"S-sure," she stammered and cursed her tongue for its betrayal. "I will be there."

Aisla smiled with a warmth that was nearly tangible.

"What of Kol? Will he attend as well?" Eimear asked.

"Who is Kol?" Aisla looked to Deaglan for answers.

"He is a ward that has arrived to us from Bitu. I planned to tell you when I saw you. It was a bit of an unexpected arrival, but nevertheless, I think it could be just the right timing for us."

"I say we have him join us," Aisla offered in a tone that made it clear she was open to a differing opinion. Eimear noticed the way she treaded lightly. It was smart of her. Aisla may be the rightful heir to the worldly realms, but she was in an unfamiliar home, borrowing resources from a family she had only just met. It was good of her to be conscious of it. "It might be good to have an opinion from another realm as well."

"I agree," Deaglan said. He stood from his chair. "I will gather my family and my council if you would meet me in our council chambers. Your friends can show you the way. We convened there before the capture of the wolf. Eimear, would you retrieve Kol from his rooms?"

A retort caught in Eimear's throat. She wouldn't dare argue with her father in front of Aisla.

But she saw exactly what he was doing. He was making it known that her watch had begun, and she could delay it no further.

Eimear knew she was being dramatic.

She knew of all the tasks her father could have assigned to his eldest daughter, keeping an eye on their ward was hardly the worst of them. But Eimear had no interest in even the smallest of roles. She feared that once she opened that door, even a crack, she would never be able to close it again.

Eimear did not want to play politics.

She did not want to return to Castle Orga, and she felt as though giving in to this new duty would open up endless possibilities for responsibilities her parents might drop upon her.

Eimear grit her teeth and sucked in a breath as she raised her fist to knock on the wooden door of Kol Asulf's rooms. If all went to plan, they would be his rooms until his final breath. In the moments before he answered the door, Eimear found herself wondering if the male felt more like a guest or a prisoner. She wondered if his new duty was a punishment or a reprieve from his previous life. Then, the door opened, and she found herself face-to-face with the male.

The daylight that filtered in through the windows behind him lit up his face brilliantly.

Kol appeared to be around her age. He was taller than any of her brothers with midnight black hair, so dark it appeared almost blue like a raven's wings. His eyes were icy blue, and his skin was paler than hers with not a blemish in sight, unlike the freckles that covered her skin like the stars on a clear night sky. He was lean, and there was a surprisingly arrogant look about him as he gazed down his nose at her. She had to crane her neck to look up at him.

"Good morning," he crooned in a low voice and tilted his head to the side as he gave her a measuring look. "Is there something I can help you with?"

"My father and the *Gheall Ceann* request your presence for a council meeting," Eimear stated plainly.

"What a request. And so soon, too."

"Input from Bitu is appreciated at our table," Eimear replied, hating the way the words came so easily to her.

"You do know the whole point of being a ward is that I no longer represent Bitu, right?" His voice was smug and condescending.

Eimear folded her arms across her chest, refusing to let the male get under her skin. "Of course I know that," Eimear snapped, narrowing her eyes at him. "But you have more of a connection to the realm than anyone else in our ranks. The more input we can gather around our table, the better."

"If you say so."

Eimear bit her tongue and tapped her foot impatiently. "Can we leave now? Or do you require a moment to get your bearings?"

The male was already wearing clothes appropriate for the council. He had on a loose black top that was tucked into matching black pants. He could have done with lacing up the top a bit higher, as the V shape dipped low, revealing a muscular chest. Eimear's eyes caught on a ruby pendant hanging around his neck, and then her gaze dragged down to the gold rings adorning his fingers. He was a decent-looking male, and he seemed to know how to dress as well. Which, in her father's council, would go a long way.

"Lead the way, Eimear Shea," he said her name in a way that emphasized the rhyme, and something about it made her stand straighter, caught off guard by the pairing of her first and last name.

"Follow me," she said before turning on her heel to make her way through the halls of her childhood home as a shadow trailed behind her.

Something she would certainly have to get used to.

4
RANIA

The morning air was warm as Rania slipped out from beneath the beige silk sheets of Captain Callum Ronan's bed.

It had become a game of theirs—like everything else in Rania's life seemed to be.

The daughter of Briongloid spent most of her midnights wrapped in his arms, only to wake early in the morning before dawn with just enough time to slink back to her own chambers before anyone could notice her absence.

She knew after their first time that she would do anything to be around him. And it wasn't just the way his body fit to hers as though he were made for her. Or the way his tender caress was a taste of Albios. She enjoyed all of those things and would never in her lifetime get enough of them, but it was truly just *him.*

Callum was funny and kind and genuine and honest. He was everything good that there was in the world, and everything that the world did not deserve. There had never been another that knew Rania, like Callum did, and she loved when he explored her—mind, body, and soul.

It was a shame to hide their love in the embrace of shadows, but it was fun, too. Rania was used to keeping secrets, and perhaps far too good at it. And while Callum deserved to be more than a secret, it somehow made every stolen kiss that much sweeter, and each whispered desire that much more tempting.

It was all worth it. They hadn't discussed the future. Rania could not bear to. When Callum tried to bring it up, she found ways to distract him, and he seemed happy enough with that.

Because, while Rania Dorcas was an unmated female, the rest of Castle Eagla believed her otherwise.

They thought her mated to the Udar Apparent of the worldly realms, and that was just what she needed them to think. She was Weylin's mate in the only way that mattered to her—title—while saving herself for the one she truly loved.

Rania wasn't quite certain how it all would work—or if it could ever work. But Weylin had given her quite a few sunrises to stall in this in-between place Rania and Callum found themselves. She could live in her own pretend world, since he had fled their mating ceremony, leaving her alone at the altar. There were questions in the air, and questions that weighed heavily upon her shoulders, but she could only take it one sunrise at a time.

In many ways, she felt as though the gods had granted her a gift. In her own twisted way, Rania saw that gift as approval of her relationship with Callum.

She was certain that couldn't truly be the case, but in the moments when her fear of reality overcame her with a panic that stole the breath from her lungs—it was what she told herself.

Besides, if it wasn't approved by the gods, how could it all feel so good, so right?

Rania held her breath as she wrapped her hand around the brass knob of her bedroom door and turned it slowly, careful not to make a sound. She crept in on stealthy feet and leaned her back against the door, closing her eyes and thanking the gods for another successful escape.

Rania released her breath. She crawled under her heavy duvet that was the color of moonlight and pulled it up to her chin. She was almost immediately slammed with the absence of Callum as she curled in on her side, missing the warmth of his body behind hers. She closed her eyes and attempted to relish the final bout of sleep she could squeeze in before her day would begin.

Rania's eyes snapped open when a knock sounded at her door.

She jolted upright and looked to the window, where the early rays of dawn were peeking out behind full clouds.

She had not overslept, at least. Rania never needed anyone knocking at her door to wake her. She had always been a self-disciplined early riser. Ever since her escapades with the Captain of the Udar Apparent's guards had begun.

Something was off.

Not even Callum came to her rooms in the early morning. He knew better than that.

Rania peeled back her covers and pulled her pale blue nightdress tighter around her tired body. Normally, she would have changed into something more appropriate before answering the door, but the knock sounded again. And aside from that, she was the mate to the Udar Apparent.

No one would dare criticize her in her own castle.

With a long exhale, Rania opened the door, only to be met by the piercing green gaze of Orla, Faolan's right hand and rumored consort. Rania had never liked the female. A chill swept through her bones as she looked at her. They rarely stood so close, and it was unsettling in a way that Rania could not explain.

"We found your mate," Orla said by way of greeting. There was a glimmer of mischief in her irises.

Orla was one of five souls who knew the truth of Rania's mating day, and she had been the one to make it all possible. Orla had used her esos as a pryer to manipulate the memories of the audience at the ceremony so that they all remembered a mating that ended in a kiss and an exchanging of vows. But Rania, Orla, Faolan, and Weylin knew the truth.

Then, Rania had of course told Callum, bringing the number to five.

"Have you really?" Rania spoke quickly, trying to conceal the pounding of her heart beneath a false excitement and eagerness. Rania still did not understand how Orla could use her esos as a pryer when ash trees had not grown on Iomlan in five generations. The knowledge that she could made Rania extra cautious around her. With no training in esos, Rania had no idea how to shield herself from it. She didn't even know which source flowed through her own veins. "Is he here?"

"No," Orla replied. "Not anywhere near, actually."

Rania tilted her head curiously, her brow furrowing in earnest. Her stomach suddenly turned with foreboding. "Is he okay?"

"For now," Orla said, and her eyes hardened with coldness. "He's managed to make himself a hostage of Fomhar."

"What?" Rania gasped, her eyes going wide and her hand flying to cover her mouth in shock.

"Not only that. He is the *mallaithe's* hostage."

"What?" Rania repeated. She swore the world around her began to move in slow motion. "How?"

"That is a question we would all like an answer to. We received the bitch's demands this morning. As the Udar Apparent's mate, Faolan requests your presence in the council room."

"Demands? Who does she have to enforce such a thing?"

"Well, for one, the Udar's son. And as of now, that is enough. Not to mention, Fomhar has now formally declared allegiance to her." Orla's eyes flashed, and she knew they both recalled the time that Rania had tried to warn them of the realm that neighbored her home. "It seems as though you might have been right about them."

Rania should have felt victorious, but she did not.

Her mind wandered to that day she had thrown open the door to a council meeting she had not been invited to. They had been discussing the Inevitable War, and she had insisted they concentrate more efforts towards Fomhar, the realms just north of Briongloid. No one had listened, choosing instead to focus on Earrach, because it was the stronger of the two realms, despite Earrach having already allied with Samhradh in the past.

"What of Eilean, then?" Rania asked, her mind racing.

The ships had been sent to retrieve the *Gheall Ceann*. There had been an agreement with the Mathair, but it seemed like something had gone terribly wrong.

"Our navy has the continent surrounded. No one is leaving, and the weapons for the wyverns are loaded and ready should a wyvern attempt to leave as well. They haven't made a move yet. They were in negotiations with the Mathair, who was stalling. Faolan sent an order to remain at peace until we can bring Weylin home. The *mallaithe* is unpredictable, and we will not risk the Udar Apparent's life."

"How did all of this happen?" Rania whispered, half to herself. Suddenly, she felt very alone and vulnerable.

Orla only pressed her lips in a thin line and scanned Rania's face. The female was unreadable, as she often was, but Rania could have sworn rage churned in the depths of her green eyes.

"Get changed and meet us in Faolan's council chamber," Orla barked the order. "And do make haste."

Rania nodded, her body itching with urgency. Orla turned

without hesitation and made her way through the castle, her black cloak trailing behind her like the wings of a bat in the night.

Foreboding rattled through Rania's fluttering pulse as she stripped out of her flimsy nightdress and slipped into a navy gown fit for the Udar Apparent's mate. Its corset was a lighter blue, and the sleeves flared at her elbows. She tied her long white hair into a low knot at the back of her neck, pulling out the strands on either side of her face.

She tidied up her room before rushing out of the door and into the eerily silent corridor.

It wasn't long before she neared Callum's room. As though they had planned it, she heard his footsteps approaching the main hallway and looked up to meet his gentle green gaze. His cheeks were flushed red, and his hair was tousled from the dregs of sleep. He was adjusting the sleeves on his beige shirt and pulling down the brown vest over the top of it. Rania's heart leapt into her throat at the mere sight of him, and under any other circumstance, she might have begged him to sneak back to his rooms with her, longing to feel the warmth of his skin on hers again.

Despite it all, Rania couldn't help but feel fortunate that they had ever met, even in the face of fear for their future.

Rania swallowed, forcing any such thoughts from her mind. She cleared her throat, and Callum looked up at her in surprise before a grin spread across his lips.

"Fancy seeing you here," she chirped.

His grin fell as he glanced about the hallway, his expression shifted to one of concern, and he shook his head. Rania did not blame him. Rania cared for Weylin, but to Callum, he was like a brother. Rania knew the love they had for one another rivaled the love she felt for her own brother, Oisin, and she cared about Oisin more than she had ever cared about anyone else in the world, even Callum.

"You heard?" Rania asked softly as he caught up to her. They began to walk forward, matching each other's hurried pace as they made their way towards the main rooms of the castle.

"Indeed," Callum said.

"I'm so sorry," she whispered. "We'll get him back."

"I sure hope so."

The rest of their walk was spent in silence until they finally reached the large oak doors that led into the meeting chambers of Castle Eagla. Callum stepped around Rania to swing open the door, allowing her to enter first.

"Thank you, good sir," a familiar voice met Rania's ears. She turned to see her brother slip in after her, teasing Callum on his way.

He was out of breath, as if he had run all the way there from his own chambers. Rania shook her head, giving Oisin a small smile.

"Glad to see you here, O," she said.

Her brother put his arm around her shoulders as they made their way to two empty seats near the middle of the table. Rania ignored all of the glances thrown her way and focused on the weight of her brother's arm around her—the familiar scent of home that clung to him in a way that it did not for her.

"We'll fix this," he whispered in a tone so convincing, she nearly believed it. But she didn't think Oisin knew what he would be fixing.

Rania nodded.

Guilt twisted in her stomach. She had not told Oisin the truth about her mating day. She could not bring herself to. Especially not after she had already told Callum, breaking her sworn secrecy the same day she had declared it. As far as Oisin knew, and as far as the rest of the realm knew, Rania was a mate grieving the absence of her newly mated. And so, Rania wore the mask of broken-hearted damsel.

And she wore it quite well, in her own humble opinion.

It wasn't hard. Rania had tried on and practiced different masks growing up in a world that had not been made for her, not until she had found an opening to make the world her own. Only it had been more complicated than that.

It always was.

Rania allowed her eyes to glaze with the early signs of tears. She wrapped her arms around herself, refusing to look anyone in the eyes as she settled into the maroon velvet chair. Her lower lip trembled slightly, but her jaw was set with determination to free her mate from the *mallaithe*.

She looked down at her hands in her lap as the rest of the seats in the room filled up. She fought not to let her gaze wander to Callum, despite the pull between them.

"I will not waste your time with salutations," Faolan spoke up, and the whole room fell silent. Malice laced each syllable. A chill traveled down Rania's spine, but she did not allow it to show. "What you need to know is my son left his own mating ceremony to settle a border dispute between some of the smaller cities bordering Brionגloid and Samhradh, riled by the event of their mating. Had we known how bad it was, we would have never sent him alone. We sent laochs scouring Samhradh for any trace of him or his horse and came up empty-handed. This morning, we received a letter via raven from none other than Aisling Iarkis, sealed with the crest of the Sheas." Faolan paused as gasps erupted through the room.

Clever, clever lies, Rania thought to herself. She didn't know if she admired the ability to lie so fluently or feared it.

"She has informed us that Weylin is in her possession. He remains in a cell beneath Castle Orga. We have been assured of his well-being, *for now.* She has sent a list of demands that we cannot possibly accept."

Rania's stomach sank to her feet. She couldn't help but lean forward in her chair, knowing that the words Faolan held could very well change the course of the Inevitable War. The course of the whole of Talam, really, during the time of the ninth generation. The whispers on the wind had long spoken of Aisling Iarkis, and the salvation or destruction of the nine realms at her hands. Rania wondered what direction they were headed, for not the first time.

Oisin tensed beside her. She dared a glance at Callum. His attention remained focused on Faolan. His jaw was clenched in anticipation, and his skin was a shade paler than normal.

"Her demands are as follows," Faolan cleared his throat before continuing, *"In exchange for your only son and heir, Weylin Myrkor, we require your ships to abandon the coast of Eilean. You will also sign a treaty of peace with Fomhar, so they shall in no way be reprimanded for their role in my scheme. Additionally, you will give up your pursuit of my life for nine years. Commit to nine years of peace, and I will spend the time resolving the matter of the prophecy once and for all. At the end of nine years, if it seems your interpretation is correct, and my life is indeed the doom of Talam, then I will bend my knee and accept your blade. If I am meant to be the salvation of the realms, then I trust you will allow me to do the job intended for me. Finally, you will return my throne to me at once. I will see it is taken to its rightful home in Eilean, and I shall sit in the seat that was my birthright. You will relinquish the crown you made in imitation of my own. Should these terms be a fair price for the life of your son, I will meet you at the border of Briongloid and Fomhar on the evening of the next full moon in Sneachta. You may bring one companion with you. Whoever else is traveling with you must wait in Briongloid. I will bring your son, along with a companion of my own. I expect a response within three sunrises, or your son will pay the consequences. Signed, the rightful heir to the worldly realms, Aisling Iarkis."*

The room fell eerily silent.

Rania's pulse hammered at her temples.

The demands were far too great, and everyone in the room recognized it. No one knew what to say.

Rania could practically feel the heat of rage radiating from Faolan across the table. The *Gheall Ceann* had gaul, but Rania did not understand what game she was playing—and that terrified her.

She anxiously waited for a response from Faolan.

Anything to break the silence.

5
WEYLIN

There were only so many ways to count the cracks in the ceiling of his surprisingly comfortable prison cell.

So, Weylin Myrkor had taken to closing his eyes and praying to gods he did not believe in that he would find sleep again.

It was midday, from what he could tell of the small window at the very top of his cell. But he was restless. Powerless. And that was something he was not used to feeling.

Weylin had certainly never considered himself to be a reckless male, yet it seemed that he certainly was, no matter how he looked at it. Callum had even tried to warn him a time or two. Perhaps when Weylin had gone by himself to ask for Rania's hand in mating, he had been reckless. If he had his laochs with him, he would have never ventured home alongside the *mallaithe*.

When he had rushed to aid Earrach in their dispute between the sylphs and the undines against his father's will, he might have been a tad brash. But at least that had gone well.

But then he had left his mate-to-be at their altar to chase a fleeting golden thread across foreign realms and through dangerous terrain with only the company of his mare, Eolas. That was clearly the most reckless thing he had ever done, and it had landed him in the arms of his enemy.

But what else had he expected? It was as though a part of him knew it would end like this, and still, he had gone with no hesitation. Willingly and eagerly.

Since then, Weylin had nothing but time to ponder every way it could have gone. He thought over all the steps he could have, should have, taken differently. It was maddening.

There was nowhere for him to run to now. Nowhere he could throw himself to rally for his cause against the *mallaithe*—who was the very reason he found himself hostage. He was almost proud of her for it. It was the best move she could have made for her own cause, but he wondered what she had planned next. Her next move would change everything—for better or for worse.

In all of his wildest dreams and most terrifying nightmares, Weylin would have never guessed that Aisla Iarkis was his *searc*—his gods-chosen match—to which no other could compare.

Or so the world tellers said.

He could have ignored it. And perhaps he should have.

But he did not know how to hide it from the watching eyes present at his mating ceremony. He didn't even know if they could see it at all and hadn't stopped to consider it. More than that, Weylin had not wanted to ignore it. And that fact made his blood run cold.

It wasn't right.

The golden thread had changed nothing about how he felt for Aisling Iarkis. It had not been a sudden burst of warm feelings or love or any of those things that Weylin did not believe in.

No, it hadn't changed a single thing. But it did validate a lot of them.

It was as though, for a moment, a weight was lifted from his shoulders. For a brief moment, he was not ashamed of the way he had grown to care for Ellora Morlee, even though she was never real, only an alias Aisling Iarkis traveled under during their time together. The fog that he had put in place to protect himself when he thought of her was lifted. The feelings hadn't appeared out of nowhere, but rather they rushed forward from the depths he had shoved them into before he had ever glimpsed that golden thread of the norns.

He could see her, almost corporeal, standing before him with her eyes of yellow-green wildfire and the freckles he had memorized. In that moment, Weylin knew the only way he could be that near to her was to follow the golden thread. He knew it would take him to her.

The moment had been fleeting.

It ended the same instant she drove her poison-tipped blade into his flesh.

Weylin had been naive to think she would have a civil conversation. He had grown up hearing of the brutes raised by wyverns on Eilean, and what could he have expected? That she would forget everything his family had done to hers?

Aisla Iarkis was as wild as the fire in her eyes.

On their journey from Briongloid to Samhradh, Weylin had been able to read her like a book. Her emotions showed in the crinkle of her brow or the scowl on her lips. But when he looked into her eyes as she betrayed him, he felt like he did not know her at all. They had been suddenly both warm and cold. Both open and closed. Both alight and covered in shadows. Flickering back and forth between paradoxes as he fell to his knees before her.

Weylin didn't have the faintest idea what she would do with him. But he did know the words he had spoken to her were true ones: he would never hurt her, for his pain would be double whatever he had dealt her.

But she was never meant to know that.

The words she had given him in return spoke a completely different message: *I could never kill you.*

There were many ways to hurt a person without killing them. In fact, there were many pains that hurt worse than death itself. As a laoch trained in combat, and what his father liked to call the art of persuasion, Weylin knew that truth all too well.

She had already hurt him when she left him in a cell beneath a castle in an enemy realm with nothing to entertain himself besides counting cracks in the ceiling. And it was only the beginning.

Weylin felt like an idiot, and he hated it.

He wished Aisla would speak to him. She hadn't uttered a word when he woke from his valerian-induced slumber. It drove him mad. Her indifference and her silence. Weylin wished she would do anything at all, even if the first words from her lips were to tell him she hated him.

He would take it. Weylin could handle yelling and screaming—hel, he would even take her blade—but he could not take her silence.

The only hint of emotion he had received from her was waking up to find her sleeping in a pile of blankets outside of his cell. The sight of her light brown hair spilling out around her like branches on a winter tree and the gentle rise and fall of the fabric cocoon she had created had fractured something inside of Weylin that he did not know how to name.

He only knew how to taunt her with it.

But it meant she cared.

Even if it was only a shred, it was enough to know she would speak to him eventually. He just hoped it would come sooner rather than later. Silence grew boring rather quickly.

At least Weylin couldn't complain about the accommodations granted to him in Castle Orga. He had been treated well, as far as prisoners go. The bed was comfortable, if a little too soft. The food they brought him was much better than the slop they fed prisoners in Castle Eagla.

Weylin knew he wasn't quite a prisoner. He was a hostage, and that came with a different set of rules entirely. He found himself curious to see what Aisling would do with the situation. It wasn't an easy one to be in—not when she had so few souls standing behind her. But now that she had found a realm with a noble family to host her, she had more than Weylin or his father had anticipated.

Faolan would be furious.

There was no doubt about that, but he would not let Weylin die. Certainly not since Weylin was his only heir. Weylin found himself grateful, and not for the first time, that he was his father's only child.

He had once longed for siblings during his childhood, when the days grew long and lonely, but he found the only one he ever needed in Callum Ronan. Weylin wondered how Callum would take the news. He hoped his father would send Callum to retrieve him when the time came—he hardly had the patience for anyone else, especially given his circumstances.

Weylin thought of Rania then and winced with guilt when he thought of the female he had left behind. His guilt deepened when he recalled the mixed look of shock and fear in her endless blue eyes.

Rania deserved better than he had given her, but really, she should be angry with the gods or the norns or whoever set such things into motion and their horrible timing.

It had been cruel of them to pull Weylin from his mating ceremony to show him who they declared as his *true mate*. The irony was blatant enough to smack anyone in the face. Weylin did not know how he would ever explain it to Rania, or anyone else, for that matter. Not that he hadn't had plenty of time to figure it out with only the company of his own thoughts on the journey back to Fomhar after he had regained consciousness.

Thinking of it often brought him back to the question he didn't have an answer to: if he returned home, would he still mate her? And would she still mate him?

The answer could very well chart the course of all of the realms forward. His mating had come with the promise of an alliance to a realm that had hated Samhradh nearly as much as Fomhar did. Weylin could only imagine Brendan Dorcas's anger when he heard that the Udar Apparent had rejected his daughter after being the one to ask for her hand.

Another thing for his own father to be furious about.

The creak of a door made Weylin sit straight up on his bed. They had just delivered his afternoon meal, and he was not expecting another so soon. Unless he was losing his mind entirely, which was very well possible, but it seemed a tad too early for that.

Still, the disturbance could mean a multitude of things, ranging from relief to horror.

The people of Fomhar had shown him no hint of violence so far, only sneers and narrowed eyes that showed their obvious disdain for him, but that was something Weylin had grown accustomed to, even within his own realm. But Weylin would not put violence past them. Not while he remained trapped behind bars—he would be a fool not to consider the all too real possibility.

He listened carefully, and nearly immediately recognized the soft cadence of her step. He had spent too much time watching her, being cautious of her, not to know it by heart. Weylin remained wary as he stood and smoothed out the beige linen pants that had been given to him.

He paced the length of his cell as he waited for her to reach the bottom of the spiral staircase.

Weylin clenched his jaw when he heard her nearing, and at last he looked up to see Aisling Iarkis approaching him. His breath hitched for a moment when she came into view. Her long, light brown hair was braided, intertwined with lilies, and hung over her shoulder. She was more put together than he had ever seen her. And for the second time since they had met, Aisling was wearing a dress, but this time it was not a night gown.

Aisling wore a gown of emerald-green, the color of her wyvern's scales. The corset hugged her waist, and the skirt flowed out like a waterfall, moving with each step she took. Layers of fabric varying in shades of green caught brilliantly in the flickering torchlight. The sleeves were loose from her shoulders until they cinched around her delicate wrists. The neckline was a deep V that plunged between her breasts. Then, there was that familiar necklace made of twine and pieces of what she had once told him were from a stag's antler, but he had a sneaking suspicion they more likely came from a wyvern.

Weylin was quite glad they were not on speaking terms because he wasn't sure he could have found the words if he wanted to.

He had always thought she acted like a *banphrionsa*. The nickname arose from the way she acted like a sheltered princess, unafraid of the world. But for the first time, she truly looked like one, too. Weylin was certain, even if she had not been his *searc*, he had never seen a more beautiful female in all of Talam.

Weylin felt her gaze before he met it. He felt it like the chill of snowfall and looked up to see her eyes that still blazed like a fire so wild it would ravage the world. Weylin knew he would be helpless to stop it, and he did not know that he wanted to.

The hair along Weylin's spine stood on end as she held his gaze, and there was a confidence there she had once lacked. He found himself glad to see it.

"I have good news for you," she spoke, and it felt as though he was hearing her voice for the first time. It was a beautiful paradox of soft and rough.

"Oh, good," Weylin replied, managing to match her even tone with his own. "I was almost certain you were here to deliver bad news."

"You might be returning home soon. If your father accepts our terms. Negotiations have officially begun."

Weylin tilted his head as he took in the update. He had not expected her to deliver her terms so quickly. He did not know if he was ready to return. There was more to be said, and more to be learned. But if Weylin knew anything about Faolan Myrkor, he knew that this was only the beginning. His father would do anything in his power to ensure the *mallaithe* got out of the situation with as little as possible. Weylin worried Aisla might not know who exactly she was up against, but he had a feeling she wouldn't listen to him, even if he tried to tell her.

"So soon? We were just getting started, *banphrionsa*."

"Don't you want to know what the terms were?" Aisling continued, clearly following her own agenda.

"Not particularly. Whatever they were, I am sure this is not the end of the conversation. My father does not like to be told what to do and will especially be opposed to any demands *you* make of all people. Come back a few exchanges from now, after he has worn you down, and we are closer to the real terms."

Anger flashed through Aisling's eyes, but she recovered quickly. "We will see."

"How are you, Aisling? It seems I have forgotten my manners during my time as your hostage," he said and tutted his tongue against his teeth for emphasis.

"I wasn't aware you had ever possessed any," she snapped. "And it's Aisla—just Aisla."

"We have nicknames now, do we?"

"No," she said, shaking her head, "everyone calls me Aisla. No one calls me Aisling. So, neither will you."

"Noted," Weylin replied coolly, noting how his indifference only riled her annoyance. "But you didn't answer my question."

"How do you think I am?" she snarled before taking a few strides forward. A loose strand of hair fell from behind her ear across her face. When she stopped, she stood close enough that if Weylin stood at the edge of his cell and reached his arm through the bars, he would just be able to graze her skin. "I'm tired. I'm angry. I'm restless. And above all, I'm terrified that I'm in over my head."

Weylin paused, shocked by her sudden show of vulnerability. When he looked closer at her and saw the dark circles lining her eyes and the way her nails were bitten down to the beds, he understood.

"In your defense," he said, lowering his voice, "I'm afraid you've been in over your head since your birth, my dear."

Aisla shot him a look, her brief moment of vulnerability dissipating as quickly as she had allowed it to show. She turned her head away from him to look at the ground.

"And you weren't?" The words were spoken quietly, and her entire demeanor shifted.

"That has always been the common thread between us, hasn't it?"

"I suppose so," Aisla replied, her voice full of defeat. Weylin watched her shoulders drop, and she began to pick at the skin around her cuticles. He wished there were words of comfort he could give her, but even if he could, he did not know if she would accept them from him

"I meant what I said," Weylin whispered. She looked up at him, confusion knitting her brow together. "Never let anyone tell you that you aren't enough, *banphrionsa.* That applies to Aisla as well as Ellora."

Weylin felt like a fool as he said the words.

He knew he should be angry. He should hate her for what she had done to him, but he also understood it. From one pawn in the world of politics to another, he had to respect her valor.

It was what she was meant to do—who they were meant to be.

Aisla's eyes glimmered with sincerity before it was overtaken by burning anger. She took another step forward. Weylin could smell the lilac and ash wood scent of her hair that not even the forests of Fomhar could wash away.

"You cannot manipulate me with your honeyed words," she snapped. "Just remember which one of us is behind bars."

"I've long known I cannot manipulate you. I wouldn't dare try."

"Nothing has changed between us," she declared as if that could erase the golden thread that bound them, even when they could not see it.

"You're right," Weylin replied, keeping the emotion from his voice. "Nothing has changed. It only makes sense now. You kissed me, remember, *banphrionsa*?"

Aisla took the final step, and her toes met the iron bars of his cell. She wrapped her small, trembling hands around the two nearest him until her knuckles turned white.

"And I've regretted it ever since," she hissed.

"Whatever you tell yourself to sleep at night," Weylin chided. "Or is that what you tell your red-haired male at night?"

It was a low blow. Weylin knew it the moment the words left his lips. That ever-present tinge of jealousy left a bitter taste in his mouth whenever he thought of the male that Aisla Iarkis had risked the entirety of Talam for. Love like that didn't happen often.

And more than that, making her angry was better than the indifference she offered him. He wanted her to feel something, and he had gotten his wish.

"You are absolutely insufferable!" she spat and bared her teeth at him, just as she once had to a pack of barghests in Briongloid. "I thought I could come down here and speak with you, but clearly, you are incapable of anything civil. I knew I would regret it, but I did not know I would so soon."

"You make it too easy," he replied with a lazy grin. He watched the muscles in her jaw tick as she clenched her teeth.

"What?" she demanded.

"To get under your skin."

Weylin heard her sharp inhale of breath before the next words left her mouth. "Gods damn you, Weylin Myrkor!"

Aisla turned on her heel to leave, and in a panicked fit of desperation, Weylin's arm shot out through the bars, and his hand closed around her wrist before she could escape him.

"Forgive me if I have a hard time understanding this dynamic between us," the words left him in a rush. "I had memorized the constellations of the freckles across your face in our time together, yet I did not know your true name."

Weylin did not know what he was saying. He just knew he had to say something that might change her view of him, if only for a moment. Her eyes flickered back and forth between his, and he wondered what she saw there. Her expression was unreadable.

"As if I knew yours," Aisla snarled and yanked her wrist free from his grasp.

Weylin's hand fell to his side, and his skin burned where it had touched hers.

6
AISLA

Aisla's jaw was still tight from her conversation with the Young Wolf as she made her way into the woods of Fomhar. She let loose a long breath and tried to shake the feeling of both irritation and shame at how easily he got the best of her.

She shook out her hands as if that could erase the feeling of his skin on hers. Aisla closed her eyes and fought to slow her racing heart. It had been a long day, and after all, he was bound to find a way underneath her skin.

She felt good about the letter she had penned after meeting with her new and first council. It had been a damn good council at that. The Sheas were helpful, but not pushy with their ideas, and Ruairi and Eire were the listening ears and sounding boards she needed them to be.

Aisla noticed that they sat back and watched before adding their own input, and Aisla would never say it, but she found their thoughts to be the most valuable.

Still, she felt even better about the plan she had concocted with Muinin. It was mostly his idea, as he liked to remind her.

When can I expect you? Aisla asked into the space in her mind that they shared. *It's getting late.*

So much complaining and not nearly enough gratitude, Muinin replied with a grunt.

Aisla could hear the flapping of the wyvern's wings around his voice that meant he was skyborne. She squinted through the night fog into the darkening star-filled sky, looking for any sign of him.

And you're sure this is a good idea?

This is the hundredth time you've asked. Minimum.

It's a big deal, Muinin.

Yes, I do think my idea is a great idea. You owe it to the people of Fomhar to be able to defend themselves if and when all Hel breaks loose.

You're right, Aisla breathed out and leaned against a tree trunk. She sat on the ground, observing bits of soil that slid along the silk of her gown.

There was no telling how Faolan Myrkor would react to Aisla's demands, or the threat to his son's well-being. They were not meant to be accepted immediately—Aisla was no fool. She was hoping for a period of negotiation with the Udar while giving herself time to continue to parse through and try to make sense of the prophecy that had been slipped beneath her pillow the sunrise after the Udar Apparent arrived to Castle Orga.

And in that time, she and Ruairi would begin training the laochs of Fomhar in their esos.

Muinin's job was to bring an ash tree from Eilean, and they would plant it in an isolated planter at the center of Castle Orga so that its roots would not spread beyond the castle or further yet to the other realms. They needed to keep its arrival and existence a secret. Aisla felt it was the best way she could thank their people for both harboring her from the Udar and aiding her in the capture of the Udar Apparent, which was one of the riskiest things they could have done.

There was a glass case prepared for the tree until Ruairi and Aisla were ready to begin training. Deaglan Shea was hand-selecting elves for their first round of training, including each of his own five children, even the youngest, Halli.

How is my father? Aisla asked down the bond.

Muinin had been keeping an eye on him and the Silenced World Tellers since Cliona had ravaged her mind following her visit to the underground library. Aisla only wished she could have been there when her father reunited with Muinin after they had both believed him dead for many moons. She could still hardly believe her father was truly alive, and knew it was taking Muinin time to come to terms with it himself. He may be Aisla's bonded wyvern, but before that, he was bonded to her father. Feargal and Muinin would never be able to reforge the bond that her grandmother had destroyed, but there was still enough love between them to fill countless lifetimes.

Though he didn't speak much of it, Aisla knew Muinin was grateful to see his previous rider once again. He had never said anything to her, but a guilt coursed through Muinin when they spoke of Feargal Iarkis. Her wyvern would forever blame himself for not realizing his own bonded was still alive. Aisla had half a mind to tell him that it wasn't his fault—there was no way he could have known—but she knew it wouldn't change how Muinin felt. She had similar feelings about not knowing her own father was alive, and it made no difference when she told herself the same things.

They couldn't turn back time.

Muinin had told her that the Silenced World Tellers were doing what they could to prepare for the Inevitable War. They would stand against their Mathair when the time came. Fortunately, Cliona had been too occupied with the foreign navy on their coast to bother with anything else. And while she had intended to be the Udar's ally, there was not much for her to offer him when her granddaughter had slipped out of her grasp and captured the Udar's son in the process.

Despite all of the anxiety and complications, Aisla found satisfaction in the predicament she had created for her grandmother. Aisla worried about how it might affect her realm as a whole, but she knew they were at a standstill while she had Weylin Myrkor. Which was why removing the navy from Eilean's coast was one of the demands she would not budge on. Aisla was thankful at least to have made friends in the library of the Silenced World Tellers, so she did not feel like she was abandoning her realm completely. Having her father there made her feel safer as well. Despite his fears, she knew Feargal was devoted to his realm and would give his life to save it from his mother.

Muinin had also been in contact with Eire's parents, as Eire's mother was a shifter and could speak mind to mind with creatures, the same way Eilis had taught Aisla. Eire's parents knew to be wary of Cliona. Aisla made the difficult decision to have Muinin tell them of the role her grandmother played in the illness that left Eire first half-dead and then as a human—stripped of her esos and long life.

Her parents were angry—they were outraged—and rightly so, but they knew better than to let Cliona know what they were privy to. Aisla trusted that.

Aisla only wished she could get them to steal back the ring that controlled the husks, but it was too risky a task to ask of them. It nagged her mind every day to know the power of that army remained with her cruel grandmother, and each passing day left her wondering if the ring alone would be enough of a barter to lock in her alliance with the Udar.

If she didn't need Aisla, it wouldn't be long before Eilean fell to Samhradh.

A chill traveled up Aisla's spine, and she rubbed her temples. Her head ached, and her mind was constantly spinning so fast, it was a wonder she hadn't lost it completely yet.

He's as well as he can be, Muinin replied in the same moment that his massive shape came into view through the fog and the dark. Relief rushed through Aisla's chest, and she stood to wait for his landing.

It was helpful that they no longer had to hide his flight. The

Myrkors already knew where Aisla was, but they wouldn't dare act against her or her wyvern while Weylin was still in her custody.

It's about time, Aisla teased as Muinin ducked his head and began his speedy descent towards her.

So impatient, he chided. *Do you have a plan for the awakening of their esos? There's been nothing like this since the early days of elves.*

Somewhat. Enough of one. Anxiety raced through Aisla at the question, but they did have a plan; she had to focus on that. It was too easy to worry about all of the things that would go wrong rather than focus on the task at hand. Aisla continued, *Ruairi will help, and I'll do what I can. We walked the Shea heirs through the art of esos as best as we could without having a source for them. They'll be the first to help us train other laochs, and we can expand from there. We prepared more than enough iron restraints to mute their esos if anyone gets out of hand. We're hoping for the best.*

Aisla was also grateful that Weylin's cell was made of iron bars, so the esos from the ash trees would not reach him. She didn't want to risk any chance he could break out of his confines. Although, as far as she was aware, he had made no attempts.

The thought of him brought forward his words that hung heavy on her heart since he spoke them. The ones she had tried to forget, despite the fact that they flickered like a warm flame within her.

I had memorized the constellations of the freckles across your face in our time together, yet I did not know your true name, Weylin had said, and he had meant it, too. That was the worst part.

It was heartbreaking in a way that left a sour taste in Aisla's mouth. The words were beautiful, and the kind one would usually hang onto like a cherished gift. But when she tried to hold them in her mind, they grew thorns and pickled her thoughts. They were his words, and Aisla could not trust the sweetness that dripped from the tongue of the usurper's son.

Despite her anger towards the Young Wolf, Aisla would continue to sleep on the floor outside of his cell, afraid of what her absence could bring. No matter how much she trusted the Sheas, there was a part of her that feared for his safety as he was truly in the home of his enemy.

Aisla was always back in her rooms before anyone knew she had slept anywhere besides her bed, and she intended to keep it that way.

It was fine when they didn't speak. Aisla hadn't wanted to break that silence, but her anger had grown until the tension between them was so thick she could slice it with her dagger. She couldn't bear it any longer, even though she had hoped it had bothered him just the same.

Even when they had traveled together under aliases in a foreign realm, she had hated the silence between them. Even when she found him to be arrogant and rude and horrible, she would rather trade insults than have him ignore her presence altogether.

And Aisla was beginning to think he might have realized that.

Just don't be naive, Muinin's voice broke through Aisla's thoughts as embarrassment heated her cheeks. *And call me if you need me.*

You remind me of that every sunrise . . . several times a sunrise, Aisla teased.

A smile lit her face, temporarily brushing aside all of the worries that plagued her as Muinin landed in the clearing. The instant the ground shook with the weight of him, Aisla flung herself towards him, throwing her arms around his neck, unable to reach around it entirely. She tightened her hold as she eased into the familiar warmth of his scales and his scent of home. Muinin chuffed and leaned into the embrace.

You're making it hard to breathe, he joked

I know you missed me, too.

Aisla pulled away reluctantly. Her eyes searched Muinin's for any hint of emotion. They were unreadable as he dropped the ash tree into the clearing. Aisla hadn't realized she was holding her breath until it gasped out of her, and her chest ached. She hoped she was ready for what she was about to unleash. Muinin lifted a wing and held out a talon to her.

Aisla tilted her head curiously, her eye catching on something metal that shone in the moonlight. Her jaw dropped when she realized what he held before her, and her feet stumbled over themselves as she stopped in her tracks.

Muinin extended the Speartha crown out to her.

Her family's crown. The true crown of the worldly realms. The crown the Myrkors had been unable to steal among everything else they had torn away from the Iarkises.

How? Aisla asked as she reached out with shaking hands and pulled the crown from a talon that was larger than her forearm.

Your father had it all this time. Hadn't you noticed the Mathair never wore it? He thought it was time it returned to the true heir, Muinin replied, his voice laden with pride, and Aisla felt her heart skip a beat. *Past time, really, if you ask me.*

"I don't know that I deserve it," Aisla whispered aloud.

She slowly ran her fingers along the cool, worn metal and across beautiful emerald stones that still glimmered in the dark of the night. Her throat was thick with emotion.

You deserve it more than any of those that came before, Muinin replied in a rare show of admiration.

His confidence brought tears to her eyes, and she leaned her forehead against his snout.

Thank you, Muinin. I couldn't do any of this without you, she said as a tear fell from her cheek and onto his scales. *I wish I believed in myself the way you do.*

Something to work on. If you don't, no one else will, Muinin said, and she knew he was right. *I should get back. I don't like staying away for long, as much as I would like to meet these gryphons you told me about.*

I don't know that they'd be so inclined to meet you. You're quite a lot larger than them.

I'm larger than nearly every creature. I don't see your point.

It's rather intimidating, and you know it. Maybe next time you can stay longer.

I should hope so, Muinin grunted. *I don't much like our current arrangements.*

You've certainly made that clear.

Aisla held the crown with a white-knuckled grip before tucking it away into the pack she had brought with her. The pack felt far heavier than the physical weight of the crown as she slung it back over her shoulder.

She followed Muinin's gaze to the ash tree he had set down. Aisla walked to it and ran her fingers along the branches. The tree was still quite young. She was instantly overwhelmed by its source rushing through her veins, replenishing that limited store of her esos. It was like a swallow of cold water on a hot summer day, and it was a relief to her weary bones. Her vision became clearer, sharper, and sound roared to life around her, as though a bubble had popped.

Stay safe, okay? Aisla spoke into her mind as Muinin beat his wings to take off again.

That's easy for me to do. Harder for you.

Aisla rolled her eyes, and Muinin's golden ones met hers. She saw the glimmer of amusement there that always warmed her.

Yeah, yeah, she muttered playfully. *Until next time, my friend.*

Aisla watched with a flicker of sorrow as Muinin disappeared as quickly as he had arrived.

Her moment of levity was over as quickly as she had found it. Everything felt heavier in the absence of Muinin.

She blinked her eyes, fighting against the instinctual desire to call her wyvern back.

Aisla unclenched her fists. She breathed in the cool air and put one foot in front of the other. Just like Ru had told her.

The journey of endless sunrises begins with the very first step.

Despite her better judgment, Aisla descended the spiral staircase into the dungeons after dinner with the Sheas.

Before dinner, they had helped her put the ash tree in the sealed case. They would start training in the morning, and Aisla could feel the blend of excitement and anxiety whispering along the wind in the castle. No one knew what to expect.

She and Ruairi planned to meet early at sunrise to plant the tree in the soil prepared for it. They talked through as many scenarios as they could think of at dinner, hoping they could handle whatever would come with the reintroduction of esos to Iomlan. Everyone in the castle had been warned. Eire had understandably excused herself from the ordeal. She had also requested to go north with the Shea male, Cillian, when the time came. It surprised Aisla, but she knew where her friend was coming from. She had protested but gave up after a pointed glance from Ruairi. Something told her the two had already discussed it, and the realization was a lonely one.

It would be hard on Eire to be around others learning to wield their esos so soon after she had lost her own. But Aisla was hesitant to see her friend so far out of reach, even though she knew Cillian would protect her like his own family. Aisla and Ruairi had only just gotten her back, and it was an unspoken reality that Eire was weaker in her new life as a human.

Aisla had almost lost her once. She couldn't bear the thought of suffering that loss again.

"It's late." Aisla's head snapped up as Weylin's familiar voice met her ears.

"How do you even keep track of time in here?" Aisla replied coldly. She tossed her blankets on the ground, preparing them for her makeshift bed.

"Window," Weylin replied, and jerked his head towards the small opening near the ceiling that filtered in faint moonlight.

Embarrassment heated Aisla's cheeks. She should have known that.

"Is it true?"

"You'll need to be more specific than that."

"I heard you're bringing ash trees to Fomhar."

Aisla froze, and her back straightened. She cleared her throat and looked up to meet Weylin's waiting amber gaze.

"Who told you?" she asked, and the iciness of her voice surprised even herself. Fear chilled her bones as the words left her lips.

"The laochs who brought my dinner," he said with a satisfied grin. "Don't worry, they didn't say it to betray their *Gheall Ceann*. More in a way to brag that they will soon know their esos, yet I will not."

"You're a fool if you thought I would trust you with it."

"Of course, I don't think that," he said, but Aisla could see there was more that he wanted to add. She listened wearily, cautiously. "But it seems lately, you're in the business of negotiating, so I thought maybe we could strike up a deal."

"I don't deal with the likes of you."

"Yet, you negotiate with my father? And believe me, my father hates you far more than I do."

"So, you hate me, yet you would not hurt me?" Aisla retorted and took a step towards the him.

Amusement chased away the brief flare of anger that flickered in his amber gaze.

"I said that before you stabbed me and dragged me in chains to the home of my enemy."

"You would hurt me now, then? Even more reason to ensure you do not feel the source of the ash tree."

"Did I say that, *banphrionsa*? You are so eager to argue with me that it makes it impossible to have a conversation with you."

"We're conversing right now," Aisla said and crossed her arms defiantly. "And that is far more than you deserve."

A muscle in Weylin's jaw twitched, and she knew she had hit a nerve. Her grin grew, and she took another daring step towards him, taunting him with the freedom that he lacked.

"Why do you have such hatred for me?" His demeanor changed. Suddenly, he was slumped, vulnerability softening his edges. For a reason Aisla could not place, guilt bubbled in the back of her throat. "Did I not save your life on more than one occasion? Did I not aid you in reaching your destination safely in a realm that I now know wanted you dead?"

"Yes, thank you for returning me to my friend, who I found maimed and tortured at the hands of your laochs," Aisla hissed, pushing past the guilt to the tunnel of rage that was never far away.

"And where was I while that was going on, *Ellora*?" He wielded the name like a weapon to be used against her as he leapt to his feet and wrapped his hands around the iron bars. *"Saving your life."* The words left him in a feral snarl.

"You act as though I asked you to!" Aisla threw her hands in the air in frustration.

"You didn't," he said, his tone calm, but his hands continued to grip the bars. His chest heaved, despite the nonchalance he pretended. "But I would have never let you die. Before I knew the truth, and even now, I still never could. Even now that I know your true name. Even now that I know the destruction you are destined to wield against the realms. I would choose *you* over Talam, *banphrionsa*, and that is quite the predicament for both of us."

Aisla was at a loss for words. She found herself breathless, as though she were running through the woods, chased by something she could not see. She didn't know what to make of this confession, only that it terrified her, and she could not address it. She would rather pretend she had never heard it at all. She felt that was the best for both of them.

"You're wrong," she said, her voice falling to a whisper when she found it. Her chest rose and fell with the anger she turned to. It was easy when he reminded her of the way the prophecy had been turned into a weapon despite the fact that no one knew its true meaning. "I will be the salvation of the realms. Even if it is the death of me."

"And a great job you've done at that," Weylin said with a snort. His eyes searched hers, as though wondering if she had really heard the words he had spoken. "I didn't know salvation came in the form of declaring war—on multiple fronts at that."

"Your family has been waiting for any reason to start a war since my birth. If it wasn't me and my wyvern, it would have been something else."

"I suppose we'll never know."

"I suppose," Aisla agreed, spite lacing her retort.

She blinked, suddenly realizing how heavy her eyelids were and how tired her eyes were. Taking a step back, she turned to settle into her makeshift bed.

"Wait," Weylin said with a sigh. Aisla looked up to meet his gaze. His eyes softened, and Aisla's heart stuttered, surprised by the glimpse of vulnerability that was erased so quickly she thought she had imagined it. "Can I ask you a question?"

"I suppose," Aisla repeated.

"Why do you continue to sleep here? Surely there are less important people they can send down here to guard me, or whatever it is that you're doing. Unless you simply miss me."

"No, that's not it," she replied quickly, then paused for a moment. "I-I've seen what happens to prisoners in dungeons. I was not there to prevent it once. And while I do not believe the people of Fomhar to be as ruthless as your own, I do not wish to see the same happen to you."

Once again, something shifted in Weylin's posture, and he lost a tad of the rigidity he held himself with. His brows creased, a subtle look of confusion knitting them together.

"Well, that was not the answer I was expecting," he replied with a gentleness she had not witnessed since he had pulled her from the roaring waves when she had nearly drowned.

"Sorry to disappoint," she muttered, half-heartedly.

She found herself wishing for a time when she was Ellora, and he was Fenian. When they were strangers without the baggage of their names, and the threads of the norns woven between them. The feeling came with a sudden overwhelming sense of grief that nearly brought her to her knees. She couldn't help but wonder if he felt it, too.

"You know that isn't what I meant," he said quietly. "I appreciate the sentiment. But I think you are safe to return to your rooms. You are correct in your assessment of the people of Fomhar. They are not like the people of Samhradh."

"So eager to be rid of me," she quipped, wishing to escape the tension and fall into their usual sarcasm. It was what she knew how to handle.

"Is it that obvious?" His signature smirk reappeared. "Since you won't yet negotiate the use of my esos, maybe we can make a different sort of deal."

Aisla opened her mouth to decline, but he cut her off.

"At least hear my terms. That's something you'll have to learn if you ever want to succeed in politicking," Weylin chided. Aisla closed her mouth and pressed her lips in a thin line, waiting for him to continue. "You go back to sleeping in your own bed, but you have to promise you'll spend one meal each day down here with me. You bring the food, I'll bring the conversation."

"How is that a deal?"

"I'm releasing you from your overnight duties. It's the least you could do for me."

"I don't think that's exactly how this—"

"Please," he interrupted, and Aisla stopped speaking when she heard the sincerity of the word. "For the love of the gods, don't argue. Just say yes."

"Okay," Aisla said, nodding her head slowly. "I promise."

"Good," Weylin said and tilted his head to the side as he met her gaze with a mischievous look dancing in his amber eyes. "You know, I've heard in Fomhar, they seal deals with a kiss. It seems only fitting since we're here."

Aisla's jaw fell open. "You've actually lost your mind."

"Not like that, *banphrionsa*," Weylin said with a *tsk* of his tongue. "You wrap your pinky around mine, and we each kiss our own thumbs."

"What kind of tradition is that?" Aisla scoffed.

"I don't know. But how can I believe your promise otherwise? It's the law of the land."

Aisla rolled her eyes.

"Here," Weylin said, ignoring her. He held out his fist between the bars, sticking his pinky towards her and his thumb towards himself.

She signed audibly and hesitantly curled her pinky around his. The moment their hands touched, her heart began to race, and she fought the urge to pull away. Weylin tightened his pinky around hers as if sensing her desire to flee. He held her gaze as he lowered his lips to his thumb.

Aisla's pulse thundered in her skull, and she swallowed around a lump in her throat. She followed his lead, and they both pressed their lips to their own thumbs. Their faces were so close, Aisla could feel the heat of his breath on her skin.

Aisla pulled away, and her hand fell to her side.

"It's a deal," Weylin Myrkor said and took a step away from her, back into the shadows of his cell. "Good night, *banphrionsa*. I will see you tomorrow."

Finding herself at a loss for words, she merely nodded. She gathered her blankets and made her way up the winding stairs, feeling a surprising lightness settle in her chest that she had not felt in a very long time.

7
EIRE

Breathing felt different when the longevity of one's life was suddenly shorter. Significantly at that.

Everything felt different, really. Colors felt more vibrant, but less sharp. The world felt bigger in an overwhelming way, as though in reminder that she could never possibly see it all. Words tasted sweeter, but stung sharper, too. And breathing felt like a way to count the passage of time—something she had never considered before.

It made her see the world in new ways. Life was more fragile, and she found herself restless in a way she hadn't been before. It was unsettling, too, in her blood. Her blood that had once been laced with the thread of her esos so tightly, it had burned with the pain of a thousand raging fires to pull the threads apart, now felt empty. Eire tried to reset her brain to not see it that way. She reminded herself that she should be thankful to be alive and that she wasn't a husk barred up in a building outside of Caillte, waiting to be called to a fight she would have no choice in.

Eire tried, but she did not always succeed. Some nights, she lost herself to the despair of it all. She cried into her pillow until sunrise, unable to sleep no matter how dark the night.

It was also isolating in a way that Eire had not anticipated. Not when she had finally been reunited with the two friends who had always felt like family. Closer than family, even.

She'd heard of their plan to bring an ash tree to Castle Orga. And it had been a great plan. She and Aisla both knew that, sooner rather than later, the people of Fomhar would need to use their weapons to stand behind their decision to harbor the *Gheall Ceann* and her fugitive. And allowing them to use their esos in that arsenal was the least they could do, really.

But it was a plan that Eire could not participate in, given the loss of her esos. Before Leighis, the goddess of healing, had offered her a new life in exchange for her esos and longer lifespan, Eire had been a master tsuna. Selfishly, she did not want to put herself through the torture of watching so much of what she had lost blossom within so many others.

Eire did not even want to be in Castle Orga while Aisla and Ruairi were training, so she had volunteered to travel north with the second-oldest Shea male, Cillian. Eire did not know her role in the Inevitable War, but she knew she would stand on Aisla's side until her dying breath. And as a founding member of whatever sort of political council Aisla had begun gathering, she could speak on behalf of Aisla when it came to the Lord and Lady of Geimhrigh.

Eire inhaled a long breath, pushing past the mountain of thoughts that were always moments away from a landslide.

"When do we depart?" she asked Cillian Shea across the table.

Her cheeks heated at the immediate realization that she had interrupted some conversation with her question, but she had needed a way out of her own mind. Her blush deepened as all eyes turned towards her, and then to Cillian. The table fell quiet, awaiting his answer. The male seemed to prefer to run things in a more casual manner than his father and eldest brother did. He had also been given full rein over the expedition to Geimhrigh. Cillian had invited the entire party out for a drink at a tavern near the castle to get to know each other. Sorin Shea, Eimear Shea, Kol the ward from Bitu, Aisla, and Ruairi had joined as well.

They had formed something of a friend group since arriving in Fomhar. And Aisla and Ruairi had, of course, remained attached to her side since she declared her intention to go north. Eire hadn't commented on it, but she secretly found comfort in the gesture.

"This sunrise," Cillian announced, and Eire swore that the entire table collectively choked on their ale.

"So soon?" his sister, Eimear, whined.

Eimear had been vocal in her complaints about Cillian leaving. They seemed the closest of the Shea children as far as Eire could tell. Each was a little rebellious in their own way, unlike Sorin, who appeared to live for the praise of his father. Eimear knew Sorin would make a good Lord of Fomhar when the time came. From what Eire understood, Eimear was also reluctant to be left alone with her duty to accompany the ward while he adjusted to life in the Shea's castle until they could trust him. The duty had been left to her since her two older siblings were preoccupied with more pressing matters, and her two younger siblings were simply too young for such a task.

"Why not?" Cillian challenged with a grin and took a gulp from his mug.

Eire felt Aisla squirm beside her. She clearly didn't approve of the abrupt timeline either, but she bit her tongue. Aisla was still finding her place in the order of things. She was the *Gheall Ceann*, but she was also a fugitive on Iomlan, taken in by the mercy of the Sheas.

"Have you even packed?" Eimear shot back.

"Sister, I have been ready for this journey for many sunrises now. I promise to send you letters by raven every step of the way. Try not to miss me too greatly."

Eimear shot him a scowl. Eire couldn't help but smile.

"I'm ready," Eire spoke up after a moment. She had never been afraid of attracting attention. In fact, before the lofa, she used to thrive off of it. She was working on finding herself again—rediscovering that voice that was so bold and unafraid, no matter what was brewing in her heart and beneath her skin.

Eire felt Aisla look at her out of the corner of her eye. Eire did not return the glance. She did not want to see her friend's anxiety and fear. She was so tired of everyone worrying about her all the time. For once, she wanted to feel capable again.

"Is there anything we can do to help you prepare for your departure?" Ruairi asked the group. He had slipped into the role of politicking so easily, Eire was almost surprised. She had never thought of him playing the game, but he played it well. Eire supposed he had the most practice out of any of them from his time in Cliona's inner council.

A shudder traveled down Eire's spine when she thought of the Mathair. Thinking about life when Ruairi had a seat at her council felt like an entirely different reality.

"You can help me load the cart for the horses when we return to the castle," Cillian responded, looking at Ruairi. "It shouldn't be much; there are only five of us going."

"Of course. Happy to help."

"You're not taking the gryphons?" Aisla spoke up.

"No. Like the other realms, Geimhrigh does not yet know of their existence. We hope to keep it that way, especially until we know which side holds their loyalty."

"Fair enough," Aisla agreed, nodding her head. "Thank you again for taking the lead on this. If any realms are to sway to our side, I believe it could be Geimhrigh, but I am aware your history with them is strained. Gods be with you," Aisla replied with an emotion Eire couldn't quite detect lacing her tone.

"It is an honor to rally in your name, Aisla," Cillian replied with a small dip of his chin.

The words made the hairs along Eire's arm stand on end. In a good way, of course. But it was strange to hear people willing to go to such great lengths for Aisla, who had always been like a sister to Eire. If anyone deserved it, she certainly did, but Eire still found it all strange, almost surreal.

"Aisla, will you go back to the castle with me? I've got a few things left to do before bed," Eire asked.

"Of course." Aisla nodded. She downed the final sip of her ale and stood to follow Eire out of the tavern, offering the rest of them her farewell.

They left Ruairi and the Shea siblings, Kol the ward, Revna the scout, Nevin the brawn, and Sten the navigator behind to finish their conversation and their drinks. If Eire was being honest, she wanted time alone with Aisla before she left. She loved Ruairi just the same, but Aisla had been so distant, Eire didn't want to leave with anything unresolved between them.

Back on Eilean, Ruairi had been the one at Eire's side when she was a husk. He visited her every day and read to her. The memory riled the familiar guilt Eire felt at how poorly she had treated him, but she wasn't herself then, and even though they hadn't talked about it, she knew Ruairi understood.

Aisla might not have come to visit her the same way, but Eire knew it was only because Aisla blamed herself for Eire's illness. As wrong as she was, Eire understood it.

Somehow, it had created a distance between them, as if Aisla was still faulting herself for what had happened. Eire needed Aisla to know she didn't blame her.

"How are you feeling?" Aisla asked as they stepped outside of the tavern, greeted by the cool air of Fomhar

"Honestly, Ash, I'm excited. I feel ready to go. I'm eager to have a purpose again and to do something to help for once. And I am glad we are leaving before the ash tree is planted in the ground," Eire admitted before changing the subject. "You and Ruairi went to Iomlan and faced the Udar along with countless other horrors. You translated a letter in the runic language that has been gone for longer than Aosta. Ruairi discovered the secret of the ring and the depths of our Mathair's betrayal. And you—you even managed to take the Udar Apparent hostage. And the whole time, I've done nothing but wait. And I'm tired of waiting. I was never made for that, and I think we both know it. Whether an elf or a human, I'm still here to make a difference, and it's about time I tried to. Leighis did not give me this life to waste it."

Eire had chosen her words carefully, wanting Aisla to understand. What she didn't say was how she couldn't help but feel as though it was all her fault, the same way that Aisla blamed herself. After all, it was her case of lofa that had spurred Aisla into action and begun the course of events that led to the Inevitable War. Not to mention everything that Ruairi had been through. Eire pushed the thought away, chewing on the inside of her lip.

"Eire," Aisla started, and Eire winced at the sympathy lacing her tone. "None of that was your fault. If the roles were reversed, you would have been out there fighting for me or Ruairi. And believe me, it's not at all as glamorous as it sounds." The final sentence was bitter, but Aisla hadn't meant it that way.

"I know it isn't," Eire protested calmly. "I know you and Ruairi both went through things I could never understand, but I'm ready to be out there with you, well, in different realms, but fighting the same fight, Ash. One day we'll have our adventure all together, but this adventure has to be mine *alone*."

"I know," Aisla said. She leaned gently into Eire, trying to lighten the mood.

"Can I ask you a question? One that you have to promise to answer honestly."

Aisla tensed beside her. "Might I know the question first?"

"Since when are we friends who lie to each other?"

"We're not," Aisla replied, quickly.

"Then tell me how you knew where the Udar Apparent would be. There's something you're hiding, and while no one else is pushing you on it, I will," Eire said, adding a playful tone to the end.

The question had been driving her mad. It made no sense how Aisla could possibly know the movements of their enemy unless a god had visited her as Leighis had visited Eire and blessed her with a miracle. And while Aisla had claimed that was what happened, Eire did not believe her.

Not because Eire had lost faith in the gods, no, her faith was stronger than ever. But any questions surrounding Aisla's visit from Realta, the goddess of celestial bodies, Aisla played off and subtly shut down. It was hardly even mentioned since they arrived at the castle with their hostage in tow. Eire knew enough about the gods to know that any gift given was one that came with a cost. That was simply the balance of things. Which meant it was something Aisla did not want the others to know she had lost—a possibility that terrified Eire.

"I-I told you already, Realta came to me in my sleep. She told me where to find him to give us an advantage in the Inevitable War. Or at the very least, to stall a little longer."

"What was she like?" Eire pushed.

"You know . . . she was beautiful, and she was, like glowing, and she radiated a power stronger than esos—"

"Aisla," Eire stopped in her tracks and turned to face her. It turned out Eire was right to suspect something, but she was wrong about what it was. Aisla wasn't hiding what she bargained away, but she was lying about how she knew where to find Weylin Myrkor. "You've never been a good liar," Eire whispered. “Even if I hadn’t had my own interaction with a goddess to judge your story by, I have been your friend way too long to not know when you’re lying.”

"I'm not lying," Aisla stated, turning to face her, but refusing to hold her gaze.

"I thought we weren't friends who lied to each other," Eire snapped.

"We're not. Eire, I can't tell you. I can't say it to anyone, because if I do, it will make it even more true."

Eire's brows furrowed in confusion, but her features softened as she noticed the tears welling in the corners of Aisla's eyes. She saw the panic pulling at her best friend and wondered what had made her this way.

"You can tell me, Ash. Whatever it is, it is too heavy for you to carry alone."

"You won't understand—"

Eire interrupted her and gently reached out and held both of Aisla's hands in her own. They were trembling, and Eire’s heart began to race, but she gripped them firmly, wishing she could take away whatever was causing Aisla to act this way.

"Don't insult me like that," Eire whispered, gently. "I have spent the last several moons as a half-alive, half-dead thing, and you never gave up on me. There is nothing you could say that I would not understand."

"H-he's my *searc,* Eire," the confession tumbled from her lips in a barely audible whisper, and the moment it did, Aisla collapsed into Eire's arms. "He's my *searc,*" she repeated, choking on tears that fell freely.

Eire swore her jaw hit the forest floor. Her mind raced faster than she could comprehend, but she pushed past her shock and wrapped her arms around Aisla as her frame began to shake with sobs and tears wet Eire's shoulders. She would have thought she heard Aisla wrong, had she not repeated herself.

"That can't be true." Eire shook her head in disbelief as she stroked the back of Aisla's head, patting down her hair in a comforting gesture.

"I wish it wasn't," she choked out, her voice strained with emotion. "A golden thread appeared to bind us together. It led me to him—just like in the World Tellers' books. It told us what I didn't want to know. But I think somehow, I already knew. I wasn't surprised. I was just devastated. But that was how I knew. I panicked. I couldn't let him get to me first."

The words were hard to understand between the gasped breaths of Aisla's sobs, but Eire understood enough. She had questions about it all, and especially what Aisla had meant when she said she already knew, but she knew it wasn't the time to ask. It was evident Eire had been right when she said it was too much for Aisla to bear alone from the rush of emotions that followed her confession.

"It's okay," Eire whispered, as she continued to hold her friend. "You're okay."

It was said that *searc* were destined by the gods to be each other's true pairing. It went beyond a simple mating. It was a bond that exceeded any level of vows that existed in the realms. Eire had no idea how the norns could be so cruel as to bind Aisla to her sworn enemy, to the one who would sooner see her dead than breathing. She knew the norns to be devious at times, but she did not think them to be so brutal. Especially not when there had been no threading of *searcs* recorded since before the Siege of Arden. *Why now and why them?*

"I wish you'd told me sooner," Eire whispered. "It's not like it's your fault."

Aisla flinched at that final word, but Eire did not know why. Aisla took a long, shaky breath and pulled out of Eire's embrace. Her cheeks were flushed and stained by the paths of her tears. Her eyes were red and puffy, and she sniffled as she rubbed at her nose with her sleeve.

She opened her mouth to say something, but Eire would never know what she was about to say, because in the same instant, an arrow flew between them. It would have pierced Aisla had she not stepped away from Eire to speak.

Aisla's eyes flew open with fear, but she wasted no time grabbing Eire's sleeve and dragging her behind a tree with a wide trunk.

They exchanged a glance, coming to terms with the vulnerable place they found themselves in.

They were under attack.

8
WEYLIN

Something was wrong.

Very wrong.

Weylin could feel it in his bones. He didn't know what it meant, but he did know that Aisla was in danger. He feared this day would come but didn't imagine it would be so soon. He knew she had taken him as a hostage too loosely. She had made herself a bigger target than she could possibly handle.

Danger scratched along the lengths of his bones, and pain seared the blood beneath his skin. There was nothing he could do but pace back and forth.

Back and forth.

Back and forth.

Back and forth.

Back and forth.

Back and forth.

Back and forth.
Back and forth.
Back and forth.
A roar ripped from his throat as he rattled the bars of his cage.
But no one came.

9
RANIA

"And you're quite certain all of this is a good idea?" Rania asked Callum for at least the hundredth time since the reading of the *Gheall Ceann*'s request, or rather, her *demands*. While the meeting had occurred several sunrises ago, she still found herself lacking faith in the plan they had committed to.

Callum chewed on his lower lip before answering. It was one of his habits Rania had come to know well.

"I know you're worried, Rania. We all are. We cannot be certain, but we have to be confident," Callum replied, sounding as diplomatic as ever. "But what else are we going to do?"

Callum's wooden sword crashed against hers, so lightly it was a dull thud through her grip. It was always *Rania* when they were training, or in the library, or walking through the corridors, and she knew it had to be. No one could know how comfortable they truly were with each other, and Rania had no intention of slipping up because she could not risk losing him. And she loved the way he said *Rania*, but it was not the same as *love, my heart, little fawn,* or *dear,* which were some of his favorite names for her when they were alone. Even the way he whispered her full name when it was just the two of them felt different—more familiar—than the way he said it anywhere else.

"Stop going easy on me!" Rania snapped, pulling herself from her own thoughts. "I already told you; I grew up with a laoch tutor. I'm no stranger to sparring. You do me a disservice by treating me as such. I need to be prepared for whatever is to come. The least you could do is assist me in preparing."

Callum and Rania had spent many hours in the training yard since her mating day. She had missed the feel of a weapon in her grip, even a wooden one. Rania was no laoch, nor did she desire to be, but she did have the skill, and it was a skill she wanted to keep sharp, especially given their circumstances. But even after so many hours together, Callum still treaded lightly. And it drove her mad.

"I understand," Callum said, pausing to scratch the back of his neck. "You're just different from the laochs I typically train with."

"How so? Because you're in love with me?" Rania teased. Callum's eyes grew wide as he glanced around the very empty training yard. Rania charged forward, forcing Callum to regain his stance once again. She made a move for his open side, and he dodged it easily. She slashed through the air and was met by his sword as he blocked her. She lunged left, then darted to the right, hoping to catch him off guard. He used her failed momentum to knock her training weapon to the ground, before grabbing her arm and twisting her around so her back was pressed against his chest and his wooden blade was pressed to her throat.

"Is this what you wanted?" His voice came in heavy breaths against her ear.

"Mmm, exactly," she crooned.

Callum leaned in towards her, the warmth of his body blazing through her from the outside in. She took a quick breath to clear her thoughts, and used the moment to elbow him in the ribs. The breath rushed from his lungs, and he doubled over, giving Rania enough time to retrieve her wooden sword and fake drive it through his gut, effectively passing him on.

"I win," she chirped, spinning her sword in her hand. "Boys are too easy."

"Not everyone will so easily fall for your charm," Callum croaked, standing straight again.

"It hasn't failed me yet," she smirked cockily, and Callum rolled his eyes. "When do we leave?" she asked, changing the subject abruptly.

"Three more sunrises," Callum replied.

Rania nodded.

The Udar had sent a raven with his terms back to Aisling, but they had not heard anything more from her. Faolan was already readying his laochs to march on Fomhar when the time was right. The *Gheall Ceann* had far fewer resources at her disposal, and Faolan was ready to remind her. In his response, he had made it known that Weylin was a mated male, and by holding him hostage in Fomhar, they would make enemies of both Samhradh and Briongloid.

Rania knew the truth of it all, but she had to remind herself that nobody else could, even her family in Briongloid. For all intents and purposes, she was Weylin Myrkor's mate. Around others, she played the role of a frightened and angry female whose mate was stolen on the night of her mating quite well. When she was with Callum, there was no need to pretend.

Faolan declared that Rania would accompany him as his chosen companion to push the emphasis of scorned mate with the *Gheall Ceann*. He believed that seeing the Lord of Briongloid's only daughter demanding her mate's return might do more than Faolan could by demanding the return of his son. He and the *mallaithe* had not met on the best of terms previously. Aisling Iarkis would not want to do anything to directly benefit him, but with two of the seven worldly realms knocking on her door, she might reconsider.

Orla, Callum, and a handful of other laochs would stay in Briongloid near the border of Fomhar while Rania and the Udar met with Aisla and her companion of choice.

Until that day, Faolan would send laochs from both Samhradh and Briongloid to surround Fomhar. They wouldn't be ready in three sunrises, but Faolan did not imagine the negotiations would end after one meeting with Aisling. No, he was playing the long game.

Once the laochs were in place, it would leave them little choice. Whether they chose to act on the threat to Weylin's life or not, they had begun a war on their own soil. Rania thought it was all rather foolish and wondered if the *Gheall Ceann* was always so irrational. It was either that, or there was something they weren't factoring in, and that possibility gnawed at Rania's anxiety.

She hated the unknown.

"You'll get to meet my parents," Rania said, trying to lighten the mood. "What an odd way to meet them."

"Odd indeed," Callum grumbled.

She knew stuff like that made him uncomfortable. Things that reminded him that what they were doing was wrong and always would be. She found that she could only cope with it by joking, while he would prefer to ignore it altogether. It weighed heavier on Callum, she knew, because Weylin was like a brother to him, and the last thing Callum would ever want was to hurt Weylin. She reminded him that they weren't truly mated as the ceremony had never finished, but that would only ease the guilt for so long.

"Don't worry, they're not horrible or dreadful, or anything like that," Rania continued.

"I never imagined they would be. You and Oisin turned out well enough."

"*I certainly* did," Rania quipped, "but whatever Oisin lacks, I more than make up for."

"Humility being one of your best traits. Right, dear?" Callum said, and Rania's heart skipped a beat, and she couldn't help but smile.

"Of course."

They gathered their training equipment and put it on the racks before making their way to the castle. They talked about the books they were reading and exchanged new titles to dive into. Rania decided she rather liked Callum's adventure books, even though she didn't always see a purpose in them. It was nice to find herself somewhere else, for no reason at all.

Inside the castle was alive with motion, so different from the empty training yard. Laochs rushed about, preparing for their movement north. The Udar appointed two of his inner council members to keep things running smoothly while they were away, and they were leaving a solid legion of laochs behind despite the ones going north and the ones already surrounding Eilean and waiting for the Udar's command to move.

It seemed Samhradh had been preparing for far longer than Rania had realized.

Rania inhaled a deep breath and pushed her shoulders back as Callum fell into step behind her. It was the natural way for them to walk in the presence of others. Rania held her chin high as the mate to the future Udar of the worldly realms, and Callum trailed her heels, ever the loyal laoch.

They parted ways as they passed his corridor, with only a brief nod in farewell.

Rania was nearly at her own rooms to change out of her training clothes and into a gown when a hand reached out and grabbed her arm. The grip was tight enough to bruise. Rania bit back a yelp as she tried and failed to yank her arm free. She whirled. Her eyes met piercing green ones, and a chill coated her bones.

"Come with me," Orla seethed between clenched teeth, tightening her grip until her nails pierced Rania's pale skin.

Rania winced. Few people in Talam frightened her, but Orla was certainly one of them. Even more so than the Udar himself. Rania's heart thundered in her chest as she nodded slowly. She allowed Orla to lead her into a nearby room.

There was something about her that never sat right with Rania. It became more apparent to Rania each day that the rumors surrounding her relationship with the Udar were true, but there was more to it than that. Rania hardly had the room to judge either of them, anyways, but there was a sinister feeling that hung about the female that Rania could not name.

When they were both inside, Orla finally released her arm, and relief rushed through Rania. It disappeared with the sound of Orla slamming the door shut behind her.

"Sit," Orla commanded. Her eyes hardened.

Rania sat, clutching her arm where the female's nails had left thin trails of blood. Rania's knees begin to tremble, but she took a deep breath and painted a practiced, easy expression on her face as she sat down.

"What is the meaning of this?" Rania asked coolly, keeping her composure.

"The meaning of this?" Orla sneered with a dark chuckle. She pulled out a chair across from Rania and sat down. She leaned forward, resting her elbows on the table between them, and her head in her hands. "I could ask you the same."

"What do you mean?" Rania asked, narrowing her gaze.

"*What* is the meaning of you trouncing about with the Ronan boy as though he is warming your bed?" Orla spoke with malice, and Rania's blood turned cold. She pushed down the rising panic and maintained her carefully practiced indifference, waiting for Orla to finish. "You think you are subtle, but you certainly are not."

"I do not know what you are talking about. *Captain* Ronan is the captain of my mate's personal guard, which means he is now the captain of mine. He is charged with watching over me in my mate's absence, and to suggest otherwise is a dangerous thing to do."

"Ha!" Orla exclaimed, cruel amusement dancing in her eyes.

"You're almost better at this than I thought you were. I know just as you do that you have no mate. Threaten me again, and I will ensure you disappear without a trace."

"That is no way to speak to—"

"The whore dares to try again?" Orla roared, slamming her hands on the table. Rania flinched away. The room seemed to darken. Rania wanted nothing more than to flee the four walls that seemed to close in on her. Her heart raced. She clenched her jaw and waited. "I am not blind to your act, even if you think you have everyone fooled. I'll make you a deal. Since it is more than obvious you ignored the Udar's direct command to keep your secret between the three of us, you are now indebted to me for keeping your secret."

Rania's nostrils flared as a mix of anger and shame and fear mingled beneath the surface of her skin. She wanted to call Orla a hypocrite, but she knew that would get her nowhere.

"In exchange for my silence, you will distance yourself from the man. If you keep it up, I will not be the only one who catches wind of your games, and now more than ever, the Udar Apparent needs the strength and loyalty of *his mate."*

She spat the final two words, and Rania fought the urge to recoil again. She had been selfish. So selfish.

Rania chewed on the inside of her lip. Orla was clearly waiting for her, and there was no point in pretending anymore. It was over far sooner than Rania had imagined it would be. But their love had always been a stolen one—it had always been running short on time.

"And if I don't?" Rania whispered, already knowing the answer. She couldn't bear the thought of ending her relationship with Callum. But even more, she couldn't bear the thought of harm coming to him.

"If you don't, I will do what should have already been done. I will wipe his mind of every memory he had of you. The fact that he has kept them this long is a gift. You will be a stranger in his eyes, and he will believe you are mated to Weylin as everyone else does. Then, I will send him off to the farthest realm of the war and to the front of the lines. We will see how he fares there."

Rania's heart dropped. Her throat dried. Panic roared back, pushing through her wave of defeat.

"But he's Weylin's best friend. He's the captain of his guard," she protested.

"Then treat him as such," Orla snarled. "Are we clear?"

Rania hesitated, biting her tongue, but there was only one answer to give: "Yes."

"Yes, what?"

Rania shifted as Orla's gaze bored into her. "We are clear." Her voice did not sound like her own.

"Good," Orla shoved away from the table. "I like you. You are strong and wise and not afraid to be the only female at the table. Don't make me change my mind. Don't make me regret giving you the gift I have."

Rania grit her teeth until her jaw hurt but said nothing. She watched Orla storm from the room like a viper in the night. Her eyes burned as she was left to wonder if she would ever feel the warmth of Callum's embrace again.

The charade couldn't last forever. But she had at least expected it to last a while longer.

She only wished she had known their last kiss would truly be their last. She would have memorized the feel of his lips and the taste of his skin. The memory fell further from her grasp with each passing moment.

Sobs escaped her lips as tears flowed freely down her cheeks.

It was childish. It was selfish. It was what she desired.

Rania's head fell into her hands, and her fingers clutched at her white-blonde hair.

10
AISLA

Aisla's heart thundered in her chest, and she choked on the remainder of her tears. Her mind and body were shifting to react in an instant.

Stay alert, Gheall Ceann, the voice that always seemed to appear at her lowest moments sounded to her.

No shit, she wanted to mumble, but Eire was looking at her, and there was no time to argue with the voice in her head.

A second arrow pierced through lilies that grew near the trunk of the tree she and Eire cowered behind. And she knew they couldn't stay in place forever.

"What do we do?" Eire whispered, fear lacing her tone.

"I'm thinking," Aisla replied. "If only we'd gone ahead and planted that ash tree."

As soon as the words left her lips, she regretted them. Eire tensed beside her. She didn't have time to apologize for the oversight, so she bent down and pulled her dagger from her boot. She clutched it, wondering how many others were in the woods with them. She had only noticed one so far, but she hadn't given it enough time to be sure. Her mind raced with endless possibilities. It was certainly difficult to fight someone at range with nothing but a dagger. She wished she could call for Ruairi and Cillian, but they were much too far from the tavern for it to have any effect.

"I didn't bring any weapons," Eire muttered under her breath.

"That's okay. I wouldn't expect we would have needed them out here."

"How many are there? Can you tell?" Eire asked.

Aisla shook her head.

She peered out from behind the tree trunk and saw a single cloaked figure before another arrow was flying towards her. She ducked behind the tree once again. Aisla assessed her options. A dagger versus a bow and arrow was not a very good fight to pick. They couldn't stand in place forever, but any time they moved, the attacker was ready. Aisla had only seen one, but that didn't mean there weren't more waiting.

"We're going to have to split up," Aisla decided. She glanced over at Eire. Her eyes widened. "I need you to distract them. Whatever you do, be quick and cautious. Stay behind the trees. Move in a zigzag. Be unpredictable."

Eire nodded slowly, her skin paling in the light of the moon. Aisla swallowed down her fear and guilt. She jerked her chin to the west, giving Eire the signal to go.

Eire took off.

She darted into the night, quick as a fox. An arrow whizzed past her, and she ducked behind a tree. Aisla's heart raced faster and faster as time seemed to nearly freeze. Sweat beaded along her brow and her palms. Again, Eire dashed out into the dark. Again, an arrow chased her. The pattern continued, Eire following an erratic and unpredictable path, just as Aisla hoped she would. She was deep enough into the woods that the attacker was forced to follow. Aisla held her breath, waiting for one more arrow. Then, she dashed from behind the tree trunk, heading for the source of the arrow. She was quiet and nimble on her feet, a practiced skill. She ran for the cloaked figure. His attention turned to her—too quickly. It was as though he was looking for her, as though he had realized Eire was not who he was after.

Aisla sucked in air as he knocked another arrow. The world began to move in slow motion. The arrow careened towards her. Aisla ducked low, dodging to the side. A second came faster than anticipated. It nicked her shoulder but did not lodge in her flesh. Aisla hissed. Her vision blurred, but she rushed onward. She was so close. If she could just make it to him and drive her blade into his heart.

Two more arrows followed. Aisla maneuvered around them. Breath heaved from her lips, and her grip tightened on her dagger as her eyes narrowed on her target.

The attacker turned, distracted by someone who could only be Eire.

Aisla hurtled forward and shouted, refusing to let Eire face him with no weapon. But she had been wrong. It was not Eire standing behind the body that fell with a thud to the forest floor, but Ruairi as he pulled his bloodied sword from the heart of the male.

Aisla let out a shuddered breath of relief as she looked up at Ruairi, and a smile turned her lips upward when she saw Eire appear next to him.

But they were both looking at her in horror. Eyes wide. Mouths open.

Aisla's brows knit in confusion. She felt something warm trickle down the corner of her open mouth.

She followed their gazes down to her abdomen. She blinked when she saw the arrow that protruded from her stomach. Her vision went blurry. As if seeing it suddenly made it real. The pain hit her like a wave in a storm. How had she not noticed?

Her hand shook violently as she grasped the shaft of the arrow.

She knew she couldn't pull it out. She fell to her knees as red blood spread across her beige dress. Pain seared her mind in flashes of white.

And then black, as she fell into open arms, and the rest of the world disappeared into the feeling of sticky red liquid on her skin.

II
RUAIRI

"Help! We need help!" Ruairi shouted over his shoulder at the laochs who had followed him from the tavern.

It had all happened so quickly.

They left the tavern not long after Eire and Aisla departed. The traveling party was eager to get back to Castle Orga to finalize their packs and rest before their long journey ahead. Before they came upon the clearing, a bad feeling had settled in the pit of Ruairi's stomach. He made out the faint outline of a cloaked figure and trotted forward to close the distance between them. His hand found the hilt of his blade as he carried onwards, and it became clear the figure was firing arrows into the night.

That was when Ruairi saw the blur that was Aisla running towards the figure. Ruairi didn't have time to think. He drew his blade and broke into a full-on sprint, ignoring the shouts from behind him. The world fell silent, besides the thunder of Ruairi's heartbeat in his ears.

Just as the male turned to face him, Ruairi drove *Fior* into his heart. Ruairi savored the brief moment he saw the light leave the male's eyes, then his attention was on Aisla.

Aisla, who had smiled at him as if he had saved her. Aisla, who had not realized he was too late.

Ruairi's ears rang as he watched her body fall to the forest floor. In an instant, he was on the ground, holding her in his arms as she bled. And bled. And bled.

Panic rippled through him in waves, his hands numb as he brushed her hair from her eyes.

Without a moment to lose, Ruairi scooped up her limp body and stood. Eire whimpered quiet sobs behind him.

"We have to take her to the castle. We aren't far," Cillian said, his voice shifting into one of command. "Our medics will be able to help her."

The air around them was heavy, bearing down upon Ruairi with each breath he took. Dark and foreboding clouds rolled through the sky, and Ruairi almost thought he imagined them, until he saw the others looking up at them as well. No one said a word.

Ruairi swallowed around a lump in his throat and nodded. He wasted no time as he took off towards the castle. He could see its looming presence through the trees. Each step dragged into eternity. He couldn't close the distance quickly enough. Aisla's head bobbed against his chest. His skull throbbed with fear and grief, but he couldn't think too long about it. He could only get her there as quickly as he could. He constantly checked for the faint beat of Aisla's heart.

It was still beating, and that was all that mattered.

"I'm so sorry," he heard Eimear whisper as she wrapped a comforting arm around Eire.

"I should have done something. It was a terrible plan. I never should have let her go through with it," Eire choked out. "It should have been me."

Ruairi's heart seized at those last words. He couldn't find the words to say in protest.

"It's not your fault," Eimear said gently.

The rest of their party remained silent as they hurried through the dark night lit only by the few stars and the light of Talam's dual moons that peeked through the clouds. Ruairi's throat tightened, and he tried to ignore the feeling of Aisla's blood wetting his shirt.

She was losing so much blood. Too much blood.

He had been too late.

Ruairi grit his teeth and continued onwards, cursing the gods in the same breath he begged them for a miracle.

Ruairi traced circles on the pad of his thumb with his forefinger as he looked down at Aisla's unconscious body. They had laid her down in the medics' wing of the castle and worked quickly to stitch up the wound, but she had already lost so much blood, they didn't know when she would wake up.

If she would wake up.

Her skin was pale. Her breaths were shallow. Her hair was damp with sweat.

"Ru," Eire whispered beside him. "Only esos can heal her now."

"I'm not a mender. And we don't know who is," he said a little more harshly than he had intended.

The thought had already crossed his mind.

The ash tree from Eilean was still enclosed in a case made by the dwarves to contain the esos before they planted it. The plan was to sink the roots into the soil the next sunrise, after the traveling party left to go north. *One thing at a time,* Deaglan Shea had suggested. They didn't know how all the elves would react to their esos awakening in their blood. They wanted a planned and coordinated time, starting within the inner council, and eventually working outwards through the castle's inhabitants.

They would train the elves of Fomhar to protect themselves for whenever the Udar inevitably lost his patience and decided to strike.

And they might have reached that time, Ruairi thought grimly as he reached out to brush Aisla's hair from her forehead.

"We have to try to find out," Eire said.

He knew she was right, but he didn't want to leave Aisla's side. He was so afraid that if he did, something bad would happen. He would never be able to live with himself if it did. He could hardly live with himself as it was. He should never have let Aisla and Eire go out into the woods on their own. Not so soon after Aisla had sent her negotiations to the Udar.

But he was doing her no favors by standing still. Something had to be done. Ruairi drew in air, filling his lungs, gathering the energy he needed to stand.

"Can you ask your father to gather his most trusted laochs?" Ruairi directed his question to Sorin Shea, who had joined them in the medic wing. "We need to find one who carries the esos of menders, but we don't want to spread news of Aisla's injury. Whoever it is will need to learn fast."

Sorin's face was grave as he nodded in affirmation and took off through the doorway.

Surely, this couldn't be the way he lost Aisla. Surely, this couldn't be the way they lost their *Gheall Ceann*. What a cruel twist of fate. And if it was, what would it mean for Talam?

But in that moment, Ruairi didn't care about the rest of the world. He only cared that the loss of Aisla Iarkis might damage him beyond repair.

He inhaled again. "I'll need your help." This time, his words were directed at Eire.

"I know," her voice held hesitancy. While she no longer had her esos, she still knew how to train in the art of it, and that was all Ruairi needed.

"Let's go, then."

Ruairi didn't allow himself to look back down at the cot where Aisla lay. Instead, he led the way through the hall toward the strange garden in the center of the castle. There was a green area with plants and trees, and the ceiling above it was a gaping hole to the outside world. It was a small piece of nature within their castle walls, and it worked perfectly for what they needed to do.

The tree sat next to the garden in the glass case that kept the esos from finding the blood of elves. All of the elves of Iomlan had thought the trees to be extinct and assumed they would never again know the esos elves were born with. It was after the War for Descendants that they disappeared, and from what Ruairi understood, they saw it as a punishment from the gods. They searched all of the six realms on the continent of Iomlan looking for a single one left, and had no luck. Little did they know, the ash trees on Eilean remained. There were fewer than before the war, but enough to continue wielding esos and training the next generations of elves.

To reintroduce ash trees to Iomlan was nothing short of a miracle. It would forever change the landscape of Talam, and Ruairi wasn't quite sure how the gods would feel about it. It was monumental, and he hated having the power of so much change in his hands, but he had no other choice.

Ruairi closed his eyes and held them shut for a moment before he pulled the small silver key from his pocket to open the case. The tree wasn't very large, and it was easy enough for him to pull out and set into the hole prepared for it. His heart pounded in his skull as he and Eire pushed dirt over the roots. Healthy, living roots were the only way for an elf to access their esos. Once they accessed it, they had a limited amount they could store within their blood to use away from the source. When that supply ran low, they had to stop or risking burning out, which led to death. It was a practiced art to understand the limits of one's esos. One that Ruairi was all too familiar with from teaching elves in scoil back on Eilean.

He wondered how long it would take for the roots to find their place. How long before esos was rushing out beyond the garden, and when the chaos would begin.

Slowly, others gathered around Ruairi where he knelt beside the tree, waiting to feel it in his own veins. He felt their curious gazes and the tension that hung in the air like invisible smoke. The room was full of the Lord of Fomhar's closest friends and council members. They would try out their esos until they found a mender within them, and that mender would be the key to Aisla's survival.

"I feel it," Cillian Shea spoke up first, turning his hand over and looking down at it, but Ruairi knew he would see no physical change.

A chill traveled down Ruairi's spine.

"It's weird," Sorin Shea mused with a frown, copying his brother's movements.

"But it feels good. It feels like when you've come across something you misplaced. Like finding something you'd once forgotten," another female Ruairi recognized, but did not know the name of, spoke up.

Murmurs continued to spark through the small gathering of elves. Ruairi's head spun as he recognized the feeling of his own esos replenishing.

"So here goes nothing," Ruairi muttered before he cleared his throat and raised his voice. "Eire and I are going to give you as much of our years of esos experience as we can fit into this evening. What you need to know first is that every unique esos comes with a feeling when you call it from your blood. For instance, as a zephys, when I call upon my esos of winds, I can hear a rush of air begin in my ears. We need a mender. If you are a mender, the sounds around you will start to sound muted. They will not disappear altogether, but voices and sounds will become distant—hard to distinguish."

"And to start pulling on your esos, we have a motto we use in scoil," Eire added, her voice strong and confident. "*Feel, but still your heart. Think, but ease your mind. Endure, but find your peace.* Esos is an intangible contradiction, and when you find yourself between all things, you will find your esos. You'll need to seek balance. I suggest getting as close as you can to the roots. Sit on the floor around the garden. Close your eyes. Clear your mind. Search for the thread you can now feel tied around your veins, and it will come to you."

Ruairi heard the way Eire's voice tightened towards the end. His heart broke for her, and he could only hope she knew how much it meant that she showed up for him, no matter how badly it hurt her to do it. She had to train them in what she had lost. Ruairi had been through a lot, but he could hardly imagine the feeling of losing his esos.

He had to imagine it would feel like losing a limb, not merely a finger.

Ruairi shook his head to clear his thoughts and watched as the elves moved about the room, getting closer to the tree. Most of them sat. Some of them closed their eyes. The air was thick with energy in a way that was almost overwhelming. It didn't help that there was so much riding on whatever happened next.

Eire and Ruairi split up, walking around to guide elves through the steps as best as they could. It was like teaching his youngest students, but even then, at least his youngest students had grown up with the feel of their esos from birth. Ruairi had also rarely instructed in esos specifically. He only filled in and typically trained the students in combat to become laochs.

He tried to be patient. Even though he could hear the passing of time in the back of his mind, that was nearly enough to drive him mad. His stomach was in knots, and he had to remind himself to keep the impatience from his voice.

His heart sank when an asher summoned drops of fire to the tips of her fingers. It fell even deeper as a terran produced a vine around the garden that quickly grew out of control. They all described the sensations that preceded their esos as the room erupted into chaos of elements and shadows, and the only pryer that was quickly escorted from the room as he clutched his head with the pressure that came with such power. The esos of mind manipulation was one Ruairi was not yet sure how he would train.

"Uh, Ruairi," a familiar female voice called meekly. Ruairi rushed towards Eimear where she sat near the ward from Bitu, who was looking at her with a soft, curious expression. "Everyone's voices—the room—it all sounds so far away."

Hope blossomed in Ruairi's chest, and his lips turned up in a grin full of hope. He held out his hand to Eimear and helped her up from the floor. Her brown eyes were wide and wild and full of wonder mixed with an emotion Ruairi couldn't quite read.

"Looks like you're the lucky one. I hope you're a fast learner," Ruairi said. His eyes flitted about the room to catch Eire's gaze. He jerked his chin towards Eimear when their eyes met. She understood his meaning and ran to Sorin Shea to give him instructions Ruairi couldn't hear. When he looked back at Eimear, she was holding her ear with a look of horror on her face. "Don't worry, that goes away once your esos settles in. Think of the physical symptoms like a warning sign before your esos reaches the surface."

Eimear nodded, though her expression remained wary.

Eire appeared at Ruairi's side, and they made their way to the medic wing. Ruairi felt the weight on his shoulders lessen at the same time doubt and fear crept into his mind.

"This is great, really," Eimear spoke up, but she didn't sound like she meant it. "I'm glad I can help. I-I just always hoped I would be a terran."

Eire laughed out loud before throwing an arm around Eimear's shoulders.

"A terran wouldn't be on her way to save the world."

Eimear half smiled, and Ruairi realized disappointment had been that other feeling flickering in Eimear's eyes.

12
EIMEAR

There was a flurry of fear and a simmer of disappointment swirling through Eimear's throbbing head as she followed Ruairi and Eire into a private room in the medic wing. She was beyond thrilled to find her esos. It was something she and every other elf on Iomlan had always dreamed of and longed for but did not ever think they would find. But it wasn't quite how she had imagined it would be.

Eimear had always believed in her heart that she was a terran. With their gifts, she could grow plants at will and manipulate the very soil beneath her feet. It felt so much like her that Eimear had practically convinced herself of her esos source long before she could ever know. It felt like a part of herself she had once held as a truth simply never existed. Which was true in a way, but a harsh reality for Eimear to face, especially when she did not have the time to.

To find out she was not a terran, but a mender, was like putting on a new pair of shoes that did not fit quite right. As a terran, she would've been in the perfect position to reside in her baile, and resume life as it had always been. Being a mender, she couldn't help but feel like her life was about to drastically change. There was a need for menders in the time of the ninth generation, and they certainly would be no help living alone in the woods. It seemed her life was destined to lead her back to her family's castle no matter how hard she tried to run from it.

At least her disappointment had delayed the panic when she realized she was expected to save the *Gheall Ceann*.

"Here," Ruairi said, calling her back to them. He ducked into an empty room in the medic wing and waited for Eimear and Eire to follow him before shutting the door behind them.

Without so much as a warning, Ruairi withdrew his blade from his belt and sliced it across his palm. A gasp escaped Eimear's lips, and her hand flew to her mouth. The sight of blood made her stomach turn. The irony was not lost on her as she cursed the gods for the terrible joke they had played. She looked at Eire, who pressed her lips into a thin line. She glared at Ruairi, clearly disapproving, but she remained silent.

"You're going to heal my hand," he commanded in a voice that she imagined he used in scoil.

"Like Hel I am," Eimear snapped back immediately. It seemed possible in theory until she looked at the open wound seeping blood. "I'm not a medic. I never have been."

"But you are a mender," Eire said, gently. "And you *always* have been. Whether you knew it or not."

Eimear opened her mouth to protest but took one glance at Ruairi's waiting gaze and closed it again. She reached out, cautiously taking his hand in hers and turning it gently.

"You're definitely bleeding," she stated, fighting to get the words out around her rising panic.

"Yes. That is correct," Ruairi agreed with a hint of irritation. "Focus inwards. The esos is stored within you now. If you can find it, you can pull it forward and bring it out to use. It will obey you if you look for it. Gently, but confidently."

"But not too confidently," Eire added with a grin.

Eimear fought the urge to roll her eyes. She nodded and closed her eyes while she inhaled a long breath. Her first thoughts were of the pressure of the two sets of eyes on her and the heat that burned her cheeks.

Focus, she reminded herself, *focus.*

She thought of that new and delicate thread she could feel wrapped around her veins. She thought of its gentle tug and pull through her blood. Eimear followed the feeling of it from her heart to the tips of her fingers, and then the world fell still. The sounds around her were muted, and her ears felt full of cotton. All except the pounding of her heart, which thundered through her ears, clear as ever. She fought to tune it out. She focused on the sound of her blood as it ran beneath her skin and finally felt the esos reach her fingertips. She blinked her eyes open, and they widened at the subtle white glow that emanated from them as the sounds around her resumed.

As she looked at it, it flickered away, like a dying flame. Disappointment sank through her.

"I can't do this," she said, feeling the fear and pressure grow in Ruairi and Eire. "Surely there is someone else in there with the esos of menders."

"Try again," Ruairi said with both sternness and patience.

Eimear sighed and closed her eyes, again tracing down the feeling.

But she tried, *again* and *again* and *again,* as the sweat built upon her brow.

"You can do this," Eire said with a heart full of hope as she gently nudged Eimear's shoulder with her own. "You healed Ruairi's hand. This is no different. Don't doubt yourself or your esos."

Eimear nodded, but her mouth was dry. She had managed to heal Ruairi's hand, and it hadn't taken nearly as long as she thought it would, but it was a much smaller wound than the one that had brought Aisla Iarkis to the doorstep of the otherly worlds.

A chill shuddered down Eimear's spine at the thought.

She gazed down at the *Gheall Ceann*, acknowledging the mortality they both shared. It was a frightening thing—how quickly a life could end—a frightening thing to know Eimear had the power to prevent it. Her stomach turned as she reached out and ran her hand over the wound that was turning dark despite the ghostly pale of Aisla's skin.

Eimear held her breath and spread her fingers wide. She sent a prayer to Leighis, hoping the goddess of healing would not abandon her now, not after she had helped them make it so far.

Then, she closed her eyes and waited for the esos to quiet the world around her.

In. Out. In. Out. In. Out. In. Out. In.

Until it was only Eire, her breath, and the whisper of her esos.

Eimear thought she felt the world inhale a sharp breath with her.

13
AISLA

Aisla knew only darkness and hushed voices just beyond her reach.

It was as though she was seeing the world through a fog so heavy that it suffocated her. She was choking. Choking until her throat burned. Her hands clutched at her neck. Her eyes went wide. It was a searing pain.

It was a pain that blinded her. Brought her to her knees. She begged the gods above that they would end it. She begged that they would save her—take her away.

Through the heat of her pain, Aisla could faintly make out a voice that called to her. It was familiar. It was male. But Aisla could not place it.

Don't die on me. Live. Fight through this. Live. You're stronger than you know. Live. Don't leave me. Live. You can't give up. Live. Talam needs you. Live. I need you. Live.

The voice was angry and afraid. It was full of rage and grief. For some reason, Aisla felt that she owed it to the voice to live. But she did not know how to. There was nothing before her to fight.

Aisla once thought death would be painless, like floating along a river, not knowing which breath would be your last. But it was not. It was the heat of a thousand suns.

It was the regret of a hundred lifetimes.

It was seemingly unending.

Until it wasn't.

Until there was a light that cleared the fog. The world unfurled before her, blurry around the edges, but visible. Aisla gasped for air that she never thought she would know again. She jolted upright as white light flooded her eyes, momentarily blinding her again.

She blinked until she could make out the shocked face of Eimear Shea, her hands trembling above Aisla's stomach. She was in Talam, then. Not Albios or Hel.

Aisla's head fell back onto the pillow.

Darkness overcame her, but the pain was gone.

14
EIRE

There was an abundance of doubt weighing on Eire's shoulders as she prepared to leave Fomhar.

It was not her home, but it had begun to feel more like one than she had in a while. Still, Fomhar was not the primary factor holding her back. No one could have predicted an assassination attempt on Aisla the sunset before she was set to leave.

Guilt ate at her when she thought of leaving her friend, especially in her condition. But she had to. Cillian delayed one sunset so she could help Ruairi clean up the mess they had left behind when they went to work with Eimear one-on-one, but he could delay no further. And Eire would not want him to on her behalf.

Aisla was alive.

That alone was a miracle, and all because of Eimear Shea. But Aisla was not fully recovered as Eire prepared to leave. It felt too soon. It *was* too soon. Eire had to remind herself that the world did not slow when the arrow struck Aisla. If anything, it served as a reminder that they were running out of time. It was more important than ever that they go north and recruit Geimhrigh to their side in the Inevitable War, if they could.

While Aisla was recovering, Ruairi would be left alone to deal with the aftermath of unleashing esos upon the castle. They were all grateful it was kept to a small population, at least. After that first day, the dwarves stayed up late into the night, crafting barriers forged of iron and the esos of shadows to keep the source contained to the castle alone.

The interior castle garden was full of bursts of fire and spurts of growth. Water poured down from clouds that should not exist indoors. It was utter chaos, and it was Ruairi alone who would have to wrangle it. But he understood, and Eimear and Kol began to help him as well. As others grasped the esos of their blood, the pressure on him would ease.

Eventually, Aisla would be able to step in, too.

Eire had to keep telling herself the medics said Aisla would recover soon. Or else she would never leave.

She felt a calling to the north so deep within her that to ignore it would be torture. She was ready to leave. Ready to find who she was once again, outside of Ruairi and Aisla and the husk they once thought her to be.

It was time.

Eire let out a sigh as she pushed open the door to Castle Orga's infirmary. She felt alone, for the first time in a long time, but in a way, she needed the feeling.

Her eyes immediately went to Aisla's bed, where she lay staring up at the ceiling. There was a journal and pen lying next to her bedside. Aisla heard the door open and winced as she pulled herself up into a sitting position. She looked up, and her gaze softened when she saw Eire.

Eire couldn't help but smile as she rushed to her friend's side. Aisla was not only a friend but the sister Eire had never had. She held Aisla's hand between her own, ignoring the deathly cold. Her eyes were brighter, and that was more than Eire had dared to hope for.

"Hey," Aisla muttered in a voice that was but an echo of her usual self, but Eire could see she was trying.

"Hey," Eire replied, rubbing her thumb over her friend's knuckles. "It's good to see you awake."

"Yeah," Aisla agreed, shifting uncomfortably before immediately changing the subject. "Who would've thought, Eimear Shea of all elves."

"Definitely not her. She was hoping to be a terran."

Aisla let out a genuine laugh at that. "That is the least surprising thing I have heard in a long time."

"I agree."

"She'll get used to it," Aisla said. "Talam needs more menders."

Eire nodded in agreement before she spoke again. "They still haven't found out who did it. We don't know if the archer acted alone or was a part of a larger group. There was no one else there, and he's passed on."

"I figured," Aisla paused, chewing on her lower lip. "Ruairi did the right thing, though."

"I agree," Eire said. Silence settled between them. "This is my last stop before I leave."

Aisla's eyes went wide at her words. "You're leaving already?"

"Yes, that was always the plan. In fact, we are even a day behind—"

"I know. I just thought—"

"That the plans would change?" Eire asked, gently interrupting.

"Yes, but no. Not because of me, but because of you. Are you okay? That was a lot. You were there with me, too."

"I was," Eire agreed. "But I'm fine. Not so much as a scratch, thanks to your hot-headedness. And this is why I need to leave, at least for now. You and Ruairi will be of no use to anyone here in Fomhar if half of your attention is always fixed on keeping me safe. I'm perfectly capable. Elf or human. You need to believe that and not worry so much about me."

"I know, but—"

"No buts, Ash. I'll be okay. Trust that—*trust me."*

"I do trust you," Aisla responded, and Eire knew she meant it.

"Good. That's all I need from you. That, and for you to heal. Talam needs its *Gheall Ceann*."

"Don't call me that," Aisla said quickly.

"If we don't believe it, who will?"

Aisla sighed but did not say anything.

"I'll miss you. But I'll be back soon. Keep in touch, okay?"

"I will," Aisla nodded, and Eire could barely stand to watch the tears well in the corners of her eyes.

"I love you, Ash," Eire said around the knot in her throat.

"I love you. Always."

Eire nodded and leaned forward to give Aisla a hug.

Eire closed her eyes and focused on the warmth of Aisla. The smell of ash and pine trees took her back home to Eilean, if only for a moment.

It was a familiarity that could not last forever.

15 WEYLIN

Weylin stalked the borders of his cage like a feral wolf, desperate for any way out.

His skin prickled with the knowledge that something *bad* was happening outside of his cell. Something horrible. Something that meant Aisla was in danger. While the thought should exhilarate him, thrill him after how she had trapped and betrayed him, it made him angry and anxious. He could think of nothing else.

He was unsettled by the sensation, and he was desperate to see her.

He was almost certain she was not of the otherly realms, but she had nearly reached them. He couldn't help but feel like he should have been there to protect her. He had done it enough times during their journey from Briongloid to Samhradh.

He hated the not knowing and the waiting.

Footsteps sounded at the top of the stairs. Weylin's heart began to pound. It wasn't her. That much he knew from the heavy steps and stench of sweat that accompanied the noise.

"Where is the *mallaithe*?" Weylin called before he could even see the face of the laoch. "What has happened to her?"

He didn't even care how hysterical he sounded.

Silence answered as the male's face came into view. His hair was dark brown and his eyes were hazel, and he had never been a fan of Weylin Myrkor. He made it clear in his sneers and snide comments when it was his turn to bring Weylin his meals.

Weylin knew there were far worse ways for the guard to show his disdain, and he was thankful he did not implement them.

"What's it to you?" the guard spoke as he neared, carrying a metal tray full of food.

Weylin wished he could grab him by the shoulders and rattle him for answers, but the bars between them made it rather impossible.

"It means a lot of things to a lot of people. She is the *mallaithe* after all," Weylin snarled back.

"Bite your tongue," the guard snapped, as he stopped just beyond reach of the bars. Weylin could smell the slightest hint of fear on him. Weylin rarely spoke to the guard, but now that he was up, now that he was something other than bored and annoyed, the guard was frightened.

Weylin grinned. "You're afraid? Of a male in a cage?" he taunted.

The guard's jaw set and his eyes shifted to something like confidence that surprised Weylin.

"I've no reason to fear you," the guard said, his entire demeanor changing as he adjusted to hold the tray in one hand, and in his free hand, he flexed his fingers until a sphere of fire flickered to life.

Well, that was unexpected, Weylin thought to himself, but only faltered for a beat.

"Neat trick," Weylin scoffed.

Which was apparently the wrong thing to say, because it cost Weylin his dinner.

In an effort to show off his *neat trick*, the guard lost control of his esos as quickly as he had summoned it. The tray clattered to the floor, sending a spread of meat and vegetables across the stone. Then, there were flames licking up the male's arms. It was so much esos, that Weylin felt the heat of it behind his cell bars. Weylin's heart thundered, wondering how far the man would go, but he refused to let it show.

The male turned his arm, observing the esos, and it quickly became apparent that he had never used so much of it before. He tried to play it off, but then his eyes went wide. A shriek of alarm escaped his lips. He shook his arms out as though to release the flames, but they only grew, and suddenly the room smelled of burning flesh.

Weylin's stomach turned, and even he was at a loss for quips.

Two pairs of footsteps thundered down the stairs as the male's shrieks turned into cries for help. Weylin could do nothing but watch in mild terror.

A male with deep red hair, whom Weylin recognized as Sorin Shea, entered the dungeon, quickly grabbing a bucket of water from the walkway and pouring it over the male. The flame slowly flickered out, but the male would have scars that would become a permanent part of him. Sorin was quick to wrap an arm around the male's shoulders. He spoke to him in an urgent, hushed tone, and guided him up the stairs. But Weylin was not listening. His attention was elsewhere on the second elf who appeared.

Aisla Iarkis.

Her eyes were narrow as she looked past Sorin and the asher who had let his esos get out of hand. She looked straight into Weylin's amber gaze, and her eyes were filled with hatred.

Weylin on the other hand, was overcome with relief, so much so, that he forgot everything else he had just witnessed.

"What did you do?" Aisla snarled, rushing around the spilled tray of food. Her eyes writhed with those familiar flames that warmed Weylin's cold heart.

She looked thinner than usual, paler, too. Her eyes were tired but still held all of the ferocity he knew her to have. Her hair hung in loose, light brown waves around her shoulders, and she wore a gown the color of the night sky. It was a blue so deep it was nearly black and shimmered with streaks of golden threading along the form-fitting bodice, and the skirt that flared at her hips. She was stunning.

As she was every time she descended from the castle above to meet him in his own personal Hel.

"What do you mean what did *I* do?" he scoffed.

"You know exactly what I mean," she growled back. She was upon his cage in an instant, her hands gripping the bars so tightly, her skin strained against the bones of her knuckles. "Why is one of your guards covered in burns?"

"Seeing as only one of us here has access to any type of flame," Weylin said with all the nonchalance he could muster, "I believe that is a question for *him*."

"I don't have time for this."

"Then why are you here?"

"We made a deal, did we not?" she said, and Weylin was taken aback for a moment.

His lip quirked up in a half smile. "To be fair, I hardly knew the deal was still on. You already missed the first few days of it."

"I was preoccupied."

"I know," he lowered his voice, hearing the pain in her own. "What happened to you?"

"Why do you care?" Her walls were coming down. The question wasn't angry or filled with malice. It was a question of defeat, and Weylin wished he knew why.

"Because, *banphrionsa*, when it happened, whatever it was, I saw a Talam without you, and it isn't a Talam I care to live in."

It was true. On the first sunset following the attack on Aisla Iarkis, Weylin had dreamed of Talam in the wake of her death, and it had been what he needed to know. She was not the *mallaithe*. It was not that he saw the world in ruins, or the skies aflame with the wrath of the gods. He saw himself, sitting next to her grave, writing a letter to her that she would never be able to read. At the time, Weylin had read the words he was writing, but he could not recall them no matter how hard he tried.

But he could still feel the pain in his chest all too vividly. The aching hole in this dream version of himself clutched onto him, eager to ruin him from the inside out.

He didn't know what to do with it. It was not truly enough to convince anyone that she was not the *mallaithe* as his father declared she was. Weylin did not care one way or the other—what her destiny truly was—he just cared that she was *alive.*

Aisla's eyes flickered with shock then desperation. She was as desperate to know her fate as anyone else. Something in Weylin shattered at the realization, because he knew if she discovered that she was their destruction and not their salvation, she would sacrifice herself without hesitation.

"What did you see? What happened to Talam?" Her voice was hesitant but eager at the same time.

"You know I hate to disappoint, but it wasn't the aftermath of the world without you," Weylin paused. "It was the aftermath of *me* without you."

Aisla's brows furrowed in confusion, then she took a step back. Her features sharpened with irritation, and any drop in her guard was replaced with tension in her jaw. As he had expected.

"You think I'm such a fool to fall for your words yet again? When will you learn?"

"When will you learn, I don't waste words on petty lies. I thought you knew me well enough by now. Have I lied to you before?"

"Fenian Daro?" She retorted with a scoff.

"Ellora Morlee?" he said back, pointedly. "Aside from an alias, I have told no other lies. It's up to you to believe that or not."

"Well, I don't," she said and broke into a coughing fit.

"I'll try again then," Weylin said with a sigh as he looked her up and down. "What happened to you?"

Aisla pressed her lips into a thin line. She toyed nervously with the necklace against her throat. Weylin nearly rolled his eyes, exhausted by this game, but then she spoke. "I was shot in the woods. Arrow clean through my chest, a little too close to my heart for comfort."

"Who?" Weylin snapped, sudden anger rushing through his veins.

"What?"

"Who shot you? My father's men? Someone from Fomhar? Who was it?"

Aisla looked at him curiously, and Weylin had the urge to find whoever it was and shove his blade through their throat.

"We don't know. They died before we could speak to them."

"That's a great way to get information," Weylin scoffed. "How bad was the wound?"

"I only live because of esos."

Weylin's eyes widened. "As bad as I thought, then."

"What do you mean 'as bad as you thought'?"

"I don't know how to explain it. I felt it when you were injured. It felt like dying, only I was aware it wasn't my pain, but yours."

Aisla tilted her head curiously, then straightened up as understanding crossed her yellow-green eyes.

"The damn *searc* thread. If I could get the cursed norns to shred it from my soul I would."

"Would you?" Weylin asked. He eyed her, searching. The words stung to hear, he couldn't deny it. "Was there not always something there? Before the *searc* thread there was still you and me, *banphrionsa*. Before the *searc* thread, *you* still kissed *me*. And I—well, I still saved your life. And I'll have you know, that was one of the few selfless acts I have committed. But I would do it again. And I wouldn't hesitate, not even after all I know. Before *everything*, I found you lying lifeless in the water, and I never got the chance to tell you how afraid I was. I thought I had lost you. I've never been so scared in my life, and I've never known relief like I knew when you breathed again. Because you were dead, Aisla. You were, and suddenly you weren't, and I didn't ever want to know that feeling again.

"Before the *searc* bond, I knew *you*. And I couldn't forget you. I was so angry after your wyvern landed. I was angry you lied. Angry you are who you are. Angry you were sacrificing everything for another male. Angry you left without hesitation, but I never stopped thinking of you. Not since I watched you fly away from my home. I grappled every day with what that meant, and even before the *searc* thread, I *knew*. I knew I could not live without you."

Weylin's heart thundered in his chest, but he refused to let it show. His tone was earnest, but hard. He hadn't meant to say all that, but he *needed* her to understand—whatever was between them was never because of an obligation to the norns and their fates.

It was settled before then. At least to him it was.

Aisla was silent as her eyes searched his with a hint of anguish. She needed to know if he spoke true. She would never surrender her own vulnerability until she knew with certainty the words he gave her were real. There was nothing more he could give her to convince her. And they both knew it.

She took a hesitant step forward, never breaking eye contact. Tears welled in the corners of her eyes. Weylin's chest tightened.

Another step, and she was within reach. It took every ounce of Weylin's self-control to keep his hands at his side as a strand of hair fell loose from behind Aisla's pointed ears. He was afraid any movement may scare her away, like a fawn in the morning woods.

"How am I supposed to believe you?" she whispered. Weylin had a feeling she was asking herself the question more than she was asking him. A single tear trailed down her freckled cheeks, and he hated to see the pain in her eyes. Then, a thought crossed his mind.

"All nine forms, yes?"

"What?" her brows furrowed again.

"You have the power to wield all nine forms of esos, don't you?"

"I-I do," she stuttered.

"Then you're a pryer. You have the power to know if I am telling the truth or not."

"I couldn't do that," she protested, shaking her head.

Weylin knew the esos was largely frowned upon, and especially when used on other elves.

"I'm telling you, you can. I give you my permission."

"You don't understand. I can't—"

She was cut off by the thundering of footsteps, and she jumped away from his cell as though touched by fire. Weylin blew air out of his nose in frustration as Aisla pulled her gaze from his and turned to face the Shea male who returned from before.

"Sorin," Aisla called, putting her hands behind her back and standing straighter. When Weylin looked closely, he saw that her hands were trembling. "Is everything okay?"

"We got a response," he said pointedly, shooting a glare at Weylin. The male must really think him a fool if he didn't think Weylin knew what he meant. His father had responded to the negotiation terms. And surely it would not be their final correspondence.

"Oh, gods," Aisla breathed out. "Let's go then. Gather the rest, we will read it together."

Sorin nodded and refused to look at Weylin again. And apparently Aisla did, too, because she strode off after the male, without a glance backwards.

"Same time tomorrow then, *banphrionsa*?" Weylin called after her, and he could only imagine the way she rolled her eyes in response.

16
CALLUM

Callum could not say whether it was the chill in the air or what he was about to witness that raised the hair along his arms. He stood among the laochs of Samhradh that had been tasked with finalizing the wyvern weapons. After an abundance of failed attempts, it seemed they finally had two working prototypes. Rania had a huge part in their creation, and he wished she were there with him now, even though he knew he shouldn't.

If they succeeded, they would begin replicating it—the final thing the Udar needed to prepare for the Inevitable War.

There was a nervous energy surrounding them. Callum shuffled his feet in the red sand beneath him. They had met near the shore outside of Castle Omra, which gave them plenty of room to test the weapons.

A whistle sounded through the air. Callum's heart thundered, and he shielded his eyes as he watched a net large enough to ensnare a dragon launch from their catapult. It soared across the sky, and when there was no target for it to trap, it fell back to the ground, slowly. Each moment of waiting made Callum's heart pound louder.

It worked, and he didn't know how he felt about it.

The laochs were silent, waiting on his word. He swallowed around a knot in his throat when the sound of sand shuffling reverberated through his bones as the net settled before them.

"Pass!" he shouted in affirmation, and felt the tension ease around him. Some shouted with joy, while others anxiously awaited the next test in silence. "Go for two!"

With a resounding crack, the ballista was fired. It was followed by a whistle sharper than the net launch as an arrow the size of a grown male arched across the blue sky. It had the force and the distance that previous versions lacked. Callum could almost imagine a wyvern in the empty space. He could almost hear its shrieks as it plummeted towards the ground.

As it took its final breath.

Callum's gaze tracked the javelin until he felt the faint tremble of its impact beneath his feet.

He could only imagine the impact a fallen wyvern would create. In that moment, Callum should have felt pride for what he had helped create. He should have felt joy that they were saving countless Samhradh lives from the wyverns. But instead, there was a lump lodged in his throat, and his hands felt cold at his sides.

"Pass!" he shouted out, if only to get it over with.

He had a coronation to attend.

While Callum had never presumed to think he could ever fully understand Rania Dorcas, he had certainly thought he was coming close. That was until she stopped speaking to him altogether. She stopped knocking on his door in the middle of the night only to slip out before dawn.

She wouldn't even meet his gaze in the corridors. She looked the other way when he spoke in council meetings. And she had refused his invitation to attend the testing of the wyvern weapons.

It was perplexing to say the least.

He should have felt relief that she had made the difficult decision for them. While Rania and Weylin were not mated, Callum was quite certain there were blurred lines regarding his relations with Gem of Dreams. In many ways, he felt like he was betraying Weylin, and Callum had always thought himself to be a loyal friend. But in other ways, he found himself justifying it. Weylin and Rania were not mated. Neither of them held affinity for the other. It was an arranged political marriage, and plenty of those ended with consorts, but Callum hated to think of himself that way.

And worst of all, he knew it was wrong because he hadn't told Weylin yet. He had wanted to talk to him about it, but never had the chance. Yet, even if Weylin was there, Callum wasn't sure if he could bring himself to. The guilt ate at him until he could hardly sleep, but still he didn't stop seeing Rania. He didn't know how he ever could.

It was wrong, so wrong, but he didn't understand how it could be, and still feel so right.

The fact that her sudden absence was consuming his every thought terrified Callum. Rania enjoyed games, but Callum was certain this was not one of them. He wished he could ask her about it, but Rania left him no opportunity to.

It was maddening.

He went over and over their last conversation in his mind, wondering if perhaps he had done or said something to upset her. But he could not recall anything. As far as he knew, they were good—in fact, better than good.

Three sunrises of silence later, Callum found himself walking behind her down the aisle for her coronation, the tension between them sharp as the edge of a knife.

She held her head high and walked with a slow but intentional gait. Everything she did was intentional. Callum knew her absence had to be as well, but he wished she would have at least communicated the why to him.

Under ordinary circumstances, Rania's coronation would be held on the ninth full moon in Sneachta after her mating to Weylin. It was tradition. It was meant to reaffirm their union on a political front once the dust had settled. The ceremony allowed the mate to take a crown, the same as the Udar Apparent did—to give Talam a unified family in waiting. Callum had always thought having four crowns in one family was rather excessive, and it seemed somehow more excessive knowing Rania had never truly mated Weylin.

It was all wrong, and for more reasons than just his love for her.

But the Udar felt that in Weylin's absence, it was best to show Fomhar that his mate was as powerful as he, and she would not remain silent while he was in their custody.

Despite everything, Callum was anxious to see Weylin return home. It may have allowed Callum more time with Rania, but his best friend's safety would always come first, and Rania knew that. It was terrifying when he disappeared without a trace during his mating ceremony. It wasn't like him. Except for the time he had left for Earrach the same way, but even then, he had left a letter for Callum to explain. Once they found out that Weylin was in the custody of the *mallaithe*, Callum feared even more for Weylin. It felt like it was quite possibly the worst-case scenario.

He still couldn't believe it. He had hardly slept since they received the letter, and there was no one for him to talk about it with. Callum was meant to be the captain of Weylin's guard before anything else, and he had somehow let this happen. All he could think about was going north to retrieve him, no matter the cost.

So, he was more than pleased when the Udar shared his plan.

Callum would lead a party to Fomhar, taking his laochs ahead of Faolan, Orla, and Rania. Callum was uncomfortable with the idea of all three of them leaving Castle Eagla, but they were taking a legion of laochs with them, and the rest of Faolan's council would stay behind with strict instructions on how to proceed in their absence.

Faolan insisted Rania come and be the one to retrieve her mate, and it seemed Faolan wouldn't go anywhere without Orla. Callum didn't know how Niamh could stand it, but he supposed it wasn't his business. Besides, it would give Rania and Oisin an opportunity to visit home, and Callum knew how desperately she had missed her realm of dreams.

"All rise!" the priestess shouted over the murmur of the crowd, calling Callum from his thoughts.

He clenched his jaw as he focused on Rania, where she stood at the center of the stage in the throne room that had been decorated hastily for the occasion. Most of it was reused from her mating day.

For her coronation, Rania wore a cream-colored dress embroidered in a golden pattern of swirls that undulated like ocean waves with each small movement. The neck was square, accentuating her sharp collar bone, and she wore a gold pendant of a wolf's head. The sleeves were tight along her upper arms and flared at her elbows.

Callum couldn't help the way his heart raced when he looked at her. She looked far more regal than Weylin ever had.

She held herself like the ruler they needed, rather than the ruler they had. Callum wondered if Faolan saw it, too. He stole a glance at the male, but his facial expression revealed nothing, per usual.

Rania's cloud-white hair was woven into small braids that formed one large and heavy one that hung over her shoulder.

His eyes bore into her back, wishing she would look at him, even once.

Callum swore he could see her inhale a long breath before turning to face the eager faces of the crowd. When she looked out at them, the people she was swearing to protect, something shifted in her gaze. Any flicker of hesitation was replaced with pride and confidence. Her shoulders pushed back straighter, and her chin tilted higher.

"We are blessed to present the mate to our Udar Apparent on her coronation day. She appears before you this sunrise to earn the crown of reigning families past," the priestess continued. "Do you, Rania Dorcas, agree to prioritize the good of Talam over all personal loyalties?"

"Until my passing on," Rania replied the words that were of expected of her in a strong voice that echoed through the room.

"Aye!" the room shouted in response, fulfilling their part.

"Do you swear to lift your blade in the name of peace and balance only as duty calls?"

"Until my passing on."

"Aye!" The crowd boomed.

"Do you swear that you accept our home as your own—that you will protect the lives of Samhradh at all costs?"

"Until my passing on," Rania's voice trembled for just a beat.

Callum didn't think anyone but him would notice.

"Aye!"

"And is it your desire to spend your life serving Talam in whatever capacity it requires—including whatever sacrifices it may require?"

"Until my passing on," Rania said around a tight throat, and Callum couldn't help but feel sorry for her. It was no simple task to have to do all of this alone in front of people she hardly knew. It had been a long time since anyone was crowned as mate to the Udar Apparent who was not born in Samhradh.

And the words she spoke were not ones to be said lightly.

"Aye!" the crowd said for the final time.

The floor beneath their feet rumbled with the sound.

Callum found Oisin Dorcas in the audience. It was not pride he saw flickering in Rania's brother's eyes. No, it was fear. It was *sympathy*.

Callum swallowed and turned his attention back to Rania as she ducked her head in gratitude to her people. Then, she turned to face the priestess, and as she did, she caught Callum's gaze. His breath caught in his throat. Her cheeks blushed pink. She looked away quickly, but it was enough.

His heart ached, and he watched, utterly helpless, as she and the priestess faced each other. The priestess lifted the small golden crown reserved for the mate to the Udar Apparent. Niamh had worn it when Faolan's father was still the Udar, and it had remained encased in the castle's gallery until Rania's coronation.

"We find you worthy. Should your words prove false today, may the gods strike you from Talam before you have the opportunity to deceive again."

"I will prove myself every day. From now until my passing on."

The room was silent. As they were meant to be.

A chill traveled down Callum's spine as Rania knelt before the priestess. His blood boiled, and he realized he never wanted to see her kneel to another again. He took a deep, calming breath. The priestess held the circlet above Rania's head.

"Rania Laoise Dorcas, first of her name, may you be a guiding light to our realm when the day comes for your mate to become our Udar. May you lead us to a better Talam!"

The room exploded in applause as the crown was placed on Rania's head. She lingered a moment, then stood to her feet.

She looked like she was born with a crown upon her head as she dragged her gaze past Callum to look at the crowd once again.

It was natural. It was right. It was how it was always meant to be.

17
AISLA

Aisla's eyes poured over the letter from the Udar again, tracing each stroke of ink as her brows furrowed in confusion.

His mate demands his return, and the rest of Briongloid is ready to back Rania Laoise Dorcas Myrkor, first of her name.

It didn't make sense. Weylin had sworn they didn't mate. Yet, they would stake war on it? Or, maybe it made perfect sense. A wolf caught in a trap would do *anything* to free itself. Lying would certainly not be out of the question.

Aisla's heart sank to her feet as she laid the paper down on the oak table, releasing it from her trembling hands. She wiped them on her legs, willing them to stop. She closed her eyes once, hoping to find the confidence to lead once again when she opened them.

"We have to meet them. I will discuss my original negotiation terms with them and try to find a middle ground we can agree upon," Aisla spoke up. The voice that left her was unfamiliar and distant. She glanced at the faces of the small council that had gathered in her name, and fear was written across each of their faces. Everyone except Ruairi, whose green eyes shone with unwavering support. "I will go with a companion of my choosing, and we will select a small group to stay in a nearby village in case all Hel breaks loose."

"Are you certain you should go?" Sorin asked, always the most cautious of them. "They pushed back on every one of our requests and flat out denied the return of the throne. Maybe his son's life isn't worth as much as we hoped."

Aisla's stomach turned. "I am certain they will honor the peace during negotiations. If nothing else, we can trust Briongloid to hold to their moral compass. But perhaps not as long as we had hoped, given the status of their only daughter."

"Aye," Lord Shea agreed, stroking his long, red beard deep in thought. "It is only right if you go as promised. Along with your one companion, following our own terms."

"Do we really think *he* will only bring one?" Sorin interjected.

"Well, that was the only stipulation agreed upon in our demands. So, I should hope so. He didn't seem to have any hesitation shutting down the rest," Aisla replied, picking at the skin that lined her fingernails.

There was a grunt of disapproval somewhere down the table to Aisla's right that she ignored.

"I volunteer to go with you to meet the Udar," Ruairi spoke up and looked around the table as if waiting for someone to challenge him.

Aisla inhaled a deep breath. She had known it would play out this way. "No, Ruairi, you're needed here. More than ever, we will need to continue training the laochs of Fomhar in esos, and the more the better."

"Eimear and Kol are perfectly capable of taking over. There are others, too, who have caught on quickly and can help as well," he said, as if prepared for her dispute.

They knew each other too well. Aisla glanced at Eimear, whose eyes were wide, but still she added: "Yeah, for sure. We can handle that."

"As much as I appreciate the willingness, Eimear, my answer remains the same. Ruairi, you will be more useful here than with me. I think we can all agree on that."

Ruairi's jaw clenched, and Aisla knew she would have to pull him aside to talk to him later. It wasn't fair to blindside him in front of everyone, but they had all read the letter together at the same time, and there had not been time to talk to him alone. Aisla had a plan, and she knew he would understand, even if he didn't want to.

"In that case," Sorin cleared his throat, and all heads turned in his direction. "I will be more than willing to escort the *Gheall Ceann* to meet with the Udar. As the Lord Apparent of Fomhar, I will be happy to speak on behalf of our realm alongside her."

"I appreciate your bravery, Sorin, and I know you would do your realm justice by my side. But I have already chosen who will accompany me." Her statement caused a flurry of chatter, despite how small her audience was.

"And who might that be?" Ruairi asked above the hum of voices, narrowing his gaze at Aisla. His gaze was weary. He trusted her plans, but that didn't mean he always liked them.

Aisla knew he would understand. She grinned as the room fell silent, everyone turning their attention on her.

Aisla's jaw was tight as she descended the stairs, clutching the edges of the stone plate. She had considered not bringing a meal at all with her but thought better of it. He would need his energy for their journey ahead.

I told you not to trust him, Muinin's deep, raspy voice echoed through her skull.

Did I ever say I did? Aisla challenged.

You never said it, but you sure acted like it.

For a reason Aisla could not name, his response resonated through her like a blow to the gut.

I don't know what you mean, Aisla shot back. *Besides, he's still in his cage, isn't he. And I haven't let him out.*

Munin's only response was a reluctant grunt.

"Well, hello, *banphrionsa*." Weylin stood and smiled as she approached. A chill traveled down her spine at the casual nickname, and her blood began to boil. "You look delightful, albeit slightly terrifying. Bad day?"

Aisla felt his eyes roam over her. She had gotten used to the feeling. Whenever she entered the room, he looked her over, as if assessing her condition. There was also something in his gaze that gave Aisla the odd sensation that he was truly seeing her, and not the *Gheall Ceann*. She had felt once that he truly did see her, as not many others did. Aisla swallowed, hoping to wash away the thought as she steeled herself to whatever words he might conjure to try to change her mood.

"You don't know just how terrifying I can be," she started, and Weylin tilted his head to the side. Their last conversation had been the most pleasant they had since his arrival in Fomhar, and she was sure he didn't understand where she was coming from. She hoped he understood then how blindsided she felt when she read the letter from his father. "Especially when it comes to liars who do not know when to stop."

"I told you already. I have not lied to you since the whole name thing. I have no motive to mislead you."

"Then explain to me why Rania Dorcas is demanding her mate be returned to her, and we now have two realms knocking at our door instead of just one."

Aisla watched his face carefully, looking for any tell. But all she saw was complete and honest shock. She didn't know how anyone could fake it so well.

He shook his head, denying the claim, which further perplexed Aisla.

"I didn't mate the female. I already told you. Why would I lie about something so easily proven? I'm no fool. You at least know that much."

"No, you are not. But you must certainly take me for one. In your father's own writing, as confirmed by Lord Dorcas, he has demanded your return to your mate, at the threat of Briongloid's retaliation. Tell me, would *your mate* appreciate the words you spoke to me just this sunrise?"

"I do not hold allegiance to her. I do not know what my father has forced her to agree to, but I have told you the *truth*."

Aisla glanced down and saw his hands curled into fists. His entire posture was defensive, and Aisla felt herself wavering. There was no sense in him doubling down, and they both knew it.

"Trust me," Weylin nearly snarled. "I don't know what else I can do to prove it. Perhaps my father is bluffing."

"How would you feel if you were me? How could I ever trust you?"

"If I were told you had mated another male, I would never believe it. Because you, Aisling Iarkis, were made for me, and I, you."

A second chill traveled the length of Aisla's spine as she kept her face unreadable and shook her head.

"I do not obey the whims of the norns nor the gods," she spat back. "I was made for no soul, but for the good of Talam."

"And neither was I, but I have known it since the first time I saved your gods damned life."

Aisla narrowed her eyes at him, wishing she could decipher the truth. She thought of his suggestion to use her esos as a pryer on him, but again the thought made bile rise to the back of her throat. She would never do it. She hardly had control of her esos as it was, and the esos of pryers was not one to be used lightly. She could do irreversible damage to his mind if she tried it and failed.

But would he offer her the option if he knew it would prove everything was a lie?

"Look at me," he spoke with urgency, but no hint of gentleness. *"Look at me.* You know me. You would know if I was lying."

Aisla couldn't help but scoff. "I don't know you, Weylin. But could anyone ever?"

She knew the words were a lie when she spoke them. She *did* know him. But she let them hang in the air as she slid his dinner plate to him with force through the small hatch door in his cell.

"Only you, *banphrionsa*. Only you." He held her gaze, not bothering to look at the food, even though she was sure he was hungry. His eyes were hard and unyielding in the same way she hoped her own were.

Aisla only shook her head before she turned on her heel to leave.

"The laochs will be here to fetch you at sunrise. Put up a fight, and you'll regret you were ever put on this world."

PART TWO
STALLING OF BLADES

18
RANIA

Rania had known there would be many new responsibilities that came with her mating to the Udar Apparent, regardless of their deception.

Still, one thing she had never imagined herself doing was standing by the Udar's side as they made their way to negotiate the ransom of his son with the *Gheall Ceann* herself.

It seemed so unlikely they had found themselves in such a position, she could hardly fathom how they would come out of it. They had ventured into unknown territory, and that was not a feeling Rania enjoyed.

Rania was thankful that her family's castle served a perfect base for them. She hadn't realized how desperately she needed to be around familiar faces, when the one person she wanted to speak to, she simply couldn't. It hit her like a wave the moment she saw her mother. She had rushed to her and fallen into her arms, not caring if the Udar saw, or what he thought of it.

Callum hardly looked her way when he went ahead with the first legion of laochs and left her behind in Samhradh with only her brother to have her back. She knew it was her own fault. Ever since Orla had threatened Callum because of his secret relationship with Rania, she knew she could not risk it. Rania had been called selfish before, and maybe she was, but she was not selfish enough to risk the male she loved just for the comfort of having him by her side.

Her throat tightened when she thought of him.

She missed the way he spoke as if he were telling a story for only her ears to hear. She missed how he looked at her with a faint shine to his green eyes as though he had never seen anything like her before. She missed the way his eyes crinkled when he smiled, and they fully shut when he laughed wholeheartedly. She missed the way his lips felt on hers and the way he held her against his chest during the few hours they'd allowed themselves.

No amount of Callum Ronan would ever be enough for Rania Dorcas. As much as she wished they could run away together and never look back, she would never forgive herself for abandoning the position she had worked her whole life to attain. And she knew Callum well enough to know he would never forgive himself for abandoning Weylin.

No, the gods had not dealt them an easy hand. And perhaps they would never know happiness as sweet as it was those first few sunrises after her faux mating ceremony, but to have them was worth all of it.

"You remember exactly what I told you, yes?" Faolan's deep voice interrupted her thoughts, and Rania subtly wiped the wetness from her eyes.

They were the first words he had spoken to her since they left behind Orla and a small group of laochs at a tavern nearest to the border.

"I do," Rania replied with a cool tone, masking all of the thoughts racing through her mind.

Faolan had decided to emphasize the grieving mate angle by

choosing Rania as his one companion to meet with Aisling Iarkis. Largely due to the fact that with Rania came the support of Briongloid. And while Briongloid may not be as strong as their other allies, like Earrach, it was a reminder to both Aisling Iarkis and Fomhar that Briongloid was no longer on their side. With only two realms backing their cause in the last war, it was a pretty significant hit. Especially considering Fomhar shared a border with Briongloid.

Rania was more than Weylin's mate. She was a force to be reckoned with. And while Faolan would never say it aloud, his choice to bring her acknowledged it.

Faolan only nodded, tense beside her. He wore the armor of Samhradh and the crown atop his head that was modeled after the one that Eilean managed to save when they lost their throne. It sent a message—and that was exactly what he wanted.

Rania wore a gown the color of Briongloid's lilac to highlight the duality of their two realms when they stood side by side in the face of the *Gheall Ceann*. It was lace and fell loosely around her hips, with beaded strands of silver. There was a dagger strapped to her waist and another hidden in her left boot that was covered by the bottom of her dress.

She was thankful for the time Callum had spent sparring with her in the courtyard before she had ceased communication with him. It was a refresher that helped her go into the confrontation with confidence. Rania had always been excellent with a blade or an arrow or whatever weapon found its way into her palm, but she had preferred her tongue and the words it unleashed.

It was common for the offspring of the lords and ladies of the seven worldly realms to train as a laoch, as it was in their nature to defend the home which they vowed to protect.

While she certainly hoped it wouldn't come down to bloodshed, it was better to be prepared than to be taken by surprise. She felt sure the *Gheall Ceann* would underestimate her, as most did, and that was to Rania's advantage.

She couldn't help but wonder who Aisling Iarkis would bring as her only companion. She had heard much of the red-haired male she had risked her life and the fate of the realms for, but there was also the chance she would bring a Shea, as they were putting plenty of their own resources at risk by helping her harbor the Udar Apparent.

Rania had not seen Sorin or Cillian or Eimear Shea since their younger siblings were merely toddlers. She had always enjoyed Eimear and her rather strange ways but assumed she would be the last Shea to volunteer for anything political. She was content to let her brothers run the game in a way Rania had never been.

In a lot of ways, Rania both admired and was envious of Eimear's free spirit.

There was a slight stutter in Faolan's step that snapped Rania's attention upwards. She lost her own footing as she saw what he had seen.

Rania's gaze was met by glaring golden eyes the size of her torso.

She stared back at the wyvern that stood far taller than the trees, its emerald scales glinting in the moonlight. The flutter in Rania's chest was not of fear but of complete awe. She had only ever seen illustrations of wyverns, and she could say with certainty that they would never do the actual beasts justice.

It was terrifying, and Rania was smart enough to know that should be her only response. Yet, she looked at the creature with curiosity, wondering how it might feel to run her hand along its snout or to sit atop it, flying above Talam as only wyverns could.

As if reading her thoughts, the wyvern blew smoke from its nostrils and loosed a low, menacing sound that could only be described as a growl.

Rania understood the meaning without ever having to converse with a wyvern before. Her gaze trailed away from the wyvern, down to the female it was there to protect. Aisling looked minuscule in comparison to the beast wrapped protectively around her.

They had not brought any of the wyvern weapons, which Rania imagined was for the best considering it was meant to be a peaceful negotiation. Still, she could not help but feel defenseless when faced with the creature.

Aisling wore black laoch leathers. Her long, light brown hair was tied in a braid that hung over her left shoulder. Freckles spattered her olive-toned face. There was a necklace at her throat that looked to be made of twine. The female held her head high as flames writhed within the yellow-green of her eyes. It was as if she herself had the soul of a wyvern.

She rested her hand on the dagger at her waist, and as if the appearance of her wyvern was not bold enough, Aisling wore the true and original Speartha crown atop her head.

A chill shuddered through Rania as the warmth of her curiosity turned to frigid terror, cold enough to freeze the blood in her veins. She refused to look at the Udar but could only imagine the rage burning through his usually icy amber gaze.

Aisling Iarkis's lips turned up in a grin that said she got exactly the reaction she wanted.

"Allow me to introduce you to my companion. Although if I recall correctly, you have met before," Aisling spoke. Her voice echoed through the clearing as she shifted her weight and glanced to her wyvern, whose gaze never left Faolan's. "This is Muinin, and he would like you to know he has a very short temper, *especially* when confronted by rulers who care more about power for the sake of power than anything else in Talam."

"I didn't realize wyverns were included in the options of companion choice," Faolan ground out, his voice grating against Rania's ear as her heart pounded in her chest.

"You didn't? Did you have your own that you would have brought? Muinin plays well with others. Most of the time."

"That's not what I meant," he spat, and Rania flinched.

"Instead of remarking on your own misunderstanding of the

terms, how about you introduce me to the female at your side who clearly has better sense than you do."

Faolan was silent for a beat, and Rania took that as her cue to speak.

"My name is Rania Dorcas," she stated, her voice ringing through the trees loud and clear.

"*Dorcas*—a traitorous name these days," Aisling interjected the moment Rania spoke her name. Her voice dripped with disgust as she finally dragged her gaze to look at Rania.

Rania bristled defensively but kept a cool tone. "I suppose it depends on who you ask," she replied with all the nonchalance in the world. "But my realm stands behind me, and that should be your only concern when it comes to the Dorcas name."

Rania's voice did not rumble with malice like Faolan's did. She didn't flex her anger and wield her rage. She spoke matter-of-factly, and it seemed to intrigue Aisling more than anything. The female tilted her head and waited.

The only sound in the clearing was steady, harsh breathing from the wyvern's nostrils, leaving behind trails of smoke so faint it resembled a morning fog. But it was enough. Enough to remind them all of the gift of the gods that dwelled within wyvern blood. The esos of ashers that they shared with the elves.

"I don't know if you realize the predicament you find yourself in," Rania continued into the silence when no one else spoke. Her voice was almost warm. Aisling's eyes narrowed, feigning no interest in political jest. "But you endangered more people than just yourself and your own loved ones when you took my mate as your hostage."

Rania could've sworn the female flinched at the word "mate," her yellow-green eyes betraying her. *Was this news to her?* Rania's heart thundered as she wondered what Weylin had told her about the mating ceremony, given he would remember it as it truly was—incomplete. *False.*

Rania ignored the feeling. They all knew they would have to cross that bridge when they could finally speak with Weylin again. She continued on with all the confidence and pride in the world. If it were all of Samhradh's word against Weylin's, they had nothing to fear. Faolan had assured her of such.

“If you return him to us, we can move past this unfortunate turn of events. And that is a mercy beyond what you deserve," Rania lowered her voice. "And if we discover that you have harmed my mate in any way, the wrath of all nine gods wouldn't be enough to save you."

Rania said the words as if she were speaking about Callum. It was the only way she could deliver them in a believable way. And apparently it worked. Fear flickered across Aisling's gaze and dissipated again as her wyvern roared in their direction. Rania's hair blew behind her shoulders, and the mist of his spit grazed her pale cheeks. The air smelled faintly of sulfur. She grit her teeth but did not wince. Faolan tensed beside her.

"Muinin doesn't take kindly to threats against his bonded," Aisling crooned.

"Enough of this game, you are a gods-damned *child*," Faolan snarled, taking a step forward. In the same moment, Rania watched the wyvern's claws flex and dig deeper into the earth. "Return my son —the heir to the seven worldly realms—or bring the wrath of the remaining five realms against a home that is not your own."

"And if I kill him first, what then? He is your only heir, is he not?"

"You wouldn't dare," Faolan's voice was rough and low.

"*I* declare the terms of his surrender. He is safe and sound, for now," Aisling said as she folded her arms across her chest. "In fact, he has been treated quite well as a hostage at the hands of the Sheas. They have *morals*, something which your brutes would know nothing about."

Rania could have sworn the air around them grew cold. The breath in her lungs turned to ice, and she felt something in her blood she could not understand. Aisling's eyes were blazing with flames, the complete contrast to the sudden chill. Her jaw was set. For a moment, Rania felt more afraid of the female than the beast behind her. She fought the natural urge to reach for her blade. One of them had to stay cordial, and it certainly wasn't going to be Faolan or the *Gheall Ceann*.

In fact, second to herself, Muinin may have been the most diplomatic so far.

"I certainly don't see my throne here," Aisling said when Faolan was silent. "That was part of our negotiation, was it not?"

"We never negotiated," Faolan growled. "You simply sent demands."

"Then why are you here?" Aisling snapped. "Certainly you aren't ignorant enough to think I will simply hand the male over to you. If so, you're even more foolish than your son."

The words brought a thought to Rania's mind, and she wasn't sure how she hadn't considered it before. Given his position as her hostage, Weylin and the *Gheall Ceann* had certainly formed some sort of relationship by now. She feared what the male could tell her about their plans and Eilean. There was no telling what sort of information Aisling could obtain using her nine sources of esos. They needed to get him home. There was no time to waste.

"Then let's negotiate," Faolan sneered, leaning back on his heels. "*My* throne is off the table."

"I wasn't aware you had your own made. Congratulations," Aisling mocked, tilting her head again. The gems of her crown glinted in the moonlight in a way that added to the taunt.

"Enough!" Faolan roared. Muinin blew smoke out of his nostrils. Rania stood straighter. "What if I give you the time you ask. I will give you one full year to try your best at the prophecy."

"Nine!" Aisling snapped. "I said *nine*. And that is only one demand. Hardly a compromise."

"One year. I will not allow Talam to fall apart due to your own refusal to see the truth. One year and that is all."

"Your confidence will be the downfall of Talam, not anything my own life brought about. Your arrogance will ruin the realms, and your pride will leave your son dead."

The moment the words left Aisling's lips, Faolan drew his sword. Aisling's only blade was in her hands, but she hardly needed it. Her wyvern took a step forward and unfurled its massive wings, covering the area in a shadow that blocked the moons of Talam. They were left in darkness. He roared again, this time tipping his head back. The sound shook the ground beneath Rania's feet.

Panic overcame Rania as she glanced over and saw the determined gleam in Faolan's amber gaze. Her palms began to sweat because she knew Faolan would curse her for the words she was about to speak, but she couldn't see another way to avoid bloodshed. Which she was quite certain was not a way to handle a hostage situation.

"Nine sunrises," Rania said. All three pairs of eyes turned on her, as if they had forgotten she was there. "In nine sunrises, we reconvene in this same place. This time, we will not return without the Udar Apparent in our custody. Until then, expect a raven with our negotiated terms before sunrise on the third morning."

"Deal," Aisling spoke before Faolan could. "You should let this female speak for you more often. She handles herself better than anyone I have met from your realm."

Rania's heart thundered as she watched a muscle tick in Faolan's jaw, knowing Aisling's words had furthered his anger towards her. The smirk that graced the female's lips told Rania that she knew it as well. Rania clenched her fists.

"You seem to forget who exactly you are dealing with," Faolan's voice was clear and firm, lacking the rough edge of rage. It was far more frightening than any tone she had ever heard him use before. Rania suddenly wondered—for not the first time, but perhaps the most earnestly—what she had gotten herself into in pursuit of a throne. "Continue to provoke a wolf, and you cannot be surprised when your head ends up severed from your body."

“Have you heard the one about wyverns?" Aisling sneered back, showing no sign of intimidation. "Look at a wyvern wrong, and your eyes will know nothing but the flames of Hel for eternity and then after."

Muinin's tail beat the ground behind her, as if in agreement. Rania glanced over to him and found his golden gaze fixed on her rather than Faolan. It was as if he saw her as the threat, and not the Udar. Rania swallowed slowly. A low growl sounded from him, and Aisling followed his gaze to Rania. She smirked again but did not say a word.

Rania remained silent as well, her pulse fluttering against her neck. Suddenly her blood felt strange, and her head was dizzy. Maybe it was because she had never known such fear.

"Nine sunrises. We will delay no further, or we will bring the laochs of five realms to your doorstep," Faolan spoke at last, eyeing the wyvern who was a very real and present threat. "On two conditions. First, my son remains unharmed, and he had better look no different than the day he left. Second, at our second meeting, companions do not include beasts."

"We'll see about that—in nine sunrises." Without another word, Aisling turned on her heel and walked away. Her cloak fluttered behind her in the wind as her wyvern took to the skies, staying just above the trees, coating the woods beneath him in darkness.

Rania's mouth went dry as Faolan turned to face her, rage hardening the planes of his face. Rania wished more than anything she was anywhere else in all of Talam.

Her blood seemed to jump beneath her skin as she tried to think of the words to say. Then, her whole body ached and nausea shot straight to her head. She doubled over, fighting off the feeling that threatened to take her.

Not here. Not alone with Faolan Myrkor. Not here.

Rania tried to stand, but the movement was too much. She fell to her knees, and suddenly the world was spinning. She felt light as her eyelids fluttered and fell shut.

Wind. Blood. Flames. Glass. The silver of a blade.

Images reeled through her mind in the span of a breath, then they were gone.

There was nothing but darkness as her head hit the soft soil of the forest floor.

19
RUAIRI

Ruairi's legs were heavy as he paced through the rows of elves practicing with their esos. His body ached from the long hours and physical demands of training, but he was happy. He had found a new sense of purpose in Fomhar, and he hadn't realized how badly he needed one. On Eilean, training laochs was one of his favorite things to do, and it came back to him as naturally as breathing.

The air was filled with the familiar smells of charred earth and fresh greenery from the mix of esos around him. There were shouts of joy and frustration and everything in between. Training the laochs of Fomhar had been an ordeal beyond what he had imagined, but one that made him feel like himself again. When he was training the youth of Eilean, they at least were acclimated from a young age to their esos.

It seemed when esos awakened in an elf of a later age, the reaction could range from severe pain to blissful relief. It often correlated to the form of esos, as though different sources reacted to their awakening in rage or gratitude and all that came between. Once the elves were finally familiar with the new feeling of their blood, Ruairi's job was to help them access it and control it, which was usually a lesson that came long after a young elf first felt their esos.

There were not many perks when it came to growing up in Eilean, where they were isolated from the rest of the worldly realms. Even before the lofa struck their realm, resources were scarce. But Ruairi saw how much of an advantage he had growing up alongside his esos. He pitied those who did not have the same experience.

Eimear and Kol had become his two best teachers, even though they did not have much experience, in the absence of Aisla and Sorin, who had both gone south to meet the Udar. The thought made Ruairi's skin itch as he anxiously rubbed his forefinger against the pad of his thumb. He trusted Aisla, and he knew she could take care of herself, but he had also seen her go up against the Udar, and it was a match that was too close for comfort. Ruairi detested the idea of her going anywhere near the male. If there was anything he could have said or done to stop it, he would have.

He found a morsel of comfort when she told him who her companion would be. If anyone prioritized her safety even more than himself, it was her massive wyvern and the flames he wielded. Muinin would never let anything happen to Aisla.

Ruairi was far less pleased when he was forced to come to terms with the fact that Weylin would also be with them. They had to be prepared to make the exchange if Aisla's terms were accepted, but no one truly thought they would be. Still, Ruairi did not like the idea of the male who wished to see Aisla dead traveling alongside her. He was grateful that Sorin brought nine of his own laochs with them, but nothing felt like it would be enough to keep the Udar from the *mallaithe* he wished to kill.

Ruairi inhaled a long breath, turning towards a female with dark brown hair who was toying with the sparks that burst from the tips of her fingers.

"Try to have patience with them," Ruairi instructed. A few heads turned in his direction when he spoke. "If you give it the time to gather, it will come out far stronger than its current form."

The female nodded, but her face was still downcast.

"Remember, you can always bring yourself nearer to the roots of the ash tree. There is no better way to strengthen your source."

At his reminder, a few elves shuffled closer to the tree. Not enough to crowd it, but the few who were losing their patience with their current circumstances.

While many of them struggled to grasp the concept, more of them were catching on. It was perhaps the most rewarding task Ruairi had ever taken on. He knew he was in part responsible for the joy on their faces when they found their esos for the first time or controlled it enough to maneuver it like the weapon it was. Under less stressful circumstances, Ruairi knew he would be having more fun with it. Still, Ruairi felt lighter than he had in a long time.

His afternoon continued on this way, coaching and guiding. Giving Eimear and Kol advice as they needed it. They had a solid number of confident wielders in all four of the elements. As expected, not a single seer had risen from the source. There had not been any since the norns revoked their esos from the elves following the betrayal of Verdandi.

Only one turned out to be a pryer, and he hadn't been able to shed a throbbing headache since his discovery. Kol was one of two shadows, while Eimear was one of the seven menders. Kol had a better grasp on his esos than the other shadow from the start. The other had encapsulated the entire room in a darkness so intense, every elf lost whatever esos they were trying to form. The elf grinned shyly when the light returned, turning her hand over and admiring the pulse of the blood in her veins.

Ruairi was exhausted by the time the last elf filtered through the door and back to their own rooms, leaving him alone with Eimear and Kol.

Ruairi had begun to notice the closeness between the two elves, despite the fight Eimear had put up against her task to watch over the ward while he was becoming acclimated to Fomhar. Kol snuck glances at Eimear whenever she wasn't looking. He gazed curiously at her when she spoke and smirked whenever her frustration grew, and her cheeks blushed red.

Eimear seemed oblivious to it. Yet, she laughed at every one of the male's jokes and leaned into him when she listened to him speak.

Kol was moody like a summer storm, while Eimear was warm like an autumn day.

"You should really take tomorrow off," Eimear spoke up, calling Ruairi from his thoughts. "You look terrible—by terrible I mean just really, really tired." Eimear tried to recover. Ruairi couldn't help but smile.

"Oh, come on, this is every day for me back home. I'm sure you guys could use the rest yourselves," Ruairi said, unable to stifle a yawn.

"Please," Eimear scoffed. "You are always here long before we arrive and rarely take the meal breaks my father insists upon."

"Time is not on our side, Eimear."

"Sure, it isn't," Kol spoke up in that nonchalant voice of his, the ends of his black hair grazing the top of his shoulders. "But we need *you* to be prepared for whatever may come as much, if not more, than we need *them* to be prepared."

Eimear nodded eagerly beside him, driving their point home.

"Fine. I won't take tomorrow off, but I will come in later. It sounds to me like you just volunteered to take the early shift."

Eimear opened her mouth to protest, but Kol cut in first, "Deal."

A knot formed in Ruairi's throat as something that was not quite jealousy ached within him. He saw their friendship, and he missed his own. Sometimes, it felt more lonely to be with Eimear and Kol than to truly be by himself. Aisla was in the south, and Eire was in the north, and he was in Fomhar, stuck in place. Waiting for news.

Waiting for anything. Their reunion had been far too short, and he couldn't help but fear they might never share the same space again.

"Ready to get dinner?" Eimear asked, tilting her head to the side as she waited for his response.

"Sounds good," Ruairi said, wearing a false smile.

Eimear's gaze lingered a beat too long, and he wondered if he was truly so easy to read. He once thought it was a trait only Aisla and Eire possessed.

20
EIRE

The sun was setting when Eire's traveling party led by Cillian Shea at last came upon Castle Oighear. The purples and oranges of the sky glinted against the sparkling white of the snow, and standing before it felt like a reward in and of itself.

"Now that, that's a castle," Sten, the navigator, said with a low whistle. He was calm and easy-going, with a quick wit that kept their group laughing through the harsh climate.

Eire couldn't help but agree, as her eyes traveled up the massive grey towers that cast a shadow across the snow. A chill ran down her spine, and her breath clouded the air before her. She hardly noticed it anymore after the sunrises they had already spent in the snowy northern realm. The gryphons had helped them get through Fomhar quicker, but they all agreed it was best not to take them past the border.

Eilean had snow occasionally, but not like this. It was quite a shock to her system, but Eire felt it had brought her closer to her traveling companions. And others even closer, Eire stole a glance to her left where Cillian stood beside Revna, his gaze lingering on her. While she marveled at the castle, he marveled at her. Eire didn't know how Revna could be so oblivious to it, but she couldn't help but adore it. Cillian was enamored with the beautiful female who hailed from a southern city in Fomhar. Revna was all sharp edges and smooth talking, and she reminded Eire of Aisla at times.

She was a comfort along the journey, and they had become fast friends.

"It sure is," Eire agreed, smiling softly. She had once dreamed of adventure such as this, although the company was not exactly who she had envisioned beside her. Life had a funny way of surprising her, and Eire had learned to stop expecting it to go according to plan. "Let's hope Lady Emil gives us a warmer welcome than her land has."

"I wouldn't expect much if her reputation has any accuracy to it," grumbled Nevin the brawn. The dwarf was the most displeased by the traveling conditions, but he carried on, nonetheless. His adoration of Aisla would have motivated him to the very ends of Talam. Eire recalled the first time they met upon their arrival to Fomhar, and she would never forget the way Nevin's eyes shone with admiration when Eimear introduced him to Aisla. "*I dutifully await the day my sword will shed the blood of enemies in your name,*" he had said, and Eimear hoped that day was far away from their current journey.

Eire enjoyed the stories of his adventures in Fomhar. Nevin's dwarven house had been the only house to make weapons for the Shea family, for as far back as the world tellers recorded. He took great pride in sharing the tales of his ancestors, and the weapons they had forged for the lords and ladies of Fomhar. Nevin told her the story of his own battle axe that was always at his side. It was the first weapon his son had a hand in creating, and they had even pressed the sigil of their house into the hilt.

Nevin had never been one for traveling, but when Deaglan Shea asked him to join them, Nevin felt the opportunity was meant for him. Deaglan knew the dwarf had a high reputation through the realms, and they might even be able to barter his forging skills in their talks with the Burkes of Geimhrigh.

"How optimistic of you," Cillian said with a playful smirk.

"You know me, ever the optimist," he snorted, then strode ahead of the group. "Regardless, I am not standing in this snow any longer than I need to."

"Fair enough." Cillian chuckled, and they all followed after Nevin towards the grey castle.

It was daunting if Eire was being honest. She had once accompanied the most wanted soul in all of Talam to a foreign castle and felt hardly any fear at all, knowing Leighis had approved of the journey. But this felt different. It felt risky. She knew Fiona—the female she had loved and watched die before her own eyes—would be proud of her, and sometimes that knowledge was what got her through the cold nights.

"Don't let him scare you." Revna appeared beside Eire, giving her a comforting smile. "He's always assuming the worst, and besides, Deaglan told Cillian that Lady Emil's bark is worse than her bite. Plus, she owes the Sheas a favor. I can't guarantee she'll aid your friend, but I would almost bet that she'll give us a good meal and a warm place to sleep. That's more than we could say for Briongloid these days. We need allies. That's why this trip is so important."

Eire swallowed and nodded at the reminder of the traitorous realm that had tossed aside their honor for the hand of the Udar Apparent in mating to their daughter. It was a transgression that would not soon be forgotten by Eilean or Fomhar. The realms had always assumed they would have Briongloid's allegiance during the time of the ninth generation after they had fought alongside one another in the War for Descendants. It seemed their loyalty was long forgotten.

They reached the stone gates that were guarded by two males, one was a dwarf and one was an elf, in heavy grey furs and beards thicker than any Eire had seen before.

"If it isn't Cillian Shea," the dwarf barked before embracing the second-eldest Shea in a hug that felt familiar.

"I swear, he knows *everyone*," Sten murmured under his breath.

"Long time no see, my friend," Cillian replied, pulling away and reaching out to shake the male's hand.

"I know our Lady has been expecting you."

"Ah, I'm glad the raven made it here. I always fear they won't make it through your everlasting winter. How do you do it?"

"I know nothing else," the dwarf replied with a hearty laugh. "And I wouldn't have it any other way."

"You wouldn't say that if you did know *anything* else."

"Maybe so. Nonetheless, you are here now, so allow me to show you in. Lady Emil and Lord Bastien were just preparing for dinner; I'm sure they can accommodate a few extra."

"Thank you, Ivar. Will you be joining us as well?"

"Wouldn't miss the chance to hear of your latest ventures."

"Good, we might need a friend."

Eire's heart thundered at his implication, but she knew he wasn't wrong. They would need more than a friend, perhaps a miracle, if they were to return to Fomhar bearing news of allies.

21
AISLA

Aisla's hands balled into fists at her side as she repeated in her mind her conversation with Faolan.

It didn't go exactly as she had planned, but none of them had expected the first negotiation to be the end of it, despite the fact that they had dragged the Young Wolf along with them, bound in iron chains and watched closely by Sorin Shea. While he was not at the negotiation with her, they had him stay nearby so that he would be easily accessible in the unlikely circumstance that an agreement was reached.

Aisla's gaze wandered over to him now. Her heart stuttered when she found him already looking back at her. His amber eyes were dimmer than usual, as if the iron dampened not only the likelihood of his esos finding him, but also the fire that blazed within him. Aisla's stomach twisted, but she clenched her jaw and looked away, turning her gaze to the road ahead.

They were walking to give their horses a break as they neared their resting place for the night. Their party was stopping in a village where Sorin Shea's childhood friend lived with his wife and young son. They owned a tavern and inn and had agreed to let them stay on both legs of their journey. Aisla's feet were weary, but her mind was alert and ready to continue home. She missed Ruairi and Eire with an ache that physically pained her.

"How much farther now?" Aisla spoke up, glancing over at Sorin, who held the reins of his white speckled mare.

"We should arrive just after sunset," he replied.

Aisla nodded. Her gaze found the skyline above the pine trees where the sun was lowering, but still a little ways from setting.

"Do you hear that?" Weylin spoke up. The sound of his voice startled her, as he had not spoken a word since they left the inn in Briongloid, where he waited with Sorin and the others while Aisla met with Faolan.

Aisla paused, glancing suspiciously at the Udar Apparent. To her surprise, he held her gaze earnestly. Concern sank in her stomach as her pointed ears strained to listen.

But she was just a moment too late.

An arrow flew past Aisla's head, nicking her ear—the sound hauntingly familiar. She inhaled sharply, and ducked behind the nearest tree. Within a breath, her own bow was strung. She would not be caught unarmed again. She glared past the string of her bow, facing the direction of the attack. She heard Sorin and his two laochs readying themselves as they all darted for cover.

"Behind me," Aisla snarled to Weylin without looking back.

"Give me a weapon and undo my chains," Weylin shot back in a harsh whisper. She heard the fear in his voice over the thundering of her heart. "I am of *much* more use to you that way."

"No time," Aisla snapped as a figure came hurtling from the woods out of the corner of her eyes.

She loosed an arrow that missed as the male raised a sword and ran for Sorin. Aisla knocked a second arrow in the same instant Weylin shouted, "Behind you!"

The words were followed by a searing pain in her shoulder. She should have never left her back uncovered. This was an ambush, not a solo archer. Aisla ducked low as she dropped her bow and gripped her blade in her trembling hand.

She heard shouts and grunts all around her, even Weylin's. Heavy guilt stirred in her stomach, knowing they had left him in a defenseless position.

Aisla couldn't think about it. She couldn't worry. *Keep him safe,* she prayed silently to any god that was listening.

Then, she moved as if the wind of the gods propelled her heels. She faced her attacker, a female twice her size with markings on her face in black paint that Aisla didn't have time to puzzle over. Aisla moved right, then left, then plunged forward with her blade, managing to bury it in the female's thigh.

The female roared in agony, but it only motivated her as she threw her weight forwards, pushing Aisla back into the fray.

Aisla's pulse quickened, and she held her ground. She dodged a strike from the female's blade and met it with her own. The sound of steel grinding against steel grated on Aisla's ears as she pulled away and took a step to her left.

"We've been following you, *mallaithe.*" The word sent a shudder through Aisla as she nearly let the fear take hold of her. It took her back to a place she never wanted to return to. A place and a voice that would haunt her dreams until her passing on.

"Well, you found me," Aisla gasped as she avoided another slash of the female's sword. "What do you want?"

"Your blood on my blade," she snarled, slashing recklessly as if to prove her point.

"I'm afraid that's a request I cannot fulfill," Aisla retorted, baring her teeth as their blades collided once again.

Aisla inhaled deeply and took a step forward. She swiped her dagger straight for the laoch's throat. It was too late when Aisla saw the female's smug grin as she predicted the movement and grabbed Aisla's wrist.

Aisla yelped in pain as the laoch tightened her hold until Aisla was forced to drop her weapon. Aisla kicked, and her foot connected with the female's gut. The impact made her drop Aisla's wrist.

Aisla used the moment to swing her fist. Her knuckles connected with the laoch's skull, resulting in a sickening crunch. Then, she moved again—faster than Aisla could keep up with.

A scream tore from Aisla's lips as the female grabbed her hair and yanked her backwards, exposing her neck. Aisla's vision went blinding white with pain, and she swung again, aimlessly, praying her fist would meet its target.

Aisla froze as she was met with the cool of a blade being pressed to her throat. Tears stung her eyes. Fear took hold of her.

I'm coming, Muinin's voice boomed through her head. *I hadn't made it far. I should have never left.*

But Aisla didn't know what the wyvern could do, not when his flames would incinerate them all.

"The gods have blessed me. They have given me the honor of being the one to bring them your head." The female spat, and flecks of spit flecked Aisla's skin.

"I'm afraid that blessing will be short-lived," a voice growled, and it took Aisla a moment to realize it didn't come from within her own head.

A weight was lifted from Aisla. A wave of nausea crashed over her in its absence. She gasped for air as she shot forward, wincing at the pain in her neck.

The female's eyes were wide with shock over the chains wrapped around her throat. Aisla watched in relief as the female flew backwards, as Weylin Myrkor used his restraints to save Aisla's life.

Aisla couldn't look away as she saw the light leave the laoch's eyes.

Weylin allowed the dead body to fall to the forest floor. In an instant, he was on Aisla. He barreled into her, pushing her into the woods until they both tumbled to the ground.

The blow knocked the breath out of her. The weight of Weylin's body pressed upon her.

Aisla didn't have time to question him or shove him off. She felt a wave of heat emanate from the clearing. She peered over his shoulder to see flames that could only belong to Muinin. Weylin had thrown himself on top of her. He had saved her life twice in a matter of moments. And this time, he knew who she was—Weylin Myrkor had known he was saving the *Gheall Ceann*, and he still did it.

Her ears rang as Weylin climbed off of her. She pushed herself to a sitting position and frantically looked around.

"Hey, hey," Weylin crouched over her, taking her face in his hands that were still bound by iron shackles. "It's okay. You're okay."

"Everyone else, I—"

"They're okay," Weylin assured, his eyes searching and full of concern. "Just breathe."

Aisla swallowed. Her chest was heaving. Her breath came in shallow pants. Her head spun.

"I'm right here," he whispered, his thumb stroking her cheek gently. "Everyone is okay. I promise. I need you to breathe."

Aisla closed her eyes and nodded. She took long, slow breaths in and out. She allowed herself to take in the fact that they were no longer in immediate danger.

"There you go."

Aisla's mouth dried and her throat tightened as she met his amber gaze. It was soft for once, tender, even. His brow furrowed with worry.

"Why did you do that? Why did you save me?"

"I thought you would know that answer by now, *banphrionsa*," he murmured.

His voice was accompanied by a warmth she had not allowed herself to feel around him. The nickname was like honey on his tongue, and Aisla longed to curl into him. She knew it would bring her a sense of comfort and safety, and in that moment, it was all she wanted. She leaned ever so slightly into his palms that cupped her face. She hoped he noticed.

I don't trust him, Muinin snarled through her mind, ripping her back to reality.

I know, but he saved my life, Muinin.

I *saved your life. All of your lives, really.*

Aisla didn't have the energy to argue.

"Are you okay?" Weylin asked quietly.

"I'm okay," she nodded. "Thank you for—"

A male grunted behind Aisla, and she knew the sound belonged to Sorin. Shame heated Aisla's cheeks as she knew they must all be looking at her now, wondering how she found herself in this position. She chewed her lower lip, wanting to finish the conversation, while her instincts screamed at her to shove Weylin away.

Weylin's jaw clenched, and he gave her a small, knowing nod as he released her face. The absence of his touch shot through her. He rocked back on his heels before standing. Weylin offered her his hand, but Sorin was already there, hand out stretched.

Aisla inhaled a long breath before accepting his help.

"Well, that was unexpected," Sorin said with a low whistle through his teeth.

Aisla could only nod as she surveyed the aftermath. She didn't know if he meant the attack or the precarious position Aisla had found herself in. Either way, she had to agree.

The ground was scorched black, and the bodies that lay there were charred and hardly recognizable. Aisla couldn't pinpoint which body was the female who nearly murdered her if she tried. There was red blood in the dirt, and chunks of grass torn up from the scuffle.

The stench of burned flesh filled her nostrils. Her stomach turned.

She turned her attention to her traveling party. Sorin looked well, aside from a split lip. Aisla's attention landed on one of the elves Sorin had brought with them, and her heart sank. The male was sitting on a rock, clutching his arm to his chest. A long jagged wound ran across his bicep, pouring dark blood. Another laoch was at work creating a bandage for him, wrapping it tightly.

This was her fault. Guilt gnawed at her until she had to turn away.

Aisla looked over at Weylin, who bore no injuries. He stepped closer to her.

"Did you recognize anyone?" Aisla directed the question to Sorin. "Or anything they wore?"

"No," Sorin shook his head with regret. "I have no idea who they were or what they wanted."

"Her," Weylin said, jerking his chin at Aisla.

“You know them then?" Sorin snarled, taking a step towards Weylin. Aisla's heart thundered as she looked back and forth between the two males.

"I didn't say that," Weylin ground out, "but you're a fool to think anything is a coincidence when it comes to *her.*"

Sorin pressed his lips into a thin line. "It's best we travel through the night. We need to get him to a proper medic—there’s no time to lose. Keep your eyes and ears wary."

Aisla nodded in agreement, finding her voice caught in her throat as fear tightened its grip around her shaking arms. She never wanted to endanger anyone else, but it felt like anyone who dared be near her found themselves in harm's way.

Shė hated it. She hated being a burden.

You're no burden, my rider, Muinin's voice entered her mind again. *You're the salvation of the realms, and they know that as well as I do.*

Aisla had no response.

They began the final leg of their journey home in defeated silence. Weylin kept pace with her, near enough to brush his arm against hers occasionally, but he didn't speak a word.

She knew it was peculiar. He had spent the journey to the border as far from her as he could within the party. Aisla knew it would raise questions with Sorin and the others. But she couldn't help but find comfort in his nearness, and she couldn't help but wish it could be like that all of the time.

22
CALLUM

Captain Callum Ronan folded his hands on the table as he surveyed the barons and baronesses seated around it. There were humans, elves, and dwarves. The room was loud as they carried on their own conversations and outrage.

He shut his eyes and rubbed his temples. His head pounded through the noise of it all. He had never been interested in politics, and he would never let Weylin live this down. If he hadn't gotten himself captured, the diplomacy part would be *his* job.

Callum opened his eyes and let out a long breath. He was in the company of the barons and baronesses of Fomhar, or at least the ones sympathetic to the Samhradh side of the war. And there were certainly more than a few.

There were enough, and that was all that mattered to Callum.

The laoch to his right, one of his own from Samhradh, shot him a sympathetic look. Callum grimaced at him before clearing his throat.

Twelve heads turned in his direction, all varying in shades of malice and frustration.

They had all expected to have the Udar Apparent in their grasp already. They had all expected their own laochs to return. There were many of them, more than enough to handle the small traveling party the *mallaithe* voyaged with.

But of course, her wyvern had come to her aid once again.

They didn't even want her. The laochs were to retrieve Weylin, then return by sunset.

Callum cursed himself for not thinking of the wyvern. He cursed himself for taking such a risk as he felt the energy of the anger in the room. He looked around at all of those he had let down.

"I give my sincerest condolences to those who suffered loss today. It was a sacrifice that will not be forgotten, and you have the favor of the Udar on your side," he spoke around a tight throat. He couldn't help but feel like a stranger in his own skin, masquerading as a figure he had no authority to be. But he could never let them see that. "We will push forward to reclaim Weylin Myrkor and have every intent to get it done swiftly. Our laochs are working on bringing several catapults and ballistas for your protection against the wyverns. I was there to witness their successful testing before I left."

"Haven't you heard?" a baron from the southeastern region of Fomhar spoke up.

"Heard what?" Callum asked as a grin spread across the male's mouth, revealing slightly brown teeth.

"Aisling Iarkis requests the presence of the barons and baronesses of Fomhar for dinner in four sunrises. I suspect it will have to do with her next round of negotiations."

Surprise dried Callum's tongue. He swallowed around a foreboding lump in his throat as his mind began to swim with the possibilities laid before him.

23
AISLA

"You nearly *died*, Ash," Ruairi emphasized the word as though Aisla wasn't acutely aware of her looming death with every heartbeat. "What happens if next time Muinin is already back on Eilean?"

I had the same question, did I not? Muinin's growl rang clear through her mind, and Aisla fought the urge to roll her eyes.

I don't need both of you jumping on me at once, she shot back at Muinin, who gave a rumble of disapproval before she focused her attention back on Ruairi.

He sat beside her, green eyes wild with fright and lined with dark circles.

"When was the last time you had a proper night's sleep?" Aisla asked. She tilted her head sideways as she changed the conversation.

"This isn't a joke," he said with a long sigh.

"Am I laughing?"

"My sleep is not the same as your life. You have to take this more seriously, Ash, you're—"

"I know," Aisla snapped, harsher than she meant to. "I know what I am. I know who I am. If you think I can forget, then you truly don't understand. My life isn't my own, and it never has been. I will protect it for the sake of the realms, but you have to understand, I cannot predict the future."

"Not for the sake of the realms, I didn't mean that." Ruairi's voice softened along with his gaze. "For *you*, Aisla. Care about your life for you and the future that you deserve to have."

Aisla didn't know if it was Ruairi's words or the look in his eyes or the exhaustion of her journey back, but her throat grew tight, and tears welled in the corners of her eyes.

"Oh, Aisla," Ruairi whispered and wrapped his arms around her from where he sat next to her on the stone bench just outside the castle walls.

She leaned in as he pulled her into his chest, cradling the back of her head with his hand and resting his chin atop her head, as he had done countless times before.

"I'm so sorry," he murmured.

The words tore the tears from her eyes as she began to sob. Her fists balled the fabric at the back of his shirt, and her whole body began to tremble with the weight of it all.

She had only nine sunrises to come up with a new offer for the Udar. She had no safe place to hide. She missed Eire and still felt the weight of her departure as if she had been the one to drive her north. And she didn't know what to make of Weylin Myrkor, and the fact that he had saved her *again* after spending his entire life raised to hate her.

And she couldn't talk to Ruairi about all of it. Most of it, yes, but he was already leading the charge on training Fomhar's laochs with their esos, and that was already more than enough work for one laoch.

She didn't want to add her own politics to his plate, let alone the matter of Weylin Myrkor.

Guilt tore at her heart as she gently pushed away from him, sniffling away the last of her tears. His firm hands took her shoulders. She looked up to meet his gaze. His eyes searched hers with all of the concern in the world buried in their green depths.

"You're my best friend, Ash. And always will be," Ruairi said. Aisla nodded. "I'm always here for you, you know that, right?"

Aisla nodded again as the knot of guilt doubled in her gut.

"Are you okay?"

No, Aisla thought to herself.

"Yes," she said aloud. "I will be."

"How can I help?" Ruairi asked, reading the deception of her answer.

"You already are. Fomhar needs to be prepared for whatever is to come."

"I can take on more," he pushed.

"No, Ru," she shook her head slowly, "you can't. When the time comes that Talam is at war, I need you at your best, and you won't be if you try to take on one more thing."

Ruairi opened his mouth as if to protest.

"Just sit with me," Aisla cut him off, allowing her shoulders to fall back. "Please."

"Okay," he said, nodding slowly.

Aisla smiled at him and shifted to sit closer to him. She leaned her head on his shoulder, appreciating the familiarity of his scent.

They watched the sun disappear beyond the tree line and listened to the birds in the trees and the rustle of leaves along the ground.

And for a moment, Aisla imagined she was home. Imagined she was in Caillte before Eire had ever fallen ill.

She closed her eyes and hoped Ruairi felt it, too.

It felt like ages since Aisla had last descended the stairs into the dungeon of Castle Orga. When, really, it had only been since the sunset before their journey to the border of Briongloid. So much had changed, and the more it changed, the less it all made sense to Aisla.

She took a deep breath, her hands trembling as she carried the tray of food set for two. Her deep green dress swished about her ankles. Aisla had finally gotten used to wearing them within Fomhar's castle.

It was nice to be in such a traditional court. It was certainly different from Eilean, but in a way, it gave Aisla a confidence she had not known before.

Yet, as her bare feet brushed the cold stone of the dungeon floor, that confidence faded. She had abandoned her shoes in her room, missing the feel of the floor beneath her toes. When she looked up, her eyes met a golden gaze that was alerted to her presence before she had been visible to him.

"You are dismissed," she spoke to the guards around the Young Wolf's cell. She needed to be alone with him tonight, even as her gut turned uncomfortably. She felt their questioning looks bore into her back.

"Are you quite certain that is a good idea?" One of the males to her left asked.

"A good idea? No, I am not certain of that," Aisla replied, calmly. "But I can guarantee you he will not harm me. And I will have to ask you to trust me."

They were silent for a moment as if debating whether it was worth it to argue.

"Understood. Just call if you need us. We'll be right outside."

"Thank you." Aisla dipped her head as they walked past her

towards the door, their judgement emanating like a wave of heat. She swallowed before she met Weylin's eyes once again.

"Good evening," he said in a voice that did not quite sound like his own. It was hesitant, something Weylin very rarely was. "What have I done to deserve the pleasure of your company, and all alone at that."

A knot that Aisla couldn't explain twisted in her stomach as she wondered at the hesitancy. She wondered if he had spent the day writhing with his own guilt for saving her life. If he regretted what he had done. She knew he had been raised to do the very opposite.

And she still couldn't understand why he had done it.

But she knew she would have done the same thing if she were in his shoes.

Aisla swallowed around the knot, dipping her head ever so slightly.

"Evening," she replied, her heart beating louder with each step she took forward. She ignored his snide comment.

"I see you haven't forgotten your promise," he said, a familiar teasing edge to his voice that eased some of the building tension in Aisla's shoulders.

"Pinky promises are not something I take lightly," she replied, and felt a thrill when the joke earned her a rare Weylin smile.

"I should hope not," he said. "My respect for you would have plummeted, perhaps beyond repair."

"I didn't know you held any for me as it is," she said before she could stop herself. Not harshly, but more as an observation.

But she hated what the words had done. How the moment they left her lips, his smile fell, and his gaze hardened.

"I'm sorry," she started, not knowing what she was sorry for.

"Don't be."

"I, um, thought I would join you tonight," she said cautiously as she balanced the tray on one hand and used the other to dig in her pocket.

The jolting jingle of keys alerted Weylin immediately. His eyebrows shot up.

"You would cage yourself with a wolf? Willingly?"

"I suppose only if that wolf is you," she said, her cheeks heating immediately. "I didn't mean it like that, just not with your father—"

"Let's not talk about my father," he interrupted quickly. "I understand what you meant."

Aisla nodded. She lifted her shaking hand, knowing with certainty Weylin could see it tremble. She pushed back the shame as the key clicked into place. The sound opened up more than just a physical door. There was something else that she knew she could not close once it had been opened.

She inhaled deeply and pushed into the room, refusing to look at Weylin again until after she had locked the door behind her. She shoved the key into the pocket of her dress, shooting Weylin a warning look. He put his hands up in the air in mock surrender.

Aisla might trust him enough to share the space with him, but she did not trust him not to flee, nor did she trust him without the iron bars that kept him from being able to reach his esos like the rest of the castle.

"I'll take that." His voice nearly made Aisla jump out of her skin, and the tray would have ended up on the floor had he not placed his large hand beside hers to take the tray from her hands.

His pinky grazed hers and sent electricity through her bones. She jerked it away as soon as Weylin had a good enough grip on the tray to carry it to the small table with two wooden chairs in the corner of the room.

"I don't often have company," Weylin said as he pulled out a chair, and it took a moment for Aisla to realize he meant for her to sit in it. She ducked her head in thanks and sat down. "You'll have to excuse the mess."

Aisla looked around his cell, and it was anything but a mess. For it being such a small living space, it was very neat. The bed was made.

The quill and parchment he was allowed was neat and tidy on the table. Very much unlike her own baile back in Caillte. The thought made her stomach churn.

"We can talk like normal, you know? We knew each other before I knew this cell," Weylin said.

"Did we, though?"

"I know that Eolas is the first horse you rode. I know that you wrinkle your nose when you laugh. I have seen you fight better than any laoch I have trained, but you can't tell Callum." Aisla didn't bother to remind him that she didn't know who Callum was—that wasn't the point. So, she listened, her tongue growing heavier with each passing moment. "I know that you enjoy red wine, and you often look up at the stars, as though there are words written in them just for you. I know you've an attitude to rival a damn badger, but the heart to sacrifice all that you are for those that you love. Yet, I know that you believe you are not enough. And I know that I would kill the soul who ever put such an idea into your pretty little head."

Tears stung Aisla's eyes as she was rendered speechless. She felt like she was pushing through a ravine, and if she reached the other side, her world would never be the same.

Could never be the same.

"I won't ask you to tell me all of the wonderful things you learned about me during our time together, but I'm sure the list would include devastatingly handsome, witty, and stronger than any male ought to be," he teased.

The corner of Aisla's lips pulled into a grin as a single tear rolled down her cheek. Weylin hesitated before he reached over to catch it. The touch made Aisla's breath catch. He withdrew slowly. Aisla met his gaze, and it held such intensity that she could hardly bear it, but she did not look away.

"But what I will say is I am more than my name. I may not be Fenian, but you surely know *Weylin* by now."

"I do," Aisla murmured softly, knowing it to be true.

Weylin was stubborn and cruel at times. But he was brave and loyal. He was proud and always thinking ahead. He cared about others in his own way, but there were few others who knew Weylin separate from the Young Wolf.

And she knew he cared for her. Not because of a golden thread sent by norns who didn't truly know either of them, but because he knew her. He knew her in a way no one else did.

"It shouldn't be like this," she whispered.

"What do you mean, *banphrionsa*?" he asked, gently, concern in his gaze. He pulled his chair closer to her, ignoring the untouched food on the table. His knees rested outside of hers, pressing on them ever so slightly.

"You should want me dead, remember?" she said. He opened his mouth to protest, but she continued before he could. "*Why* did you save my life? I think this was all easier when we were on opposite sides —when we knew where we stood."

"First of all, I know where I stand, and I have made that more than clear by now. It is you who needs to answer that question for yourself. Secondly, I think we both know we were never destined for *easy* lives," Weylin paused before continuing, "and finally, I saved your life, because I couldn't live with myself if I didn't. I wouldn't want to live in a Talam without Aisling Iarkis."

When he said her full name, a chill traveled down her spine, and the world seemed to slow for just a moment. Because when he said her name, he said it in a way that made it feel brand new. The name had once belonged to her parents, and the memory was too heavy for her to bear. When Weylin said it, she did not hear her pain and devastation. She heard hope, and she heard love.

"I-I don't know what to say," Aisla replied, breathless as Weylin leaned in closer.

Her eyes fluttered shut for a moment, and she had the sudden feeling that she was dreaming, because this couldn't be real. This couldn't be Weylin.

Or could it?

Her head was light when she opened her eyes and was met with his narrow gaze, full of something that looked an awful lot like fear. Aisla parted her lips to speak.

"Say you're mine," Weylin whispered, and Aisla's heart stuttered a beat. "Or say you'll never be. I cannot continue to wonder where your heart lies. Not when everything depends on your answer."

The air was thick with silence. It pressed on Aisla until her nausea grew, and she knew she had to say something.

"I know it does," Aisla replied. "Which is why I cannot give you an answer."

Weylin's face fell before he nodded in understanding, but pain lingered in his eyes for only a moment. Aisla would have done anything to erase it. She wanted him, but the words of the prophecy—*a union or a dissolution of power will chart the course of vanished stars*—lingered in the back of her mind, beating like a drum.

"I wish it were easier for us, Weylin," she said, gently. "But the realms think you are mated. What am I to do with that?"

"I don't know why anyone would think that. I've already told you I left Rania at the altar. Nothing was made final in the eyes of the gods or any mortal. I swear it on my own name," he said. Aisla cringed when he said *that* name, but she could not say why. She recalled the female with otherworldly beauty that Aisla could never possess. "I can't help you if you don't trust me."

"I do trust you. But you have to see how it looks to me," she pleaded.

Weylin pursed his lips, deep in thought.

"What are you planning to do with me?" he asked, changing the subject.

Aisla averted her gaze. "I'm working on it."

"Use me," he said, without hesitation. Aisla startled, whipping her head to look at him once again. "Return me and use me, *banphrionsa*. Let me help you."

"I don't want to use you," she said, shaking her head.

Weylin chuckled. He extended a hand and gently took her chin, forcing her to hold his gaze. His eyes roved over her face, resting on her lips for the briefest of moments. Aisla held her breath.

"Have you no concept of politicking? You've been using me since the moment you dug your poisoned dagger beneath my skin."

"I—"

Weylin moved his thumb to rest atop her lips, quieting her. The touch warmed her skin, and her cheeks burned.

"You're an excellent laoch, but a terrible politician, my dear. And that's one of the many things I admire about you. Use your wit. I know it's there. I've been a pawn in your game for a while now. What's a little longer?"

"I'm sorry," she said as he released the pressure of his thumb. "I don't regret stabbing you and poisoning you, but I am sorry."

"I'd be disappointed if you did regret it," he gave a small laugh again. "It was the right move."

"What an odd thing to say," she mused.

"A thank you would suffice."

She smiled at him.

"How do you want me to use you?" she asked, hesitantly.

"Why, that is a very bold question to ask." He smirked, raising the corner of his mouth.

"Politically, I meant politically. Because you said—"

"I know what I said. Politics tomorrow, please. The past few nights have left me exhausted with all of the walking and all of the *saving your life*. I don't want to talk about politics tonight, but I will help. I promise."

Aisla nodded, then held out her hand to him, pinky out. Weylin's smirk widened as he wrapped his pinky around hers. They raised their hands, holding each other's gaze as they pressed their thumbs to their own lips.

Their fists lowered, and before Aisla could say anything more,

Weylin wrapped his warm hand around the back of her neck. He gently pulled her towards him and placed a soft kiss on her forehead.

The gesture was enough to send Aisla's heart racing. Her nails bit into her skin as she balled her hands into fists, fighting the urge to wrap her arms around him. She wanted to allow herself to be held by him and swept into his arms that had kept her safe. She longed for more, but she couldn't.

He felt like home in the strangest of ways, but he reeked of danger and decisions she could not undo.

24
EIRE

Even the interior of Castle Oighear was cold.

A shiver traveled up Eire's arms as she glanced around the large oak table. Revna's leg shook nervously beside her. Revna was entirely out of her element and certainly didn't hide it. Cillian was next to her. He looked just like his father as he waited for the Lady of Geimhrigh to speak.

Nevin was on Eire's other side, his expression stoic as ever. He set his battle axe on the table, running a thumb over the sigil of his house. Eire swallowed nervously. Next to Nevin was Sten, who had not hesitated to begin eating the meal set before them.

They were a formidable group. Eire found herself honored to be among them, even if she often found herself missing Aisla and Ruairi dearly. She had proven to herself that she could find somewhere to be useful—somewhere to belong—and she hadn't realized how badly she needed that.

Emil Burke cleared her throat, commanding the already near-silent room. Her husband looked at her with admiration in his eyes. She was the matriarch of Geimhrigh as she was the one who carried the Burke name into their mating.

Upon arrival they had been invited to dine with the Burkes, and no one knew what exactly to expect. The meal had started in silence, everyone focusing on the stew set before them. It was delicious, and Eire could not help but enjoy it, despite the tension traveling through each soul at the table on a thread strung tight.

"I was not sure you would actually follow through, Cillian Shea," she said.

Cillian nodded his head, as if expecting the comment. "The Sheas honor their word. I know the Burkes do as well. We always intended to make this journey. I apologize for the delay in our arrival. We had unexpected company."

Emil raised an eyebrow but did not further implore.

"Can I assume this visit has to do with the Inevitable War? We don't have the time to dance around the subject."

"You are correct," Cillian agreed.

"I assume your father has the good sense to choose the right side this time," she said, her voice as icy as her realm.

Eire's heart dropped. In the Siege of Arden, the Burkes were known as the last to join the Udar's side. They were hesitant at best, preferring to stay out of the conflict altogether. They only joined at the threat of the Udar at the time, and the war was already almost a certain loss for Eilean. Eire assumed the lady would at least hear them out. She fought to keep the panic from her face. She trusted Cillian to handle it; she had to. She crossed her hands in her lap, nervously toying with her thumbs.

"We *are* on the right side," Cillian said with confidence that momentarily replaced Eire's fear with pride. "We were only hoping you might join us."

Emil let out a harsh laugh. Eire's gaze remained on Cillian. He did not flinch.

"And how the Hel do you imagine backing the *mallaithe* is going to put you on the winning side. She has already lost Briongloid. Leaving only your own pathetic realm and Eilean—or what remains of it."

Eire held her breath at the mention of her home realm. She worried every day for them. Only the power Aisla held over Faolan with Weylin as her hostage brought her comfort. She knew it could not last forever, but she hoped it lasted long enough for Feargal Iarkis and her own parents to rally the forces they would need to stand against Cliona and the laochs of Samhradh. Eire noticed a muscle tick in Cillian's neck. She admired the way he otherwise kept his composure. Revna's leg ceased shaking between them. She was completely still, as if waiting for something to happen.

"We have wyverns," Cillian retorted. And the words he said next were not a part of any plan Eire had been made aware of. "And, we have esos."

Revna gasped, letting Eire know she was not alone on the outskirts of this plan. Emil and Bastien both sat up straighter. Emil tilted her head curiously and smirked. She leaned forward, resting her chin on her fist. For all the realms knew, the source of esos had long gone extinct. Eire did not know what Cillian was thinking giving away that information. She blinked the surprise from her face, knowing they needed to present as a unit. Eire had to trust Cillian. She had so far.

"Now you have my attention," Emil crooned. "Go on."

"Eilean never lost their ash trees, and we have obtained one from the *Gheall Ceann* herself. Our laochs are training with it, readying themselves for the Inevitable War," Cillian said.

Eire heard Nevin choke on his wine, and it took everything in Eire to keep her mouth from falling open in shock. There was a moment of silence, and Eire knew they were being evaluated. She squirmed in her seat as sweat began to bead along her brow.

"And the Udar is unaware?"

"He hasn't the slightest idea."

"So what? We agree to back Eilean and then we will be granted a single ash tree?"

"Sign a formal pact to side with Fomhar and the *Gheall Ceann* and give us a ward to return home with. In exchange, you will have the protection of the wyverns and three ash trees. You must also agree to keep the ash trees far from your border with Bitu."

Eire toyed with the corner of the cloth napkin in her lap. She listened closely, anticipation crawling across her skin.

"And if I don't agree?"

"Your realm will be the first to burn," Cillian said coolly. Eire's eyes widened, and she bit her tongue to prevent a gasp of shock. "You know too much as it is. And with Briongloid tied so closely with the Samhradh at this point, our laochs will march north, see how quickly the Udar responds to protect his least favorite ally."

"Are you threatening me?"

"Yes. We are in the midst of a war like no other before it. If you think this will be the first threat I will deal out, you are sorely mistaken," Cillian continued, leaning forward and folding his hands on the table. "But it is not just a threat I am making. I made an offer as well, and if you ask me, it is much more appealing. A good deal, really. What would you give to know which esos the gods have blessed your blood with? For all those that you love to finally feel whole again?"

The Lady of Geimhrigh was silent for a moment, clearly considering the power. Eire's throat burned. Every word was a reminder of that which she was not—whole. And she never would be again.

"And what authority do you have to extend such an offer? I should think only Aisling Iarkis herself could do such a thing," Emil spoke at last.

"You are correct. It is not for me to offer," Cillian finished and turned to Eire. Eire's cheeks heated, and panic bloomed in her chest. She dropped the napkin, and it silently fell to the floor. "But my friend, Eire Trygg, is here on behalf of the *Gheall Ceann*. She holds the highest rank at this table. And *she* can extend such an offer."

Eire felt all eyes turn to her. She had never taken issue with being the center of attention. She had always enjoyed it far more than Aisla or Ruairi had.

But she had never been in a situation such as this. And this kind of attention was enough to make her want to sink into the depths of Talam.

Eire took a long, slow breath.

Eire trusted Cillian.

Aisla trusted Eire.

So, surely Aisla would trust Cillian, right?

"His words are true," Eire said, her voice strong and her chin tilted ever so slightly up. "Agree to our terms, and three ash trees will be delivered to your castle gates with haste."

Emil held her gaze with an intensity that almost made Eire flinch away, but she refused to. Instead, Eire smiled at her sweetly, fighting her iciness with a warmth of her own.

The female sized her up for a moment, and Eire had the distinct feeling of being undressed while fully clothed. She refused to let the female see through her. She clenched her jaw.

The Lady of Geimhrigh grinned.

"You drive a hard bargain. I will sleep on it, and we can reconvene at sunrise. For now, enjoy the meal prepared for you. You all look like you could use it."

Eire's heart fell to her feet at the same moment a joyous relief flooded her brain.

She didn't say *no*.

25
AISLA

Aisla was restless as she settled into bed after her dinner with the barons and baronesses of Fomhar.

They were colder than she had anticipated.

Where Deaglan Shea had accepted her with open arms and revered her in an almost startling way, his barons seemed split down the middle. Half of them treated her much the same, and for that she was grateful. But others did not speak. Their eyes roved her from her head to her toes in the elegant silk dress she had worn, but not a word left their lips. It was almost more unnerving than if they had said something. She could take their taunts and arguments, and she was willing to converse with them, but the silence felt as if they had already made up their minds about her in some way.

They held their tongues, as if evaluating her silently. Aisla hated it.

She felt like a book they wanted to not only read, but study. Aisla had never wanted to be a political figure, and her grandmother had certainly not prepared her for it.

She supposed the norns wove their threads without the preferences of the elves in mind. In fact, sometimes Aisla thought the norns kept their preferences in mind only to give them exactly what they didn't want.

The meeting had resulted in a stalemate of sorts. The barons and baronesses were all to stay the night in Castle Orga, and they would reconvene the following evening after everyone took space to think.

Some demanded far more than the Udar would ever be willing to concede, while others were willing to comply. No one suggested offering up her life, but she had the sneaking suspicion there were several that wanted to. She did not blame them.

All of the elves, dwarves, and humans in the room expressed verbal agreement on backing her in the war, and for that, she was beyond grateful, even if some of them granted it begrudgingly. If the lords and ladies of Fomhar had broken out into a dispute over her place in the prophecy as her own realm had, she didn't know what she would do.

She left them to think about how many laochs they would be willing to deploy, and what kind of rations they could contribute to the cause. They would need as many laochs as they could get, given that they were far outnumbered when it came to allies. Aisla was able to offer wyverns and ash trees. They also discussed the exposure of the gryphons—another topic that was split down the middle in terms of agreement.

The gryphons had been Fomhar's secret since the War for Descendants. Although they would be a valuable asset during the war to come, Aisla would never dare make that decision for them. That was something she wanted them to agree upon as a realm.

Muinin? she called into the chasm of her mind.

He was always there, but he was not always listening. He respected her privacy, but she sometimes wished he were there for every moment. If only so she had someone there to tell her she was still sane.

Yes, I am here, he spoke, his voice tired in her mind.

Do you think we have a chance? she asked, speaking aloud the question she had asked herself since the moment she first stepped on Iomlan.

It felt like a lifetime ago. Her life before Weylin Myrkor.

Of course, Muinin replied with a confidence that could not be faked. *You will only do yourself and those who follow you a disservice by thinking you don't.*

Aisla swallowed. *How is it back home? How's my father?*

Eilean is fine. They are still surrounded, but no one has made a move since the wolf was put in your custody. Cliona has been negotiating, though. What the terms are, I have not heard. They won't do anything rash until Weylin is safe, Muinin said, and a faint relief filled Aisla's chest. *Your father is well. You would be proud of him. He continues to rally those in your favor. He's even left the library with Eilis. They are making their way south to those who survived the lofa.*

Aisla smiled, thinking of her father and her friend. She turned on her side, her eyelids growing heavy.

"I just hope he's proud of me," she murmured, not realizing she spoke the words aloud.

He is, my bonded. Rest; your days are only going to get busier.

That's what I'm afraid of, Aisla whispered, but it was not long before she was enveloped in darkness all-consuming.

When Aisla awoke, her eyelids were even heavier than when she had fallen asleep.

And the ground was . . . hard.

Panic erupted in Aisla's blood as she jolted upwards and felt a tight strain against her wrist. She immediately recognized the effect of iron muting her esos.

She tried to scream, but cloth filled her mouth. Aisla struggled to sit up. She looked around the unfamiliar room.

It was dark and musty. Torchlight flickered from one corner, illuminating the tight space. Her mind was spinning in a blend of fear and fogginess. She blinked, trying to clear her vision. She had been poisoned—that much she was certain of.

By who? For how long? Where did they take her?

The questions ran through her mind as she tried to free herself from the iron shackles. She kicked and flailed, feeling more helpless than ever.

Her body grew tired. It took double her effort to fight through the effects of the poison. Her wrists were rubbed raw from her struggle. She fell back onto the ground, wishing she could wake up from the nightmare she had found herself in.

Aisla's heart sank into her stomach.

26
RANIA

"I'm so glad you're home, even if only for a little while," Brigid Dorcas crooned as she ran her pearl comb through Rania's long, silver hair.

"Considering the circumstances," Rania replied, trying to hide her bitterness. But she'd felt only bitterness since Callum had been taken from her. Since he had not even tried to fight to bring her with him. Since she had no idea if he was dead or alive, only that it was the night his plan to abduct the *Gheall Ceann* from her borrowed room in the Fomhar castle was to play out. "I wish I weren't home, Mother. Although, I am grateful for the chance to see you and Father."

"I know," her mother said, trying her best to understand something she never could. "I cannot imagine how it would feel to lose your mate so soon after finding him."

He's not my mate! The words rested on the tip of Rania's tongue and grew ever closer to freeing themselves the longer she spent in the comfort of her own home. But she supposed her mother's words rang true in more than one way.

Rania didn't think she would feel quite so strongly about Weylin's disappearance if it hadn't caused such a commotion. Lives were at stake, and not only his own.

Rania thought she would be content to keep up the charade until her dying breath, but that was before she realized what a nuisance he was. She had to remind herself that this was what she wanted for all of her life. It was what she had worked so hard for. And more than that, Callum's life now depended on her commitment to that life.

Only, he didn't know it.

She had wished to tell him the reason for her distance, but she never got the time.

Because now, he was gone, and she didn't know if she would ever see him again. Pain shot through her as she shoved away the thoughts that she refused to allow herself to dwell on.

"Have you heard from Oisin?" Rania cleared her throat, changing the subject.

"He wrote to check in on you. I wrote him back and let him know you made it safely," Brigid replied, her nimble fingers weaving Rania's hair into a long, elegant braid. "I wish he could have come with you."

"Me, too, Mother."

Her brother kept her sane during her time in Castle Omra, especially in Callum's absence.

Ever since she and Callum had rescued Oisin from the Gnashing Wolf, he had really gotten himself together. It felt like a lifetime ago with all that had changed. Oisin had even abandoned his endless pattern of one night stands. He had a boyfriend, and Rania approved. The man was gentle and kind. He worked in the castle's library, and Rania had introduced them when Oisin went with her one day. He rarely stepped foot in a library of his own accord.

Oisin stepped up in Callum's absence and continued to train with her and accompanied her to her meals. When he asked where

Callum was, she simply told him that he was needed for the assembling of the catapults and ballistae. It was true, and Oisin didn't think much of it.

A knock sounded at her bedroom door.

"Come in," her mother called instinctively.

Rania shot her mother a look, wishing she had asked who it was first. Brigid Dorcas simply shrugged in response.

The door opened, and Orla walked into the room, her pale face unreadable. Rania's heart began to thunder as her mother quickly tied off her braid at the end.

Rania stood to her feet. Orla's presence always roused Rania's fear.

"It appears as though your mate may be one step closer to home," she said, a glint of satisfaction dancing in the green of her irises.

"Really?" Rania asked, joy and anxiety warring within her. It was good news, she told herself. "How so?"

"Our dear friend, *Callum*," she replied, her voice edged with a threat that made Rania wince internally. "Turns out he's a better schemer than any of us had thought him to be."

"He's okay, though?"

"Your mate is quite well, our insiders have informed us," she said, pointedly.

Rania bit her tongue and waited for Orla to continue.

"They would have gone straight for him if it weren't for the host of guards posted outside the dungeons. We figured that would be the case, though. If they'd treated their precious *Gheall Ceann* with half as much concern, maybe they'd still have her."

"What does Faolan plan to do?" Rania asked cautiously, folding her arms across her chest. She wasn't certain the Udar would find his son's life worth the *Gheall Ceann*'s. In fact, she rather thought he wouldn't.

Orla narrowed her eyes ever so slightly. "What would you have him do?" she asked.

A test.

Rania felt her mother tense beside her, but she remained silent, waiting for Rania to answer.

"I would have him return my mate—his son—no matter the cost."

Orla's lip turned up ever so slightly as if to say, *correct answer.* Relief sagged Rania's shoulders. She tried not to let it show.

"Of course you would," Orla said. Rania did not miss her double meaning. Nor did she miss the way her mother remained tense beside her.

And what explanation could Rania give her when Orla left? None. There was nothing she could offer her mother that would not put Callum's life at risk.

Rania bowed her head in a gesture that could have been seen as relief, but it was defeat.

Rania, who had spent her entire life learning and fighting so that she might always be the one in control of it, was trapped. Her heart thundered in her chest as she imagined a mouse's would when caught in the gaze of a snake.

27
WEYLIN

When Weylin opened his eyes, a sense of unease fell over him. He was still in his cell, but it felt different.

A chill filled the silent air, and with it, a sense of doom.

"Weylin," a soft voice whispered his name. There was pain in that voice.

His heart leapt at the sound. He sat up in his bed and turned to find Aisla standing in his cell once again. He swore she was not there a moment ago.

He paused as he took her in, sensing something was wrong—*very* wrong. Her brow was drawn together in fear, her skin was pale, and her hands were tucked behind her back. She wore a cream-colored night gown that clung to the sweat on her body. She was trembling.

Weylin stood and crossed the cell without hesitation. When he neared, she fell into his arms, wrapping her own around him, something she had never done before. She pressed herself into his chest, clutching at the back of his shirt with desperation. He breathed in her familiar scent of iris and sea breeze.

"You're not really here, are you?" he whispered even as he pulled her closer, his hand cupping the back of her neck. He held her tightly to him, wishing he could protect her from the world.

"No," she replied in a broken voice. "I don't even know that I'm in Sruthar any longer."

If she thought she was no longer in the capital of Fomhar, something was indeed *very* wrong.

"What?" Weylin snapped, his blood racing with the urge to act. "What do you mean?"

Aisla took a shuddering breath and pulled away slightly. When she moved, Weylin noticed a dark purple bruise blooming along her neck and collarbone.

"Who did this to you?" he snarled and immediately regretted it when he felt her wince.

"I don't know," she replied, shaking her head.

"Look at me, *banphrionsa*." Her hands tightened on his shirt at the nickname. She swallowed and raised her yellow-green eyes to meet his gaze. The fire within flickered faintly, as if a candle on its last leg. He lifted his hands to gently hold either side of her face, his thumbs grazing her cheeks if only to ground himself. "Please, what has happened to you?"

"It's happening again," she whimpered. "They're turning against me. I went to sleep after the meeting with the barons of Fomhar, and I woke up in an unfamiliar place. It has to be a cellar, but I don't know where. I only know they poisoned me and took me from my bed and brought me here. One of them came in with a mask covering the lower half of his face, and I-I didn't recognize him by eyes alone. It was just he and I in the cellar. He got his hands on me. He did this. Nearly strangled me until a man stopped him. A man I recognize from your castle."

"From Samhradh?" Weylin's eyes searched hers, wishing he could do more to help. "Was he a laoch?"

"Yes. I think," Aisla whispered. "I don't know. He wasn't in the throne room with us that day, but when I was leaving your castle, I went back for *Oidhe*, and—and he told me to tell Ruairi he's glad he got out. He has brown hair. He looks around our age—"

"Callum," Weylin said, immediately remembering the sympathy Callum found for the red-haired male. Anger and relief warred within his chest. Callum wouldn't let anyone torture her, that much he was certain of. The man had morals higher than anyone else in Castle Eagla. But he also recognized Callum had played a role to some extent in the abduction of his *searc*. "He won't let them kill you. Not while you're the key to my return. He won't let them hurt you, either, not if he's aware. Aisla, trust Callum. You don't have to tell him anything, but don't let yourself be alone with anyone without his knowledge. Tell him," Weylin paused and cursed under his breath. *What could she tell him?* "Tell him 'Saga'. That's the name of his horse—there's no way you would know that otherwise."

"I will," she said, cautiously. And for the first time, Weylin could hear the trust in her words, no matter how fragile it was between them. "Weylin, please help me."

The sweet sound of his name on her lips was soured by the desperate plea that followed. Anger filled him until he wanted to wrench apart the iron bars of his cage, but he could not. He had to be strong for her—*smart* for her.

"I will, *banphrionsa*," he whispered. "I swear on my life I will, and believe it or not, that goes even further than a pinky promise."

The ghost of a smile graced her pale lips as she nodded.

"Thank you." The words were barely audible.

"By now, you should know better than to thank me for such things."

"When you go back, try to remember every detail of every interaction. Voices, eye colors, hair colors, even the smells," he prodded gently. "Anything that could help us identify where you are. Can you do that for me?"

Aisla nodded. "How do I know I'll be able to get back to you—like this?"

"I don't know. We've never really had control of it, have we?" Weylin chewed on the inside of his lip as he considered the question. "We'll figure it out. One way or another, we'll find each other again like this. I trust you. I trust *us*."

"Okay," she said, softly. "Weylin, I—"

Weylin would never know the words she was about to say.

In an instant, she was yanked from his grasp. He reached for her, but there was nothing left of her to hold onto.

A roar built in his chest full of rage, but he pushed it down. He pushed it down if only for her, and the fact that she needed him to keep calm.

She needed him.

Weylin jolted up in bed, his fist curled into his blankets, gripping so tightly his knuckles ached.

He inhaled one deep breath and stood. He walked with intent to the front of his cell. Weylin did not rattle the bars of his cage like he wished to.

No, he opened his mouth and spoke with all of the poise he could muster.

"Morning or sweet dreams, I suppose," he said, catching the attention of the guard dozing off at his post. "I require a favor."

"And why should we grant you that?" he sneered.

Weylin fought the urge to roll his eyes.

"Because your *Gheall Ceann*'s life depends on it," he said. This got the male's attention. His eyes widened, but they filled with disbelief just as quickly. "You don't have to believe me, but I know a handful of people—very powerful people, in fact—that would be quite angry with you if you could have helped but stood idly by out of pride."

Weylin watched the male's jaw clench.

"What do you want?"

"The red-haired male. The one she keeps by her side from her home. Ruairi. I need to speak to him. With haste, if you will."

28
RUAIRI

There were few things that surprised Ruairi Vilulf. Not after everything that had happened since the moment Eire had fallen from her wyvern.

But Ruairi could say with absolute certainty that he was shocked to his core when a laoch showed up to interrupt his training with the elves to inform him that Weylin Myrkor had requested him. Ruairi hadn't seen the male since they had entered the gates of Fomhar with him in tow.

He hadn't cared to see him.

He could hardly look at him without seeing the traces of Weylin's tyrant of a father in every feature he possessed. Every reminder of the Udar only took Ruairi back to that place where he had lost so much of himself—pieces he feared he would never get back.

His hand ached as if in reminder. Ruairi fought the urge to look down at the nub where his pinky finger had once been. But that certainly wasn't the worst thing he had lost.

A breath left Ruairi's lips as he worked to calm his racing heart. Dread filled his stomach and made him want to turn back, but it was too late.

Ruairi had always known he couldn't avoid the male forever, but he hadn't intended to face him that sunrise.

His thumb traced circles along the pad of his forefinger as he descended the final stair and made his way through the cold dungeon, the cape he had been given by the Sheas trailing behind his steps.

Weylin was perched at the edge of the bed, face in his hands, when Callum approached. At the sound of his footsteps, the male looked up.

Ruairi was taken aback at the wild look in his eyes. His black hair looked unkempt, and his knee bounced nervously before he jumped to his feet.

As if on instinct, Ruairi's feet stuttered a moment at the male's approach. The amber eyes before him—while they bore an expression that Ruairi had never before seen on the Udar's face—took him back to Samhradh. His head was suddenly lighter.

Ruairi swallowed around the lump in his throat and took a step forward, fighting through the feeling.

"What do you want?" he asked, without introduction.

He didn't think he needed one.

"Have you seen Aisla today?" Weylin answered his question with one of his own.

A feeling of nausea hit Ruairi all at once. It stirred an anger within him. He balled his hands into fists.

He knew it was the name she preferred since her parents'—well, just her mother's—passing, but it still felt like a nickname. And for the male to speak it indicated a type of familiarity that made Ruairi sick to his stomach.

"No," Ruairi answered honestly but tersely. "I haven't. But that is not uncommon these days. She is rather busy, as you might imagine. She certainly doesn't have time for the likes of you."

Something flashed through the male's eyes. It was not an emotion Ruairi could name, and it was one that he had not expected.

The male's odd behavior was setting off alarm bells in Ruairi's head, but he felt the urge to stay and hear him out. It was all too strange to ignore.

"Has anyone else seen her today? I can tell you know that the answer is *no*," he said, his voice grim. "I suppose at this point—there is no point in asking you questions—really, I called upon you to tell *you* something."

Weylin's voice was clear and strong, but the way he stumbled over his words gave away the nerves that lay beneath. A chill traveled Ruairi's spine as his words settled upon him.

"Enough of these games. Get on with it. What are you trying to say?"

"She isn't in this castle," he blurted. Ruairi's brows drew together curiously. "You won't find her in this city at all."

"What do you mean?" Ruairi asked, completely baffled by his claims.

Ruairi had joined Aisla for a drink after their meeting with the barons and baronesses of the realm. It had not gone how she had hoped, and she hadn't spoken much, but Ruairi had walked with her to her room. He had seen her just before bed.

"I mean, she's been taken," Weylin said at last. He looked up at Ruairi with eyes that both pleaded with him and challenged him to understand. "And we need to go find her."

Ruairi opened his mouth to say something, then closed it again. He didn't know what to say.

A laugh bubbled to his lips and before he could stop it, it escaped.

"I don't know what game you're playing at, Wolf, but I'm not falling for it."

Ruairi turned to leave but was immediately halted by Weylin's voice.

"Fine," his reply was short and packed with frustration. "If you don't believe me, go look for her, and if you do not find her, then it is you who will live with the fact that you wasted precious time on your pride and ego."

Ruairi whirled back around and stormed right up to the bars of the male's cell.

"Why do you care? Why would you want to help her?" Ruairi snarled, his mind a mix of emotions that he could hardly contain.

Fear. Anger. Anxiety. Disbelief. Confusion.

"Because—" the male started then swore under his breath, "because I just do. I am not who you think I am. I could have killed her on more than one occasion, surely you know that much by now. Yet, she lives. That ought to be proof enough that her life is of some value to me. And from what I have gathered from our minimal interactions, I would assume her life is of some value to you as well."

"She's everything to me," Ruairi interrupted, furious at the fact that the Udar Apparent would ever compare his concern for her to his own.

The male's nostrils flared in response.

"If you speak true, then listen to me!" he snapped back, his patience visibly waning. "She was kidnapped in her sleep by the barons of Fomhar who are plotting against her. I don't know exactly where—"

Ruairi laughed again, his mind spinning with madness.

"And how in the world would you know such a thing? Because you orchestrated it? This is all absolutely preposterous. I cannot even begin to understand the game you are playing at."

"No," Weylin growled. "She appeared to me in a dream."

"You must be losing your mind in this place. I almost feel sorry for you. Even after everything your laochs did to me, I was able to keep my sanity," Ruairi scoffed.

"You're not listening!" The male snapped, rattling the bars of his cage. Ruairi flinched before he could stop himself. Regret flashed across Weylin's eyes, and he released the bars. "I need you to take this seriously, if you care for her as you say you do. We need to find her before my father gets his hands on her."

Ruairi tilted his head, the last part getting his attention. His palms began to sweat. He still didn't know if he believed the male. How could he?

"Release me and organize a party to search the homes of the barons who showed her disdain," Weylin spoke with confidence. "I will hear from her again, and I can help you find her.

"So that's what all of this is? An elaborate escape plan?"

"Wrap me in iron if you must. Tie me to you with a chain if that will give you peace of mind. Whether you like it or not, you need me right now."

Ruairi chewed on his lower lip. He cursed and looked to the ground at their feet.

"Okay," he agreed with disdain. "Okay. If I do not find her, then we will organize a search party and go to the homes of the barons as you suggest. Is there anything more you can give me?"

"Myself," he snapped. "You'll need me."

"I don't need you," Ruairi retorted.

"So the *mallaithe* has visited you in your sleep as well," Weylin challenged.

The answer was no, but the male already knew that. Ruairi's stomach stirred with anger, and he curled his hands into fists as he felt the rush of esos within his blood.

What he wouldn't give to wield it now, to slowly pull the air from Weylin's lungs and leave him gasping for it.

But Ruairi would never do that to an unarmed man. He was better than they were. He had to be.

"I'll think about it," Ruairi said at last.

"I'll be here then," Weylin said through gritted teeth. "Please act with haste."

Ruairi pushed down every retort he wanted to throw back. He left with a haunting feeling that clung to him like a ghost.

Why did the Udar Apparent care so much about Aisla? As far as Ruairi knew, he had spent his whole life wishing her dead and would continue to until she breathed her last breath.

But there was no mistaking the genuine concern. It made Ruairi's gut turn with unease. Something was not right. None of it was.

And if he was telling the truth, why or how could Aisla ever visit the male during his hours of sleep?

Ruairi had certainly never heard of such esos.

29
CALLUM

The air was cool despite the coming summer when Callum prepared himself to open the door to the cellar. The chill seemed to find him each time he visited Aisling Iarkis, no matter how hard he tried to shake it.

He closed his eyes, asking himself for not the first time how he had wound up in such a position. He opened them again, and with shaking hands, he turned the knob.

She was right where he had left her—huddled against the wall where her ankle was shackled. She was trembling and pale.

While she had not been away from Sruthar for long, the female already appeared visibly weaker. But still, the fire in her gaze persisted.

Ever since Callum had walked in to find one of the barons of Fomhar alone with Aisling, he had been more diligent about checking in and monitoring where the keys to her room went. Only he and Bragi, the owner of the tower they were using near the border of Briongloid, were meant to have them.

Callum ensured Bragi got an earful after the situation that had nearly ruined everything. The baron had gone mad in a frenzy, thinking he would take the matter of the prophecy into his own hands, and the bruises and cuts still lined Aisling's throat and collarbone. The baron had gone in with a dagger, and Callum still did not know how the female had managed to keep him at bay with her hands tied behind her back. Her room was in disarray with the signs of a struggle when Callum arrived, having heard her screams from his room down the hall.

Prophecy be damned, Callum knew the male had almost lost them their key to Weylin's safe return.

Aisling looked up at him at last, blinking away the last dregs of sleep. He hadn't meant to wake her, but it was already well past the breakfast hour. Her brows furrowed, then she jumped as if remembering where she was. She pulled her knees in tighter to her chest. Her jaw clenched.

A chill raised the hair along his spine as he knelt down next to her. He clutched the plate of food, not knowing what to say or do.

He hated this part.

Aisling flinched away from him, almost instinctively.

"I won't hurt you," he said, hoping she believed him. "I hope you know that by now."

"What worse could you do to me?" she snarled, her voice coming out far stronger than she appeared. "You are preparing to give me over to the one soul who would show me things worse than death. Whatever happens to me, you're to blame."

Callum felt the blood drain from his face, and his stomach turned. He cleared his throat, sliding the plate to her. He sat down next to her, leaning against the wall.

He stayed there a moment, the tension in the room thick enough to make him sweat. Callum had no words of comfort to give her, and he didn't know why he even felt the need to.

"He won't kill you," he said. "You have to know that. Your people still have Weylin, and that's why you're here."

"So had I never touched that male, you're saying the Udar would have left me alone?" she scoffed.

"Well, no," Callum replied. "Probably not. But now he's forced to. You'll be protected as long as Weylin is in Fomhar."

"There are things worse than death," she said, her voice cracking at the end. The first hint of true fear she had allowed to seep into her voice, and it twisted something in Callum's soul. Who was he to allow this? "But you already know that, don't you? I remember you. You knew Ruairi."

The name immediately conjured an image of the red-haired male Callum had brought to the Udar as a captive. He found a spot on the floor to fixate on as the familiar heavy feeling settled on his chest.

Callum would never forget the moment the *Gheall Ceann*'s blade pierced his shoulder, and he stood by and watched her leave. He never told Weylin.

"I never touched him," Callum said with glum resolve.

Aisla let out a dry laugh that rasped through her throat.

"Is that how you absolve yourself of guilt? You don't commit the punishment. You merely deliver the victims." She sneered. Her voice was no longer loud or full of force. The female leaned her head against the wall, speaking with an odd mix of defeat and condescension. "Your hands might be clean of blood, but your soul is not. It's as stained as those who pressed the blade to his flesh, and those who will soon find pleasure in my pain as well. You aren't better than them. No, if anything, you're just as bad, only more of a coward."

Callum's stomach was in knots. His throat constricted, and his eyes burned as her words struck a part of him that he had locked away. A part of him that he fought to keep at a distance, but she was not wrong.

And Callum could hardly admit it to himself.

What was he doing? What kind of monster had he become?

Time seemed to slow as he turned to look at her. He startled when he realized she was staring at him. Her yellow-green eyes looked tired and worn, lacking the hate that propelled the words from her lips. And it was almost harder to face.

"I-I shouldn't be down here," he mumbled rather than the apology that rested on the tip of his tongue.

He gathered himself to stand on shaky legs. "Enjoy your meal."

"Wait!" she yelped. Callum looked back as he heard the sound of chains scraping across stone. She scrambled to sit up taller as if possessed by a sudden spirit of self-preservation. "Weylin—he's your friend, right? He's spoken of you."

Callum's hair rose along his arms as his step faltered.

"Yes, you could say that." *He's my best friend. He's my brother. I do everything I do for him, and still I think he would be disappointed to see me now,* Callum wanted to say.

"He told me to trust you. He told me you would protect me. He told me to tell you that, so that you would know that my—" She paused as if searching for words. Her eyes were wide and frantic, and her forefinger drummed on her elbow where her arms were crossed in her lap. "My life is important to him. He wanted you to know that."

“How do I know you’re not just making that up? A lot of people will say a lot of things when their lives are on the line.”

“Saga,” the female blurted, and Callum’s heart stuttered. “That is your horse’s name right? Weylin told me that.”

"What are you saying?" Callum asked, his mind reeling with this sudden confession. Weylin couldn't have possibly gotten a letter to her. There weren't even windows in the cellars for ravens to deliver messages. And Aisla certainly hadn't known that she was going to be taken from Castle Orga.

"I can't say anything else," she said, chewing on her lower lip. She looked at him, not with pleading in her eyes, but with determination. "I've told you what you need to know. If you choose not to believe me, then it is out of my hands."

She leaned against the wall once more. Her eyes fell closed, not in defeat, but in acceptance. He saw it in the way the crease in her brow loosened.

Callum didn't know what to make of any of it. His heart thundered in his chest. His fingers itched with the need to act—to do something. How could he not believe her? The proof was undeniable the moment she spoke his horse's name.

He ran his fingers through his unruly brown curls. A nervous energy filled his stomach as he cursed under his breath.

Before he could think on it longer, Callum darted to her side and fell to his knees. He didn't look at her. He didn't want to know whether her eyes widened with shock or her lips turned up with smug satisfaction as his fingers found the lock around her ankle, the key already in his hand.

He heard a sharp inhale of breath from her lips, and the sound was followed by the sound of the cellar door clanging open.

Callum's blood roared in his ears as he leapt to his feet. He curled his hand into a fist, concealing the key within it. His eyes darted towards the shackles around the female's ankle.

A mix of relief and regret rushed through him at the sight of the lock, still in place.

Callum swallowed as he turned his full attention to Baron Bragi, who was staring at him curiously.

"Everything okay here, Captain Ronan?" he asked, raising an eyebrow.

"Of course," Callum replied with all of the stoicism he could muster. "Just bringing breakfast."

The baron nodded slowly, eyeing the untouched plate beside her. Then Bragi looked at *her*.

Aisling narrowed her gaze at the baron and bared her teeth. A moment later, her hand flew out from her side and flipped the plate full of dinner, sending it flying across the floor, spraying a mix of gravy, potatoes, and chicken.

Callum winced, but the baron—the baron took heavy steps towards her before kneeling in front of her. Aisling did not shrink away from him. Callum's heart thundered as he watched, frozen with fear and shock.

The male reached out and held her chin in his hand, forcing her to look at him, not that she appeared to be looking away anytime soon.

"You ungrateful bitch," he snarled, shaking her chin.

Callum felt the urge to do something, say something, but his feet were frozen in place, and his tongue was too heavy to move.

Then, Aisling spit in the male's face, and Callum's heart fell through the ground.

He lunged for the male, knowing what came next wouldn't be good for anyone, but it was too late. Before Callum could do anything, Bragi's fist connected with her face. A sickening crack echoed through the room as her head snapped back and connected with the cement wall. Not so much as a cry of pain came from the female.

She only sat up and rubbed the back of her hand across her bloody nose. Callum grabbed the baron by the elbow and yanked him from the floor.

"That's enough," he snapped, finally finding his voice, but it was too late. And he knew it was when he looked in her eyes and saw rage that flickered with the force of a thousand fires.

Callum dragged his gaze from hers. He dragged the male through the door as he spewed curses at her.

Callum didn't look back.

But still, he felt her eyes full of hate following him long after the door fell shut behind him.

You're no better than them. In fact, if anything you're more of a coward.

Callum couldn't shake the words from his shoulders. And more than that, he couldn't shake the damning feeling that they were true.

30
EIMEAR

"I told you the seeds need to be a bit deeper to take root," Eimear scolded playfully as she leaned over to see Kol's rather poor work.

"And they are deeper than the last time you said that," Kol looked over his shoulder at her, a playful smirk playing across his lips.

A blush crept into Eimear's cheeks when his gaze met hers. There was an intensity in his icy blue eyes that seemed to light up whenever she looked into them, but she couldn't explain it. She had never been one to fawn over boys, or even girls for that matter. Eimear had more important matters to attend to than her feelings.

She had secretly thought she might live a life as a spinster, tied down by no one but the woods she would reside in and the garden she would tend to. It was a fool's wish, as she knew her status as the eldest daughter of a noble family would never let that happen. She figured when it came down to it, her hand would be promised to another for some political reason or another.

Regardless, Eimear had never taken interest in finding her own match.

"What are you thinking?" Kol asked, interrupting her thoughts, which only deepened her blush.

"Nothing," she said, a little too quickly.

"If I know anything about you," he said, "it is that you certainly never think of *nothing*."

Kol did, in fact, know a lot about her. More than most people ever cared to learn. He had spent time with her in her favorite places listening to her stories. She could tell that Kol missed his home, but he was not bitter or angry. He was curious and interested in everything Eimear had to tell him. He didn't share as many of his own stories, but Eimear didn't want to push. She imagined it would be hard to speak of a place one might never see again. So, she distracted him, as best as she could, and hoped that he had begun to feel a little more at home in Fomhar.

"Whatever," she said dismissively. She knelt beside him, letting her knees push into the cool dirt. "Here, I'll show you how it's done."

"Please do," his voice rumbled with amusement.

Eimear ignored him as she used her bare hand to dig a hole in the soil. It was quite possibly her favorite feeling in the world. She ignored the heat of his gaze that fixed on her, rather than the demonstration she was giving him in the dirt.

"You're not paying attention," she remarked without looking at him.

"Oh, I am."

Eimear rolled her eyes and turned to find his face surprisingly close to her own.

She let out a small gasp, which brought a smile to his lips. Eimear opened her mouth to say something, but she didn't know what.

She leaned forward as if on instinct, and he did the same. And suddenly all she could smell was the smoke of fire and rich scent of amber that clung to him like a shadow. It was intoxicating, and she didn't know how she would escape it, or if she ever wanted to.

Kol reached forward, tucking an unruly red curl behind her ear. Everywhere his skin touched blazed a fire along her own. She wondered if it was normal to feel that way, or if it was something special just the two of them shared.

Before Eimear's lips could brush his, Kol's eyes widened and he leaned back, reaching for the blade at his hip.

"What is it?" she asked, her brows creasing.

As soon as the words left her, Kol's hand shot out to cover her mouth. Fear grasped Eimear as she realized something was very wrong.

"Be quiet," Kol commanded in a stern whisper that was barely audible despite the fact he was a breath away from her. "Follow my lead."

Eimear nodded as Kol slowly removed his hand. He looked around, and that was when Eimear heard it, a rustling in the woods coming from the south.

There were plenty of creatures in the woods, and very few of them scared Eimear, but whatever it was sounded big. The sun was setting, making it difficult to see as far.

Without a word, Kol extended his hand to her. Eimear took it and allowed him to lead her to the other side of the clearing closer to the castle. Each step was slow and careful. Eimear watched Kol's feet so she could follow his path precisely, careful to avoid any twigs or fallen branches that could alert whatever creature it may be.

"Maybe it's just a bear," Eimear whispered. "The black bears are friendly enough."

"I don't think so."

"How do you know?"

"Just trust me, okay?" Kol said as he pulled her behind a wide oak tree. "And be quiet."

Eimear did not reply.

"Stay still. Did you bring a weapon?"

Eimear pressed her lips in a thin line, feeling embarrassed as she answered, "No."

"That's okay. But it means you really have to listen when I say to stay here."

Before Eimear could so much as nod, Kol stepped around the tree and into the clearing.

In the same instant, a barghest came barrelling through the trees. Eimear gasped, but she could not look away.

Kol dodged out of the way and turned to face the beast that glared at him with glowing yellow eyes. The beast looked terrifying, even more so than regular barghests. His hide was mottled with scars, and he was sickly thin. Most of them remained in a pack, but this one had the look of an outcast.

In Eimear's heart of hearts, she couldn't help but feel sorry for the creature.

But Eimear would still choose Kol over the beast. She swallowed, not loving his odds as fear pounded through her skull.

Kol held his arms at his side, and black shadows rolled off of him in waves. Eimear's eyes widened. She had seen Kol learning his esos, and he had picked up on it faster than most, but she had never seen such power before. Not at the volume that was pouring forth as the shadows grew, nearly enveloping the clearing.

Kol looked perfectly calm, and Eimear could've sworn she saw shadows dancing in the depths of his own blue eyes. The barghest snarled and lunged for him. Eimear nearly screamed at him when Kol did not move to get out of the way.

Then Kol clenched his fists, and the shadows swirled in response. They rushed the barghest before it reached Kol. The scream the creature let out was like nothing Eimear had ever heard before. It choked on Kol's esos as Kol watched, without a hint of fear. A thud vibrated through the ground as the beast hit the floor, writhing as shadows coursed through the creature and around it, until the cries of pain ceased.

Eimear watched as its eyes rolled back into its head, and its entire body stilled.

Her throat was tight and tears stung her eyes, but all she could think about was Kol.

She rushed from behind the tree and threw herself at him, wrapping her arms around him. He caught her, lifting her feet off the ground as he embraced her, his breaths heavy on her neck.

He had been so confident—so unafraid—but all Eimear could think of was the barghest tearing him limb from limb. It was such a relief that he was still standing, she hardly had the time to process what had truly happened.

"You're alive," she gasped in near disbelief.

"And so are you," he whispered back, but did not let her go. His hand cradled the back of her head, holding her to him in a way that felt safe.

"Are there more?" she mumbled into his shirt, adrenaline still coursing through her.

"No. No more."

Eimear inhaled a breath of relief that filled her lungs, then abruptly shoved away from Kol. She saw the immediate hurt in his eyes.

"Now tell me, what the Hel was that?" Her voice was still a whisper but one that rose to a high pitch. Her mind was spinning.

"I used the esos I had available to me," he insisted, holding his hands up in surrender. Eimear's eyes scanned the air around them, but there were no lingering shadows. "We've been training for this. It was the fastest way to dispatch the beast. I couldn't risk him getting to you, and one blade against a barghest is a bit of a reach."

"It's not about you using the esos. It's about *how* you used the esos. That was insane. You should *not* be able to do that!"

"I don't know what you mean."

"It was too controlled—too powerful."

"Desperate times sometimes bring that out of you," Kol said

dismissively. He crossed his arms, the ever-perfect portrait of nonchalance. Eimear didn't know how he could be nonchalant about any of it. "Now, let's get out of here before it gets too dark out. They are most often found in packs. We got lucky, but I wouldn't push our luck. We shouldn't have stayed out this late, anyways."

"How did you know it was a barghest and not a bear?" Eimear continued, ignoring him. "I could hardly tell the difference, and barghests aren't common in these parts. My father will be horrified to hear it."

"We have a lot of them in Bitu. I can tell their scent apart from a bear's."

"Teach me," Eimear said and crossed her arms, refusing to move.

"What?"

"I said, *teach* me."

"Ruairi is teaching you," Kol said. "He is better with his esos than I am."

"I want to be as good at mending as you are at whatever that was," she insisted.

"Fine. I will teach you. But we still have to help Ruairi."

"Of course," Eimear said. "I just want to be able to help when the time comes. Especially with mending."

The corner of Kol's lip lifted into a smirk. "What is this—Eimear Shea desires to partake in the Inevitable War?"

"I-I didn't say that. I just want to help people."

"I know," Kol said, his gaze softening, he took a step toward her, closing the distance between them. "You are too good for this world, Eimear. How am I ever going to protect you from it?"

"What a silly thing to say. There are many parts of this world that are still wonderful, despite what is going on. The animals and the plants, the sound the wind makes when it travels through the leaves—just to name a few."

"Yet none of these things are as beautiful as you."

Eimear froze, her mouth still open. Her cheeks grew warm, and she found herself at a loss for words. Butterflies stirred in her stomach, and she longed for him to finish what they started and press his lips to hers.

"Come on, Eimear," Kol said with a chuckle. "Let's get you home before any other olc creatures come looking to test our esos."

He put an arm around her shoulders and pulled her into his side. He placed a gentle kiss atop her head before starting off towards the castle. It wasn't exactly what she wanted, but it was close enough.

Eimear had never felt more safe—despite the terror that shadows often brought.

31
AISLA

Aisla's stomach had ceased its grumbling. Her hunger had become more of a constant presence, like a shadow, rather than a fleeting pain that came in waves of audible reminders.

The first few sunrises she had expended all of her energy taunting guards and probing them for information they would not give. She observed every laoch they sent in and watched for any weak points. One had left with her bite marks on his ankle and a slew of curse words in his wake.

Aisla tested every door hinge and looked for a key on each guard that entered. It was all to no avail. She had not the energy to try anything new.

She curled into herself and couldn't help but wonder what her grandmother would think of her now. If she could see the pathetic heap of flesh and bones Aisla had become despite how hard she had tried to be strong. She had spat and fought and cursed and roared, until she had nothing left.

Until she was nothing.

The one who had shown her kindness for the briefest of moments —the one Weylin had told her to trust—he had not been back.

She had been close, so close.

No one had brought her a single meal since then, either. She wondered if the male was punished for his decency. She wondered if maybe that was why he had not returned.

She didn't care. Every soul in this damned tower could rot in Hel for all she cared.

Aisla longed to call upon Muinin. She knew if she did, he would not hesitate to burn the place to the ground. He would not hesitate to burn the whole cursed village for what they had done to her.

But they had already made threats against her wyvern. When they taunted how powerless she was, they mentioned weapons made specifically to combat wyverns. They called them catapults and ballistas—one was used to capture wyverns, and the other to kill them. It was clear they feared she would call Muinin down upon their home, and Aisla could not tell if they were bluffing or not. She could not risk it, not until she had more information, which she had tried to pry out of them. Until she knew, it was not worth risking Muinin's life. Not only would it be a pain Aisla did not know if she was able to bear, but Muinin was an invaluable resource to their cause. Her connection to him had helped them communicate to Feargal and the Silenced World Tellers, as well as Eire's and Ruairi's parents who continued to help them in Caillte.

If the weapons were real, it was something that certainly further complicated the war she had wrought upon the realms.

The wyverns had always been their greatest advantage. She had to hope they had more wyverns than weapons, but that would still be risking the lives of wyverns. Something she was not keen to do.

My bonded, wyverns have risked their lives in wars long before this cursed prophecy ever existed, Muinin pushed through her thoughts. The sound of his voice in her head was enough to tighten her dry throat. *Besides that, I am faster than their weapons. Please, allow me.*

No, Aisla said back forcefully. She was grateful they could speak this way. She was afraid her own voice was no longer capable of forming even a syllable. *I cannot risk you. The realms cannot.*

I could say the same to you, he snorted with defiance.

They won't kill me, Aisla insisted, even though she often wondered if death would be better than whatever was to come. *Not while Weylin is in Fomhar. The realms are watching.*

There are indeed fates worse than death, my bonded, Muinin said, gentler.

But the gentleness hurt worse. It only confirmed her already festering fears.

Come on, Muinin, she tried to think the words lightly, but they came out harshly. *I'm the* Gheall Ceann *after all. Wasn't I practically born for trials such as these?*

That doesn't mean you deserve them.

And Ruairi didn't deserve what happened to him. Eire didn't deserve what happened to her. My mother didn't deserve her fate either. I've learned not to expect anything to make sense when it comes to the games of the gods. They couldn't care less about what we assume we do or do not deserve, Aisla said with a scoff down the bond. *I don't deserve you either, but here we are.*

Hmm, Muinin grumbled, not in agreement, but in thought. *Have you spoken to your male again?*

My male? Aisla asked, startled. *The one who tried to free me?*

Don't play the fool with me. Surely you don't think I am unaware of the one you visit in your sleep. His voice was disapproving at worst, judgmental at best.

It's not like I can control that! she snapped in frustration at the reminder of her complete lack of privacy when it came to the bond with her wyvern.

There were certainly positives and negatives to it.

You didn't answer the question, he pushed.

No, she bit back. I haven't. *Not since the first sunset here.*

Maybe you should try.

Aisla would've rolled her eyes if she had the energy.

I do, she said. *All the time I do.*

It was as if even her mind didn't have the energy to find him. It was terrifying to be so alone, but at least there was Muinin.

Why don't I try to tell them where you are?

I don't know of a shifter there. And besides that, none of them have the bond with you required to hear your voice.

Muinin huffed with frustration.

Muinin, before you—and still, even after I started to hear you—there is this female in my mind. Do you know anything about it?

Voices in your head? That's concerning, Muinin said dryly. *In all seriousness, no. I do not know.*

She used to help me sometimes. When I felt lost or alone or defeated. It was never a solution, but just a comforting voice—encouragement. She sang to me once, too, Aisla said, remembering the memory fondly, despite the circumstances that surrounded it.

Maybe she will come again, Aisla. If there ever were a time, it is now.

Aisla nodded in agreement. Her eyes burned with the sting of tears that could not fall. She hurt everywhere, felt both heavy and light in every bone of her body.

She had not the will to shout at the gods, but she swore to herself, not for the first time, that she would make them pay.

Whatever it took, the gods would not get away with their crimes against those she loved.

Aisla curled deeper into herself. Her eyelids were heavy and her body shook with the chill of the cellar.

She drifted into the darkness of a dreamless sleep.

Her mind was empty, and there was no heavier feeling.

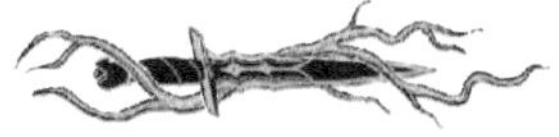

Aisla blinked her eyes open as rough hands gripped her bicep hard enough to bruise. She opened her mouth to shout at them, but no sound came out.

She was surrounded by laochs, all with their weapons aimed at her. As if she were any threat at all in her state. Not to mention the iron chains around her wrists, ankles, and neck. The male gripping her arm was burly with deep red hair. She recognized him as a baron from the meeting, and her stomach wrenched.

She was yanked to her feet, but she immediately crumbled to the floor. A choked sob lodged in her throat, unable to escape. Her body felt unfamiliar to her—it was so weak and no longer obeyed her will.

Laughs scattered through the air, deepening that thread of anger wound tightly through her veins.

She couldn't even get back up. She would have been humiliated if she had the energy to care how they viewed her.

They remedied the situation by having two laochs haul her to her feet and drag her limp body between them, supporting her weight.

"It's your big day," one of them sneered in a voice like venom.

Foreboding tore through Aisla. A big day certainly couldn't be a good thing under the circumstances.

"Shall we tell her, or will that ruin the surprise?" another voice called, but Aisla could not locate it. She could not even look up.

They dragged her through the fort, and all Aisla could see was the stone floor passing beneath her as her head hung low.

"No, let's leave it a surprise," another voice. Or was it the same as the first one?

"We'll be there by sunrise anyway," someone said. Aisla had no idea what time of day it was or what that meant for her. "It gives her just enough time to imagine where she's going."

Aisla didn't want to. She didn't want to think of all the things they could be doing to her, so she closed her eyes.

Aisla did not flinch as they dragged her body across a large horse. She did not stir at any point during the long, uncomfortable journey through the night.

She merely waited. And refrained from sending any prayers to the nine gods.

32
RANIA

As a little girl, Rania Dorcas had dreamt of castles and gardens and balls and crowns.

She had wanted to have it all—all the things that came with power and status. She had positioned herself in such a way to ensure that she could. She would be the perfect match for the Udar Apparent. She had enough practice taking care of her own family matters behind the scenes.

There had never been an expectation of love for her, despite the example her mother and father had given her of a pure and selfless and beautiful love.

Rania wanted a voice. She wanted to be more than the shadow of her brother, and she had accomplished that. Only, she had never taken the time to consider that all of her previous scheming could lead to the brutality of what had to happen.

At first, when Weylin visited Briongloid in late winter, it was so easy.

Easy in a way that felt not unlikely but rather earned. As if it were easy to reward all of Rania's hard work.

Because she knew how to wield a sword as well as her words. Because she studied history and strategy in nearly every free moment and used the rest of her time to study the male gaze.

It had been easy to find herself in Weylin Myrkor's arms because she had made it so.

Or so that is what she told herself.

But Rania could not see the future. If she could, she would know that it had all been easy, not because her work had paid off, but that her sacrifices had yet to be made.

She had sacrificed the dignity of her family. That was made abundantly clear the moment her mother's eye was ripped from her socket by a dove of Eabha in a visceral mess.

She had sacrificed her heart when she stood at the altar rather than choose the one she loved. There was no plainer way to tell Callum that he meant so little to her, no matter how far from the truth that was. But she had done it anyway, for reasons she could not explain.

As Rania tore her eyes away from the female laying on the ground at their feet, she swallowed down the bile that crawled up her tight throat.

She knew she was making yet another sacrifice. A sacrifice of her morals.

Rania's body grew numb, as if she could distance herself from the skin that held her there. Any sense of morality she thought herself to possess slipped away like a flower torn from her loose grip when she took in the *Gheall Ceann* laid before them like a lamb to the slaughter.

A living, breathing one at that.

A starved, damaged, broken, and bruised one at that.

The worst part was that Rania knew she would not say anything to stop it. A muffled voice screamed within her. It was not a harsh, shrieking scream. But a low, mournful screech, that dragged through her insides, scraping her from within. It made her want to itch her skin, but it was too easy to silence.

A part of her wanted to say that there was nothing she could do to stop it, but everyone had a choice. Rania had made hers. And she was too far down that path to turn back. The reality that she was in far over her head crashed into her before she had the time to fully understand that she was not in control as she had one thought she was.

The female hardly moved. She did not tremble or shake. If Rania had not seen the labored breath trembling through her, she might have thought her dead.

Shame forced Rania's eyes to look away. She found a speck of dirt on the ground and focused all of her attention on it.

Callum had arrived as well. Rania could not bring herself to look at him. She refused to acknowledge he had been a part of this, in whatever capacity.

Like a part of herself in some strange way, Rania could feel him. She could feel his own guilt and shame, and she knew in her heart that he had never laid a hand on Aisling Iarkis.

He had once told her of the red-haired elf who found himself in the dungeons of Samhradh's castle. Callum still carried that guilt like a weight upon his back. And she knew, if it were not for Weylin, Callum would not have participated in the capture of the *Gheall Ceann*.

But Callum would do anything to save his best friend. The loyalty was admirable, but Rania still couldn't stomach what it had led to.

Under all of the terrible and heavy feelings filling her blood until she felt like she might crumble beneath the weight of them, Rania still held her head high. She would not let Faolan see her falter.

Rania did not know what he would do if she did.

"The *Gheall Ceann* as you requested, my Udar," a male spoke, but it was not a voice she recognized.

A baron of Fomhar then.

Traitor. Coward. Turn-tide.

Rania longed to shout the words at him, but it would only make her a hypocrite, for she was far worse than any of them. Still, she had not realized how much discord there was within Fomhar itself. The realm had always presented a unified front. Her family had always known where they stood in terms of the prophecy, and there was no hint of rebellion within.

"Let me make certain it is her," Faolan said.

"Oh, I can assure—" the first voice started, but Faolan merely held up a hand in silence.

Rania's heart thundered in her chest as she watched the scene unfold before her, as though she were seeing it through eyes that were not her own.

Orla stood between them, ever calm and unreadable.

Faolan walked forward until he reached Aisling. He looked down at her, but she did not stir. A victorious smirk pulled at the corner of his lips. Rania's stomach turned.

He knelt slowly, lowering himself to the ground where the *Gheall Ceann* lay. Several laochs moved their hands instinctively to the hilt of their swords as he did so. Rania's breath caught in her throat.

The next few moments seemed to happen in slow motion.

Faolan reached his hand out to tuck Aisling's hair behind her ear —in a sickeningly gentle way—to reveal her face beneath the mess of light brown hair.

Approval shone in his eyes for the briefest of moments.

The moment he pulled his hand away. Aisling's own darted out to latch onto his wrist. Rania stumbled back a step in shock.

Somehow, Aisling mustered up the energy to lash out. In a movement completely otherworldly, the female flung herself forward. Rania could not see what was going on between the two bodies and did not care to move closer to them.

Faolan let out a roar of pain and shock. Someone kicked Aisla, but she did not budge from where she had Faolan pinned to the ground.

Then, someone grabbed her hair and yanked. Aisling's body flew backwards from the force of it. She fell to the floor with a thud that shook the ground. Rania swore she heard a bone crack. Aisling looked once again for all the world as if she were no longer of the worldly realms.

She lay there motionless.

Rania looked back to Faolan and saw the silver glint of a bloodied butter knife in his hand. Her eyes found the spot just above his heart where blood stained his shirt. Rania's breathing slowed as she processed what had happened.

"A damned butter knife? You thought you would end me with a *butter knife*? How foolish you are, and how foolish you continue to be." He prowled forward, stepping over her body.

He leaned over her and grabbed her face in his hand. Her eyes were closed.

"Look at me," he spoke with lethal calm and waited a moment. "I said, *look at me*!" His voice rose to a shout that rattled the torches along the walls.

Rania saw Aisling's eyes flutter open, and for the briefest moment, she recognized fear within. That fear was replaced so quickly by a pure and raw hatred—Rania almost thought she had imagined it.

"Have you nothing to say for yourself?" Faolan growled.

Aisling was silent for a moment. "It is *you* who will be the ruin of the realms," she rasped out in a voice hardly recognizable as her own.

She began to cough with the effort of speaking but was abruptly cut off as Faolan flung her head back against the floor. A crack sounded through the room. Rania flinched.

Blood pooled around the *Gheall Ceann* like a dark, cursed halo.

Faolan stood and raised his foot.

Rania squeezed her eyes shut, unable to bear a moment more. But she would never forget the sounds of each time Faolan's foot met the female's unconscious body.

No matter how hard she tried.

Sobs racked through Rania's shaking body as she leaned against the wall of the toilet room, having just emptied her stomach.

She wanted to pound her fists against the wall. But she had neither the courage nor the energy. She sat there, crumbled into herself, and cursed herself for her own silence.

Rania had always thought that when the time came to end the *Gheall Ceann*, she would be able to handle it. While it felt rather wrong to take a life for a reason other than the unfortunate circumstances of her birth, it would put an end to needless war and violence.

The prophecy had never been clear to Rania, or anyone for that matter, and while Rania held a deep belief in the gods, a part of her had never believed the prophecy to be their doing. It felt more mortal than immortal to her. She didn't think the end of the nine realms would come with or without Aisla, so if ending her life was what it took to bring peace to the warring realms, then it was an understandable and necessary sacrifice.

But the things Faolan Myrkor had done to her—the way he took pleasure in her pain—Rania had never imagined she would witness such things. Whatever Rania had thought her life of political ambition would lead to, she had never imagined such atrocities. It made her angry and sad and overwhelmed by a guilt so intense it made her physically sick.

And she would curse her own naivety until her final breath.

Her father had been a stern man, but a gentle one, too. He had never raised a hand to her or her brother. He spoke to both his council and his laochs with command but also respect. He would never bring another soul pain.

He wanted justice, not suffering.

And while Rania had known Faolan was a different sort of male than her father, she had not been prepared for it all.

Rania clutched her knees tighter to her chest. She dug her nails into her skin until there were five red crescent moons on each of her thighs.

She wanted to forget. She wanted to go back to a time before she had ever journeyed south to Samhradh.

The sound of footsteps echoed in her ears, and it took Rania a moment to realize they were in her room. She hadn't even heard the door.

She frantically wiped the tears from her eyes on the back of her hand, leaving behind smears of black kohl. Then, the soft sound of the doorknob turning echoed through her bones, followed by a sliver of light entering the toilet room. She held her breath.

At any moment, Orla was going to see her as a weeping mess on the floor and probably send her to the dungeons to punish her for her weakness—in her own home.

Rania looked up and met green eyes that were warm like the sun, not cold like the depths of Hel.

Her breath caught in her throat as relief washed through her. She no longer cared about her weakness or her appearance, because she knew Callum wouldn't either.

"Oh, my love," the words left Callum's lips in the same instant he dropped to his knees before her.

Rania had no words. She merely stared back at him and swallowed around a lump. His eyes filled with a feeling she couldn't face, so she was forced to look away. There was so much grief and pain and fear—fear for her that she did not deserve.

What did she have to fear?

She looked down at her knees.

Callum did not say a word. He reached out and gently wrapped his arms around her, pulling her into his warmth.

In the safety of his arms, Rania fell apart. She was not the put-together eldest daughter she always tried to be. She was broken and messy, and there was hardly a semblance of the female Rania presented to Talam left. She laid herself bare before Callum, unafraid. Rania dropped all of the weight she had felt and put it before him. He took it.

He rubbed her back and ran his fingers through her tangled mess of white-blonde hair until she crawled into his lap and clung to him, hands balled in the fabric of his shirt.

He held her until her sobs ceased and her eyelids grew heavy, but she was not ready for sleep.

Callum's head rested on hers. His fingers ran gently up and down her spine, each touch warming her chilled bones with electricity down her skin. She wished she could live in the moment forever. Rania wished that was all there was—she and Callum alone in the world.

She leaned against his hard chest and nestled into the crook of his neck.

"Callum," she said, needing to say his name.

"Rania," he whispered back in a voice thick with emotion.

"I was worried sick about you," she said.

"You shouldn't have," he replied. "I was well protected."

Rania was silent.

"Besides, you were barely speaking to me before I left. I didn't know what to make of that."

Guilt twisted in Rania's stomach. There was so much she needed to tell Callum, so much she wished she already had. If anything had happened to him when he left, and she had been treating him like that . . . Rania couldn't finish the thought. She had no more tears to shed.

"Orla," Rania said at last. "She's onto us. She threatened you. You shouldn't even be here."

Callum tensed around her. He was silent for a moment. Rania closed her eyes and listened to the steady *beat, beat, beat* of his heart.

"What if we ran away, Rania, just you and me?" he spoke up at last.

Rania blinked in surprise, even though Callum could not see her.

"We couldn't possibly—" she started before cutting herself off. "What about Weylin?"

"I've given Faolan what he needs to see his son returned home," Callum replied. "Weylin will be back soon enough. He doesn't need me. Your safety matters more to me. He'll understand."

"You seem to forget my relationship to him," Rania pointed out gently. She breezed past the part where Callum said she mattered more. Weylin was like a brother to him, and she didn't want to think about what it meant that he said that to her. If she did, then she might well and truly run away with him. Rania Dorcas couldn't afford to think like a lovesick fool. "His understanding might be a reach."

"I don't care," Callum responded. "I hate to see you this way. Leave here with me. We can go and start our own life, just us two. You're all I need."

Rania nearly interjected to say she had a family, and her disobedience could endanger them. But then she remembered Callum's lack of family, at least in the ways that mattered. They had given him over to the Udar at such a young age to be forged into a weapon. She couldn't imagine he held much affinity for them.

She pushed away slightly and leaned back to look him in the eyes. Eyes that she could lose herself in if she let herself.

You're all I need, he had said.

And Rania had never wanted to hear those words so badly. She had never known how powerful they could be as her whole body began to burn with the heat of them. She leaned forward and pressed her lips to his, gently. The kiss tasted like salt as she realized it was her tears between their lips.

Callum's arm moved up her spine to hold the back of her head. She wrapped her arms around his neck—their lips moving in perfect harmony like a song they had sung a million times before as she parted her lips for him.

The tenderness of his touch was enough to say all of the words they never could. But it wasn't enough. Rania turned and positioned herself so she was straddling his hips, one knee on either side of his waist. Her arms remained around his neck as he pulled her closer.

Rania didn't realize when the kiss went from a gentle whisper to a roaring shout of need as they grasped at each other as if they were being pulled away by an invisible force.

A gasp escaped her lips as Callum stood, holding her the entire time. He carried her as though she were weightless and continued to kiss her with a fervor she could never get enough of.

He laid her onto the bed, tenderly, bracing the impact with his arms. Rania broke the kiss for a moment, pulling back and leaning into the familiar comfort of her own bed.

She looked at Callum, eyes wide and warm. Concern drew his brows together, then Rania smiled at him, and he smiled back, the corners of his eyes crinkling.

And she knew only one thing. "I love you, Callum Ronan."

She whispered the words and felt a single tear slide down her cheek. Callum reached out and held her face in his strong hand, wiping away the tear with a gentle thumb.

Rania had never meant the words more than in that moment.

"My Rania," he whispered in a husky voice that made Rania's breath catch in her throat. "I love you more than should be possible."

Rania smiled again and reached out to grab the collar of his shirt. She pulled him down atop her and found his lips again.

"Are you mine?" he asked between kisses, his breath heavy on her lips.

"I'm yours," Rania replied without hesitation. "I'm yours," she repeated because she knew he needed it.

PART THREE
SHATTER OF OATHS

33
EIRE

The sun was shining, and highlighted by the white of the snow beneath her feet, it was nearly blinding Eire. She held her hand to her forehead to shield the intensity of it as she, Cillian, and Revna watched the gryphon descend with a small ash tree clutched in its grip.

They had started planting trees in Fomhar to spread as needed, and when they were ready for the roots to leave the castle walls. Aisla and Deaglan Shea had agreed to send the source of esos if Geimhrigh accepted the terms. After a night of deliberation, they had—much to Eire's relief.

Lady Emil may have seemed stoic and unafraid of the times to come, but Eire knew that every realm was desperate in its own way when it came to the Inevitable War. Even if Geimhrigh did not intend to get involved, there would come a time when it was unavoidable, and they would need a way to defend themselves. An offer of esos and wyverns was too good to pass up.

Eire was still a little surprised Cillian had come up with the idea, seemingly without informing anyone else, but she had to give him credit nonetheless. Most of Aisla's council felt certain they would not be able to secure an alliance with Geimhrigh, and to prove them wrong was no small task.

They would offer whatever it took, within reason, to guarantee allies.

"Oh, Colm, how I've missed you," Cillian shouted as he jogged to meet his gryphon. He threw his arms around his neck, burying his face in his thick brown fur and feathers.

Colm dropped the sapling, and Revna darted forward to retrieve it, not taking any chance it could connect with the ground and grow a source outside of the castle. Lady Emil had agreed to train her most trusted laochs privately first, the same way the Sheas had.

It seemed Eire would be unable to avoid training the elves in esos, no matter which realm she chose. She had resigned herself to the task, despite Cillian reassuring her she didn't have to. If it was something that would benefit Aisla and her cause, Eire could manage.

All of them volunteered to help, of course, but none of them came close to matching Eire's experience, and they all knew it. Still, in time, Eire knew they would make great teachers.

Eire smiled, watching Colm and Cillian reunite. It made her miss Combha so dearly. She wished she could speak to her the way Aisla could with Muinin, but even that was not the same as flying through the skies together, above the trees with the wind blowing through Eire's dark curls.

Eire cast a glance at Revna to see that she was smiling at Cillian, too. But her gaze was full of affection, even adoration. Eire knew that she would not be looking at him that way if she knew Eire was watching.

No, the female seemed to prefer stolen, secret glances at the red-haired elf.

"What's this?" Cillian asked, catching Eire's attention.

Eire stepped towards them as Cillian's gryphon let out a rough squawking sound. Eire froze as Cillian pulled a rolled piece of parchment from the gryphon's claws.

His eyes grew wide, and his mouth fell slightly agape.

His eyes went first to Eire, and Eire felt her heart sink into her chest.

No bad news, she pleaded to the gods she now knew listened. *No bad news, please.* But even as she prayed the words, she wondered if a single soul could be granted more than one miracle in a lifetime.

Revna snatched the paper from Cillian's hands, breaking through the tension running taut through the clearing. Eire's chest constricted as she watched Revna's brown eyes scan the page. The female's face paled, and Eire couldn't take it any longer.

"What is it?" Eire asked. No one spoke up. Eire heard her blood rushing in her ears. "Let me see it," she said more harshly than she had intended. "Please," she added.

Revna chewed on her lower lip, a nervous habit Eire had picked up on. Revna glanced at Cillian, who gave her a nearly imperceptible nod. She walked forward, closing the distance to Eire, and placed the parchment in her grasp with a trembling hand.

Eire swallowed as she unfurled it and held it before her. She ignored the looks exchanged between Revna and Cillian and began to read.

My dear son,

I regret writing you this letter for more reasons than one. I know you are celebrating your success in Geimhrigh and preparing to take on the task of reintroducing esos to their realm, but things back home have taken a turn for the worse. I fear saying too much, so I will only write what you need to know. The Gheall Ceann has been taken from within our walls, and it seems to have been planned by the barons in our own realms. We are actively working towards a plan for her return.

I should ask that your party remain in Geimhrigh to help when the ash tree takes root, but I would not blame Eire if she chooses to return. I am sure Colm can take her, if that is what she desires. Please assure her either way, we will save her friend. It is our top priority, and we expect a resolution sooner than later.

Be wary and be wise.

Love,

Your Father

Eire couldn't hear her own thoughts over the pounding of her heart in her eardrums.

She gripped the letter like a lifeline for several beats. She felt numb as she released it, letting it fall to her side.

No more pain, please. She had pleaded. But even this was worse than any fear that had come to Eire's mind.

Tears stung the corners of her eyes.

She met Revna's gaze and saw nothing but sympathy shining in her wide brown eyes. That alone was too much. Eire's head began to spin, and she felt light.

Cillian and Revna rushed to her side. Revna pulled her into an embrace, while Cillian placed a steadying hand on her back.

"Aisla," Eire whispered, because no other word came to her mind but that one on repeat.

It continued racing on an endless loop until Eire had to grit her teeth. Her pulse raced. Her head ached with a splitting pain.

Revna held her tighter, whispering comforting words, but Eire could not make them out.

"Gods be with her," Eire choked out, swallowing down the panic that had built within her, forcing herself to slow down. "And they will be—I know they will."

"We'll find her," Revna agreed. "Deaglan won't let anything happen to her. She didn't come all this way for nothing. She'll be okay."

Eire didn't know if okay was the right word. Not when she thought about Ruairi.

Eire may have been well on her way to becoming a husk when Ruairi returned from Iomlan, but in the time since, Eire had gathered enough to know he had changed in ways she could never understand. He had changed under the pressure of pain.

Ruairi had never explicitly brought it up, but there were moments when he forgot he didn't talk about it. Moments where the familiarity of their friendship outweighed his fear of burdening her.

Eire didn't want to think about the same things happening to Aisla.

She couldn't bear to imagine the yellow-green of Aisla's eyes lacking the fire that was as much a part of her as Muinin was.

34
WEYLIN

The nights of dreamless sleep almost felt like torture to Weylin Myrkor.

It was the third sunrise since Aisla had visited him in his sleep. And every night, he lay his head upon his pillow, praying to the cursed gods that he would find her blazing yellow-green eyes amid the darkness.

So when he finally did, it felt as though the gates of Albios had opened just for him. If there were such a place, where the worthy souls went after their passing on, Weylin knew it would feel like looking into her eyes.

But then, he took in the rest of her.

She was there in his room, as she always seemed to be the one to find him, but she was curled up against the wall, beaten and bruised. Her face was so swollen, he hardly recognized her, and dried blood clung to several gashes across her freckled olive skin.

Weylin dropped to his knees beside her and pulled her into his lap, cradling her against his chest as if on instinct. His touch was gentle, but his blood raged with more anger than he knew himself capable of. He would tear apart the nine realms for what had been done to her.

He would gladly rip the throat out of each of their nine gods, too.

"*Banphrionsa*," he whispered. "Who did this to you?" He asked it with lethal calm as he stroked her knotted hair, gently undoing some of the tangled mess. His throat tightened with the knowledge that he already knew the answer.

He almost didn't want to hear her say it. But he had to.

"Udar," the word was a croak from her dry lips.

She could have said *your father*, but she didn't, and for that he was grateful, even as his rage grew with each passing breath. His blood began to boil, and it ached in a painful way at his lack of esos. If he had it, he would use whatever form he possessed to rip through the realms until she was back in his arms.

Until he could carry her far away from all of the pain.

"I'm so sorry," he whispered, knowing the words would never be enough. But he would show her. He would do whatever it took.

"Briongloid," she rasped. She winced with the word as it rattled through her ribcage. Weylin could only imagine what damage had been done there.

"Shhhh," he hummed, but his mind focused on that one word. He wanted to ask more, but he didn't want to make her speak. "Nod yes or no if you can," he said. "You're in Briongloid now?"

Aisla nodded her head: *yes*.

"Can you call Muinin?"

Aisla paused, then shook her head: *no*.

"Are there any windows in your room?"

No.

"Do you know where in Briongloid you are?"

She nodded: *yes*. "Castle," she managed to say.

Weylin gritted his teeth. That would make his job awfully difficult.

"Stay strong for me, *banphrionsa*. Just like you have been. You are so strong—stronger than you know. These realms do not deserve you." *Nor do I,* he added to himself. "Hold onto that, and I will come get you. I swear it."

Aisla nodded and leaned further into him. Weylin's throat was tight with emotions he could not name.

"I would take your place if I could," he murmured and meant it. "I would not hesitate to."

As if in response, Aisla reached out and grabbed his hand, but it was hardly a grab. She had no the strength to do anything more than place her hand atop his. Weylin gently closed his hands around hers, trying to give her some of his warmth.

"Wait for me," he whispered. "I'll be there soon."

Aisla shifted to look at him, but before their eyes could meet again, Weylin was roused from his sleep.

The Young Wolf woke with a roar. His eyes flew wide open, and his chest heaved.

"Whoa, whoa, easy," came a vaguely familiar voice from his bedside. "You sleep like the dead."

Weylin turned to meet Ruairi's green gaze. He calmed his breathing, if for no reason other than he needed the male's help.

"I had good reason to," Weylin muttered back, rubbing the sleep from his eyes. "I was busy."

Ruairi's expression went from confused to understanding to disgusted within moments. Weylin ignored it, knowing it wasn't worth his energy.

"I know where she is," Weylin said, sitting up.

He felt vulnerable with the male standing here in his cell, knowing he walked in while Weylin was completely unaware, but Weylin had gotten used to the feeling of being out of control of his life since Aisla had buried her poison-tipped dagger in his thigh.

"And so do I," Ruairi shot back.

Weylin raised a brow at him.

"Castle Tromlui," they answered in unison, and something like hope blossomed in Weylin's chest for the briefest of moments.

Then, he recalled the feeling of Aisla's broken body in his arms. She had been weak and frail and so far away from the female he had grown to know.

"How do you know?" Weylin asked.

"Fomhar has eyes," Ruairi replied, rather secretively.

Weylin rolled his eyes. "And these eyes couldn't have stopped their precious *Gheall Ceann* from being taken from their own castle?"

"Trust me, I'm far from happy about it myself. But there is nothing we can do about that now," Ruairi sneered back. Weylin silently noted that the male did not ask him how he knew where she was. "Lord Shea has arranged a party of laochs for us. We are going to retrieve her."

"And we are just going to waltz into Briongloid, a realm now firmly standing behind the Udar, and take her back?"

Ruairi looked at him quizzically, as if there was a key piece to all of this he should have understood, but did not.

It hit Weylin moments before the words left Ruairi's lips.

"Not *taking* her. Trading her back," Ruairi said. "One Udar Apparent for one *Gheall Ceann*."

It should have been obvious to Weylin. It only made sense.

Still, he felt his heart drop into his stomach. He was yet again a pawn in plans that were not his own. And this time, those plans would take him far away from Aisla.

He hated the plan but knew it was their most viable option. Would he be reunited with her only to be taken away again?

"Fine," Weylin spoke through gritted teeth. "But you must swear to me one thing, and I, in return, swear to go along with your plan."

"I'm listening," Ruairi said, with no small amount of hesitancy.

35
AISLA

"Well, looks like your luck might be turning around." One of the laochs that was on rotation sneered as he walked up to Aisla's cell.

Aisla did not even turn towards him. She lay on the ground, curled into herself. Her body ached. Her olive skin was coated in bruises varying in shades of yellow, purple, blue, and brown, depending on how recent the blows were.

Dried blood lined the floor around her. It had spilled from her lips, her head, her hands, and her nose.

Faolan had always been a cruel male in her eyes, but he had been a faraway, distant figure. A metaphorical manifestation of all that she had to fight against. But now . . . now she knew the male and knew that his cruelty ran deeper than she imagined. Now she knew his face in a way she never wanted to.

She knew the evil glint in his eye whenever she took his blows. She did not cower, not once. She kept her head up when she took the beating. As high as it could while starving and battered. She spat and she fought and she cursed until her throat was too dry to utter a sound.

She refused to give him what he wanted.

He tried to get her to call Muinin again and again, but she never did. She never even considered it. Then he wanted to know about Fomhar. She did not give in—no matter what he tried to get the information from her.

Aisla knew she was a shell of herself. A shell that was wholly incapable of saving Talam. She already knew battles had broken out in Fomhar. She heard the news from laochs on their rotations.

It's all my fault. The words repeated in her mind as her head throbbed.

Muinin rarely offered words of comfort anymore. She had stopped responding to him.

What Aisla did know, with every fiber of her being, was that Weylin was nothing like his father. No, the sort of evil that ran through the Udar's blood had not reached his son. Their amber eyes that once felt similar could not be further apart. Even the way they grinned held no similarity.

"Did you hear me?" the laoch asked, rattling the bars of her cell as though she were but a caged animal.

Aisla didn't move. She heard the metal key scrape inside the lock until it clicked open. Her eyes remained shut despite the sound of footsteps approaching. Soon, there was a hot breath on her neck.

A harsh voice growled in her ear, "I said it *looks like your luck might be turning around.*"

He snickered with emphasis on the word *luck*, knowing she felt anything but.

Aisla knew there were only two solutions that would get her out, and both would result in something terrible. There was no winning in the situation. It was a battle lost for Aisla—and one she could not afford to lose.

The male began to haul her to her feet. Even if Aisla wanted to assist him, she did not have the energy to. She was limp in his arms, her body sagging to the floor as if it longed to return to its previous position.

"Useless bitch," the male swore, trying once again to lift her to her feet—feet that did not work. "Use your legs! You've got places to be."

She couldn't, but she didn't bother to tell him that.

"Aye!" the male snapped as she crumpled to the floor again. She would have felt shame—should have felt shame—if she had the will to feel anything at all. "Callum, get over here and help me lift the wench. We're to bring her to the Udar immediately."

A second pair of hands touched Aisla. A gentler but stronger pair. She recognized the name immediately as Weylin's trusted friend. Though she could not say he had earned her trust in any way, he was always kinder to her than the rest. He had never raised his voice or raised a hand to her.

He carried her with ease in his arms. He did not say a word, but she felt the strangest sense of comfort that it was, in fact, him of all the laochs.

The feeling made her want to shove away from him. To scratch his face until its beauty no longer remained. Instead, she leaned into his chest, unable to help herself.

She was carried through halls and up stairs that she could not follow. Eventually, they entered a room. Aisla could hear voices talking but could not make out their words.

She recognized the familiar voice of the Udar and was consumed by an instinctual urge to vomit.

"There she is," Faolan crooned. "The *Gheall Ceann* herself, gracing us with her presence. At last, you will help me get my son back. It's about time you've been of some use to me."

Option one then, Aisla thought grimly. The one where they would exchange pawn for pawn, playing the extravagant and deadly game of the gods.

The one where Weylin would be taken from her and returned to his father. And there was nothing Aisla could do to save him.

She was helpless.

36
RUAIRI

The Inevitable War was what they called it, and the Inevitable War it was. Each moment brought them closer to a destiny they had been working to delay.

Ruairi and Weylin and the laochs that Lord Shea had sent with them were hardly outside of the city walls when they found themselves confronted with bloodshed. Lord Shea had warned Ruairi that Faolan's forces would advance with their hostages. Ruairi didn't think anyone had anticipated just how quickly that would happen.

They had Weylin, and Faolan had Aisla. Hands were tied, and shackles were loosened at the same time.

Ruairi cast a sideways glance at Weylin, who had been armed with a blade, and dressed in armor for their journey. He wore a cloak and a mask pulled up to his nose to disguise himself from any laochs that might recognize him. It was also a handy way to cover the iron collar wrapped around his throat, to ensure he would not feel the esos running through his veins. The dwarves had crafted it along with wrist and ankle cuffs for extra measure.

Ruairi had not been in favor of returning the Young Wolf's blade to him. It seemed a terrible idea as far as Ruairi was concerned, but when they found themselves confronted with conflict so quickly, he was glad that they had.

Ruairi inhaled and unsheathed his weapon. They would have to help. They could hardly push past the scene and pretend that there was nothing going on.

Aisla needed them, but Fomhar did, too.

"I've got my eyes on you," Ruairi growled in a low voice to Weylin, whose blade was already in his grasp.

"I would expect nothing less," he quipped before diving into the fray.

Ruairi couldn't help but wonder what it said of the male that he would be so quick to turn on his own people. He didn't know what else he expected the heir to do, but it seemed wrong. Very wrong.

Ruairi brushed the thought away and launched into battle alongside the other laochs in their traveling party.

Metal clashed against metal. Shouts of pain and grunts of effort reverberated through the trees. Bodies fell. Blood spilled.

Ruairi pushed on, driving back the laochs from Samhradh. He kept near Weylin, knowing that without him, they stood little chance of getting Aisla back.

And that was all that mattered to him.

"Retreat!" A voice called at last, and it was a voice that belonged to a female dwarf in maroon Samhradh armor.

Relief blossomed through Ruairi. They had not been anticipating the arrival of Ruairi's party, and that was exactly what Fomhar's laochs needed.

A small win, but every small win would count towards the greater victory to come.

Of that much, Ruairi was certain.

"We've sent a raven ahead of us," Ruairi spoke up, leaning against the tree where they had made camp. Weylin Myrkor lounged beside him, an anxious energy emanating from him. It felt almost unnatural.

"Now let's hope my father has the sense to agree with you," Weylin grumbled around the piece of sweet grass he sucked between his teeth.

"It's only asking for a neutral location," Ruairi replied. "Surely he can see the sense in that."

"I agree. But my father is not known for being a sensible man."

"That, I can also agree with," Ruairi said with a wince.

Weylin turned to look at him. The glance lasted for the briefest of moments, but Ruairi swore he saw something like humanity in the male's amber gaze, and he hated it.

"I need to apologize to you," Weylin said in a tone that was matter-of-fact. "I regret what happened to you within my walls. My father is a cruel male. I know that better than any other. But you should not have to know that fact so intimately. If it was me, well, let's just say I would handle things differently, even prisoners. I do not plan to rule the realms the way my father has, even though most expect me to. I find I enjoy proving people wrong."

Ruairi's throat grew dry. He rarely talked about his time in Samhradh, let alone with the son of the male who had orchestrated his torture.

Not only that, but Ruairi had scarcely stopped to think what it might have been like to grow up with a father like that. He had only assumed they were one and the same, and surely if Weylin was just like his father, we would be rewarded, not punished.

But maybe Ruairi had been wrong.

"Thank you," Ruairi said at last. "But I must say, the throne you intend to sit is Aisla's by birthright, and I will fight for her until my final breath. But I think you would do better upon it than your father, for what it's worth."

Weylin let out a humorless chuckle. Ruairi thought the conversation was over, but after a few moments of silence, Weylin said, "I agree. For what it's worth."

"Wh-what?" Ruairi stammered, turning to look at the male. He was certain his facial expression was one of utter shock and confusion.

"I said I agree," he stated. "Not the part that I would be better than my father, while I hope that is true, the bar is quite low, but I agree. The throne is meant to be Aisla's."

Ruairi found himself at a loss for words.

None of it made sense. Not in the slightest. This male was meant to hate her. To want her dead. To want to be the one to do it.

Yet, he claimed that his very throne belonged to her? It had to be manipulation. It had to be a trap. But who was he manipulating if Aisla was already gone?

"I don't know what game you're playing at, Wolf," Ruairi sneered, "but I'm not buying it."

"It isn't a game," Weylin snapped back. "You have no idea who she is to me, and you've no idea what I would do for her. I don't care if you believe me or not."

"You don't even know her," Ruairi spat.

Weylin opened his mouth and shut it again, but Ruairi did not miss the way his nostrils flared in irritation.

"What is your plan then, beginning to end? I think it is time you fill me in as I am quite certain I will be playing a rather pivotal role."

Ruairi was thankful for the change in conversation. He was far from understanding what it all meant, but he didn't need to—didn't want to.

"As long as the Udar agrees, we will meet on neutral ground in a city along the border between Fomhar and Briongloid. I have suggested each side bring a party of nine—the number of the gods.

Eight souls, and then our hostages for exchange. This gives us each our laochs and a sense of comfortability. Back up if things go awry," Ruairi explained, knowing how poorly the meeting between Aisla and Faolan had gone last time.

"And the wyvern?" Weylin said as if reading his mind.

"No wyverns," Ruairi said. "We have ears and eyes in Samhradh that warned us of the weapons they have crafted to take down the wyverns—their catapults and ballistae. And we cannot take that risk so early into the war that has only begun."

"So my role is just to show up and be prepared to return to my father's open arms," Weylin said dryly.

"Did you have something else in mind?" Ruairi asked, voice laced with sarcasm.

Weylin paused. "No," he said, almost definitively and full of defeat.

Ruairi did not reply. He felt the conversation had ended.

"Will I have a moment to say goodbye to her?" he asked, taking Ruairi off guard.

"Why would you ask such a thing?"

"Please," he said instead of answering the question. The sincerity of his voice made the skin along Ruairi's spine stand on end. There was something so wrong about it. "I will play along with your plan, however you want me to, if you will just give me this."

"Fine, as far as I'm concerned, you can have it, but good luck with your father."

Weylin nodded in agreement. "One other thing," he said, and Ruairi sighed.

"Don't forget what you swore to me. Take care of her. And never *ever* let my father get his hands on her again," Weylin asked, holding Ruairi's gaze with an intensity that made him want to look away.

He did not. "You don't have to tell me that. All I've wanted to do is protect her since long before she ever set foot on Iomlan."

37
AISLA

Before departing Castle Tromlui, they had shoved a meal down Aisla's throat. Along with several mugs of water. It was a good meal, too. Far better than the meals they ate in Eilean following the lofa.

The poison her grandmother had spread against her own people.

But Aisla did not enjoy it for the flavor. No, all she could focus on was the bits of energy it brought back to her system. Her stomach had shrunk so much, she could hardly finish it, and ended up throwing up shortly after, only to be fed again.

Then, they sent her to a room with a maid.

Aisla stumbled into the room, her legs still weak but at last able to support her.

She looked around the ornate room, a welcome change from her own living quarters since her arrival at Tromlui. The walls of the space were a pale lilac, and the quilt was beautiful shades of teal threaded with silver, creating the outline of stags. Aisla blinked at the sun shining in through the window. She had not seen it in several sunrises. It smelled fresh in the room, too. Not that the windows were open, but it was better than whatever musty place they had thrown her into.

Her gaze caught on a dress lying on the bed. It was a beautiful gown, made of beautiful sage green silk and embroideries of gold. It had a corset with a square neckline, and it flared at the waist. It was a gown fit for a true *banphrionsa*.

Aisla's stomach turned.

"No," she snarled through her raspy throat. It was the first word she had said since Callum had carried her from her cell. She turned to face the maid.

"Miss, you must understand, I have been instructed that you *must* wear it," she said, her eyes darting towards the dress. Her hands shook. Under other circumstances, Aisla would have felt pity for the female who clearly feared the Udar.

"No!" Aisla snapped again, turning for the door.

"Please," the maid begged, blocking her way. "Please, miss, he has my son. I need you to comply."

Aisla ground her teeth together. She did not want to be the Udar's plaything. She did not want to be mocked. He thought to dress her in her colors—the colors of Eilean—and parade her into the arms of her allies, when beneath the charade, her skin was still littered with cuts and bruises from the evidence of his hospitality.

He thought to highlight her failures by dressing her up as who she should have been. Who they needed her to be, but underneath the finery, she was in no state to lead anyone.

"The dress doesn't define you," the maid whispered as if afraid someone were listening. "His actions do not define you. They never did. Only you can do that. Do this: carry your head high and your chin up. If he wants to dress you up as the *Gheall Ceann*—then you walk as the *Gheall Ceann*. Your strength is greater than what meets the eye. Show him that."

Aisla turned to stare at the female. Her mouth opened slightly in surprise. They were bold words from a maid controlled by the Udar.

And they were words that struck Aisla's heart. She swallowed around a lump in her throat.

"I am no one's savior," she whispered back, voice full of defeat. "I cannot save myself or anyone I love."

The maid's face fell, but she nodded as if she understood. Guilt clenched Aisla's gut at the evident disappointment in her gaze.

"Don't let them know that," she said.

It was Aisla's turn to nod. She wouldn't.

It was a long day spent walking in the uncomfortable dress she had been forced to wear. They had nearly arrived at the place that both parties had agreed upon as neutral ground. It was still in Briongloid, but closer to the border with Fomhar. The area was far from any real civilization, which meant they were less likely to have laochs at the ready nearby.

Each party would consist of nine souls—wyverns excluded—even though Aisla had the feeling Faolan would prefer Aisla call upon her wyvern this time. He seemed much more keen to meet Muinin thanks to whatever horrid weapon had been constructed to combat them.

Apart from Aisla and Faolan, he had chosen Callum, Rania, the odd female that was constantly at his side who they called Orla, and another cruel laoch she recognized from Castle Tromlui but hadn't bothered to learn the name of, along with three other laochs that were entirely unfamiliar to Aisla.

Aisla wondered who would be standing with Ruairi, aside from Weylin. The thought made her stomach uneasy and her head light, despite the food and water they continued to shove at her as they walked. She wished there was no one coming for her. She wished she could handle it by herself, reducing the risk of anyone else getting involved. But she knew that was not how it worked. She wished she and Muinin could handle it themselves like they had last time.

But she knew she would not survive a life without Muinin and could hardly bear the thought. She wanted to keep him as far from their wyvern weapons as possible.

What little faith you have in me, Muinin's voice rumbled through her skull. He spoke as if he couldn't help himself. He had been silent for a while, as Aisla had given him nothing to say or to respond to. She had wrestled with her own guilt over blocking him out, but she knew he understood.

It's not about faith, Aisla retorted.

Ahh, Muinin hummed, *she speaks.*

I'm sorry, Muinin, she said. *It was all I could do to keep breathing, let alone carry a conversation.*

No need for apologies, he said with a hint of sternness. *I understand your silence, but that does not mean I enjoyed it.*

How are things on Eilean? Aisla asked the question that had been burning at the back of her tongue. She was almost afraid to ask it while she was in Tromlui. She didn't want anything about her home realm at the surface of her mind.

More ships arrived yesterday, Muinin said, cautiously as if afraid to deepen her sense of dread and defeat. *We are completely surrounded, but still, nobody has made a move to attack.*

They're waiting on you. On your exchange with the Udar Apparent. And I'm sure your grandmother is bargaining as best as she can without you to offer. Your father's sources haven't been able to gather much information from her council. Some say they haven't even convened recently. She is trying to sort it all out herself. Your father and Eilis continue to rally in your favor. Their number grows with each passing sunset.

Am I doing the right thing? she asked, her heart quaking with fear she was too afraid to let herself feel.

The right thing? I don't know. But the only thing I am quite certain of is there is no way around it. You need to leave the clutches of the Udar, or all the realms are doomed. There is no way to do it without returning the Young Wolf—no practical way at least. It means they have no more reason to wait and will surely launch their attacks, but we always knew this would happen. We have been preparing.

Does Eilean stand a chance? Aisla asked, her throat burning.

Yes, Muinin answered with more confidence than she expected, given their situation. *The wyverns rally behind you, save for a few. Your father has worked hard to turn the tide in your favor.*

Aisla swallowed. *My grandmother—does she know about my father, yet?*

No, Muinin replied. *Not yet. Your father is a well-connected man, and he has been able to use his friends and the parents of your own friends to do the work needed in Caillte. He dares not venture there, yet. In the south, they are recovering from the lofa and training more laochs than ever in both esos and their blades. The wyverns are bonding to those who back you as well; those who don't, they tend to stay away from.*

Good, Aisla replied. Her tongue was heavy with emotion, and the corners of her eyes stung. She didn't know if proud was the right word, but it was something close to it.

Your father has made mistakes. Mistakes that a lot of bonded wyverns might burn him alive for, Muinin said, and Aisla's jaw nearly fell open at that, especially considering Feargal Iarkis was Muinin's bonded rider before she was. *But he always knew what was going on. He always knew you were safe. He could have done more—should have done more—but he's been preparing for a time like this. And the Silenced World Tellers will make formidable allies in the war to come.*

I know. I have long forgiven him.

You make people believe in a better Talam. Don't forget that. It will take sacrifice and hard decisions, but you are so much more than they know.

I don't think I can agree with that, she said with a grimace, continuing to put one foot in front of the other.

I don't need you to agree. I just need you to trust me.

That, I suppose I can do, Aisla said.

Good, Muinin replied shortly. There was something in his voice she could not pinpoint. Something unusual for him. *I'm always here if you need me.*

I know, Aisla said, ignoring the foreboding stirring her blood. *Thank you.*

Muinin replied with a grunt, then Aisla was left once again with only her own thoughts and fears. She tuned out the voices around her. It was all small talk about things that did not matter to her. None were ignorant enough to discuss anything of importance with the *Gheall Ceann* in their midst.

Aisla stole a glance to her left and saw Rania, the female from Briongloid. She sat rod straight, ever the female destined to mate the Udar Apparent. Her long white-blonde hair hung down her back, with several small braids woven into it. She wore a silver tiara with glittering diamonds.

The sight of her made Aisla's stomach turn. They had rarely interacted during Aisla's time in her home, but Aisla would never forget the blue of her eyes as she watched the Udar enact his torment.

There were countless questions Aisla wanted to ask the female, but one thing Aisla felt almost instinctively: Rania considered herself to be Weylin's mate. And the way the rest of the castle acted around her, they believed the same. But Aisla couldn't help but recall the time Weylin had assured her otherwise. She had seen the truth in his eyes.

The thought should have made Aisla angry, but instead it left her confused. She didn't know what to make of the situation.

She didn't know someone could be such a convincing liar and didn't want to believe he was.

Not after the moments she spent cradled in his arms. Not after the way he held her as if her pain was equivalent to Talam itself falling apart.

It was easier to be vulnerable when she appeared to him in a dream. Somehow, it made it easier to pretend he was not the son of the cruelest male she had ever known and that she was not the daughter of the Iarkis line they sought to end.

She wished she could have stayed there forever in his arms. She longed to pretend that the rest of Talam did not exist. If only for a while, she wanted to shed the burdens placed upon her since birth. She wished she could pretend once again that they were simply Ellora and Fenian.

Aisla didn't want to believe it could all be fake. She couldn't convince herself no matter how hard she tried.

She tore her gaze from the female and looked ahead.

Her throat clenched as she saw figures in the distance. Aisla's eyes immediately found the brilliant red hair of Ruairi glinting under the dual moons. Her palms began to sweat.

A sudden and unfamiliar flare of energy coursed through her veins at the sight. If only she could run into Ruairi's open arms. If only she were allowed to fall apart in the comfort of his embrace that was as familiar as home. But she could not.

The world was heavy as the weight of it came crashing down on Aisla's shoulders.

Callum tensed beside her.

Aisla looked again and saw Weylin. Her breath caught in her throat, and her heart seemed to slow its rhythmic beating. She was grateful to see that the Sheas had continued to treat him well in her absence.

She caught the nearly imperceptible tick of the muscles in his jaw when he saw her. Shame heated her cheeks for the briefest of moments when she considered how he might see her.

Battered. Bruised. Broken.

But she was more than that. She was Aisla Iarkis, and she would be enough.

She held her chin a little higher, hoping Weylin understood. If he pitied her—if he made her look inferior—it would only give Faolan what he wanted.

Weylin nodded so slightly that Aisla did not know if she imagined it. His hand twitched at his side.

Aisla did not know if he longed for his blade, or if he was thinking of the warmth of her hand in his. She considered both before dragging her gaze away.

She didn't see Eire or Eimear among their party. It came as both a shock and a relief to her.

She only recognized Sorin Shea, who took an evident step back as he let Ruairi take the lead.

Aisla looked again at Ruairi, but his gaze was locked onto the Udar. It was so full of hatred and malice and disgust that Aisla nearly didn't recognize him.

She didn't blame him, not in the slightest. However much Ruairi hated the male, Aisla knew she hated him tenfold.

Before Faolan had ever laid a hand on her, Aisla had hated him with a burning rage fueled by the fire of a thousand suns for all the pain Ruairi had endured.

There would be a day he would take his last breath—just like any other mortal. Aisla prayed to the nine gods above that the honor of his death would be at her hand.

I don't like this, Muinin's voice rumbled through her skull. *I have a bad feeling.*

Well, that makes two of us. And certainly more, Aisla replied, glancing at the anxious faces around the clearing. *What else are we to do?*

His silence was answer enough.

"My son," Faolan spoke first, much to no one's surprise. "It is good to see you are well. You've given your realm quite the fright. Your mate as well."

Aisla's stomach churned. She didn't know where to look. Her eyes roamed over the faces of her allies, looking for reassurance until she found Weylin's gaze on her once again.

Full of rage, full of wonder, full of fear. She watched his jaw clench as he answered his father, but his eyes did not leave hers. She did not hear the words he spoke. She was too busy trying to read his gaze.

I am here. You are not alone. I am here. Aisla's head grew light at the words he seemed to convey to her.

He had to stop. Faolan couldn't know what she was to him. What he was to her.

But Aisla couldn't look away either. She wondered if these would be the last moments she laid eyes on him in the flesh outside of her dreams.

If next they met on the battlefield, what would he do?

The thought raised the hair along her arms as she swallowed.

"It is fortunate for us that the Sheas treat their hostages better than we treat ours, isn't it?" he said pointedly, pulling his eyes from hers and calling Aisla from her thoughts.

She blinked as she readjusted her aching head to the scene unfolding around her. Aisla could feel the tension in the clearing as more than one soul shifted uncomfortably in the silence.

"Their weakness is not mine," Faolan replied, his voice dripping with disgust.

"An abuse of power is not what most would consider a show of strength," Weylin snapped back, his hands balling to fists at his side. "It is the strength of the Sheas that they do not feel the need to exert their authority through inflicting pain."

Stop, Aisla pleaded silently, willing him to understand. *Stop. You'll ruin everything.*

"You'd be wise to shut your damned mouth," Faolan roared, "or have you grown soft to the *mallaithe*? That's something we can easily fix."

The words made Aisla's stomach turn as she tried not to think too hard about them.

"Enough," Ruairi snapped, taking a step towards Weylin. Ruairi grabbed the male roughly by the arm and shoved him forwards towards Faolan. Aisla was shocked that Weylin didn't fight back and wondered how much of this had been planned. "We didn't come here to witness this familial bickering. *His* life for *hers*, you agreed. Let's get this over with."

Aisla caught Rania straightening out of the corner of her eye. There couldn't be many people who would dare speak to the Udar that way.

"Fine," Faolan spoke the word like a snarl. "Take your cursed *mallaithe*. It will not be long before she meets her end anyway."

Aisla's body went rigid as Faolan approached. Before she could walk forward of her own accord, he grabbed her bicep hard enough to bruise and tugged her forward.

Aisla yelped from the pain that shot through her already battered body. Her knees buckled, but she did not fall. Faolan dragged her towards her allies and threw her to the ground. She heard gasps and shouts. She recognized the raised voices of Ruairi, Weylin, and Sorin, but she did not hear their words.

Her whole body heated with shame where she lay crumpled in the grass before her people. Then, strong arms wrapped around her. Strong familiar arms. Aisla smelled ashwood and mint. She reached out to fist her hands in the fabric of his shirt. Pulling herself into Ruairi's chest.

"I know," he whispered in a voice choked with emotion. "I know. Let's get you out of here."

Aisla nodded as she allowed Ruairi help her to her feet. She knew he could have carried her, but she was grateful he did not. She did not want to look weak in front of all of those who had risked their lives for her, at least not any weaker than she already appeared.

She wanted to be strong for them, but her strength was waning.

She stood with Ruairi's arms wrapped around her shoulders, providing both a warmth and stability that she desperately needed.

"He will pay for what he has done," Ruairi hissed, half to himself.

"I'm okay," she whispered back in a voice that grated along her throat. "I'm okay, Ru. Thank you for coming."

"Aisla, I will always come," he replied as though it was the simplest thing in the world. "Always."

Aisla nodded, unable to reply. She acknowledged once again that she would never deserve Ruairi Vilulf.

Aisla stole a look over her shoulder and saw Weylin with his father, exchanging words she could not hear. Their facial expressions told her more than enough. Fear turned in the pit of her stomach. Ruairi followed her gaze.

Then came the barely perceptible sound of an arrow soaring through the still air. If she hadn't turned, she would have never noticed it. She had no time to act, but Ruairi did.

A scream split the air, so harsh and full of pain, it took Aisla a moment to recognize it as her own as the arrow shot through the chest that should have been hers.

Aisla fell to the ground with Ruairi. She collapsed alongside him, immediately pulling his crumpled body into her lap. She didn't know anything else that was going on around her as the world erupted into chaos. She only knew Weylin stood over them as a shield, ensuring their safety from his side. But he had been too late.

"Ru," Aisla whispered, tears streaming down her dirtied cheeks. "Ru, what were you thinking?"

"You have to live, Ash," he choked out, blood spilling from his mouth. Aisla stole a glance at the arrow lodged just above his heart. There was no doubt it was a fatal wound. It couldn't be real. Aisla couldn't accept it. "For the realms. *For me.*"

"I can't do it without you," she sobbed, cradling his limp body closer to her chest. "Not in this world or any other, Ru. Please don't leave me. Don't leave. I need you. I need you here."

Aisla's words escaped as breathless pants. She was numb. All she knew was Ruairi and his scent that filled her nostrils. All she knew was Ruairi and the warmth of his blood staining her clothes.

Ruairi's eyes were glassy. Aisla could see the life fading from them. All she wanted to do was grab it from the air and give it back to him. This couldn't be. It was never meant to be like this.

It was always meant to be Ruairi, Eire, and Aisla. She could accept no other possibility.

"I love you," Ruairi's words came out as barely a whisper. He coughed, choking on his blood. Aisla shushed him gently. She reached to brush his damp red hair off his forehead. "Show them—show them who Aisling Iarkis is."

His body went limp. His heart stopped beating.

Aisla felt Talam tearing along the seams. She felt the loss in her bones. In her blood. In her heart that was ripping with an agony so severe, she could hardly think.

"No, no, no," Aisla pleaded, choking on her snot. "I don't know, Ru. I don't know who I am without you."

There were no more words for him to give her.

"Please, please," she begged, searching his green eyes frantically for a spark of life. "No, no, no. Please no."

She shook her head with madness as she pulled Ruairi's lifeless body into her chest.

"No!" she screamed, and the whole world fell silent for a moment.

Just a moment, and then there was an unnaturally loud sound of wind whooshing through the air. It was followed immediately by the piercing sound of glass shattering into a million pieces.

Her heart pounded in her temples. She did not loosen her grip on Ruairi. Aisla looked up and saw what she had done.

She had turned the air into shards of wind. Physical and jagged and lethal. The pieces were flying towards Faolan and his traveling party. She felt Weylin's presence behind her. Out of her path of destruction.

Aisla's blood boiled with rage as she watched the glass of her esos pierce through the bodies of her enemies. Without the source of roots nearby, Aisla was only able to pull from what was stored within her. A voice in the back of her mind reminded her that she was limited, but she could hardly hear it.

Aisla did not know who had fired the arrow. She did not care. They all deserved to pay for the deplorable act they had committed. Six bodies fell to the ground. Dark blood pooled around the many holes on their flesh.

There were two missing.

That was when Aisla saw Orla. The female had grabbed onto Faolan, and somehow they had evaded Aisla's attack. The shards flew around them, as if the Udar and Orla were surrounded by an impenetrable bubble invisible to the eye.

Somehow, they still lived while Ruairi did not.

Her anger intensified, and she nearly lost herself to it.

Then, she felt the weight of Weylin's arms wrapped around her shaking body. He had been holding her the whole time. And he was unharmed. His breaths were hot on her neck, and the beating of his heart pounded against her back.

"It's okay," he whispered into her ear, "you're okay."

She wondered how many times he had repeated those words, and how many times she had missed them behind her deafening anger.

"No," Aisla protested weakly, making a half-hearted attempt to escape his embrace, but Weylin held her still. "They should be dead!" she screeched. "Why are they not dead?"

"I don't know," he answered. "I will find out. I have to go with them now, my *banphrionsa*. Sorin will take care of you."

"No," she said frantically. Reality came crashing in like the waves against the sand on Eilean. "You can't leave, too. You can't."

"I wish I didn't have to." Aisla heard the truth in his voice. She heard it in the tightness that spoke of his own internal battle.

"Then don't," she said, "please."

He pressed a kiss to the back of her head where no one could see what he had done.

"Don't leave," she whispered again, losing all of her fight. She felt her body loosening with defeat in each passing breath. "Don't leave me."

"Don't forget," he whispered in a tone that felt an awful lot like goodbye. "Look for me in your dreams."

Aisla gripped his arm tighter, as if that could make him stay. But she was weak—so weak—he hardly had to pull himself free. More words were exchanged between them, but Aisla scarcely had the mental capacity to hang onto them. Though she wished she had. There were gaps she would never recall, but she remembered the feeling.

And it felt like losing him.

"I'm sorry," were his final words to her.

His warmth was quickly replaced by Sorin Shea. The male put his hand on her shoulder, comforting her the way a brother might.

He was not Ruairi. He never would be.

"We have to leave," he said to her in a gentle voice.

"They're outnumbered," Aisla insisted. "Finish this, now."

"Whatever *she* is, we have no chance against her like this," Sorin said, and Aisla didn't have to ask who he was talking about. "This isn't over. I promise it's not, but today is not the day. We have to get you out of here alive. That's what Ruairi would want."

The sound of his name tore a painful sob through Aisla as she fell into Sorin's embrace. She didn't know how she could ever lift herself from the ground.

"I'm so sorry, Aisla," he said with all the sincerity in the world, which somehow made it worse. "We need to leave now."

Aisla didn't want to. She wanted to stay and cut the Udar into a million pieces to be fed to the wolves. She wanted to hurt him the way he had hurt her, but she knew there was nothing that Faolan cared about that could cause him the pain Ruairi's death had caused her.

Aisla was pulled from her thoughts when the sound of Muinin's roar echoed through her skull. It took her a moment to realize it was only in her head and not real. Panic flooded her veins, making her lightheaded.

No! Aisla shouted to him, unsure if it came out or stayed in her mind. *Stay where you are!*

You called me, he answered in a voice so deep it shook her core.

I didn't mean to, Aisla said. *Please, just stay away. I cannot bear to lose you, too.*

I hate this, Muinin snarled. *I hate that I cannot be there with you. Damn their ballistae. For all we know, they don't work.*

For all we know, they do, Aisla snapped back. *That is not a risk I am willing to take. You have to trust me. I cannot argue with you right now.*

Muinin's silence was all the answer Aisla needed.

38
RANIA

The last thing Rania remembered before the air around them splintered into shards was the slowing of time.

A moment before it happened, the air fell still. It was full of a tangible static as the red-haired male dropped to the forest floor, and the *Gheall Ceann* fell to her knees with him. Their fall was followed by a blood curdling female scream. Rania's hands were cold as ice as they trembled and moved to cover her mouth in shock.

This was not a part of any plan she had been made aware of.

She turned to Callum, needing to see his face. It was immediately clear that he was not part of this, either. His mouth dropped agape. Shock, rage, anger, sorrow warred in the green of his irises. Rania stepped towards him. She yelped when her hands burned with chill. Then, she saw the esos play out moments before it happened.

She couldn't explain it. She thought maybe she had imagined it, and it was an interference of the gods that had saved her life. They had certainly interfered when Eabha's doves had come crashing into her castle during her betrothal celebration.

She could only thank the gods for the odd premonition as she lunged for Callum. She tackled him to the ground with her. Rania was thankful for the element of surprise that allowed her to take him down with her. Otherwise, he was far stronger than she was.

"What are you doing?" he asked, and for a moment Rania wondered if she had lost her mind.

Then, she heard the crackle through the air like a lightning strike. The hair along her spine stood on end. She heard the unmistakable sound of breaking glass and grabbed Callum's head forcing him back to the ground. She pressed her body against the soil, covering her head with her hands.

She heard it all. Sounds she would never forget.

It began with a cry from Aisling Iarkis. A cry full of more emotions than Rania had ever known in her short life. Then, there were the yells of the soldiers that came instantaneously with the sound of tearing flesh as they were pierced through with the physical embodiment of Aisling's esos. She heard gurgles when they choked on their own blood. Calls for help. Gasped final breaths. The thuds of bodies hitting the grassy floor.

Then, there was a near silence.

All except for the sobs of the female cradling the red-haired male's body.

Rania's heart pounded in her chest. She was too afraid to look up. Her whole body trembled. She inched closer to Callum until their bodies were pressed side by side.

A jolt of relief wracked her body when she felt his heavy breaths against her rib cage.

"You're okay," she breathed out as if to reassure herself.

Callum's hand found hers, gripping it so tightly it nearly hurt. "We're okay," he assured, gently. Silence passed between them that seemed to stretch into eternity. "How did you know, Rania?"

He didn't ask the question accusingly. He didn't sound upset. He sounded in awe, as though she had hung the moons.

"I don't know," she replied, honestly, breathlessly.

In the moments that followed her confession, Rania suddenly became conscious of her proximity to Callum, which made her think of Orla.

Her head snapped up, needing to know who had survived and who had not.

Only two wolves stood tall. Faolan and Orla. Of course they did.

Something like disappointment boiled in Rania's gut, immediately followed by guilt. Her eyes roved onward, looking for the missing wolf, until she noticed Weylin hunched over Aisling. His arms protectively around her. Rania had not the sense or the time to try to understand what she was seeing, but she tucked the sight away for later.

She scrambled away from Callum's side and to her feet as Orla's glare burned a hole through her, even with everything else happening around them. After she got to her feet, Rania looked closer at Faolan and Orla and noticed that neither of them had so much as a speck of blood on their skin or clothes.

How? Was all Rania could think. She looked at the ground beneath their feet and noticed a distinct circle around their feet, free of the shards that littered the rest of the clearing. She looked down at her own pale arms and saw the flecks of blood staining it like freckles. It was not her own, but the sight of it still made her stomach turn.

Rania took a deep breath and made her way to Orla's side. Breathless and speechless.

Orla clenched her jaw and looked at Faolan, whose gaze was fixed on his son, who still sat on the ground holding Aisling while she held the red-haired elf.

On her second look, Rania saw it, something that could not be denied.

Weylin Myrkor held Aisling as she cried. The Udar Apparent brushed the tears from the cheeks of the *mallaithe*. The Young Wolf consoled the *Gheall Ceann* with a gentleness and tenderness Rania had only seen in Callum's eyes when he looked at her.

The blood in her veins froze. Not because she was angry—although she had enough sense to realize she should be—but because she was terrified.

What this meant for Talam, gods only knew.

39
WEYLIN

It was blinding pain.

Weylin knew it belonged to his *searc*, but he felt it as if it was his own.

It was enough to break him, but Weylin clenched his jaw and straightened his shoulders. He held the female he loved while she sobbed for the male she had loved.

Weylin did not know the extent of what lay between them, but her love for Ruairi had never been more evident to him. Weylin was not jealous or angry. He was only focused on keeping her from breaking. And his own heart felt shattered for her.

"Shhh, my *banphrionsa*. I'm so sorry," he repeated, whispering into her ear, not caring who saw. "It will all be okay. You're okay."

The moment her grief had consumed her, the entire world had felt it. Her esos had exploded from her, turning the air into a physical thing, then shattering it into pieces to maim and kill.

And that is exactly what she did. Although he knew it was not unwarranted, it was still terrifying in a way.

Weylin swallowed, not knowing what came next. He folded his body around her to protect her from his father. For the time being, at least.

He pulled her tighter into his chest, wishing he could absorb the pain. He craned his neck to look at her. Her freckled cheeks were wet with tears and her eyes scrunched tight with sorrow and anger. He reached his thumb out, and electricity shot through his skin as he wiped her tears away.

The feeling of her heart that usually thundered when their skin touched, drummed a slow rhythm. It was a rhythm of mourning and all-consuming grief. It was enough to thicken the knot already in his throat.

Weylin inhaled her scent of iris and sea breeze. He closed his eyes and allowed himself to pretend for just a breath that this was a moment of peace. Not one of destruction. He wanted to memorize the feel of her skin. The smell of her long, unruly brown hair. The way she fit into his arms in a way that confirmed everything Weylin believed.

Because he knew what he had to do next.

He knew it like a curse placed upon him.

"Don't forget," he whispered when he could finally speak. "I'm with you. No matter what you see or what you hear, remember. I'm with you, my *banphrionsa*. Until Talam is dust, I am yours. Look for me in your dreams."

He felt Aisla stiffen beneath him. He heard her sniffle.

"No," she whispered in a broken voice he hardly recognized as hers when the realization hit. "You can't leave me, too."

Weylin felt the cracks along his heart tear. "Trust me," he murmured and planted a gentle kiss on her temple. She did not flinch away. "I know I haven't earned it. I know I don't deserve it, but please. *Trust* me."

"Don't do this to me," she began to shake her head slowly. "I cannot do this alone."

"You are not alone," he said and reached out to take her hand in his, gently as if it was the first time he had ever touched her. "I am with you. Your friends and your allies, they are with you. And you are stronger than you know. Stronger than the best of us. You are enough. Don't let anyone tell you otherwise."

"This feels like farewell," she said, her voice suddenly empty and cold. She sounded faraway.

"I won't let it be," he said and swallowed the doubt stuck in his throat. "You and me—we will always find each other."

"How can you know that?"

"The same way you do," he said, and released her hand. "I'm sorry," were the last words he said to her before he rose to his feet.

Tears burned the corners of Weylin's eyes. A feeling wholly unfamiliar to him. His throat was scratchy as the sands of Samhradh. His blood burned with an emotion he could not put into words. He swallowed once and closed his eyes.

When he opened them, he looked directly at Sorin Shea, who stared at him with wide, shocked eyes. Weylin only nodded towards Aisling, and Sorin understood.

He made his way to her side, taking Weylin's place. Weylin turned to face his father and fully assessed the damage for the first time.

Dark blood shone in the moonlight, spattering the green forest floor. Four bodies lay splayed out amongst the blood, their limbs angled in unnatural ways. Their skin was riddled with holes, blood seeping from around the material that looked every bit like glass, but Weylin knew it was not.

He did not know what to call it, but the wrath of the *Gheall Ceann*.

The sight was enough to make his stomach turn. Relief blossomed in his chest when he caught Callum's gaze where he stood beside Rania, ever the protector.

The relief was quickly replaced by nausea when he saw the looks they gave him. The shock that made him wonder how he could ever fix this. He kept his body angled between his father and Aisling, to ensure his father would not try anything else.

He was certain his father had not been the one to loose the arrow, but he would not put it past his father to try something else in desperation.

Finally, he met his father's waiting gaze. The red anger he found there was enough to make him want to look away. But he did not, he clenched his jaw and stared back.

"This was meant to be a peaceful exchange," Weylin snarled, feeding his own anger.

"And let an opportunity to end the *mallaithe* once and for all go to waste?" his father roared back, his voice echoing through the clearing.

"How did that go for you?" Weylin threw his hands up, indicating the mess that surrounded them. "Was it worth it?"

"Clearly," Faolan replied, looking over Weylin towards Aisling and Ruairi.

Weylin knew nothing but the blinding rage that filled his veins. He flew at his father, wrapping his hand around his throat before anyone could react.

He distantly heard Rania gasp, but otherwise, the world was silent to Weylin.

His father stared at him with taunting eyes, as if daring him to try to end him. And Weylin was more than tempted to.

His breath heaved from his chest as he felt his father's pulse against his hand.

Weylin did not know what he intended to do nor what he intended to say as his eyes flitted back and forth between his father's which were a sickening mirror of his own. The realization hit him like a wall and caused his grip to loosen.

He would never know what happened next. Within a breath he

was on his knees filled with a pain he could not describe. His insides burned with an icy cold. His mind was nothing but blackness. His hands gripped his head and a yell tore from his lips.

He was going to die. He was certain of it.

Not by a blade like he had always imagined, but by a power that could only be esos. But only Aisling and the laochs from Fomhar had esos stored from their contact with the roots of the ash trees.

It made no sense. Nothing did except the pain he would never forget.

Then, as quickly as it came over him, it left him. His vision came back slowly, as if peeling back a curtain to the world before him. His ears rang and he swayed on his knees as the green grass and brown bark of the trees formed before him.

He tilted his head back and looked up. He was met with a glowing green gaze that felt so entirely other worldly he thought perhaps he had passed on after all. Then, a face formed before him.

Orla.

His brows furrowed in confusion before he fell to the ground, losing the world once again to darkness.

40
EIMEAR

Sweat glistened along Eimear's brow as she faced Kol across the training ring—a place she had not often found herself. She supposed if ever there was a reason to pick up a blade, it was certainly time.

Her fingers tapped on her thigh in a steady rhythm. Her body was rife with nerves while she awaited the return of her eldest brother and his traveling party. She could feel the weight of all of their plans falling apart in her muscles and her bones. The *Gheall Ceann* had been captured. They would soon lose the leverage of their hostage and had lost out on all of Aisla's demands with it. And the chaos had all erupted from within her own realm. Barons and baronesses of Fomhar turning against her father was not something she ever expected to happen.

But fear could do terrible things to a soul, and she knew that fear ran rampant through the realms as the ninth generation was upon them.

The fate of the nine realms hung in the balance, and Eimear thought even the whispers on the wind had stilled in anticipation. Everything felt just slightly off. It was like viewing the world through a lens tinted a color that was just enough to skew her perception. Not enough to really change anything.

Eimear took a shuddered breath and twirled her wooden practice weapon absentmindedly.

"You okay?" Kol's voice called her from her thoughts.

She opened her mouth to reply, but she did not know what to say. At her expression, he set his own wooden sword down and made his way over to her.

She didn't understand it, but he had a way of reading her like no one else ever had. With a family as large as hers, Eimear often found herself lost. It wasn't that she minded it. In fact, Eimear preferred to fade into the background when it came to family matters.

But sometimes Eimear wondered how it would feel to be noticed. To be someone that others would look for when they entered a room.

Somehow, Kol did exactly that. He saw her at a time when she had not been looking to be seen.

He noticed everything about her. Every change of her mood and every inflection of her voice. He watched her with careful intensity. Not too strong or overbearing, but enough to understand her.

"I wasn't done yet," Eimear protested as he came and stood beside her. His eyes searched hers, and she looked away.

"I needed a break," he said with a shrug of his shoulders.

"Liar. You never need a break."

"Haven't you ever been told not to speak in absolutes? There is a time and a place for everything, and right now, I need a break."

"Well, I don't," Eimear said. She dropped her blade to the sand at her feet. "Time to move on to esos then?"

Eimear had made huge strides in her esos, and while it still wasn't the source she had longed for, Kol had taught her to appreciate it in new ways. She could heal, but she could wield light, too, the way that Kol wielded his darkness.

Eimear blinked her eyes and waited for the familiar feeling of the world falling mute around her. When she opened her eyes again, a glowing sphere of light hovered above her palm. She tilted it around and used her free hand to pull at it, shaping it into a blade like she had been practicing. The power hummed in her grasp. It felt like the warmth of sunshine, though she knew to others it would feel like a blazing heat harsh enough to leave burns.

"My favorite trick," Eimear chirped, turning the esos over in her hand. She looked up at Kol. His striking blue eyes shone with admiration. He tilted his head and the corner of his lip pulled up into a smirk.

"You're a fast learner."

"That might be the first time those words have ever been spoken about me."

"Maybe you just needed the right teacher."

The words brought a blush to Eimear's freckled cheeks. "Maybe," she agreed, unable to hold back a smile.

"Now, will you please tell me what's on your mind? Stop trying to change the subject."

Eimear let out a sigh of frustration and allowed her esos to disappear back into herself. It returned to her blood like a swig of ice water on a warm day.

"I just—I don't like waiting. And it feels like that's all I've been doing lately."

"I don't think anyone likes waiting, Eimear. But you've done more than that. You're using the time in between to better your own skills, as well as others. That's something."

"I know, but sometimes that doesn't feel like enough," Eimear said, pausing to find the right words to articulate all she had been feeling. "I just keep feeling like we're tunneling down a path that we won't be able to undo. And every step forward leads us closer to the salvation or the demise of the realms. I want to dig my hands into the sides of the tunnel—slow us down somehow. It feels so out of our control."

"It does," he agreed, and Eimear stopped for a moment to look at him, surprised at his agreement. "I won't lie to you. But what I can say, Little Red, is that you have done far more than most."

Eimear found herself speechless for a moment. Kol reached out and tucked a piece of her unruly red hair behind her ear, his fingertip brushing her skin, and she couldn't help but lean into it.

When he pulled back, the absence left her feeling cold inside. He studied her for a moment, waiting for her to speak.

"What do you mean?" she asked at last.

"You gave Aisling a safe place to land. Without you, she might have been captured long before now. Without you, they wouldn't have the Udar Apparent to bargain with."

Eimear felt heat rush to her cheeks. She hadn't thought of it that way. And when she did, a small burst of pride bubbled in her chest.

"Thank you," she said.

"Please," he started, "it is you who I should be thanking. Try not to worry yourself over things that are yet to pass, okay?"

"That is far easier said than done," she quipped.

"Don't I know it," he said with a humorless chuckle.

"Do you ever miss home?" Eimear blurted, wanting to change the subject. It was something she had been wondering about for a while, but she had almost felt bad asking it. It was her family's fault, after all, that he was not in his own home.

He smiled at her thoughtfully before replying. "Not as much as I thought I would, if I'm being honest."

Eimear opened her mouth to ask another question, but she never had the chance to.

"Eimear!" Her stomach dropped at the familiar sound of her

father's voice. She jumped away from Kol as if they had been doing far more than exchanging words. Her cheeks burned red as she put her hands nervously behind her back.

She glanced up to see her father in the distance striding towards them from the castle, her mother on his heels.

Her feet were moving before her mind was, but a gentle hand on her wrist stopped her. She turned to face Kol, whose eyes were suddenly wide and full of concern.

"Whatever happens—I need you to know it will be okay," he whispered the words, urgently. Eimear's brow furrowed in confusion. "You will be okay."

Kol slipped his hands into hers for the briefest of moments and gave it a reassuring squeeze.

In that moment, Eimear felt at peace. Like when she would gaze at the pond beyond her home in the evenings. Peace like a flight atop her gryphon in the autumn. Peace like lying in her bed wrapped in the quilt her grandmother had made her.

Then, he removed his hand and looked ahead as if he had said nothing. Eimear's own hand twitched reflexively, wanting to reach back out for him. But she knew her father would never approve. She swallowed and turned her attention back to her parents.

A feeling of foreboding rippled across her skin. Eimear picked up her pace and trotted forward, closing the distance between them.

"What's going on?" she panted when she reached them. "Is everyone okay?"

She felt Kol walk up behind her, his presence like armor.

Her father hesitated. "Cillian has written from the north. He and the others are safe there. Training with esos has begun."

"Sorin?" Eimear blurted, knowing he was the most at risk. "Is he okay?"

It was a relief to hear from Cillian, but he was not the brother lingering on her mind the past few sunrises.

"Sorin sent a raven ahead of them. He is okay. As is the *Gheall Ceann*," her father said. Relief swelled through Eimear, but she knew there was something her father was still hiding from her.

"So, why did you come find me? What is going on?"

"We wanted you to hear it from us first. Before the talk spreads through the castle," her mother said, her eyes glistening with unshed tears.

"Hear what?" Eimear asked around a knot in her throat.

"Ruairi is not returning with them. His soul has gone to rest in Albios," her father said. The world began to spin. "I know you had come to know him as a good friend during your time training the laochs together."

Her father kept talking, but Eimear hardly understood the words. She had been fortunate to experience such little death in her life so far, and the news of Ruairi's death hit her like a blow to the gut. It left her searching for air to fill her lungs with. She could only imagine how Eire and Aisla must feel.

"That can't be true. He was strong—he was capable. It shouldn't have happened to him," Eimear stammered.

"I know. No one could have predicted this."

Tears began to stream down her face, but she hardly felt them.

"Come here, my dear." Her father pulled her into his chest. His strong hand ran up and down her back in a comforting rhythm. Soon her mother's arms joined the embrace.

Eimear did not know how long they stood there. It could have been a moment or an eternity.

Her mind was spinning, as suddenly it all seemed too real—too close to home. Ruairi would not be the first to lose his life for the *Gheall Ceann*. Suddenly, Eimear remembered why Kol had arrived in Fomhar in the first place. He was a ward sent to go to war with the Sheas to pay back a debt.

It was bad enough her brothers were out there. It wouldn't be long before Kol would join them. He was always a laoch, and Eimear would have to come to terms with that, no matter how badly she would rather continue on as they had. The thought made her nauseous, and she felt selfish for even thinking it.

Everything was changing. Eimear didn't care how Kol felt about absolutes. It seemed quite certain that nothing would remain the same in the moons to come.

41
AISLA

The world was no longer worth saving, as far as Aisla Iarkis was concerned.

There was not a soul left worthy of it.

There had been one. One soul that was good and kind and forgiving and brave and loyal and true. And all of the things Aisla wished she could be, but he no longer walked the worldly realms.

She wanted to give up. She wanted to scream. She wanted to shout and cry and smash her fists against the trees until they bled and the skin tore from her flesh.

She wanted to walk away and continue to walk until her feet could no longer carry her—until she took her passing breath.

But in whatever heart she had left, Aisla knew that was not what Ruairi wanted.

Ruairi was gone because he believed in her—because he believed in Talam. If he was with her, he would tell her to put one foot in front of the other. But the problem was, he wasn't there.

A journey of endless sunrises begins with the very first step. She could hear his voice in her mind.

Aisla wanted to scoff at the notion. She wanted to forget the way he said the words—insisted on them—anytime she had her doubts.

Her hands curled into fists at her sides as she teetered between anger and grief, trying to comprehend how they were different feelings but felt so similar.

Sorin had hardly left her side since they left Briongloid. He didn't speak much, but neither did she. They were nearly back to Castle Omra. She hadn't eaten. Hadn't slept. She could hardly think of anything besides the feeling of *his* body cradled in her arms, and the feeling of *his* final breath leaving his body. All the while, a rage was building within her so strong, she didn't know if she could ever escape it.

Aisla stopped.

Her chest pounded. Her esos thundered just outside of her control. Her mind spun. Everything blurred. She leaned against a tree. She felt Sorin's hand on her shoulder in the same instant she emptied the contents of her stomach onto the forest floor. She had nothing left. It was all bile and saliva, but she couldn't stop.

Tears streamed down her cheeks. She didn't feel them. She didn't feel anything. She must have fallen to her knees, because suddenly, Sorin was kneeling beside her, cradling her head while she cried.

Her sobs were silent. She had no voice left to grieve with—her throat was raw from screaming. Snot dripped down to her chin. Her whole body was numb. She distantly felt Sorin wipe her face with the fabric of his shirt.

She should have been ashamed, but she didn't have the energy to be. Her body shook violently as Sorin tried to steady her.

She cursed the gods in her mind. She cursed Faolan Myrkor and his green-eyed viper.

Aisla Iarkis swore her vengeance against every last one of them. If it was the very last thing she did, she would wager her grief and turn it into a rage sharper than any weapon at her disposal.

Then, she cursed herself and her family line.

Aisla did not know how long they spent on the ground beside the tree. But somehow, she made it back to Omra with Sorin supporting her weight when she needed him to. She was grateful for his silent strength.

When they arrived, he walked her to her room. A lady's maid was there waiting to run her bath. She had not run into anyone else on the way to her rooms. Which she was sure was intentional, and she was relieved. She couldn't imagine having to see anyone, let alone speak to them. She was not ready to face their pitying eyes, or those that knew Ruairi, and were grieving, too. No one had known him as she had.

The lady's maid bowed her head and laid clothes on Aisla's bed before silently exiting the room.

Aisla's shoulders fell, burdened by the weight she carried that grew heavier with each passing sunrise. She let out a long, shaky breath before she slipped out of her clothes. She bundled them up and shoved them into the waste bin in her room. She never wanted to lay eyes upon them again.

The bathroom floor was cool against her aching, bare feet.

The bath water was warm when she sank into it, wishing she could disappear beneath the surface. Aisla looked down at the varying shades of bruises still littering her body. Her fingers traced over the gashes that remained and the ones that would scar. The lesions and wounds brought back a flood of memories she did not want to face. Aisla shoved them back, further into her mind as far as she could.

She grabbed a wash cloth from the table beside the porcelain tub and clutched it in her shaking hand. She pressed it to her skin. Her throat was thick with emotion as she scrubbed the length of her arms and her legs. It didn't take long for the once clean water to discolor with grime and Ruairi's blood that washed away from beneath her fingernails. She did not acknowledge the pain that accompanied each time she pressed on a bruise. Her skin was red where she rubbed, wishing she could remove it from her bones and start anew.

The water was cold by the time she emerged. Aisla felt the slightest bit lighter, no longer burdened by the physical evidence of her worst moments.

She climbed into bed, beneath the heavy blanket that had been washed while she was away, and wondered if she would ever find the will to leave it again.

Talam needs you. Your friends need you, a voice sounded from the depths of the prison of her mind.

For a brief moment, Aisla thought it was Ru. Then, she recognized the voice. The voice that had not visited her in many sunrises.

"Now you want to speak?" she muttered aloud. Her chest filled with anger. "You're useless. All you do is remind me of all that burdens me."

That is not my intent, Gheall Ceann, the voice replied. *I apologize for my absence. It is hard to find you most days.*

"What does that even mean?" Aisla asked, angrily.

I cannot say—

"Then go away!" Aisla shouted, the words scraping against her throat. "Leave me alone!"

Aisla didn't care who heard her. She didn't care who thought her mad, because maybe she was. It was only because they had made her that way.

The voice went silent in response, and as much as she had asked for it, she felt even more upset in its absence.

She had closed down her bond to Muinin since it happened. She couldn't feel his pain on top of her own. She didn't want to talk to Muinin or anyone else. Aisla could feel him occasionally, clawing along that thread that glittered in her mind, but she did not budge. He knew she was okay, and that had to be enough.

Aisla wanted to be alone.

She was tired, oh so tired.

When she finally drifted into a heavy sleep, she dreamt of Ruairi and the stars. Nothing more, nothing less.

42
CALLUM

A chill hung in the air as Callum waited beneath the massive oak tree. He wrapped his cloak tighter around himself. He leaned his head back against the bark, longing for his bed, but willing to wait a little longer.

He didn't know what was going on with Rania. He understood Orla had interfered and threatened his life, and he knew that Weylin's return would further change things between them. But after everything they saw, everything he knew was coming, he did not want to linger in the unknown any longer.

Not when it came to her.

He had been waiting for longer than he anticipated. It was well into the midnight hours, but Callum always loved the night sky and the stars. He enjoyed the turning of the moon phases and watching Braon and Sneachta make their trek across the dark sky.

Callum knew even if he was in the comfort of his own bed, he would not be sleeping. He had hardly slept since the exchange of the hostages. He would never be able to erase the death of the red-haired male from his mind. It all seemed to happen in slow motion. And Callum would have done anything to take it back. He hadn't deserved that. The arrow was not meant for him.

Yet, the male had known that. He sacrificed his life for Aisling Iarkis, willingly. The thought raised the hair along his arms. It was strange to think of her as anything other than the enemy.

But she was loved. She had friends and family. She had a cause and a life. She didn't just appear out of nowhere. She'd had nineteen years of life to form connections and relationships. Just one year less than Callum had.

Callum couldn't help but think about all the years her male would never see. It made Callum's chest burn with an emotion he could only call guilt.

Aisling's scream would forever be ingrained in his mind. A scream of pure grief and rage and such total devastation. Callum could feel it in his own soul.

Then there was the way her esos had turned the very air into a weapon. She had nearly killed everyone on their side, save for Faolan and Orla—who Callum was growing more and more suspicious of.

And Rania, who had somehow known to duck before anything had happened. He didn't understand it and almost thought he had imagined it, but no, if she hadn't reacted when she did, they would be walking in the otherworldly realms, too.

Aisling hadn't been wrong when she called him a coward, but he still wrestled with the idea that he was just as bad as the other laochs. If he thought too hard about it, he didn't know what he would do. He had nowhere to go. If anything, he could only hope to disappear into a realm far away and leave this life behind. But there was always Weylin, and now there was Rania.

Callum had never wanted an extraordinary life, and it seemed each sunrise grew more complicated. He knew this would be one of his last before he was sent to the battlefields. Soon, no realm would be safe from the Inevitable War, and all that he had ever trained for.

"What are you doing there?" Callum jumped at the sound of *her* voice.

"You scared the life out of me," he breathed out, as Rania lowered herself to the ground beside him.

Her white-blonde hair fell loosely around her shoulders, something he did not see often at Castle Eagla as it was usually pulled back in braids or pinned atop her head. She wore a simple maroon nightgown and a black cloak overtop of it. Her eyes were tired, and there was none of the kohl she often wore on her face.

Callum thought she looked beautiful this way.

So beautiful he found himself at a loss for words when her eyes met his. Her eyes that were as blue as the sky on a clear summer day, and Callum realized no color had ever looked so right to him before.

"Are you okay?" she asked, tilting her head curiously.

"Yes. No. I don't know," he stammered. "I've missed you, incredibly so."

Her cheeks blushed pink under the bright light of the moons. "I shouldn't even be here now," she said, gently. "Orla."

The name was a harsh reminder of the reality they found themselves in.

"I know. I just needed to see you."

"I did, too," she admitted. "I was happy to receive your letter—relieved even. We just have to be careful. Even now, *especially* now, that Weylin is back."

Callum couldn't help the guilt and jealousy that flared within him when Rania said his name. He was her mate, in some strange unofficial way, which made Callum's feelings towards her wrong on so many levels. But Callum couldn't stand the idea of them sharing a bed, even though Rania had told him already that they kept separate sleeping chambers.

Callum knew it wouldn't be that way forever.

As if sensing his fears, she leaned closer into him, resting her head on his shoulder. The familiar warmth of her was enough to calm his racing nerves. He ached for so much more than what they could have. He swallowed around a knot in his throat.

"I've been so worried about you," she whispered, her own voice thick with emotion.

"Me? Why?"

"What do you mean why?" she nearly snapped. "You've been practically on the front lines of all of this."

"If you think this was the front lines, then—"

"You know what I mean," she cut him off. "I hate every moment of it—being separated. I never knew where you were and if you were okay, and I couldn't dare ask about you, not while Orla is waiting for any reason to fault me. I've never liked not knowing, and I especially don't like the not knowing whether your heart still beats."

"I'm sorry, Rania. I never want to cause you unnecessary stress, but this is the position I serve. It will only get worse from here."

"I know," she said, resigned. "That doesn't mean I like it."

A comfortable silence passed between them, but there were so many words they had yet to say.

"I thought about you," Callum murmured. "Every moment that I was away from you—you were on my mind."

"And you were on mine," she whispered and reached out, taking his hand between hers that were icy cold. She laced her fingers through his.

Callum leaned his head back, letting his eyes fall shut, wishing they could stay there forever.

"Where do we go from here?" he asked, suddenly terrified to hear her answer.

"You tell me," she said, avoiding the question, something she so rarely did.

"I fear that you now outrank me, milady," he teased, wrapping an arm around her shoulders and pulling her closer. "I am not the one giving the orders."

"Oh, hush," she said with a laugh as she nuzzled into his side.

The silence returned like a third soul between them. Neither of them answered the question Callum had posed. Eventually, Rania opted to fill the silence, and once she did, neither of them could stop, as if a dam had broken. They talked about the constellations and the springs in Brionglоid. They talked about their families and memories from childhood. They laughed like Callum hadn't laughed in ages. They ended up lying in the dirt, Rania's head resting on his arm and her body curled in towards him, her eyes following his every word as he looked out at the night sky.

They talked about everything but the Inevitable War and the gods and Weylin's return and everything they were afraid of.

"What's one thing nobody knows about you?" she asked, suddenly as if she had been wondering about it for a while. But Rania had a way of saying a lot of things like that. It was her genuine curiosity—one of the many things Callum loved about her.

"Isn't that obvious?" He turned his head towards her and saw her eyebrows knitted together in confusion. "I love you. Not many people know that."

Callum saw her cheeks blush as a grin spread across her lips. Her eyes stared into his own so deeply, he felt she might see his every thought, and if so, she would know he only thought of her.

She didn't say anything, but she reached out and put her hand on the side of his face, brushing her thumb across his lips. He placed a gentle kiss on it. She leaned forward and pressed her lips to his.

A relief so deep flooded Callum as he wrapped his arms around her, pulling her onto his chest. Her knees were on either side of his waist and their lips never parted. She kissed him slowly, warmly. It felt different than ever before. The distance had brought them closer than ever, but at the same time, Callum never wanted to be parted from her again.

It was better than he had been dreaming of. He was only pulled out of the trance she had put him under when he tasted salt. His eyes opened, and he saw a tear trailing down her cheek.

He pulled away, and her eyes fluttered open in surprise. Her lips were pink and swollen. Her eyes were wide and brimming with tears. He gently wiped them from her cheeks, holding her face in his hands as she leaned into it.

"What is wrong, my love?"

"I can't help but feel every moment we share is stolen. I wish it didn't have to be this way."

"I know. I wish the whole world could know," he whispered. "It seems a shame to keep our love in the dark."

He saw her protest bubble to the surface, but he didn't want to hear it. He couldn't hear it, so he kissed her again. Harder this time, as if it would be their very last.

Her hands found his hair, tugging gently as a moan escaped his lips. His own roamed her body as she leaned into every touch of his calloused hands. He could never get enough of her. Each touch felt both brand new and as familiar as home to him.

"I love you," she murmured onto his lips. "I love you more than the stars in the sky."

Callum's heart cracked into pieces only Rania could heal. His throat was too tight for words, so he showed her how much he loved her with each moment they shared that night beneath the brilliant moons of Talam and a sky full of flickering stars.

43
AISLA

There was a soft knock on Aisla's door that woke her from her slumber.

She did not know how long she slept, but her eyelids did not feel so heavy even though her eyes were still swollen and puffy. When she sat up, she felt a glimmer of strength returning to her, despite the fact her muscles ached all over, and there were still bruises and cuts that had not yet faded. She had a long way to go to get back to where she was before her time in Castle Tromlui, but she had not realized the toll exhaustion had taken on her.

Aisla swallowed as she pulled herself all the way up, leaning against the headboard just as her door opened.

Eire peered around the door at her. A rush of relief and sorrow and guilt surged through Aisla, so violently the wind was knocked from her lungs. Eire simply smiled; her beautiful blue eyes were red, as if she, too, had been crying. Aisla's throat tightened. She made to get up, but Eire shook her head to stop her. She made her way over to

Aisla's bed, slipping her shoes off before crawling under the covers and sliding in next to her.

The silence between them pounded through Aisla's skull.

Eire leaned her head on Aisla's shoulder. The mere touch was enough to bring tears to Aisla's eyes again. She had missed her best friend so much, but she had wished they were reuniting under different circumstances.

"I'm so sorry," Eire said gently. "I came as soon as I heard."

"You shouldn't have," Aisla rasped in a voice that she hardly recognized as her own. "I'm okay. I know how much the mission meant to you. You were doing big things."

"Do you know what means a lot more to me?" Eire asked and continued without waiting for a response. "You. And Ruairi."

Hearing his name on Eire's lips made Aisla nauseous with grief. With Eire beside her, she felt her rage ebbing and replaced by a sorrow that only Eire could share in. Aisla didn't know if she was ready to face it.

"Oh, Eire," Aisla murmured. "He didn't deserve any of this."

"I know," Eire replied softly. "He was the best of us. But he loved you, and he would always protect you. If it had been you and not him . . . Aisla, he would have never been able to live with himself. It's not right, none of it is. But we still have each other."

"Thank you for being here."

"There is no where else I would rather be."

They sat in silence for a while, resting in the solidarity of the friendship only they knew. It aroused so much of the grief Aisla had tried to push away, but it also brought her a strange sense of comfort. Eire had always been a light in her life, and even in the darkest of times, she continued to shine.

"I-I've been worried about you," she spoke up, breaking the silence. "They told me you aren't eating, and you've hardly left your rooms."

"I'm okay," Aisla assured, instinctively.

"No, you're not," Eire replied, with a sad smile. "But that's okay. No one expects you to be. I know I'm not and I won't be for a long time. I just wanted to let you know, you're not alone. I'm here if you need me."

Aisla nodded in thanks. Her tongue was too heavy to reply.

"Everyone is, really," she continued. "The Sheas are all grieving with you, although I know it isn't the same for them. He was . . . he was the best of them, and that was easy enough for anyone to see."

The knot in Aisla's throat thickened. A single tear fell silently down her cheek, and she couldn't help but wonder how she had anything left to produce them.

Eire reached out and took Aisla's hand in hers, rubbing gentle comforting circles on the back of it. Aisla remembered a time when Ruairi had done that, in a clearing back in Eilean when he had been trying to help her with her esos.

Aisla's breath caught for a moment at the thought.

"What's going on out there?" Aisla asked, unable to pretend the outside world no longer existed.

She felt Eire tense beside her, and her heart dropped.

"Please," Eire started. "Just take care of yourself right now. Out there can wait for right now."

"But it can't, can it?" Aisla said with a humorless chuckle. "It never could."

"It can," Eire said after a brief hesitation. "And it will. They have their Udar Apparent back. They will be stalled for a time."

"Stalled, or whole again?" The mention of the Udar Apparent made her insides turn, and her head felt lighter.

She hated to think about him. Aisla hated that she grieved him in a way entirely different and less intensely than Ruairi. He still walked the worldly realms, but she did not know when or if she would ever see him again.

Aisla would never forget the warmth of his arms around her in her darkest moment. She could still hear his voice in her ear. The words he spoke had never been clear to her. She wished she had been more present and was able to hold onto them, but her mind was so far away. Aisla wanted Weylin there with her. The path before her was daunting and nearly impossible, but she felt if he was with her, they would figure it out.

She couldn't do it alone. Not without both of them.

Aisla's hands trembled. Eire stopped her circles and held her hand with a firmer grip. She turned to look at Aisla, and Aisla was shocked to see a steely resolve in Eire's gaze, as though her anger had chased away her sorrow.

"But be honest with yourself, do you really want the world to wait? You're still Aisla, and I know that this is hard, in fact it feels impossible right now, but let that drive you. Let them know who you are. I know it is what Ruairi would want you to do. I know the world needs its *Gheall Ceann*, but don't forget who *Aisling Iarkis* is. If you do, it will be all too easy for Talam to tell you who she is, and I don't think any of us wants that. You are still *you*. Hang onto that and don't let anyone take it from you. And I'll be here to remind you, whenever you need it."

Her words soothed Aisla's weary heart and gave her a renewed sense of purpose she now realized was needed. She nodded in agreement, feeling her chest lighten ever so slightly.

"Thank you, Eire," Aisla said.

"No need to thank me," Eire replied as she reached out and wiped a tear from Aisla's cheek. "It's what we do, right? I remind you what you're capable of, and you remind me. Let's make Ruairi proud, Ash."

When Eire left Aisla's rooms, Aisla noticed she had left a plate of beef, potatoes, and beans on her bedside table. Aisla smiled to herself and picked up a fork and took a bite. She knew she would need her energy, and eating was the first step.

She ate as much of the food as she could, then climbed into the bath.

When she got out, Aisla was beginning to feel more like herself again, even if she would never really be the same.

She inhaled a long, steadying breath and looked at herself in the mirror. She did not recognize the face that looked back at her.

She looked older, thinner, somehow stronger and weaker at the same time. Her yellow-green eyes were hardened and lacking all of their warmth. Her face was pale from the lack of sun, and her hair was matted and dull.

She swallowed around the knot in her throat that seemed ever present.

That's my bonded, Muinin's voice rumbled through her mind.

She had allowed him back in as soon as Eire left. When she felt she could no longer be alone in her silence—in her grieving and misery—she reached for him. He was there, like he always was, and he didn't even scold her for her silence. She couldn't help but smile at his familiar voice.

I missed you, Aisla said. *I'm sorry it took me so long. But I'm ready now.*

She wanted to protect the realms. She wanted to fight for them. She wanted to be the warrior and the leader they believed her to be.

Aisla wanted vengeance. Vengeance and control of her own fate.

I know you are. Don't forget, I'm with you, even when you can't see me.

I know, Aisla repeated. *Don't do anything stupid.*

That's meant to be my line, he teased, and Aisla felt the tension in her shoulders loosen ever so slightly.

How's Eilean? she asked, as she often did.

Eerily quiet, he responded, per usual.

The Udar had made no move to attack her home realm, and while that should give her a grain of peace, it left her feeling restless and uneasy. She could only assume a bargain was made for their safety, and given Cliona still possessed the ring that Faolan so desperately wanted . . .

Aisla could barely think about it. She felt Muinin's anger ripple through her at the thought.

Ruairi had never wanted the ring to end up in her grandmother's care. For him, Aisla vowed to get it back, if it was the last thing she did.

She would destroy it for Ruairi, and for Eire, along with all of the other victims of her grandmother's poison.

Are we doing this? Aisla asked.

I should be asking you that, came Muinin's retort.

True.

Aisla wrung her hands nervously as she turned to her bed, where she had laid out the gift from Lord and Lady Shea.

It was beautiful—maybe the most beautiful thing she had ever seen.

The dwarves had made the armor of black metal plates, and beneath those were an assortment of dragon scales, woven together to create a protective layer over her leathers. The scales came from Fomhar's few reserves remaining from the time when wyverns used to roam all of Talam. Aisla swore to replenish their stocks after the war. They brushed her off, and no one spoke their fears aloud, wondering if there would be an *after* the war.

Aisla slipped out of her nightgown and pulled her new and improved black leathers on first. Then, she began dressing herself in the surprisingly light armor.

It was comfortable, despite its materials, and it fit her as if she had worn it her whole life. When she finished, she looked again in the mirror, and somehow, she looked more like herself than she ever had.

She thought her mother would be proud to see her like this. And her father, too.

She was twisting her long hair into a braid over her shoulder when her gaze caught on a box sitting on her dresser that she had missed when opening the armor from the Sheas.

Aisla tilted her head as she walked over to it. The box was deep green with a golden ribbon around it. It was long and narrow. She pulled the ribbon loose, then removed the lid of the box. An audible gasp escaped Aisla when she saw the hilt of a sword peaking out from the cloth it was wrapped in. She noticed a folded piece of parchment lying atop the bundle. She picked up the note and opened it to read.

Aisla,

I know you have been missing Oidhe, so I had this blade made for you. It's a bit of a long overdue upgrade. The Gheall Ceann deserves a heftier blade than a dagger. I hope it will protect you in case I am ever not around to.

Love,

Ru

Aisla clutched the note to her heart as silent tears streamed down her cheeks. Ruairi thought of everything. She would never deserve him. No one could.

Aisla set down the note and pulled the blade out from the cloth with shaking hands. It was nearly an exact replica of *Oidhe*, with its crystal handle and silver engravings that crawled along the blade to form a pair of wyvern wings, but it was bigger. She held in her hands her very first sword.

Her very last gift from Ruairi Vilulf.

44
WEYLIN

Sweat dripped from Weylin's chin as he stared across the ring at his laoch. They had been training since after dinner, and the sun had long since set.

Weylin was exhausted. In his mind and body.

He had hardly slept since Ruairi Vilulf was ripped from the worldly realms. He had hardly eaten either.

Every dream was filled with the sound of his *searc*'s agony. And every waking moment was a reminder of her absence.

She shouldn't be alone after all that had happened. And Weylin should not be sleeping under the same roof as the male that had orchestrated her attempted murder which had ultimately taken Ruairi's life instead.

Because there was nothing else he could do, Weylin trained until it hurt. He sparred and he ran and he worked his body until his muscles were so tired, he could hardly continue on.

The most ironic part about it all was that Weylin did not even know what he was training for.

He had spent his entire life training to defeat the *Gheall Ceann*. Everything he knew hinged on the fact that her death would save the realms.

But Weylin knew, beyond a shadow of a doubt, he would see the realms go up in flames before he saw the light leave Aisling Iarkis's yellow-green eyes.

Weylin didn't know what else to do, and because he was restless and angry and full of energy he could not release, he trained.

He paused to use the bottom of his shirt to wipe the sweat from his eyes.

"Again!" he shouted to the laoch who was his third sparring partner of the evening. And so it began.

Weylin rushed his opponent, and they began their dance of wooden swords. He moved effortlessly like a wolf on the hunt. His movements were careful—practiced and precise. He let his mind go. He sparred away every thought that raced through his mind. He tuned out all of the noise and was simply Weylin Myrkor, the Young Wolf.

It was the middle of the night when Weylin finally laid his wooden sword on the training rack.

There was only the faint glow of Talam's dual moons illuminating the bright sky. Weylin dreaded what came next—the hours he would lie awake looking at the ceiling, waiting for a sleep that would not find him. He had all but given up hope of seeing Aisla in his dreams again. He used to lie in bed, waiting for her, but it only led to disappointment, and that made it harder for him to find sleep.

Weylin ran his fingers through his hair made wet by sweat and turned around to face his castle.

The outline of a female standing at the edge of the training ring closest to the castle made him stop in his tracks. There was no one else in sight.

For the briefest of moments, Weylin thought she was Aisla, and his heart jumped into his throat. He squinted his eyes and quickly realized just how wrong he was. He recognized the petite frame of Orla, his father's right hand.

The female unnerved him, but he rarely interacted with her. He left her alone, and she left him alone. He knew how much his mother detested the female. His father had never loved his mother, but there was a time he had respected her enough to be discreet when it came to his affection for Orla. That time had long since passed.

Weylin was not fool enough to confront his father about it.

"How long have you been here?" he called across the ring as he approached her.

His nerves were on edge and heightened by the fact that she had somehow managed to sneak up on him. He was usually more aware than that. He knew his mind had been wandering, but he should not have let it get to that point.

"Long enough," she replied, her voice carrying on the wind. "You overwork yourself."

"Impossible," he retorted, his voice a growl.

He reached her, and her eyes locked onto his, looking at him with an expression he could not place. It made his skin crawl.

"What do you want?" he asked with not a touch of warmth in his voice.

"A conversation."

"Is that not what's happening right now?"

"Follow me," she said, ignoring his remark.

"No. I'm going to bed. It's too late for conversations. Try me tomorrow."

He turned to walk in the direction of his own wing of the castle when her icy cold hand locked onto his arm. She gripped him so tightly, it hurt. He tried to yank his arm away, but she did not release him. She did not even budge.

"Let go of me, you bitch," Weylin snarled.

"You will not speak to me that way," she snapped, surprising Weylin. She was always so calm and unreadable. "I said, follow me. If you choose to disobey again, I will see to it that your father finds out—"

Weylin scoffed and rolled his eyes. "You cannot threaten me with my father's disapproval. I am far beyond that."

"You did not let me finish. I will see to it that your father knows who the *mallaithe* is to you."

Weylin stiffened. Every muscle in his body went taut. The night was silent except for the thundering of his heart against his ribcage.

"I don't know what you're talking about," he lied between clenched teeth.

She released his arm at the same moment. A shrill, chilling laugh erupted from her. "Oh, you are ever the fool, Weylin Myrkor."

Weylin glared at her, unsure of how to respond. All he knew was that he had to tread carefully.

"Now, will you follow me?"

Weylin clenched his jaw in response.

"Use your words, dear; I haven't got all night."

"Fine," he growled. He had been left with no other choice.

Orla grinned in approval.

She did not look back as she took off across the training grounds towards her wing of the castle. Weylin followed behind her like a leashed dog, his nerves heightening with each step as alarm bells sounded in his mind.

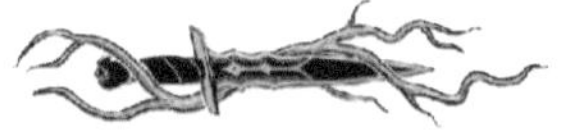

Weylin leaned back in his wooden chair across from Orla, an unreadable expression on both of their faces.

He had managed to gather himself into indifference. The walk had been silent and tense, but Weylin had expected nothing else.

"You have me," he said, feigning boredom. "Now, what do you want? I would much prefer to be in my bed right now."

"I've already told you," she said in her airy voice. She leaned forward, elbows on the table, and rested her head in her hands. Her bright green eyes were full of mischief and a foreboding feeling riled in Weylin's gut. "A conversation."

"Go on then."

"You're so much like your father," she said with a knowing grimace.

The words sent a ripple of anger through Weylin. He clenched the armrest of his chair so tightly, he could feel the wood splinter beneath his grip.

He hated being compared to his father. He always had, and now he had even more reason to. His father was evil—the very worst kind of male. He violated the sanctity of a treaty of peace that was meant to last during their exchange. He attacked them unarmed. And if it hadn't been Ruairi, it would've been Aisla.

Weylin couldn't bear the thought. He couldn't let himself linger there or he would have torn the whole office apart.

There was another part of him that was enraged by the sense of familiarity she used when she spoke about his father. She was not his mother and had no right to speak as if she was. His mother was gentle and kind, and she cared so deeply with a heart that was never meant for a world this cruel.

She deserved a better mate and a better son. She deserved a better life, and he wished he could give that to her.

"I didn't know such a statement would insult you so deeply," she mused, assessing him with her eyes that were almost too green. Mischief danced within their depths. Weylin knew she was enjoying his reaction, but he couldn't help himself.

"Then you don't really know me," he retorted.

"That is regrettably true."

Something in Orla shifted. A moment of vulnerability. It was one of the only times he had seen her speak with sincerity. He shifted uncomfortably in his chair. He had this odd sensation that he was walking into a trap. He wanted a way out, but it seemed he was in too deep.

"Weylin, there is something I have wanted to tell you for a long time. Something I should have told you sooner, and maybe we could have avoided all of this mess."

Weylin leaned forward, his pulse suddenly quickening and his palms sweating with anticipation and uncertainty.

If he had known what she was going to say next, he would have left the room and chosen never to hear the words that would change his life.

"You are my son, Weylin, and you should have never been led to believe otherwise."

The whole world went still. Weylin's arms fell limp at his side.

"What?" He breathed out as he felt the blood rush from his face.

"There is so much you do not know, my child. So much that has been hidden from you."

"Why should I believe anything you say? This is all madness!" Weylin had found his voice again. He was angry. He was shouting. He didn't care who heard.

"Hold your tongue. You don't know who you're speaking to."

"I'm speaking to a filthy snake who slithered into my father's bedroom while he was a mated man," he roared. "But that does not make me your son. You weren't even around then."

The words had no sooner left his mouth before Orla stood in front of him, and the room darkened with shadows. She looked different when she stood. Younger somehow, but wiser, too. There were subtle differences in her demeanor that made him feel as though his eyes were playing tricks on him. He would have blamed it on his lack of sleep if he couldn't feel the very power radiating from her.

The changes continued, playing out before his eyes in slow motion. Orla's black hair darkened to the color of the night sky and unraveled from its updo, hovering about her head as though there was a breeze in the room. Her green eyes began to glow brightly. Her pale skin was suddenly flawless and beautiful. It was unreal. It was otherworldly. Her clothes rippled away into a heavy black gown that was fit for a queen, and a black crown appeared atop her head. It glimmered with emerald and onyx stones.

Her presence was terrifying. Weylin knew in the back of his mind he should be putting together the pieces laid in front of him, but he could not see past his blinding anger. He also knew if he had any sense about him, he should have been horrified. He should have cowered against the wall behind him, pressing as far away from the terrible creature before him, but he did not fear her.

He shot up, his fists balled at his side.

He was standing for no longer than a moment when a familiar and searing white pain crashed into him as scalding hot as a fire. He grabbed at his ears, wanting it to stop. He fell to his knees. He didn't feel the impact. He knew nothing but pain and emptiness.

He grit his teeth, refusing to scream.

The pain loosened, but it kept a hold on him like shackles she could control without lifting a finger. He felt Orla hovering over him. He looked up at her and immediately the pain returned. He groaned through it, wondering if he could possibly survive it and hating that he could go out like this. On his knees on the floor of his own castle.

"Bow!" A voice boomed throughout the room. It was deeper than the typical unnervingly high pitched voice of Orla. It was authoritative. Weylin had no choice as he curled into himself on the floor. It made him sick to his stomach to bow to her, and if he ever held any amount of respect for her, it was rapidly fading.

"You will speak to me with regard," the voice returned.

The pain ebbed.

"Rise," she commanded.

Weylin tried and failed.

His body was not fully under control after what she had done to him. The pain had subsided, but it had left him in a state of weakness. He could barely lift his head.

"Rise!" she repeated.

Weylin made no attempt to move.

A hand yanked Weylin up by the collar and deposited him back in his seat. He curled forward in pain, panting heavy breaths.

"What in the Hel are you?" He seethed between breaths.

"You're getting there, but it is my other son who rules that domain."

Weylin's breath caught in his throat as he took a moment to process her words.

"That can't be."

"The blood of the gods runs through your veins, dog. And you've done nothing to deserve it. You have repeatedly brought shame to me."

"What?" he snapped, forcing the word out between his clenched teeth.

His mind reeled. A mix of the residue of the pain and confusion at her words.

"Must I spell it out for you?" She grabbed a fist full of his hair and yanked his head back so he was looking up at her, into her terrible green eyes.

Sionna.

"Sionna is my name."

She spoke in the same instant the pieces fell together for him.

She must have seen the realization in his eyes, because a cruel grin spread across her lips that were painted black.

"I see you're starting to understand," she crooned and dropped his head. Weylin winced as she returned to the chair across from him. "I will say, I thought you would have figured it out sooner, if I'm being honest."

He looked up, holding her gaze, and it all began to make sense, but he couldn't accept the first thing she had told him.

"I'm not your son. My mother is Niamh Myrkor. I do not have the blood of gods."

"Haven't you always known you were different? Special in a way others your age were not?"

"I trained my whole life. I worked harder than anyone else I know." Weylin sneered, baring his teeth at her. She merely smiled.

"You're not wrong." She nodded, then shifted her attention to her nails which she began to pick at nonchalantly. "But you were born with natural strength, too. And when ash trees return to Iomlan, your esos will rival that of the Iarkis bitch."

An involuntary snarl ripped from Weylin's throat. Her eyes flicked back to his with a cruel grin.

"Your attachment to her is not something any of us saw coming," she said the words not with anger, but curiosity.

It unnerved Weylin even more. He bit his tongue so hard he tasted the metal tang of blood.

"It will certainly make things interesting," she continued. "Your brother did not report any interactions between you in Fomhar. He told me he was watching but had not seen anything out of the ordinary. So, imagine my surprise to see you caressing her and comforting her with such tenderness and care. Your little stint back in Briongloid told me all that I needed to know."

"My brother?" he asked, immediately.

Her eyes lit up further, as though excited to torment him with a new revelation. "That's right. You did not know I sent my dark prince to watch over you. That whole plan did not go very smoothly. Ifreann, my son, you might have known him as Kol of Bitu. Same mother, different fathers—"

"You are not my mother!" Weylin interrupted, nearly leaping from his seat again, but he had not the energy to. His mind began to reel with the new information. He had not personally interacted with Kol, but he had heard of him. He was sent as a ward from Bitu when the Sheas called in a favor. He was in their castle and knew far more than the Prince of Hel should, if Sionna was telling the truth.

"Oh, you bore me," she said, feigning a yawn. Everything that she did only further enraged him. And she knew it. "I can prove it any way you'd want to. I can show you a memory of your birth. I can take your blood and have the norns confirm it as mine. Or I can have your mother tell you the whole nasty truth herself, but that might be a bit much on her poor, broken mind. Don't you think so?"

"Leave her alone," he seethed, suddenly panicked.

"Do you believe me yet?"

Weylin did.

He didn't want to, but he couldn't deny it. Not when she sat before him, so clearly not of the worldly realms.

"Must I remind you again? Use your words, child."

"I do," Weylin ground out, afraid of the pain she could inflict on him once again.

"Good," she said with a sigh. "Now, I have a few questions for you."

Weylin swallowed, suddenly truly afraid for the first time. Without thinking, he ran for the door, knowing nothing good was coming. It slammed shut and would not budge. He pounded on it, knowing he had information she could not know. He had memories and secrets he needed to protect.

"Don't be so pathetic," she snarled, without moving from her seat. "Sit back down, or I will force you to."

Weylin ignored her and was rewarded with that familiar pain that only burned brighter. Suddenly, his body was moving not of his own accord. Each step hurt like helfire. Each movement felt like it could be his last. When the pain lifted, he was once again face to face with his mother, Sionna, goddess of mischief and war.

"Let's try this again. Shall we?"

Weylin clenched his jaw in response.

"Who is Aisling Iarkis to you?"

45
AISLA

Aisla's nostrils burned with the stench of blood. And the stench took her back to a moment she wanted to rip from the depths of her mind.

It only drove her further.

Her ears filled with chaos of battle. Metal banging against metal. Shouts of fury. Cries of pain. Yells of victory. Aisla was silent as she brought her blade down upon the male in front of her, slicing his head clean from his shoulders.

Her new blade felt like an extension of herself. She swore it hummed with an energy that echoed through her bones. It was not *Oidhe*, but it called to her in a different way. The renewal of esos to their realm had given the dwarves a new material to work with. The steel melded with their esos, working in unison.

She called the blade *Dioltas.* It was the aosta term for *vengeance*. It was the word that spiraled through her mind on repeat as she surged forward into the fray.

She was careful with her esos—they all were. Their source could not be replenished out on the battlefield. The only ash trees in Iomlan remained in the castles of Fomhar and Geimhrigh, locked away so that the laochs sent from Samhradh could not access it.

Sorin commanded the laochs in the area. They were not far outside the capital. Their primary goal was to push them back, as far away from Sruthar as they could. Faolan was punishing them for the role they played in the kidnapping of the Young Wolf, that much was evident.

Aisla growled as another female made eye contact with her. She approached with a vicious gleam in her eyes. Aisla grinned, meeting the challenge. She was not the *Gheall Ceann*. She was not Aisling Iaarkis. She was not anyone of importance. The dwarves had ensured her helmet would conceal her identity. No one knew the very soul they were at war to claim was fighting within their mist, except for her own laochs. Aisla refused to stay at the castle and do nothing. She could not.

She was a loach doing what laochs did—what she had trained her whole life to do. What Ruairi and Eire had trained all their lives for.

Her purpose was reinvigorated as she surged forward, gripping her blade so tightly her knuckles ached against her skin. She parried right then left. The female slashed her blade, narrowly missing Aisla's neck.

Aisla thrust forward, then kicked out, knocking the female off her feet. She stumbled backward, nearly righting herself until her feet caught on a branch. She hit the ground and Aisla buried her sword in her heart without hesitation. She would always hate the feeling of her blade sinking into flesh, but she knew it was a necessary evil.

Aisla flinched, but only slightly. Every death on the battlefield was for Ruairi. Everything she did was for him and always would be.

Aisla withdrew her blade, looking around for her next opponent. She found herself looking under every helmet, meeting every gaze she could, wondering if she would meet *his* amber eyes.

She knew his father would never send him out this far, but Aisla couldn't help but hope to see him. One day, she knew they would have to face each other in combat. She just hoped they were still on the same side when the time came.

She still didn't feel confident that she knew what he would do. If he would choose her or his home. The thought made her weary, but he had told her to trust him, so she tried her best to.

A loud roar sounded above her head.

Aisla reached down that golden thread to Muinin instinctively at the same time she looked to the sky.

Muinin? she called as a shadow fell over them all.

It's not me, he replied, his voice panicked and low.

The whole world seemed to freeze for a breath. It was a moment that would change Talam for eternity, and Aisla began to wonder how much Talam actually had left in eternity.

Because when she looked to the sky, she saw a creature of nightmares.

A wyvern with a dark grey, mottled body, larger than Muinin. It roared a rattling sound that shook the ground. It was decaying in places, and it looked eerily similar to Eire during her time in the infirmary. The resemblance to the victims of her grandmother's poison was uncanny.

Aisla's knees grew weak as she struggled to stay on her feet. Everyone else was looking up as well, even the Samhradh laochs seemed to be taken aback.

No one had seen this coming.

They had wyverns. Wyverns controlled by the ring that had last been held by her grandmother. A bargaining chip Aisla had let fall out of her grasp.

Muinin? Aisla repeated, frantically.

We're coming, Muinin replied, and Aisla could hear the rush in his voice. She didn't know if it was the right call given the threats of their catapults and ballistae and the cursed wyverns overhead, but she had to trust Muinin. She knew he and the other wyverns were smart enough to protect themselves. Fomhar needed the wyverns to protect them.

She had no time to discuss further. She turned and darted as fast as she could through the woods, hearing the retreat of thundering footsteps around her as the heat of the wyvern's esos filled the air. Except, it wasn't warm. It was freezing cold. A chill drove up Aisla's spine. She ignored it as she pushed forward, hoping the rest of their laochs followed suit.

A large boulder loomed ahead of her, and she locked onto it. She sprinted faster than she knew she was capable of and swung behind it, falling to the ground and huddling behind the rock.

She winced as the blast exploded around her hiding spot, chilling her to her core. The rock was not enveloped by flames, but shadows as dark as the night. They burst around her like flames of midnight, and fear rattled through her.

That's when she heard the choking of a laoch nearby, followed by another. They were suffocated by the shadows.

Aisla leaned further into the rock, squeezing her eyes shut and praying out to the gods above for mercy.

It is not your time, young one, the voice returned, and the sound of it filled Aisla with a mix of annoyance and relief that she could not explain. *But you will need your wyverns.*

When night fell, the sky was black and endless.

There were no stars and no moons. It was eerie. There was no explanation for it, besides an act of the gods. It felt like a punishment.

None of them knew what to do. A weary truce had fallen among both sides with the blinding dark. They retreated to their own camps. The wyvern had left after they all fled. Aisla imagined its esos couldn't last long without ash trees either, and it seemed that whoever controlled it had called it back.

Muinin had arrived under the cover of night, along with several others. They nestled among the trees, making the laochs of Fomhar uneasy being that they were so unfamiliar with the beasts.

Aisla could not help but think of the words of the prophecy and wonder if another omen was unfurling before them: the absence of the lights in the sky. It made her head light. She glanced at the candle beside her bedroll in the small tent she stayed in.

The gods had once provided them so that mortals would never know true darkness.

Now they did.

Aisla was filled with a foreboding that only intensified with every passing moment.

Tears slipped down her cheeks in silence. She leaned against the warmth of Muinin who was pressed up against the side of her tent. His presence was so much in contrast to the cold of the wyvern husk.

"What did I do? What if they're right about me?" she said aloud in a broken whisper.

It was at night when she felt the most afraid and alone. During the day she wore a mask. The mask of a laoch that was the easiest for her to don.

There is nothing you could have done that would have resulted in a better outcome, Muinin's voice sounded in her mind. *This was always going to happen.*

I could have saved him, she replied immediately. *I know I could've.*

The gods take what they want, my bonded. You are only a mortal, even if you are the best of them.

Aisla did not bother arguing. She didn't have the energy to.

This is only the beginning, isn't it?

The beginning of the end, I fear.

Aisla's throat grew tight as she closed her eyes. Exhaustion got the better of her as she drifted off to sleep.

On that dark and cold night, she dreamed.

Aisla dreamed for the first time since Ruairi's soul was ripped from the worldly realms.

TAISTEALAI

There was a chill in the air while Taistealai paced back and forth through the trees of the Deithe forest. He had scaled the *Crann Na Beatha* after silently observing the conversation between the Viper Goddess and the Young Wolf. It was the first time Taistealai had nearly been unable to hold himself back from breaking free of the shadows. But he did not trust Sionna, and he knew she had harbored a grudge against him for many generations. With no one around to stop her, Taistealai feared to think what she might do to him.

He did not understand how the gods had been so oblivious to her involvement. It seemed her influence ran far deeper than they thought. They were all aware that Sionna had gotten in the ears of the mortals, and that was fair game. It was the same way Taran continued to speak to the *Gheall Ceann*, or Leighis had elected to help the female elf called Eire save her friends. Muir's own children had tried to sabotage Aisling Iarkis on more than one occasion, and Realta had worked with Leighis to protect Aisling and her friends on their flight to Iomlan. To know that Sionna and Ifreann both had taken on mortal forms to walk Talam and play their own roles in the ninth generation went beyond the acceptable involvement. Not to mention the fact that she had given birth to a demi-god, something that was forbidden since Sionna had first done it, leading to the birth of Ifreann. It was horrifying, and Taistealai had yet to know how Eabha would punish her. If Sionna refused to return to Albios, there was little they could do.

Taistealai had watched Ifreann as a mortal named Kol during his visits to Fomhar to observe the *Gheall Ceann*. He had not seen as much as he would have liked, but he had no idea that Kol was the god of death in disguise. From what he had seen, Ifreann had been helping Fomhar—and it didn't make any sense.

Taistealai could only hope that the god had a change of heart, otherwise the Myrkors had gained an immortal on their side acting as both a spy and a saboteur. Steadying his breaths, Taistealai paused his pacing. He would need to enter Hallamor with a clear mind.

The woods around him were dark and covered in a haze. The air smelled of pine and the smoke of a hearth fire. The two-tailed four-eyed squirrel sunk his claws into the cool earth, wishing he had intervened sooner. He couldn't help but feel as though he had failed them all in his role as messenger between the worldly and otherly realms.

Eabha, the mother goddess of wisdom, had called a second meeting of the nine gods in light of the ever-changing political landscape in Talam. She had been short in her invitation, and Taistealai did not know what to expect.

In the games of the gods, there would be two sides, and that was becoming more and more clear to Taistealai. It would not be wyvern versus wolf when it came to the immortals. No, there would be those who thought Talam was worth dying for, and those who would see Talam burn.

With a final long exhale, Taistealai finished his trek to the meeting place of the gods.

The familiar chill of the marble steps soothed his growing nerves.

When he entered the great room of Eabha's home, he was struck by the warmth of the fire that chased away the cool forest air that lingered on his russet fur. He felt the attention turn on him and looked up to see seven gods gathered in the ornate room—unsurprisingly missing both Sionna and her son.

"Hello, my little friend," Cion the Kind, the god of love, greeted him first as he always did. He was leaning back in the beige-colored chaise he often occupied. He had the calmest presence of the gods, and Taistealai often found himself gravitating towards Eabha's mate. "I wish we were meeting under better circumstances."

"As do I." Taistealai ducked his head in greeting. His ears twitched at the thick silence in the room.

When he raised his chin, he looked around at the gods. Eabha sat next to Cion with her ankles crossed in her velvet purple chair. Taran was on Cion's other side, perched at the edge of her seat, tension evident in her posture. Leighis and Realta shared a small couch—Leighis disguising her nerves much better than the younger goddess beside her. Muir, Leighis's twin, sat as far from them as possible, an expression impossible to discern clouding his features. And finally, there was Airdeall, protector of immortals, leaning against the hearth as she gazed into the fire, her eyes far away from this place.

"If you're here to tell us about Sionna's deception and disgrace, we have already been informed," Eabha spoke solemnly. Her voice full of the heaviness that came with her burden of wisdom.

The information startled Taistealai. It was rare that the gods discovered the happenings of Talam before he brought it to them.

"How?"

"The norns came to me the sunrise before she revealed herself to the heir," Eabha replied. Taistealai could not help the pang of betrayal that shot through him. The norns should have told him first—that was the way it went. Conversations between the gods and the norns were far and few between.

"What is to be done?"

"What *can* be done?" Muir spoke up. As much as Taistealai struggled with the god of the seas, he couldn't help but feel empathy for the male who arrived without two of his strongest allies.

Sionna, Muir, and Ifreann had always kept close, and closer in the time of the ninth generation. The three had always been in opposition to Taran, Leighis, and Realta, while the remaining three gods did not pick sides. They merely tried to keep the peace.

Taistealai had to give Muir credit for showing up at all.

"I suppose that is why we are here, isn't it?" Leighis retorted, shooting daggers at her twin.

"Enough." Eabha's voice boomed through the hall, making Taistealai's paws tremble as he sat back onto his haunches. "What is done cannot be undone. Moving forward, I can only expect more of you will become involved despite my insistence that we leave the mortals to their own disputes."

"How can we when Sionna and her wretched son have so clearly taken matters into their own hands?" Taran snarled. Her hands were balled into fists at her side.

"Do what you will, but do not expect me to come to your aid," Eabha replied. She sized up her eldest daughter with tired eyes. "Taran, I understand your feud with your sister has existed long before the prophecy came to be, but I must ask you to think before acting out of emotion. I am not blind to your own involvement and personal attachment to the Iarkis girl. Tread carefully."

Taistealai saw a muscle tick in Taran's sharp jaw, but she wisely held her tongue.

"If I may," Taistealai spoke up, his voice wavering. "I have come with a suggestion. A precaution if you will."

"You have our ears," Cion said.

Taistealai fought the urge to scurry away under the pressure of their expectations. It felt all too familiar to the time he had read the prophecy to them, furthering Sionna's anger with him.

"The norns have told me little of what is to come, aside from the prophecy I have already shared." Taistealai had not yet informed the gods that he had shared the prophecy with Aisling, and he did not intend to. He was the messenger to both sides, and he was not obligated to share the messages he passed on to mortals. At the same time, anxiety ate at him when he thought about it, wondering if by knowing, Aisla would somehow change the events foretold. For better or for worse. "But I know Talam has never seen a conflict such as this. One that has and will result in the involvement of the gods."

Taistealai paused, waiting for interruptions or protests. When none came, his heart thundered in his chest.

"I would suggest we send one of you to another world during the conflict," he continued and felt the collective shock ripple through the room. "This ensures at least one of the old gods is safe and stays out of the conflict. While I expect you all to see the other side of the ninth generation, it is unwise to ignore the possibility foretold in the prophecy."

"Who would you suggest we send away?" Eabha asked with a shocking level of calmness.

Taistealai's claws clicked nervously on the marble floor beneath his feet. He swallowed as he stole a glance at the goddess of celestial bodies.

"I would propose Realta."

The moment the words left his lips, protests went up. Eabha silenced them with a slam of her cane against the floor.

"I would ask that you share your reasoning with us."

"Realta is the youngest goddess. She would have the easiest time blending in with mortals elsewhere. Aside from that, the absence of the stars, moons, and sun would be a glaring sign to the mortals.

Realta provided them as a way to save them from true darkness, and their removal will be an omen of the disapproval of the gods. A reminder that they are being watched and the gods deal punishment as they see fit."

"Absolutely not," Taran interjected. "Send someone else away if you must."

"Are you volunteering yourself?" Eabha said, turning a challenging gaze on the female whose eyes danced with anger.

"No—that is not the case."

"Taistealai presents a solid argument," Eabha continued, ignoring the outburst. "Realta, what say you?"

They all turned to stare at the young goddess, and Taistealai almost felt bad for putting the pressure on her.

"If it is what you desire, then I will go. But I will go to a world of my own choosing."

Taistealai tilted his head curiously, unaware that the female had her eyes on another world.

"That seems agreeable," Eabha replied, leaning her head thoughtfully on her hand.

Muir seemed eager to interject but said nothing. Taran and Leighis glared at Realta, while she actively avoided looking at them. Taistealai did not know if he had made the right suggestion, but it seemed imperative to preserve the sanctity of the old gods in some way, and Realta seemed like the only practical choice.

"And Sionna—have you heard from her?" Taistealai asked, directing the question to Eabha who surely had invited the goddess of mischief and war.

"I have not."

Taistealai nodded, having expected no other answer. Defeat clung to the air like a curse waiting to erupt.

"Sorry I am late." Taistealai jumped at the sound of the male's voice as Ifreann approached from behind him.

Taistealai scurried out of his way, curiously observing the calm composure of the god of death. He reeked of the mortal realms, and Taistealai knew the other gods smelled it, too. They sneered at him as he made his way through the room towards an empty black armchair near Muir.

"You've never been known for your timeliness," Cion mused, cutting through the tension in the air. "But I had begun to think you would not show at all. Your mother is yet to be seen as well."

"I am not here to discuss my mother," Ifreann replied. He looked down, turning over his hand and picked at a nail. "I am here to share my side of the story. You may not believe me, but I had no idea of the parentage of the Young Wolf. We spent time within the same walls, and I did not know he was my brother. That was a secret my mother kept from me."

"Are there other secrets she did share with you?" Taran interjected.

Ifreann sighed and dragged his gaze to meet that of his aunt's. "I already told you, I am not here to discuss my mother. That is a conversation you will have to have with her yourself."

"Then why are you here, Ifreann?" Eabha asked before Taran could interrupt again.

"I am here with a proposition of my own. I have spent more time among the mortals than all of you combined, and believe my voice deserves to be heard."

Taistealai sat up straighter. His tails twitched back and forth with anticipation.

"We are listening," Eabha spoke. She narrowed her gaze at Ifreann as he leaned back in his chair casually.

"I propose a deal—one that will benefit everyone in this room. I ask that you grant Eimear Shea immortality to rule the realm of Hel by my side. In return, I will carry on as Kol, the ward of Bitu. The alias gives me access to the *Gheall Ceann* as well as some of the most influential ruling families of Talam. Not only can I spy as our friend Taistealai here does, but I can influence their actions. I have developed trust among them, and I now have ties to both sides of the conflict. I will consult with you each full moon in Braon, and act according to the best interest of *all* of the gods."

The air around them stilled as everyone waited with bated breath. Only Eabha could give him an answer, as only she was capable of granting immortality—as she once had with Ifreann himself.

THANK YOU FOR READING SHARDS OF WIND

Share your feedback on social media using #CrownsOfTalam. I would love to hear from you! Connect with me on Instagram and TikTok @LEVanVeen. To keep in touch and be the first to hear news about the final book in *The Crowns of Talam* series, scan the QR code to visit my website and scroll to the bottom to join my email list!

If you enjoyed *Shards of Wind*, please consider leaving an honest review on Goodreads, Amazon, or any platform of your choosing.

Your feedback is so important to me and helps indie authors reach a larger audience!

PRONUNCIATION GUIDE + GLOSSARY

World Lore:

Airgead [*air • eh • gid*] — currency of Talam

Atruach [*ah • tru • uh*] —an honor binding agreement

Anamacha [*on • om • ah • huh*] — souls

Anamarbh [*on • om • arb*] — Faolan's sword

Aosta [*ee • sta*] — the ancient tongue

Arden [*are • den*] — the true throne

Baile [*ball • luh*] — houses in cities

Banphrionsa [*bon • frin • suh*] — term of old for princess

Banrion [*bon • reen*] — term of old for queen

Barghest [*bar • guest*] — wolf-like beast; malicious children of Ifreann

Braon [*breen*] — one of the dual moons of Talam

Crann Na Beatha [*cron, nuh, bah • ha*] — the tree of life

Dioluine [*dee • loo • nay*] — immunity herb

Dioltas [*dee • ull • tuss*] — the name of Aisla's new sword given to her by Ruairi

Eitilt Go Maith [*eh • tilt, go, ma*] — term of old for "fly well"

Esos [*ess • ohs*] — magic

Fior [*fee • er*] — Ruairi's sword

Gheall Ceann [*gal, kee • own*] — the promised one

Laoch [*lee • ock*] — warrior

Lofa [*loff • uh*] — disease plaguing Eilean

Mallaithe [*mall • uh • hey*] — term of old for cursed

Mathair [*mo • her*] — ruler of Eilean

Nimhebas [*neeve • bas*] — death poison

Norns [*norns*] — ancient beings who name and prophesy the fate of each elf upon birth; they also know the fate of all beings, mortal and immortal

Nua [*new • ah*] — the common tongue

Oidhe [*oy • de • hey*] — Aisla's dagger given to her by Ruairi

Priomh [*preeve*] — a chief in a tribal community

Puball [*puh • bull*] — tent structures, often found in villages

Realta [*rell • tah*] — the crown of stars; the original crown from Eilean

Ri [*ree*] — term of old for queen

Scoil [*scoll*] — school for elves

Searc [*shark*] — true mates

Sneachta [*sh • knock • tuh*] — one of the dual moons of Talam

Speartha [*spare • tha*] — the crown of skies; the replica crown from Iomlan

Stoirme [*ster • rum*] — Aisla and Ruairi's ship

Teigh [*chay*] —used to urge a horse forward

Uamhan [*oo • on*] — Weylin's sword

Udar [*oo • der*] — ruler of all seven worldly realms

Undine [*un • deen*] — sirens that live in deep waters; malicious children of Muir

Valerian [*val • air • ee • in*] — herb that causes drowsiness

Names:

Aileen Shea [*ay • leen, shay*] — Lady of Fomhar

Aisling (Aisla) Iarkis [*ash • ling, (ash • la), ee • ark • iss*] — the promised one

Aine Iarkis [*awn • ya, ee • ark • iss*] — Aisla's mother

Alfson [*ulf • sun*] — Sorin's gryphon

Bastien Burke [*bass • tee • en, birk*] — Lord of Geimhrigh

Bela Unfrig [*bay • lah, un • frig*] — Lady of Bitu

Brendan Dorcas [*bren • den, door • cass*] — Lord of Briongloid

Brigid Dorcas [*bridge • id, door • cass*] — Lady of Briongloid

Callum Ronan [*cal • um, roan • in*] — captain of the Udar Apparent's personal guard

Cillian Shea [*kill • ian, shay*] — Deaglan Shea's middle son

Cliona Iarkis [*clee • own • uh, ee • ark • iss*] — Mathair of Eilean

Colm [*coal • m*] — Cillian's gryphon

Comhbha [*co • wa*] — Eire's wyvern

Conroy Myrkor [*con • roy, mur • core*] — Weylin's uncle

Corren Kyne [*core • ren, kine*] — Lord Apparent of Earrach

Deaglan Shea [*deck • lin, shay*] — Lord of Fomhar

Eilis [*isle • esh*] — guardian of the library of the Silenced World Tellers

Eimear Shea [*ee • mur, shay*] —Deaglan Shea's eldest daughter

Eire Trygg [*air • uh, trig*] — Aisla's best friend

Emil Burke [*ee • mill, birk*] — Lady of Geimhrigh

Eolas [*o • liss*] — Weylin's horse

Faolan Myrkor [*fay • lan, mur • core*] — Udar of the seven worldly realms

Feargal Iarkis [*ferr • gal, ee • ark • iss*] — Aisla's father

Gaotha [*gwee • ha*] — Ruairi's wyvern

Halli Shea [*hal • lee, shay*] — Deaglan Shea's youngest daughter

Intinn [*in • chin*] — one of Eabha's doves

Kol Asulf [*coal, a • sulf*] — ward from Bitu living in Fomhar

Laisren [*lays • rin*] — Priomh of Spiorad

Luas [*loo • iss*] — Rania's horse

Maira [*may • ra*] — Eimear's gryphon

Muinin [*mun • een*] — Aisla's wyvern

Nevin [*nev • in*] — member of Eire's traveling party; fondly known as 'the brawn'

Niamh Myrkor [*neeve, mur • core*] — Lady of Samhradh

Noland Kyne [*no • lund, kine*] — Lord Apparent of Earrach

Orla [*or • lah*] — right hand to the Udar

Oisin Dorcas [*oh • sheen, door • cass*] — heir to the seat in Briongloid

Rania Dorcas [*ruh • knee • uh, door • cass*] — daughter of the Lord of Briongloid

Revna [*rev • na*] — member of Eire's traveling party; fondly known as 'the scout'

Roark Shea [*rork, shay*] — Deaglan Shea's youngest son

Ruairi Vilulf [*roo • ree, vill • ulf*] — Aisla's best friend

Saga [*sah • guh*] — Callum's horse

Sinead Bracken [*shin • aid, brack • en*] — bartender in Briseadhceo

Smaoinigh [*smwe • chee*] — one of Eabha's doves

Sorin Shea [*soar • in, shay*] — Lord Apparent of Fomhar

Sten [*sten*] — member of Eire's traveling party; fondly known as 'the navigator'

Taistealai [*tash • tuh • lee*] — messenger between the worldly realms and the otherly realms

Weylin Myrkor [*way • lynn, mur • core*] — Udar Apparent of the seven worldly realms

Gods/Goddesses:

Airdeall [*are • dull*] — goddess of the heavens; protector of the gods

Cion [*key • un*] — god of beauty, love, and fate

Eabha [*ay • va*] — goddess of wisdom, mother of the gods

Ifreann [*if • run*] — god of death and Hel

Leighis [*lay • sh*] — goddess of healing, harvest, and hunt

Muir [*moor*] — god of waters

Realta [*ray • all • ta*] — goddess of celestial bodies

Sionna [*see • on • uh*] — goddess of mischief and war

Taran [*tear • in*] — goddess of thunder and justice; protector of humanity

Locations:

Albios [*all • bee • oss*] — the heavens; one of the two otherly realms

Anseo [*ann • show*] — mid-sized city in Samhradh

Bitu [*bite • oo*] — northeastern worldly realm

Blathriel [*blath • ree • ell*] — capital of Earrach

Briongloid [*bring • loyd*] — southwestern worldly realm

Briseadhceo [*brish • oo • cho*] — mid-sized city in Briongloid

Caillte [*call • chuh*] — capital of Eilean

Cluain [*clu • en*] — small city outside of Omra

Cruthu [*cruh • who*] — castle in Bitu

Deithe [*day • thuh*] — dense forest at the top of Crann Na Beatha in Albios

Eagla [*ogg • luh*] — castle in Samhradh

Earrach [*are • rah*] — southeastern worldly realm

Eilean [*eye • lee • an*] — an island to the southwest of Iomlan; in exile following the War for Descendants; one of the seven worldly realms

Farraige [*far • uh • gay*] — castle in Eilean

Fas [*foss*] — castle in Earrach

Fomhar [*fove • err*] — northwestern worldly realm

Fuar [*for*] — capital of Geimhrigh

Geimhrigh [*gev • ree*] — northern most worldly realm

Hallamor [*haul • uh • moor*] — the capital of Albios; home of Eabha and Cion; meeting place of the gods

Hel [*hell*] — the underworld; one of the two otherly realms

Iomlan [*um • lawn*] — the main continent

Oighear [*ire*] — castle in Geimhrigh

Omra [*ome • ruh*] — capital of Samhradh

Orga [*ore • gah*] — castle in Fomhar

Samhradh [*sour • rah*] — southernmost worldly realm

Scamall [*scom • ull*] — capital of Briongloid

Scamhog [*ska • wog*] — capital of Bitu

Speir [*spare*] — midsized city in Briongloid

Spiorad [*spear • id*] — village on Briongloid and Samhradh border

Sruthar [*suh • roo • thar*] — capital of Fomhar

Talam [*tall • um*] — the world that consists of the seven worldly realms and the two otherly realms

Trasnu [*trass • new*] — small coastal city in Briongloid

Tromlui [*trom • ly*] — castle in Briongloid

Tus [*toos*] — forest in Caillte near the northern coast

Tusnua [*toos • new • ah*] — ocean between Eilean and Iomlan

DON'T MISS THE
EPIC CONCLUSION
TO AISLA'S
JOURNEY IN

EMPIRE OF DUSK

BOOK FOUR IN
THE CROWNS OF TALAM

COMING
SOON

ACKNOWLEDGMENTS

When I say this book would have been impossible to finish without the support of my loving community of family, friends, readers, and dogs, I mean it with my whole heart. Each book I write seems to come with a fear of failure, but with the encouragement around me, I began to believe in this story again. I have and always will love Talam and Aisla, but I often worry about not doing her story justice. In time, I had this feeling of deja vu, when I remembered to trust in the voices that have carried this journey so far while writing *Blood of Ember* as well. Through the eyes of Aisla, Weylin, Rania, Ruairi, Eire, Callum, Eimear, and Taistealai, I found the joy of writing once again. I could not do any of this without them. Spending time in their world feels like coming home, as wild as that may sound.

Always in my corner, my loving husband, Eron, provided gentle nudges and encouragement along the way. He has believed in Talam every step that I take forward, and I can say without a doubt, he makes this crazy dream of mine seem not so crazy after all. That alone is more than I could ever ask for.

My mum never fails to remind me of the little me who dreamed of nothing more than writing stories, and I am so grateful she has believed in me ever since. Thank you, Caeh, for entertaining my random thoughts and questions.

And to Nana for being the first to read this manuscript in its entirety, and being willing to read through my midnight chapter dumps the next morning. I could not have done any of this without you. Papa, thank you for being a voice of reason when my emotions threaten to run wild.

I am grateful for my four-legged companions, Yoshi, Obi, and Luna, tolerating my late-night writing habits and bringing me such joy each and every day.

Tori, your voice notes kept me going through each step of the process, and I hope you know you are now stuck with me forever. I appreciate your friendship during all of the ups and downs of both life and indie publishing. Sarah, you are both a cherished friend and an inspiration to me—your help with this novel was absolutely invaluable. Thank you for being you, and someone I can always lean on. To Haley—a friend who has changed my life in the best of ways—thank you for always being there for me. You filled a hole in my life that I didn't realize existed, and have kept me sane ever since.

To my friends who have supported my writing aspirations since long before I published *Under Cold Moons*—Jade, Kat, Ireland, Kate, Ricki, Zoe, Victoria, Maddy, Sievey, Beasley, Faith, Jasmine, Taylor, Maddy, and Erica—thank you for always being by my side. And to the new friends I have made since publishing—Bex, Susanna, Therese, Desiree, Sarah Elizabeth, Grace, Kona, Candice, Kate, Erin, Allison, Samantha, Kristen, Amanda, Karina, Maria, and every other reader who gave Talam a chance—thank you for continuing to bring me courage.

I want to also thank Jessica Tobin, Jessica Edwards, Tess Johnson, Brienne La Flair, and the team at Burning Pages Bookstore, who have shown me and Talam so much love since opening their doors in my hometown. And thank you also to the wonderful and supportive friends I have made through the Burning Pages book club: Morgan, Samantha, Annie, Katie, Veronica, Caity, Kristyn, Stevie, Bethany, Sara, and Kimberly.

I am beyond grateful for all of the creative and talented hands that played massive roles in bringing *Shards of Wind* to life. Thank you K.D. Guthauser, Becky Wallace, Jennifer Murgia, Alyssa Hurlbert, and Drew Flanagan. The lessons taught by my undergrad professors continue to influence my writing, and I am so grateful for the expertise shared by all of them, but namely, Nina de Gramont, Emily Smith, Tim Bass, Bekki Lee, David Gessner, Sayantani Dasgupta, and Michael Ramos.

Every time I sit down to write, I still think about my trips to Ireland and Scotland in 2022 and 2024. They largely inspired the landscape of Talam and brought the story to life in my mind. I am constantly inspired by Norse and Irish mythology, language, and culture, which influence the world of Talam.

To my readers who have made it with me to book three, thank you for all of your support—I look forward to our next adventure into Talam.

Above all, I want to thank my Heavenly Father for guiding my steps and placing His loving hand upon me. I find my strength and hope in Him and could not do it any other way.

ABOUT THE AUTHOR

L.E. Van Veen lives with her husband and three dogs in coastal North Carolina, although she spends a good deal of time lost in fictional lands. She has enjoyed stories set in different worlds for as long as she can remember and has long dreamed of building her own. After studying Creative Writing at UNC Wilmington, she began work on her debut novel, *Under Cold Moons*, an epic fantasy novel inspired by years spent dreaming.

www.ingramcontent.com/pod-product-compliance
Lightning Source LLC
Chambersburg PA
CBHW020904060726
47591CB00004B/1079